EDGE *of* WILD

a novel by
D. K. Stone

Danika Stone

Stonehouse Books
www.stonehousepublishing.ca
Alberta, Canada
Copyright © 2015 by D. K. Stone
Designed by Janet King

Although Waterton Park is a real location, the characters, situations and events portrayed in Edge of Wild are all fictitious. Any resemblance to real persons, living or dead, is purely coincidental. Any commentary on historical or public figures is purely fictional and has no basis in fact.

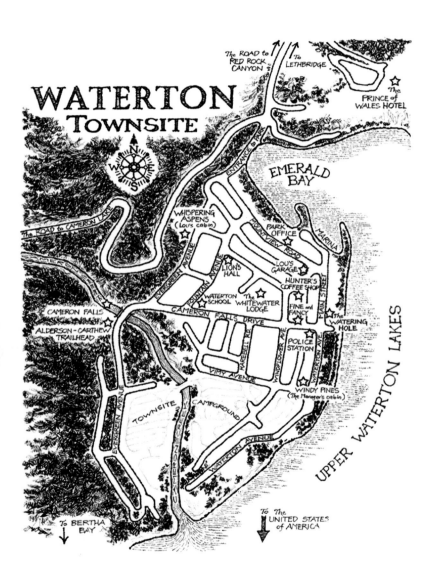

PROLOGUE

Jeff was packing to leave when he heard the noise outside the window. It was a low keening sound, the sort of moan that would have sent a city slicker like him running a year ago. But not now. No, tonight, he picked up the wooden bat next to the door and walked out onto the porch.

Jeff's time in the mountains had changed him. He was far more confident in who he was nowadays; the solitude of Waterton had done that. Other changes were less certain. He was preparing to throw away a career at Coldcreek Enterprises, for one thing. And last spring, he would have had misgivings about walking out into the darkness after hearing ... something.

Tonight he did it without a second thought.

He stood, staring out into the sooty black. Waiting. The sound didn't return, but his mind was abuzz with it. Jeff replayed it over and over, subtly adding to it, filtering it, until he was certain Tucker's whine was somewhere in the remembered sound. Jeff had bought the cougar hound pup from a local rancher last spring, when the problems had begun. "Cougars can be trouble 'round these parts," a Park warden had warned when the bloody kill had appeared on this very porch. A dog seemed like the best way to deal with it. Jeff hadn't expected to love the long-eared mutt so much.

The dog had disappeared a week ago.

In the darkness, far beyond the porch's golden light, a branch broke.

"Tucker?" Jeff called, his hand tightening on the bat. "That you, boy?"

He whistled, but there was no response. Jeff turned in a slow circle, taking in the protective perimeter of porch light and the door to the house, still ajar, and the warm light of the kitchen. Uncurtained windows framed the room beyond. Jeff frowned. A year in the mountains had made him indifferent to privacy.

Another branch broke, this time a little further out, nearer to the garage.

"Tuck...?"

Jeff stepped down to the yard, heart pounding. Coming here had been a lifetime opportunity: project manager for the building of the Whitewater Lodge, the biggest hotel complex the hamlet had ever seen. Jeff wished he'd known how difficult that goal would be to accomplish.

The issues had started immediately, weather putting the project weeks behind schedule. The construction crew had been outsourced from Calgary, but the men hadn't been prepared for building in extreme mountain conditions. "No one builds in the winter," the townsfolk smirked. Pipes burst. Workers quit. Still Jeff pushed forward.

And then the other things began.

In the darkness, something moved. Whatever it was had circled round the far side of the garage, keeping to the shadows. The presence was uneasy and so was he. Rolling sweaty fingers over the bat's grip, Jeff moved in.

This time he would know.

Jeff's lifetime opportunity had turned into a nightmare. Even after the snowy weather had cleared, the troubles continued. Everything that could go wrong with the unfinished hotel, had. He had opened one wing of the lodge despite misgivings.

It was a disaster.

Balancing that small section of rooms while finishing the remaining two wings was impossible. He'd borrowed money to finish, but the loan wasn't nearly enough. The rest of the town ran as if it was still 1950. The townsfolk didn't like him. Didn't want him here. Warden Grant McNealy had blamed a cougar for the dead animal on his porch. But there'd been the trouble with broken cabin windows. "The wind." And then the break-ins at the Whitewater Lodge. "Seasonal workers." All of it conveniently discredited, but Jeff didn't believe that anymore. Not after Tucker had disappeared off the chain in the yard last week. He knew the reason now.

Someone wanted him out.

Jeff made almost a complete circuit of the yard, pushing further into the darkness, but the bushes were silent. He whistled once more, knowing there'd be no answer, and then stopped, taut with frustration. With a sigh, he turned back around and froze.

A shadowy figure stood on the porch.

Jeff took a shaky breath, lifting the end of the bat and widening his stance. With the light behind, he couldn't see who it was.

"What do you want?" he called.

The figure on the porch smiled, teeth white against the shadows. "Just to talk..."

CHAPTER ONE

*"Love is a fire. But whether it is going to warm your hearth or
burn down your house, you can never tell."*
~Joan Crawford

Louise Newman always knew she was different than other children. It wasn't a question. She just was. As far back as she could remember her sleep was interrupted by dreams so real they seemed alive. Bits and pieces of other lives intruded into her mind after she awoke, their voices whispering to her.

"I dreamed of a woman with eyes too full of water," five-year-old Louise announced one morning. "She walked out into Emerald Bay and tried to drink the lake."

"Louise!" her mother gasped, hand covering her heart. "You shouldn't say such things."

"People tried to pull her out," Louise said, pointing to the window and the flat shimmer of water beyond. "But she drowned anyway. I saw it."

Her mother looked from Louise, to her husband, to the butsudan in the corner of the room. "Memories of another life mean you've come back for a reason," she said warily.

Lou Newman, a self-declared atheist, lifted his gaze from his plate and grimaced. "Hardly, Yuki. Kids have crazy dreams. Louise just has an overactive imagination."

"But it wasn't a dream," she argued. "It was real, Daddy. I remember!"

"Well, just don't go around telling everyone," he said. "They'll think you're off your rocker, baby."

There were other things Louise just *knew*: like the man down the street who had a different family in a different town, and her classmate who'd killed his pet rabbit in the shed, then lied and said it had run away. Each realization separated young Louise from her peers; each memory that wasn't her own, pulling her a little further to the side. Teased for her peculiar differences, she became an observer of life's chaos rather than a participant. Her mother was open to her daughter's visions, though Louise knew that they worried her. "You need to make sure you walk the right path," Yuki said.

Even at the hardest times, Louise tried to remember that.

Louise attended Waterton's small, two-room school until sixth grade, its highest level. For the remainder of her childhood, she was shuttled to Cardston, the nearest town with a school. Trapped on a school bus for an hour each morning and each evening, she devoured book after book. She explored a hundred worlds, indifferent to her peers and the passing of the universe. She went through her parents' bookshelves, moving onto the school's small library, then Cardston's public library, and onward from there, receiving tomes via inter-library loans as years passed. She lived through these stories, her mind lost in the subtle variation of human existence. She understood them, could see them. *Knew them.*

The belief that she'd been born hundreds of times before never wavered.

She left Waterton the summer after graduating from high school, taking courses at the University of Alberta with the anxious feeling that she shouldn't be there. Eventually the emotion settled like a stone, deep in her chest, leaving her jumping every time the phone rang in the apartment.

A few weeks after Christmas, Yuki was diagnosed with breast cancer. Louise came home, knowing it was to stay. Spring brought radiation treatments and chemotherapy, along with songbirds and wildflowers. Summer added tourists to the mix. Louise helped her father with the garage during the day, and helped her mother with dying at night. She knew the end was near, just as she knew she needed to be there at her mother's side. And so she did what she'd been called to do: hold Yuki's hand as she passed from this world to the next.

"What's the point?" her father muttered brokenly the day of the funeral. In the last months his shoulders had curled like an autumn leaf.

"The point is that we're not alive unless we also die," Louise said. Heartbroken, she lifted the urn, spreading her mother's ashes into the wind, watching them dance like smoke, then disappear across the surface of upper Waterton Lake.

Her father never answered.

Years passed, and Louise settled into the role life had given her. She took lovers and let them go. Made friends and watched them leave the town behind. The stories she read became a lens through which to understand the world. Disconnected, she stayed on the outside of conflict, offering words of solace and hope to those she loved. It put her on the edge of life, looking inward, rather than fording the stream with the rest.

By the time her father joined his wife in the next world, and Louise was the only 'Lou' in town, she'd more than accepted that this was her place. The townsfolk, with their long-standing ways and hard-won trust, were her family. The summer visitors, with their chaotic lives and endless troubles, were her calling.

And, for the most part, she was happy.

*   *   *

When Richard Evans arrived in Waterton in mid-April, 1999, the town was shrouded in white. Dressed for the grey dullness of New York spring, his feet were soaked the moment he climbed out of his car. The parking lot of the newly-constructed hotel was covered in ankle-deep slush, the 'open' sign flashing like a beacon in the mid-afternoon gloom. Wind howled through tall pine trees, picking up bits of snow and casting them like pebbles against anything solid. Squinting, he did a quick survey of his home for the next six months.

Barren hardly covered it.

"Fuck it all." The words were dashed away by the icy breeze, leaving only the shape of the sound behind.

While the other Canadian communities Rich had driven through looked like the America he'd left, the town of Waterton was strangely out of time. The Rocky Mountains formed a hollow bowl in which the Park was situated, huddled against the border with the United States. A chain of lakes flowed between craggy precipices. It was fringed by an elbow of flatland which held a scattering of buildings. Pockets of trees appeared between the houses, the forest greedily encroaching on civilization. While most buildings were quaint and small, built in the Alpine style, a few others were heavy-set log cabins with rotting, moss-covered roofs, heaving under advanced age. By comparison, the unfinished Whitewater Lodge, the centre-point in town, was a glaring edifice to modernity. The outer 'C' of the mountain hamlet wrapped the newly-built lodge like arms. These appendages were connected by the clasped hands of a small business centre, the line of Cameron Creek crossing through it like the cédille on a French 'Ç'. It was surrounded by a wall of trees.

For visitors, Waterton was a sparkling gem in the unexpected setting of the Rockies, untouched and pure. But Rich cared for none of its beauty. He was here for a job, nothing else. The silvered, desolate beauty of the landscape was lost on him.

Ears burning with frostbite, Rich headed to the trunk. His jacket—the heaviest he owned—was cut through by daggers of wind, the gusts sharpened as they descended down rocky cliffs and across the icy lake. He'd been warned that spring came late to the Rockies, even here in the southern end of Canada. With numbed fingers he tugged his laptop and suitcase from the sports car's shallow trunk and trudged up the slick path to the main building.

He already wanted to go home.

* * *

The strains of *The Price is Right* theme song filled Rich's ears as he swung open the front door. There was no doorman to take his bags, no welcoming hubbub of happy guests. The couches on either side of the stone fireplace were bare; the sole occupant of the shabbily-decorated great room was a young woman who sat behind the counter, beer can in hand.

"Mr. Evans!" the night clerk squeaked in horror. "You're early!"

Rich grimaced. *This* was the mess that his predecessor, Jeff Chan, had left behind when he'd abandoned his post last fall.

The young woman was off the stool, had tucked the open beer under the counter, and flicked off the television behind her before he'd made it off the welcome mat. She ran a quick hand over her clothes, doing up a button on her blazer while he took the few short steps up to the counter.

"We were told you'd be in tomorrow morning," she said anxiously. "I didn't realize flights came into Lethbridge this late."

"They don't," he said, gaze flicking to her name-tag: *Amanda*. "I drove."

Her lashes flared wide. "All the way from New York?"

"No," he growled. "I flew into Calgary, picked up my car, and drove the rest of the way."

"Well, I'm glad the weather cooperated for you," she said, falsely bright. "There's been lots of snow this year. The upper lake froze over."

Rich made a noise that could have been an answer or an expression of irritation. He dropped his bags on the floor with a thud, layering the rug with a coating of snow.

"Key," he snapped.

Amanda's expression wavered. "Key to...?"

"To my room," he said, hand outstretched. "I'm here for the next six months; I'm not sleeping in a tent."

She dug through a nearby drawer, pulling out a rusted skeleton key. "Aha!" Amanda said. "There it is!"

Rich frowned down at it. "This isn't a room key."

She giggled, leaning onto the counter so that her cleavage thrust forward.

"Of course not, Mr. Evans. It's the manager's cottage. You know, the place they bought when this ol' thing," she swirled her hands above her head, "was getting finished."

"Whitewater has a separate house for the manager?"

"Not a house," she purred, "a cabin."

CHAPTER TWO

Dawn came too quickly, and Rich struggled to awaken when the alarm went off. He shaved and showered, putting on his second-best suit and heaviest top-coat, then headed out into the early morning haze. Around him, sun-tipped ridges soared, looming golden over the far southern edge of town where the manager's cabin was located. He shielded his eyes, taking in his home for the foreseeable future.

His was the last cabin before the campground, beyond that was untouched forest. The two-storey house had cross-timbered peaks and faded stucco, its roof covered with uneven cedar shakes. Against the majestic sky, it looked like a doll's house, while eight blocks away—dead centre in the target of the small town—the straight angles and bold lines of the newly-constructed Whitewater Lodge perched like an ungainly bird against the backdrop of lofty peaks. It looked, Rich decided, like an unfinished drawing from a discarded Frank Lloyd Wright sketchbook, but even from this distance, dark blotches on the surface marred the illusion of perfection. Pieces of siding were peeling under the onslaught of wind. Seeing it, Rich grimaced. He buttoned his coat and trudged down the front steps. What he saw beyond the porch had him stumbling to a stop.

There were footprints in the snow.

His eyes widened in indignation. The path moved from the road, up to the porch, and then, most disturbingly, *around the house*. There wasn't a fence on the property, so it wasn't exactly trespassing, but the fact that someone had come onto the lot irritated him. He stood for several seconds, weighing whether to walk or drive. Before he'd decided, something moved through the bushes at the side of his property, chittering angrily. The sound startled him into action.

He jogged across the yard, snow leaching over the side of his shoes and past the thin layer of his socks. "Deal with it when I get home," he muttered, sliding the key into the car's door and climbing inside.

He didn't return for sixteen hours.

By that time, the restless wind had shaped the snow into soft dunes, the area where the footprints had crossed the lot scoured bare. Rich followed the edge of the shadowy porch, searching for a hint of the intruder's tracks.

"Oh for Chrissake," he snarled.

The spot around the windows was covered by drifted snow, and any hopes that the police might take impressions of the footprints was quickly dashed. Instead, Rich made a mental note to check out the cabin's security systems, and headed inside. That thought was quickly lost under a backlog of tasks: organizing the staff time-sheets, ordering items for the upcoming long weekend, and reviewing the previous winter's ledgers. By the time he fell asleep, still clothed, the footprints and any concern from them were long buried.

It took Rich less than a week to realize that this job was going to be a hell of a lot more difficult than he'd expected. With last summer's fiasco—one wing of the hotel open, while the rest were a drain on any revenue, followed by Chan's disappearance in the fall—he had expected the position to be a challenge. He hadn't realized he'd have the entire town to contend with.

With the hotel finally complete—*roughed in*—his mind corrected, he was there to get this new business off the ground for the coming summer. It should have been a simple task. The Park was in a pristine spot and no one had taken advantage of the potential revenue. There were no four or five star hotels in Waterton. Rich figured even three stars was pushing their ranking. And that meant that the wealthiest visitors simply didn't stay. They drifted in, stayed a night at the archaic Prince of Wales Hotel, located high on a hill overlooking the town, then left again, happy to be on their way.

Rich intended to change this.

The problem was Waterton itself. The mountains surrounding it were a barrier to the rest of the world, blocking most cell phone reception, and causing insurmountable issues with internet access and cable television. The third night after arriving, he'd attended his first Chamber of Commerce meeting, where a bed and breakfast owner named Susan Varley had growled that people came to escape from their lives.

"Like a cruise ship," she said, her wrinkled face grooved with annoyance. "You don't want to bring in the troubles from the outside world." The woman's grandmotherly appearance was at odds with her acid tongue.

"This town is hardly a cruise liner," he retorted, "and even out on a ship in the middle of nowhere, you can certainly have access to internet if you want to pay for it."

With that, the room erupted into chaos, and the rest of the discussion splintered into a thousand different lines. A stout businesswoman with a penchant for lurid clothing was the only one who'd spoken to him after that. Everyone else had been stone-faced after the meeting was adjourned.

No one had shaken his hand.

Rich wasn't making friends, but he didn't care. His job was to drag the Whitewater Lodge into the twenty-first century by the time the millennium arrived. Having driven there, Rich knew the area was surrounded by prairie; the nearest city, which boasted less than 80,000 people, an hour and a half away. Technology was antiquated and nothing satellite-related worked with any certainty. The mountains were too high, and the businesses too low. Waterton wasn't like Banff, with the quick-draw from Calgary, or like Denver, which was a city unto itself.

This place was a trap.

It was pristine but stark, the walls too high to look over to see the goldmine inside. *Or the rotten core*, Rich thought in disgust. But that was okay, he decided. He'd hate it, but he'd do it anyhow.

That was what he'd been hired to do, after all.

* * *

Louise Newman sat on the floor of the garage that was both her livelihood and passion, clipboard in hand. It wasn't yet 8:00 a.m., but she'd already been in the store for more than an hour and her back and knees ached from kneeling on the tiled floors. She added another hatch-mark onto the list and a sheet of black hair fell across her eyes. She tucked it back over her shoulder, twisting it absently into a loose knot as the bells on the door chimed.

"Just a sec'!" she called as she clambered to her feet.

Hunter Slate stood at the counter, leafing through the magazines next to the till. His rusted orange pickup truck was outside at the pump, three drooling mongrel dogs hanging out the windows, barking whenever a car drove by.

"Morning, Hunter. Should've known by the ruckus it was you," she said with a laugh.

Hunter's face broke into a wrinkled grin as he saw her. He was dressed for the outdoors, his plaid hunting jacket loose despite the chill, chin stubbled, grey hair shaggy.

"Thought maybe you'd taken off on us," he teased. "Didn't see you hiding back there."

Lou slapped her hands against her pants, dust rising. "Oh, I'd let you know if I was going anywhere." She nodded to the truck beyond the window. Two of Hunter's dogs snapped and lunged at one another, the other baying at the overcast sky. "You heading out today?" It wasn't hunting season, but the dogs in the truck suggested that was exactly what was happening.

"Colt's got cougar trouble again," Hunter explained. "Thought me 'n the dogs could give him a hand."

Lou pursed her lips, exasperated. Colton Calhoun was a backcountry guide whose stables were located on the wide plain next to the Waterton River, a ten minute drive outside of town. With his easy laughter and rugged good looks, Colt had an uncanny ability to talk himself out of (and into) trouble. That quirk hadn't changed since their schooldays.

"Did Colt at least call Grant about the cougar?" she asked dryly.

Hunter's mouth quirked up. While he wasn't a conservationist, Hunter could usually be cajoled into doing the right thing. "Thing is, Lou," he said, shrugging, "Colt's grazing his horses out on his cousin's ranch. The cougar's on private property, not the Park's. I wouldn't be headin' out otherwise."

"Of course not."

Hunter grinned, pulling out a faded billfold and tapping it once on the counter over the lottery tickets and the scratch and wins.

"Course not," he repeated, unabashed. "Wouldn't be right, y'know."

Lou couldn't help the snort that escaped her lips.

"So if I could fill'er up, hon, I'll just be on my way."

Lou reached under the counter, flicking the pump release.

"You got it, Hunter."

* * *

Lou was in the shop, elbow deep in the innards of a dying Dodge, when Mila's face appeared at the edge of the door. The teen's hair was pulled back into a tight ponytail, her jaw popping a wad of gum.

"You got someone for the garage," she called.

Lou peered over to see a silver BMW sports car limping its way across the gravelled lot. The vehicle was idling high, engine whining, and Lou's mind ticked through the potential issues as it approached. The whine rose to a roar when the driver slammed it into park.

"Doesn't sound good," Lou said with a grin.

The stranger, tall and blond, eyed her uncertainly as he stepped out of the car. His cheekbones were cut high above a straight-edged jaw, an aristocratic nose paired with pale eyes glittering like shards of ice. The well-known image of Sir Edmund Hillary mounting Everest flashed to mind, but quickly faded when Lou took in the rest of his attire. It took only a second for her mind to add up the expensive suit and silk tie to know the Whitewater Lodge's new manager was standing in her garage.

"Started idling kind of high on the way down from the lake," he said. "You know that lake back over..." He gestured vaguely toward the mountain range behind them.

"Cameron?"

He gave her a weak smile. "Right. Cameron. It started doing it there and it hasn't lowered yet."

Lou nodded. The road from Cameron Lake would put most cars through a workout, but this one appeared new. "Well, I won't know for sure until I look, so take it into the stall and we'll see what's going on."

The uneasy expression returned and his mouth twisted scornfully. She waited, certain he was going to say something. Lou'd heard it too many times before: *a woman doing a man's work.* She'd already decided how she was going to cut him down if he did. Instead, he said nothing, just put the car in gear and eased it forward. She smiled and followed.

Lou had a feeling about him.

Lou's Garage was both the sole gas station and repair shop for the town, the sloping roof, white stucco and red trim reminiscent of a Swiss gift shop rather than an industrial mechanic. The building was poised between the entrance road and the town's minuscule downtown. Rich had driven past it numerous times since he'd arrived in Waterton. He'd never set foot inside it until today.

Rich had rarely felt so out of place. The garage, with its oil stains and grime, was a minefield. If he'd been in his weekend jeans, he would have liked it, but being here now, forced into the role of voyeur as the woman's glossy black mane disappeared behind the hood, he felt trapped.

He waited next to the car, moving out of the mechanic's way as she brushed past for the umpteenth time. Rich knew her name now. She was Louise Newman, the 'Lou' of Lou's Garage. She wasn't at all what he'd been expecting. She was slightly built, narrow through the hips and chest, and she moved with feline grace. Her long hair was tied back in a red bandanna, bringing attention to the slant of her almond-shaped, amber-coloured eyes. She made him a little uncomfortable, but he'd certainly met enough attractive women in his years in New York. What disconcerted him was the way that the conversation kept jumping from place to place.

"Enjoying the weather lately?" she asked. "It's nice that spring's finally on its way."

"Sort of ... hadn't really noticed," Rich admitted.

"Hadn't noticed the weather'd changed, or hadn't noticed that it was spring?" Lou asked, winking at him as she reached into the engine.

"I, um ... the weather," he said, crossing and uncrossing his arms.

Rich leaned back against the workbench, then stepped away once more, checking the back of his pants for marks. Finding none, he settled in place, watching her work. If she wasn't picking apart his engine, he'd be inclined to think she looked like someone he'd meet in a boardroom, though she clearly knew what she was doing under the hood of a car.

She lifted her head as if she'd heard his thoughts, catching Rich staring. He held her gaze, waiting for her to drop her eyes. It was what most women would do.

Lou didn't.

She clucked her tongue. "You're not doing a good job hiding it."

"Hiding what?"

She pointed at him with the wrench she held. Her grin was wide and mischievous, unsettling him with its certainty. "Might as well 'fess up. Dressed like that you're either a tourist or the new manager of Whitewater."

Rich opened his mouth to argue but changed his mind.

Lou leaned under the car's open hood. "Doesn't seem to be the accelerator pump," she muttered. "Not the coolant system either ... might still be the carburetor, but can't be sure. Fuel pressure seems okay for now. I can adjust the ignition timing, and see if that works."

She popped up from behind the hood.

"You could go for a coffee, you know. This might take a while."

His face fell. "Really? How long?"

"As long as it takes. Not even sure what's wrong."

"Shit."

Lou unhooked a pair of faded mechanic's coveralls from the side of the garage and handed them to him. "Don't worry, Mr. Evans," she said wryly, "I'll be charging for the task, not the time."

"Rich."

"Okay, Rich. If you have things to do, then go." She gestured to the coveralls. "Or you could stay if you wanted."

He glanced outside. The day was bright and full of spring sunshine, the last of the snow tucked in the building's bluish shadows. He could go back to the Whitewater Lodge. There were accounts to balance, and the manager's cabin to unpack. Staff to retrain and repairs to organize. Truth was, there were any number of other tasks calling for his attention.

His gaze moved back to the dim garage. Once, long ago, he'd spent hours in a shop not much different than this. The thought left him aching. He held the stained coveralls, the fabric tattered and heavy in his hands, fighting the urge to stay.

When he didn't move, Lou spoke. "This reminds me of a story I once heard about a long journey through the mountains."

His brows quirked sceptically. "A story?"

"It's one my father told me. It involved a group of men that came to this area when it was first being settled." She turned back to the engine, hands moving on their own, her mind drifting to another time. "This was around the time of Kootenai Brown," she said, peeking at him. "He was an old man then, but he knew the wilderness, and settlers would come to him for advice. One day, three men came into town, looking to set up claims."

"Claims for?" Rich's lips pursed, annoyance appearing under his polite façade.

"For ranching, or prospecting," she said with a shrug. "Not sure." Her attention shifted as she moved through the engine, dismantling it in her mind. "Kootenai suggested they head out past Bellevue Hill and move into that valley. There was plenty of wildlife there, lots of game to hunt, fresh water, trees. They settled in the valley by the Crandell Mountain Campground. It was a good spot and they had a crude camp in a few weeks. They cleared the land, panned for gold, worked from sunup to sundown."

Something brushed Lou's elbow and she turned. Rich was staring into the engine, something akin to pain creasing his brow. He glanced up, catching her watching him, and the expression disappeared, disaffection returning.

"They were working?" he prompted.

"Yes, and one day," Lou said, "one of the three settlers, a man by the name of Ephraim Thompson, went out to get them supplies. He'd been trading with the Blood Tribe and had stopped in to visit with Kootenai before heading home. By the time he left, the weather was starting to change. Cloud cover came over the mountain, settling in and making the old trails look completely different."

She looked over at Rich again. His hands were tight at his sides, his attention on the engine.

"Ephraim knew he should be close to the camp, but he couldn't seem to find his way," Lou continued. "Partway there, the brush around him grew thicker, and he realized that he had somehow found his way onto a game trail, rather than the path he'd been following all along. When Ephraim realized he was going the wrong way, he had to make a choice, to either turn back and find his way to camp, or keep going and see where the path led. The horse was heaving under the strain of the packs, but Ephraim could have pressed on."

She paused, fiddling with the distributor cap. It was bound tight, and Lou fought to release it. She had just begun to check the ignition wires when Rich spoke.

"So what did he do?" His voice was softer than she expected.

"He left the horse next to a small creek," Lou said. "You might know the place, if you've driven that way. It's called 'Lost Horse Creek.' While the horse rested, Ephraim followed the path on up the valley. It led him to the source of the creek that came through their camp, someplace that he'd never been before ... probably someplace no one had visited, ever."

She lifted her gaze. Rich's expression was dubious. "What was it?"

"It was Red Rock Canyon. One of the most beautiful places in Waterton ... in the Rockies, for that matter. And it was there, waiting for him to find it. As long as he was willing to look for it."

The lines around Rich's mouth deepened. "So what's that supposed to mean?" he sneered. "I'm supposed to just sit here in your garage and be happy about it?"

Lou walked to where the toolboxes sat in neat stacks. "No," she said, returning items. "It's just a story."

"Just a story," he repeated. She didn't have to be watching him to hear the insult in the tone.

Lou returned to the driver's side of the car, leaned across the seat and turned the ignition. The car started with a purr. She stood up, smiling to herself.

"You can pay up front, Mr. Evans. Your car's fixed."

At the till, a teen took Rich's Visa card, pulling out an old-fashioned credit card machine that he recalled using back when he'd been in college a decade earlier. She inserted his card, slamming the cover back and forth, then offered it to him to sign. He shook his head in amusement. *Only in Waterton,* he thought.

The cost of the repairs, listed as: *Adjusted the ignition timing and checked hoses and the carburetor. Seems fine,* was far less than he expected. Rich looked up at the clock above the doorway, his eyes widening in shock.

An hour had passed and he hadn't once thought about leaving.

* * *

Long past midnight, the stony silence of the mountain was shattered. A lurching shadow stretched across the trail, a man's form appearing by degrees. Middle-aged and overweight, he forced his body on without mercy. Stones flicked under fumbling feet, twigs broke, but his pace never wavered. He couldn't stop. If he did, he'd die.

The man peered over his shoulder. In the muddy half-light, the darkness was alive; narrow bands of moonlight danced between looming trees. Was that a man or a rock? From this distance, he couldn't tell, but he didn't slow to find out. Free from his captor, he careened down the path, stumbling on wobbly legs, lungs on fire.

Sudden laughter taunted him from the shadows. A whine—high-pitched and terrified—echoed in the man's ears. It took him a moment to realize that *he* was the one making the sound.

"There are animals in these woods," a voice shouted. "They'll find you even if I don't."

"No!" the man yelped, his terror surging into all-out panic. He zigzagged off the darkened trail into the solid black of the underbrush, stumbling, falling, and then standing again. The canopy closed in, blocking the faint starlight. Every noise was amplified, the pounding of his heart crashing like cymbals. He froze, trying desperately to control his breathing. If he could hide, then he'd be safe until—

Behind him, the bushes crackled as someone stepped into the forest.

"Come out, come out, wherever you are," a singsong voice taunted.

The man tore forward blindly. Twigs slashed his face, blood stinging his eyes. He tripped on a hidden log, falling headlong into a tangle of brush. The laughter—appallingly near—echoed louder. Crawling to his feet, he sprinted from his hiding spot. The bushes that had caught his clothes abruptly let go and he stumbled through, falling to his knees on an open patch of ground.

It was quieter here, the faint sound of a wind rising around him. A veil of clouds had closed in since he'd entered the trees; even the moon was hidden. The man bolted. If he could get far enough away he could hide until morning, figure out where he was, and find his way back to town.

"Oh Jesus, Jesus," the man whispered. "Please—"

The earth fell away from his feet, and then slammed back against him. Knives of rocks stabbed through flailing arms as he pin-wheeled down a cliff face, landing with a horrifying crunch at the bottom. Excruciating pain brought with it a strange calmness. He was broken ... *everywhere*. One leg was twisted at an impossible angle, his mouth full of the salt-tang of blood. But below his waist, there was no feeling at all. He took a rattling breath, staring upward. In that moment, the clouds parted, moonlight flooding the trail from which he'd just fallen.

A figure waited for him at the top.

CHAPTER THREE

The next few days trickled by for Rich. With the snow receding, there were no more footprints, though one night he'd woken up near midnight, *certain* he'd heard someone on the porch. He headed downstairs, adding another note to his ever-growing mental list: *see about an alarm*, but when he'd turned on the porch light, no one was there.

The garage door was partially ajar when he rushed off to work the next morning. Given the unrelenting wind, Rich assumed that it'd blown open in the night. He was too busy to worry.

The hotel had begun to transform under his guidance: sullen-faced workers who'd met him at the first staff meeting slowly changed into the type of employees he could rely on. The night staff, on their way home, nodded when Rich arrived just after dawn each morning; cleaning ladies smiled coyly when he met them in the hallways, giggling behind their hands once he passed. But for every step forward, a new issue arose. It felt like unravelling a Gordian knot which retied each night.

After one morning's staff meeting, Rich stormed back to the main desk, Amanda rushing to keep up. "I can't plan out the staff schedules if no one tells me when they need their personal days until the last minute," he snapped, throwing the now-defunct staffing sheets onto the desk. "It doesn't *work* that way!"

"You need to talk to them, Mr. Evans."

"I do talk to them."

"Oh no," she laughed. "You talk *at* them. There's a difference."

He spun on her. "What's that supposed to mean?"

She gave him a cheeky grin. "You might try stopping a minute. Make small talk. Shoot the breeze once in a while."

"Shoot the breeze," he repeated.

"Exactly!"

Rich's lips curled into a snarl. "And how would that help?"

Amanda's expression wilted. "Oh, never mind," she sighed. "I'll talk to them for you."

Rich opened his mouth, then closed it again as an elderly couple came bustling through the main doors, a doorman with bags in tow. Rich waited while Amanda chattered to them, taking their credit card information and filling them in on scenic locales in the Park. As they headed away, she peeked over her shoulder, catching Rich waiting.

"Sorry, Mr. Evans. Did you need something else?"

"Thanks for the advice, Amanda," he said, lifting his hands in defeat. "I'll give it a try."

She grinned, and Rich headed back into his office, making a mental note to talk to the staff. *Small talk*, he thought wearily. *If only there was more time to schedule it in.*

Every hour seemed compressed. Part of Rich's day was spent scheduling the seasonal employees and reviewing the current approach to the hotel. Someone was skimming off the top and he intended to find out who. His first guess, Amanda Sloane, was quickly scratched from the list. She wasn't incompetent, as he'd originally assumed. Her warm manner and quick smile smoothed issues with guests, but she couldn't keep a secret for the life of her. Whoever was shorting the books could and did. There were various other employees with access to funds, and each day brought Rich closer to finding them.

Missing funds were just the start. While reorganizing the office he'd inherited, Rich had stumbled across a hefty unpaid loan for the Whitewater Lodge, co-signed by Jeff Chan, the previous manager. As Chan's replacement, the financial complications should have been easy to solve, but Chan had dropped off the radar—and the face of the earth—the previous fall. As Amanda put it, Chan had "taken off just after Thanksgiving, without even stopping to say goodbye." Despite a two-week police investigation and a private investigator hired by Coldcreek Enterprises who'd carried out his own search, no one had seen Chan since. Seething, Rich had contacted Coldcreek's financing team to check into the legitimacy of Chan's loan. The documents showed that the company which had provided the loan wasn't a bank, but a company called Borderline Industries. The elusive business had a number of financial agreements in Waterton and controlled an unexpected number of leases in the area surrounding the Whitewater Lodge.

A call to the Park office had only added to the confusion. Whatever Borderline Industries actually was, no one seemed to have contact information. When Rich demanded to talk to the official in charge of leases, his phone call had been passed from one staff member to another until, an hour later, he still found himself on hold. Furious, Rich made himself a note to check on the leases surrounding the Whitewater Lodge in person.

After organizing the maelstrom of paperwork, Rich put his attention to the Whitewater's technical issues. He headed to Main Street—located halfway between the lodge and his cabin—opting

to walk the four blocks rather than drive. His first stop was the police station, an antiquated two-storey building surrounded by a low
stone wall and a gravelled drive. With dark wood trim and peaked
dormers, it reminded Rich of the old promotional images of the
Canadian Pacific Railway. Once inside, Rich was directed to a narrow counter where he stood in a line of tourists carrying parking
tickets. After fifteen minutes of waiting, Rich reached the front of
the queue and made a report about the trespasser. The stone-faced
officer took his information, muttering that he'd swing by and "keep
an eye on the place."

Rich's second stop was at Fine and Fancy. The store was owned
by Audrika Kulkarni, the sole business owner who'd spoken to him
after the Chamber of Commerce meeting. Audrika's shop was one
of the many businesses that lined the Main Street. Though relatively
bare of shoppers, the tree-lined avenue was filled with the sound
of the marina, and the rumble of motorboat engines and buzz of
jet skis mingled with the strains of music on outdoor patios. Rich
wanted to talk to Audrika about hiring people to work on the internet and connectivity issue. She stood behind the counter, nodding
as he went through reasons to do it.

"Your last manager tried the same thing," she said as Rich finished. "Brought in some technicians from Lethbridge to look at the
issue."

"He did?"

"Chan did a lot of things. Made a lot of enemies, too." Her eyes
were black and beetled, at odds with her feline smile. "Wouldn't
suggest making the same mistakes, Mr. Evans."

Rich wanted to ask her more about Chan's enemies, but a bus-
load of tourists arrived and suddenly the shop was abuzz with en-
ergy. He stood at the side, watching Audrika pull trinkets out from

behind the counter, her manner all sunshine and chatter. Rich nodded to himself. The town definitely had potential, if you could get people to visit.

He walked back to the cabin to drop off a few items he'd purchased to appease Audrika and headed to his car. In New York, Rich would have walked, but with the town half-wilderness, a car felt safer when he knew he'd be getting home after nightfall. The lots here were overgrown with bushes, wild animals grazing on lawns, oblivious to the civilization which pressed in on them. The thought of running into a bear while walking in the dark had been niggling the back of his mind since he'd first arrived. According to the notes left by his predecessor, it had happened to him more than once.

For the rest of the afternoon, Rich sat in Whitewater's large industrial kitchen, checklist on lap, ticking off the items that needed to be corrected before the health inspector visited. The almost-forgotten food next to him was certainly acceptable, but this was no five-star hotel.

Not yet.

By the time he headed home in the strange, lingering twilight of the mountains, it was almost eight o'clock. The cabin was dark and empty, and he drove the car slowly, leaving it outside the garage at the end of the property. He turned off the engine, but didn't get out, letting his mind wander. His thoughts were full of Ephraim's story and the woman who'd told it, Louise Newman. He could imagine her now: the bow of her lips, the angle of her eyebrows, like slashes of punctuation above solemn eyes. *Gold*, his mind whispered. In his reverie, his gaze lifted and then snapped to attention.

There was a light in the upstairs window.

Riding a wave of shock and indignation, Rich reached for the cell phone in his breast pocket.

No reception.

Rich groaned, his mind flickering through possibilities. He needed a phone—*a goddamned hard-wired phone!*—before he could call anyone. But the house next door was still boarded up for the off-season and the nearest place after that was the Whitewater Lodge, eight blocks away. The upstairs light flicked off.

Without a second thought, Rich stepped out of the car.

He was halfway across the lawn when the door swung open and a shadowy figure appeared on the porch. "Hey!" Rich roared. "What the hell do you think you're—?"

The silhouette was in motion before he'd finished shouting. There was a crash as the intruder—tall and moving fast—jumped off the end of the porch into the darkness. Rich Evans had run track in high school and he pursued without delay. He sprinted after the trespasser, adrenaline pushing him faster than he'd moved in years.

The area around the manager's cottage was thick with foliage. The figure moved straight into the underbrush, twigs snapping as he headed inland, following the creek toward Cameron Falls, a place where the cabins ended and the forest began. Rich knew if the trespasser got that far, it was over. There were simply too many places to hide, too many paths to follow. Whoever this was knew the area.

Rich didn't.

Furious, Rich pushed harder, his breath coming in rapid pants, thighs burning. He knew in the back of his mind he should let the guy go, that the right thing to do was to stop running and go back to the house, but his anger urged him forward. The frustrations of the weeks of work, staffing issues, and building crises rose inside him, a wildfire burning away every other consideration.

Up ahead, the shadow veered toward the trees where mountains met plateau. He darted behind the cabins, dodging toward the road. Rich followed, nearly careening headlong into a swing set and losing precious time doing it. The sound of the waterfall was a distant rumble in his ears, the air heavy with humidity. His mind ordered him to go faster, but his legs were wobbly with exertion, heart pounding so hard it felt like it would burst.

There was a flash of russet and two startled deer bounded past. Rich's head jerked in surprise, but he didn't slow. He could no longer see the figure ahead of him, but the ground canted downward, his speed increasing as he moved toward the falls. Suddenly the greenery fell away, replaced by open ground, the roar of Cameron Falls deafening. A flicker of movement—gold this time—caught his attention on the cliff face next to the waterfall, and Rich stumbled to a halt.

There were cougars, three of them, and they were watching him.

He recalled reading Jeffrey Chan's last email to Coldcreek Enterprises, sent a week before the wayward manager had disappeared. *"Waterton is too primitive, and I don't feel I'm adequately prepared to manage a hotel in the area. There is dangerous wildlife in the townsite. My dog was killed by a cougar while chained in my yard."* Rich was panting, the sweat across his back icy. He was the only thing in the small clearing, except for the three cougars. One was the mother, the other two her half-grown cubs.

That's why the deer were running, he realized in belated horror.

The mother raised her head in interest and took two steps down the steep incline, muscles rippling under loose hide. Cunning eyes held his gaze. Rich took a single step backward, and then another, random snippets of information flashing in his mind. Cougars could take down much larger animals than themselves. They were known to be clever and enjoyed the hunt. Swift and deadly, the surest way to be chased was to turn and run.

Rich stopped in his tracks. He didn't have a chance. He was already winded.

With a calmness born from exhaustion and terror, the shaking of his body stilled, his heart slowing. The cougars were burnished gold in the moonlight, their shapes bright against the damp grey cliff. The two cubs moved across the ragged edge of the rocky outcrop, their mother a stone's throw below. Rich gasped as the female in front jumped to a lower ledge, balancing on the small precipice. She watched him warily, her head moving back and forth as if trying to ascertain what he was, and whether he was worth the bother. Rich waited out her attention, his mind skittering, looking desperately for an escape.

He couldn't see one.

Somewhere in the townsite—far enough, Rich would think later, that it felt like it was miles away—a dog's keening howl rose into the night air. The cougar shimmered like quicksilver. She lunged back up the rock, hissing at her cubs. The three of them moved across the stone face like wraiths, disappearing into the shadows of the undergrowth, leaving him alone on the path below.

Nerves shattered, Rich wheezed, his body humming. Everything felt brighter and sharper somehow. The air was cold, the wind carrying the tang of spray toward him. He lifted his gaze to the waterfall, seeing for the first time the picturesque cascade of falls.

This, Rich thought, *is how Ephraim felt.*

* * *

Lou stood at the kitchen sink, her eyes unfocused on her hazy reflection in the window. Outside the sky was fading from steely blue to indigo. The mountain range beyond was a solid sheet of black, cut out by a child's sloppy scissors. She was unsettled tonight, and cleaning tended to help, whether here in the cabin or back at the garage. Her gaze moved restlessly over the ragged peaks she knew so well: Crandell and Bertha on either side of the hollow where Cameron Falls ran; the wall of trees where her property ended and wilderness began. It was too quiet tonight; a dog's howl the only thing interrupting the silence.

Her mind had been nervously circling a half-realized emotion ever since she'd had coffee with Hunter this afternoon. People were already unhappy with Rich Evans' attempts to modernize the town, and according to Hunter, several locals were spoiling for a fight. The thought left Lou's stomach churning. It was a familiar sentiment, one she'd fought when Jeff Chan and Waterton's locals had locked horns last year. Lou's fingers slipped on a glass and it dropped back under the soapy water, thudding hollowly on the bottom of the sink. Lou hadn't known Chan personally, but she'd felt the effects of the growing conflict. When he'd disappeared, leaving his post at the Whitewater Lodge unattended, the town's calm had returned. Eyes still on the range, she picked up the glass in one hand and reached out with the other, twisting the knob for the faucet. Unnaturally cold water sluiced over her fingers.

Lou gasped, submerged by memory.

She stood in the knee-deep mud of a rural road, a man across from her. The two of them were dressed in ochre monks' robes, their feet bare, heads shaven. Lou's companion shouted at her to grab the rope, but she could barely hear him above the pounding rain. Without warning, the muddy pit at her feet exploded into motion. There, a water ox was trapped by the slurry of water and soil, its mouth foaming, eyes rolling in panic.

"Keep it steady!" her companion yelled. "Pull harder!" His words emerged in a language Lou didn't know, but could

suddenly understand.

She heaved. The hemp fibres sliced through her hands, leaving the rope wet with blood. In the gore on the rutted road, the animal lunged again, its horns slashing precariously near to the other man's legs. The ox roared, charging and falling.

"It's too strong!" Lou shouted.

The animal bellowed as it thrashed, pulling the two monks forward. The tip of one horn caught on Lou's robe, bringing her down. She scrambled backwards just as the animal swung back, close enough she could feel its warm breath.

"You need to control it!" the other monk yelled, voice shrill with fear.

Her bloodied hands tightened on the muddy rope, but it slid through her torn fingers.

"I can't!"

The animal turned again, its attention on her. She watched in dread as one hoof lifted from the mire, the beast moving in—

Lou jerked backwards, the glass falling from her fingers and shattering at her feet. The water was still running in the sink, full almost to the brim. She reached forward, turning it off with a trembling hand. She swallowed convulsively, the memory too real. She could taste that life, feel it pressing around her, and she waited until the steady beating of its heart faded and only echoes remained.

She'd had visions off and on her whole life. Occasionally they were the dull tug of a toothache, forgotten almost immediately. Other times they arced like a live wire, leaving her caught in between. But even more rarely than that, they foretold something to come.

This was one of those times.

Once, she would have talked to her mother about the dream, letting Yuki's words roll over her like waves, soothing her fears. Now she had no one, but the urge for comfort was stronger than her need for privacy. Heart pounding, she turned and picked up the phone, dialling Hunter's number.

The phone rang three times before he picked up. She let out a relieved breath as the old man's voice broke through the receiver.

"H'lo?"

"Hi, Hunter," she said, "it's me."

"Hey, hon. How are you?"

She looked at the kitchen window. Outside the sky was now charcoal, the mountain range an unbroken black shape, the howling dog silent.

"Um ... had a weird day, I suppose. It left me feeling a bit off." She had known Hunter Slate almost her entire life, and she knew there were things he wasn't comfortable with. Lou kept her innermost thoughts from him the same as she did with everyone else. "I wanted to make sure you were okay."

He let out a snort. "Checkin' on me, hmm? I'm not that old, you know."

She smiled, turning her back to the window and the darkness it framed. "Well, yes, sort of," she admitted with a laugh. "I'm sure you'd do the same for me."

His voice returned, quieter. "'Course I would, Lou. Not even a question."

"Thanks," she said, "that means a lot to me. Really." She took a steadying breath. Lou didn't like conflict, and she knew this would cause it. "You know, Hunter, I was thinking about what happened last year."

"Oh?"

Seconds dragged out, with only Hunter's wheezing breath rattling the receiver.

Lou kept her voice light. "The stuff with Chan. The way people got up in arms when he started changing things."

"Mmmph," Hunter muttered. "Brought the trouble on himself, if you ask me."

"Well, yes and no," she said. "But I was thinking about how all the trouble started when he arrived, and now that the new manager is here—"

"Lookit, Lou," Hunter interrupted, his voice taking on the hardened timbre she remembered from her childhood, when he and her father had argued. "You got something to ask me about Chan, then you come say it to my face. 'Cause I ain't done a thing to be ashamed of."

"I wasn't saying—"

"You know damned well you were, and I won't have it. Chan was a troublemaker from the start, and I'm glad he's gone."

Lou squeezed her eyes shut, heart pounding. The feeling was back—the gloom pressing inward—except now it was tangled with guilt. "Sorry, Hunter, I never meant to suggest you'd—" She let the rest go unsaid. "Look, I'm just hoping that things stay ... *calm*, now that the new manager's arrived."

Several heartbeats passed before Hunter answered.

"S'pose that'll be up to him then, won't it?"

Lou let out a weary sigh, her thoughts on Rich Evans. "Yes, I imagine so."

* * *

Rich and a bleary-eyed police officer stood in the upstairs bedroom of the manager's cabin. Piles of paper were strewn across the hardwood floor; desk drawers pulled out and tossed onto the bed. A large scrape marred one wall where the intruder had forced open the safe, knocking it to its side as he did.

"Hell of a mess," the officer grumbled, lifting up the police report and leafing through it.

Rich had already identified the missing papers: documents regarding bulk purchases for Whitewater's kitchens, a folder of employee files, Chan's loan agreement, and all the notes he'd gathered on Borderline Industries. It was a huge step backward; everything Rich had worked on was gone. Given the items taken, the police had begun looking at people with ties to the Whitewater Lodge. The only staff member still unaccounted for at this hour was one of the kitchen staff, twenty-year-old Lucas Sorenson.

"Your statement says you chased the perpetrator down to Cameron Falls," the officer said, "but you lost him after that."

"Uh-huh." Rich squinted at his name-tag: *Constable Flagstone*, forcing himself to remember it.

"Should have just called it in," Flagstone said, "but you probably know that, being from the city."

"Yes," Rich ground out, "I know that."

"Or driven," he added. "Lou tells me you've got a nice enough car."

Rich's eyes widened. "The guy was on foot!"

The officer shrugged, glancing back at the report. "Also says you saw a cougar up there at the Falls. I'll need to let Warden McNealy know about that."

"Yes. Three of them."

"You're a damned lucky man to walk away from that," he snorted. "Running 'round in the dark by yourself." The officer's smirk told Rich the rest of what he wanted to say: *damned city slicker.*

"Do cougars usually come this close to town?" Rich asked.

Flagstone eyed him curiously. "The cougars have been here forever," he said, flipping the report closed. "We're the ones who've moved into their territory."

A woman's voice echoed up the stairs before Rich could answer. "Jimmy! You up there? Perkins just called!"

Flagstone walked carefully down the risers, head ducked to avoid the angled slope of the eaves. Scowling, Rich followed. A uniformed woman with two long, black braids waited in the kitchen, her cheeks flushed with excitement.

"You've got to see this," she said, pushing a piece of paper into Constable Flagstone's hands. All Rich could see was a series of shorthand notes, but whatever the man read concerned him.

"Shit."

"What is it?" Rich asked.

"An update from the Pincher Creek RCMP."

"RCMP?"

Flagstone gave him a tight smile. "The Royal Canadian Mounted Police," he said. "A squad car just picked up the Sorenson kid on the highway outside the Park.

CHAPTER FOUR

Twenty-eight year-old Constable Sadie Black Plume squatted at the edge of the ravine, her attention on the broad expanse of broken rock below. The scree slope below the Lineham trail was littered with stone shards from the mountainside above; jagged bits, larger than shale, treacherously sharp. At the bottom lay a carcass, broken and bloodied, its white ribs poking out from a half-eaten torso. Two hikers had noticed a bear feeding on it this morning and had contacted the Park Office. Grant McNealy, the warden, had made a grisly discovery when he'd come to close the trail.

It wasn't a deer or a sheep at the bottom of the cliff. *It was a man.*

"Goddammit," Sadie muttered. She lifted the field glasses to her eyes, then dropped them down, frustration rising. It was a chilly spring day, but the coldness she felt had nothing to do with the weather.

"No one's filed a missing person's report," a voice said. "Whoever it is, no one knows he's gone yet." The toe of Jim's boots appeared on the ground next to Sadie and she glanced up. "Stupid tourists," Jim grumbled. "Wish they'd just stay home."

The corpse was ravaged beyond recognition, limbs scattered across the scree slope by carrion eaters. Jim offered his hand but Sadie ignored it. She scrambled upright, backing away from the cliff's edge. It was going to be a hell of a climb to get down to the body.

"You ready to head down and check out the scene?" she asked.

Jim nodded. "You'd think people'd be smarter," he said. "Guy out here, hiking alone. Must've fallen off the cliff and been found by a bear."

Sadie looked back down the path. "Grant thinks he might have been attacked while he was on the trail." She pointed to the woods. "There's a path through the trees, scuff marks on the rocks at the edge, like he was running."

"Or tripped."

"Either way, it's an awful way to die."

"Stupid, is what it is," Jim said. He peered over the cusp of the deadly slope. "Weird..."

"What's that?"

He shaded his eyes with his hand, squinting. "Don't think the guy's wearing shoes."

"Huh," Sadie muttered, lifting the binoculars once more. "Not sure. Too much blood to tell."

"Can't see a damned thing from up here," Jim said. "Need a way down."

Sadie nodded and they headed back the way they'd come. There was an outcrop of trees and brush a little lower on the trail. It would be a punishing climb, but they'd stand a better chance of making it to the body without breaking a leg if they went this way. Sadie turned sideways on the trail, taking a single, sliding step into the bushes. She stumbled through the foliage, catching herself on the trees as she dropped in elevation. A few feet away, Jim followed.

For a time they climbed in silence, their passage marked by crunching twigs.

"I'll check the body for ID," Jim panted, "if you want to take photos of the scene." He was ten years older and fifty pounds heavier than Sadie; the hike was already taking its toll. His sides heaved, rings of perspiration darkening the fabric under his arms.

Sadie rolled her eyes. "It's fine, Jimmy. I've seen my fair share of bodies. You don't have to coddle—" She stopped in her tracks, heart pounding. "Stop!"

Jim went motionless at her command. "What do you see?" His tone was all business, his hand on his gun.

"Look up ahead," she said. "Those branches are broken. And there on the slope; see that mark on the rock? I think that's a footprint." Her eyes were bright despite the filtered light. "Something came this way already."

"The hikers who found him?" Jim asked.

"Nope. They never left the trail."

"Grant come down to check on the site?"

"Only from up above," she said. "He called for us as soon as he saw what it was."

Jim peered around them, voice dropping. "The bear?"

"Maybe, or maybe someone else was with this guy when he fell."

With cautious steps, both officers crept forward, leaving the cool shadow of the trees and stepping into warm sunlight. They walked slowly toward the corpse, avoiding the black lines of dried blood which trailed across the slope. The scene sprang into focus as they neared. What appeared to be the dead man's ragged shirt wasn't clothing, but the stripped remains of muscle and flesh. From this lowered perspective, the scene was visible in gory detail. His dismembered limbs were bare, twigs caught in his hair, scratches across the gouged remains of his bloody face.

The man was naked.

Sadie lifted her camera, snapping pictures of the scene while Jim crouched next to a gnawed arm. "This wasn't an accident," he announced.

"What's that?" Sadie asked distractedly.

"Look at the wrist."

Sadie peered through the lens, snapping photographs. "Severed," she hissed.

Jim stood slowly and stretched his back. "The guy's teeth have been smashed in too. Clothes gone. No shoes."

Sadie lowered the camera, face blanching. "Whoever did this didn't want him to be identified."

Saying it aloud, the day grew colder.

For an interminable hour they secured and documented the murder scene. With the photographs taken and the bloody trail marked through the trees, a picture of the man's violent ending had emerged. He'd spent his last minutes on the run, only stopping when he'd fallen over the cliff. His pursuer had taken the same path as Jim and Sadie, shooting the man twice at point-blank range in the back of the head, then dismembering the body and removing all identifying features.

"Just don't understand it," Sadie said as they put the last evidence kit aside.

"Understand what?"

"Why kill the guy *here* of all places?"

"Don't relish the thought of climbing back up to the trail?" Jim teased.

"That's not it at all," she said. "It's been bugging me since we got here. This body was left out in the open. Whoever did this to him didn't have to leave him like that."

Jim's smile faded. "Keep going."

"Whoever came after this guy could've dragged the victim into the trees. Nobody would've noticed the blood on the rocks. I was looking right at it and I didn't see it until we got down to the bottom. Didn't need to shoot him either. Could've just left the guy out here in the open. He was so bashed up, he wouldn't have lasted until morning. Everyone would've assumed he fell."

"True." Jim nodded.

"This bastard chose this place, Jimmy. He chose to climb down through the trees after the guy fell. And he chose this mother-fucking scree slope to leave him on for someone else to find."

Jim squinted up at the barren slope and the trail above them. A storm cloud passed in front of the sun, leaving them standing in icy shadow. In the last hour, the air had grown heavy with the scent of coming rain.

"He *wanted* people to see what he'd done," Jim muttered.

* * *

Rich was in a terrible mood. The entire morning had been overcast, the rain alternating between a fine drizzle and torrential downpour, but never lifting. With May's arrival, muddy spring appeared, swollen buds exploding into the first blush of green on bare, black branches. The days were growing incrementally warmer, but the change of seasons did nothing for Rich's mood. Through the slash of windshield wipers he searched for the Park's main office, driving his car from the town's single entrance, along the lakeshore with its cabins, past the marina and Lou's Garage to the barren main street, before turning at the RCMP station, circling past the theatre, and retracing his steps to the entrance once more.

He followed the circuit twice, temper rising with each pass.

Rich had just pulled his car over to the curb across from Lou's Garage, intending to go ask Louise Newman for directions (something which irked him more than he wanted to admit), when he realized that the cabin on Mountview Avenue wasn't just another house, but an administration building. The office faced the marina. It had a jutting bow window, stone foundation and angled roof, blending chameleon-like into the cabins which surrounded it.

Rich gathered a folder of papers and tucked it under his coat. A blanket of moisture enveloped him the moment he stepped onto the street. Rain buzzed on the rooftops, fat drops snapping against the pavement and soaking his shoes. Swearing, he dodged puddles and aimed for the small entranceway which he hoped was the front door. To his relief, it was.

He ducked inside, wiping his water-soaked shoes on the mat. The interior of the Park office was filled with generations-old office furniture, the walls covered in faded black and white prints, nothing like the shiny, modern offices of Coldcreek Enterprises in New York. Behind the front counter, a woman with a helmet of tight curls tapped away at an older model computer. Other staff moved around the small office, engrossed in their tasks.

The receptionist's fingers paused as he neared. "Bonjour. Good morning," she said pleasantly. "Can I help you, sir?"

"Yes, you can," Rich said, laying a list of lot numbers and names on the counter. "I'd like to go through the real property reports and lease agreements for the lots along Cameron Falls Drive and Fountain Avenue."

The receptionist's pencilled brows pulled together as she scanned the list. "Are you planning to purchase a cabin in Waterton?"

"Not buying," Rich said, pushing the paper forward. "But I need the records for these lots."

The woman stared at the paper as if it was a snake. "Land developer?"

"No."

"Lawyer?"

"No. Just here for the records," Rich repeated. He tapped the list with his forefinger. "I want to see the documents for these cabins and land-holders."

The woman frowned. "What do you need them for?"

"I'm doing some research into the leases in the centre of town."

"Why?"

Rich grit his teeth. "Because I have an issue with the company which controls a number of these leases."

"What kind of issue?"

"I'm not here to discuss it, I'm here to—"

The woman's hands rose up in exasperation. "Unless I know what the problem is, I don't see how I can help you."

"The Whitewater Lodge has some business with Borderline Industries—the company in control of those leases," he said testily. "I'm having some difficulty locating the contact information. So far as I can tell, no one seems to actually know *what* Borderline is."

The discussion began to draw the attention of the other people around the office. Several paused in their tasks, watching the interaction with obvious interest.

The receptionist glared at Rich. "This isn't our issue, sir."

"Actually, it is, because Borderline Industries owns a number of leases in this Park. Now, can you pull those records for me, or not?"

"I'll need some identification first."

Rich set his bag on the counter, searching through his breast pocket until he found his New York driver's license. "Will this do?"

The woman glanced at the card before pushing the papers back toward him. "I'm sorry, Mr. Evans, but you're at the wrong place," she said icily. "You should be over at the Historical Society. It's on Main Street."

"They're the ones who told me that this is where the documents are housed," he said. "Now, I need to see those lease agreements."

The woman returned to her typing. "I'm afraid I can't help you with that."

"Excuse me?" Rich coughed. "Are you refusing?"

The other people in the room went silent.

"You'll have to look elsewhere," the receptionist said, her fingers a blur on the keyboard. "I can't do anything for you."

Rich braced his hands on the counter, looming forward. "Those files are public record," he barked. "I'm a member of the public, and I want to see them!"

A suited man appeared in the doorway of an interior office, peering out worriedly.

The woman's fingers paused again. "The records are public for Canadian citizens," she replied coolly. "And you, sir, are an American."

With a muttered swear, Rich reached into his bag, pulling out a hand-held video camera he'd used earlier this morning to document the shoddy millwork in the east wing. He flicked on the power button and hit 'record', holding the camera aloft.

"Are you refusing to provide me records?" Rich asked loudly. There was an audible gasp from the people in the office.

"Get that camera out of here!" the man in the doorway shouted.

Rich kept recording.

"Leases in the Park are public record," Rich said. "Are you refusing to give me access to them?"

The woman's eyes were wide circles. She glanced over her shoulder to the man in the suit. "I-I never said that."

"You said that I couldn't access them because I was an American," Rich said. "That isn't true. I know. I checked before I came."

The suited man strode forward, red-cheeked and indignant. "What's going on here?"

Rich swivelled to film him next. "I'm trying to access the lease agreements for Waterton. Your receptionist seems to be under the impression they aren't available to Americans. Would you care to comment on that..." Rich zoomed in on the engraved name-tag on the man's lapel. "...Superintendent Barton?"

The superintendent's face paled and he took a half-step backward. "I-I'm sorry. I think there must have been some kind of a mistake."

"Mr. Evans is the new manager of the Whitewater," the receptionist explained. "He's looking into lease records for the area."

The superintendent cleared his throat. "Well, let's get those for him."

Rich's mouth twisted into an angry smile. "Thank you. I appreciate your cooperation."

"You'll need to turn that off," the superintendent said, nodding to the camera. "This is a government office, after all."

"Of course," Rich replied. He set the camera onto the counter at his side but left it recording.

Superintendent Barton sidled closer, his girth blocking the camera's lens. "We would be happy to help you," he said, "but first we'll need you to fill out some documentation."

"Hoops," Rich said.

The superintendent laughed nervously. "Not hoops, no. They're official forms. Everyone who requests public records would do the same." He turned to the receptionist. "If you could get out the requisition forms for our guest?"

She glared at Rich before reaching into the drawer at her side and pulling out a pile of photocopied forms. She slapped them down on the counter in front of him.

"One for each lease you want access to," she said with a cold smile. "And I need them filled out in triplicate."

* * *

It was just after noon when Rich knocked on the door of the Bertha Mountain Bed and Breakfast. The converted cabin was located at the far south-western edge of the town's 'C', far beyond the falls where Rich had seen the cougars. Overgrown by foliage, the building hung precariously, twenty feet up a tree-covered slope, and had to be reached by climbing an unevenly laid set of narrow stone stairs. By the time Rich reached the door (and belatedly noticed there was a second access road behind the cabin, on grade with the door) his knee was aching. *Need to get back into running,* Rich thought, *but when?*

With all the Whitewater's issues, Rich's free time was at a premium. When he'd agreed to the transfer, he'd imagined long afternoons hiking in the mountains, but the reality was quite the opposite. Living in New York, he'd had far more leisure time than in Waterton. Just this morning, Rich had spent two hours sifting through the purchase history for the Whitewater, leaving him with more questions than answers: untracked deliveries, requisitions lacking signatures, staff members with no employee numbers. With Lucas Sorenson in custody, Rich hoped that at least some of those concerns would be answered. For now, he would focus on the leasing agreement, tracking down the owners of properties in the surrounding area. Susan Varley was the first.

Rich lifted his hand and knocked a second time.

"C'mon in," a voice called. "Door's open."

Susan Varley, the proprietor of the bed and breakfast, glanced up from her perch at the front desk as he stepped onto the uneven floor of the foyer. She held a cup of tea in one hand, a dog-eared copy of *Birds of Alberta* in the other. "Mr. Evans," she said with a wary smile. "What brings you 'round these parts?"

"I've been contacting the other business owners in the area. I was wondering if we could talk for a few minutes?"

She grumbled noncommittally, her book still in hand.

"I thought you might be able to give me a little advice," Rich said.

Susan peered over the top of her book, snorting as if the thought amused her. "Advice, huh? Well, that's a surprise."

"I have a few questions about properties around town. Mr. Chan, the last manager, arranged things a bit ... differently than I'd expected." Susan didn't answer. Rich leaned on the counter. "Any chance you'd be willing to answer a couple questions regarding your lease?"

She set the book down. "My lease is no one's business but my own."

"But I just wanted to ask if—"

"You just don't get it, do you?" Susan interrupted.

"Get what?"

She crossed her arms, brows knitting together. "It isn't about your fancy hotel, Mr. Evans. Not really."

Rich's smile faded and he schooled his face into a polite mask. "Then what is it about?"

Susan's voice grew harsh. "You're not the first person to want to change this town," she said. "Waterton's a pretty enough place for tourists, I'll give you that. But all of you city types, you don't get why we don't want you here. That's half the problem."

A line of muscle began to tick in Rich's jaw. "And what's the other half?"

"You show up here and expect us all to change: You, Chan, any number of others who've come and gone." Susan shook her head.

"You've got no respect for the way things are done here. None at all."

"Ms. Varley, I'm just trying to—"

"You all live in a world that moves fast, and Waterton doesn't." She uncrossed her arms and picked up her book again. "City folk," she said sourly, disappearing behind the curled pages. "You're all the same."

All aspects of Susan's demeanour—from her down-turned lips to the way she hid behind her birding book—had dismissed him, but Rich waited.

"It's going to happen whether you like it or not," he said quietly.

The top of the book dropped to display Susan's wrinkled gaze. "What's that?"

"Change," Rich said. "It's inevitable."

The lines of her face sharpened; she leaned back, glaring at him hawk-like from her perch behind the desk. "You think so, hmm?"

"Change and the truth, Ms. Varley. They come whether you want them or not," he said as he headed for the door. "I'll see myself out."

Susan waited until she saw Rich disappear up the lane before she picked up the phone beside her. She dialled from memory.

"H'lo?"

"Mr. Evans just showed up at my bed and breakfast."

"Oh really?"

Her expression darkened. "He was pestering me about lease agreements."

The voice on the other end grew cold. "Well, we can't be having that now, can we?"

CHAPTER FIVE

May was shaping up to be an utter failure.

News had broken about the murder of an unidentified man on Lineham trail, fuelling concerns about criminal activity in the Park. An autopsy had shown the victim had died from two gunshot wounds to the head. The person or persons who had chased the man through the trees and then dismembered his body was still at large, leaving Waterton awash with controversy. Suddenly there were reporters from as far away as Edmonton on street corners, setting up long shots of the meagre tourist trade and making inflammatory statements. Decades-old stories about Prohibition-era rum running were front page news once more.

This was far from Rich's only concern.

Of the documents stolen by Lucas Sorenson, only a few items had been recovered. Rich's notes, a detailed map of the Whitewater Lodge, and the specifics of the loan Jeff Chan had arranged the previous year had disappeared. The missing funds were gone. Most surprising was that despite an offer of a plea bargain, Lucas had refused to cooperate.

"We'll interview him again," Constable Flagstone assured Rich. "Just give him a couple days to stew in the Lethbridge jail and he'll talk."

"There was something going on with Chan," Rich insisted. "I need those papers back."

"Leave the investigation to us," Constable Black Plume said. "If the papers are still around, we'll find them for you. The Sorenson kid will roll. I'm sure of it."

As the long weekend neared, the spring weather grew increasingly unpredictable; bright in the morning only to drop to near-freezing at night. The trend kept away day-trippers who usually bumped up the lagging tourist trade. Rich scrolled through the reservations screen in growing dismay.

"That's it?" he said. "We're still more than a third open."

"Not everyone reserves a room," Amanda assured him. "We'll pick up a few more by the weekend."

"But those who plan to stay, do." Rich's hands tightened in fists at his side. "Dammit!"

"We might fill up," Amanda said, smiling hopefully. "It could happen."

"Doubtful."

"Even if we don't, we're still doing better than some of the other hotels in town, sir."

Rich closed the file, stomping away. "I don't care about the other hotels, just Whitewater!"

The promotions budget for the month was gone, but Rich needed to do more. If the newspaper and magazine ads weren't bringing visitors in, maybe a radio ad or television spot would. Rich slammed his office door, yet another item added to his already full plate.

Thursday afternoon, the dark clouds closed in, and by Friday morning a heavy rain was falling. The mountain peaks were hazy sentinels, disappearing into misty fog that clung to the valley. Hotel reservations dwindled with each passing day. Most businesses reported a fifty percent vacancy rate to the Chamber of Commerce. Even with last-minute bookings, the Whitewater Lodge was looking at an abysmal seventy-five percent occupancy rate.

Rich didn't think the weekend could get much worse, but Saturday afternoon he discovered he was wrong. He was sitting in Whitewater's empty lounge, reworking the hotel's computer system, when the phone at the server station rang. Rich glanced around. The only waiter was polishing glasses behind the bar, so he answered it himself.

"You've reached the Campfire Lounge at the Whitewater Lodge," Rich answered. "How may I assist you?"

"Mr. Evans?" came Amanda Sloane's breathy voice. "That you?"

"Speaking."

"Oh, thank God!" she sighed. "I've been calling every wing of the hotel trying to find you. Thought maybe you'd gone off in your car somewhere! I tried to find you this morning, too. Nando said he'd seen you in the kitchens, but when we couldn't find you, Andrew thought maybe you'd gone downtown. I checked for a note, but you hadn't signed out of the office so I—"

"Amanda," he answered dryly. "Is there a point to this?"

"Oh, yes! Yes, of course, sir!" she laughed. "There was a call for you at the front desk a couple hours ago. I left you a voice message on your Whitewater staff account, but I don't know if you got it yet."

Rich turned to check the time. It was just after four p.m. He'd been there since ten-thirty in the morning, he realized in dismay. There were too many things to do and never enough time.

"No, not yet."

"There was a woman on the phone asking about you just before noon. The call came in from Lethbridge, I think. I explained that you were on site, the way you asked me to, but she kept insisting she wanted to talk to you personally. And I tried to contact you on your cell phone, sir, *I did*! But you know how the reception is around here and I couldn't get the call to go through..."

Rich sighed. This was going to be a long conversation.

"...and the caller didn't want to leave a message for you, but I thought that you should know there was someone looking for you. So I left that message for you myself," she said cheerily.

"And this is important because...?"

"Because she's standing here in the lobby now!"

Rich put a hand to his temple, the first hint of a headache pulsing behind one eye. "Sorry, who is?"

"The woman who wanted to talk to you earlier, but couldn't find you," Amanda explained. "Seems she drove into town. She's here waiting for you." Her voice dropped. "Long brown hair, fancy clothes. You might want to come see her. She doesn't look like someone who likes to wait."

Shoulders tensing, Rich's suspicions started to rise. He'd left his whole life behind in New York, but not all of it neatly. In the rush, he'd made some hasty decisions, both professional and personal. He hadn't regretted the choices, but he also hadn't called anyone in the city in the weeks since he'd arrived. If there was an unexpected woman standing in the Whitewater's lobby, he bet he knew who she was.

"Amanda, does this woman have a name?" he asked coolly. He could imagine the smirk on Gabby's face.

"She says her name is Miss Gabrielle Rice."

He winced. "Tell Ms. Rice I'll be right down."

* * *

Red Rock Canyon was one of the two winding roads which headed away from the townsite to go deep into the untouched mountains along the far western side of the Park's border. The exposed reddish-purple rock of the creek shone crimson when wet, while along the roadside, verdant grassland met yellow aspen on softly sloping ridges. Rich had been meaning to visit the site ever since Lou had told him Ephraim's story, but he'd never had the chance. Driving back from the canyon, he barely noticed the passing scenery.

Everything was going wrong today. Gabrielle sat fuming in the passenger seat, her cloying perfume pervading the car's interior.

"I can't believe you!" she hissed. "I came all the way out here to … to the middle of fucking nowhere, and you don't even give a shit!"

Rich's lips pursed and his right hand slammed the car into third gear as he accelerated. Outside, the bright green and yellow canopy of late spring pulsed as it whipped by, Rich's hands white-knuckled on the wheel.

"I told you things weren't working out," he said. "I told you I was leaving. End of story."

"What you told me," she answered shrilly, "is that you didn't *know* what you wanted!"

Rich coughed, but didn't otherwise respond. The car picked up speed, passing the other vehicles on the road.

"Can you just slow down?" she snapped.

He tapped the brakes and the car shimmied.

"I can't wait around for you forever," she said. "I've got a life, too."

Rich laughed angrily, switching gears again as the car hit an open area of road. On either side of the vehicle, dense forest rose up mountain's slopes, the overcast sky a woollen blanket snagged across the peaks.

"I don't want you to wait. I didn't want it when I left, and I certainly don't want it now."

Ahead the road veered left, a sign for "Crandell Campground" appearing on the right. He dropped down a gear, slowing the car, but the volume of the engine didn't lower. It was idling too high, the sound rising.

"Oh, for Christ's sake!" Rich snarled.

"What's wrong?"

"The fucking engine again! Had the same trouble before."

They hit a pothole and the car jumped then slammed back down, jarring Rich's clenched teeth.

"Be careful!" Gabby squealed.

Outside, the leaves were a swirl. Reaching another open patch of road, Rich slammed the car into fourth. He hit slick asphalt and the car skidded. They were going too fast, on a road that was too goddamned narrow, but he felt alive!

"Take me back to town," Gabby ordered. "I'm leaving!"

The engine's drone had risen to an all-out roar.

Rich's jaw tightened in an angry smile. "Gladly."

* * *

Lou was inside the gas station, handing change to an elderly couple, when she heard the sound. It was an engine running too fast and too loud.

"Rich Evans," she breathed. She knew it.

Leaving Brendan to run the till, she headed out the door, catching sight of the silver sports car coming down Windflower Avenue. An unexpected grin tugged at her lips. It'd been three weeks since she'd repaired his car and she'd been wondering what Rich had been up to lately. His name had become a fixture of Waterton gossip as he singlehandedly turned the Whitewater Lodge inside out, bullying contractors into completing unfinished work on time and at no cost to him, reorganizing the staff with fervour, and revamping the behemoth's entire management system. It made Lou wonder what kind of experiences made a man as driven as he was. Some part of her hoped she'd have a chance to find out.

As Lou watched, Rich slowed the car on the gravelled drive behind the garage. The engine's roar rose until it was the scream of a band saw, then fell silent. Rich slammed the door behind him before striding forward.

"Heard you coming," Lou said, pushing a long strand of hair off her face.

Rich's lips were a white slash of frustration, shoulders hunched. "More engine trouble," he growled. "It's worse this time."

"I can tell."

Rich glared in mute fury at the mountains that surrounded them. The rain had stopped, but ghostly clouds wove their way through the valley, blocking out the sun.

"Bad fucking luck!"

"Maybe," Lou said with a low chuckle.

"What's that supposed to mean?"

"There is no luck. Just what you make of it."

He stared at her, blue eyes steely. "And how do you figure that?"

Lou stepped right in front of him, catching the way his brows rose in surprise. He didn't expect people to push back. He was used to being in control.

"Bring the car into the garage," she said, "and maybe I'll tell you."

* * *

Rich sat on the floor of the garage, indifferent to the dust, his attention on the woman beside him. His car was elevated on the hydraulic lift, Lou lying underneath, and he passed her tools as she called for them.

"There once was a farmer with just one son," Lou said, her voice echoing under the fuselage of the car. "The farmer was the poorest man in the village and only owned one horse. One day that horse ran away. 'What bad luck,' the neighbours said, but the old farmer simply nodded and said: 'Maybe'..."

Rich had trouble concentrating on her words. Her long legs and tapered hands, fingernails ringed with dirt, were distracting. He sat, his knee almost brushing her thigh, his hand near enough to touch hers, though he didn't. His rotten mood hadn't passed.

"A few days later, the runaway horse returned," Lou said, "bringing three wild horses along with it. They were worth more money than the farmer and his son had ever had. 'What good luck!' the neighbours said when they found out about his windfall. 'Maybe,' the farmer answered."

The story abruptly stopped and Lou's open palm appeared near Rich's hip, fingers waggling. "Quarter inch ratchet, please."

Rich dug through the toolbox. It'd been years since he'd worked on a car, but he could recognize the implements on sight. He pressed the correct size into Lou's palm, letting his fingers linger there longer than needed. If she noticed, she didn't say.

"The farmer's son decided to break the wild horses so they could be used on the farm. The first day he tried to ride one, he was thrown and his leg was broken. 'Such bad luck!' the neighbours insisted. 'Maybe,' the farmer said."

"I think I've heard this story somewhere," Rich said, his gaze on the curve of Lou's hip. From this position, he could admire her figure without her catching him. He liked what he saw.

"The next day, the army passed near the farm," Lou continued. "They were drafting all young able-bodied men from the villages as they headed to war. Many were taken, but the farmer's son, with his broken leg, was left behind. The neighbours said, 'such good luck,' and the farmer replied—"

"Maybe," Rich finished, tapping Lou's calf with his foot.

Her laughter bubbled up and Rich fought down a smile.

"I'm going to have to think of better stories if you already know them," she said dryly.

"I like the story just fine."

Lou's legs brushed past him as she emerged without warning. Seeing him sitting on the floor next to the car, she grinned. "I figured you'd pulled over a stool or something," she said, eyeing the soiled knees of his pants.

He shrugged. "Just seemed easier to sit while I passed you tools."

Lou ran her eyes down Rich's frame. "I assumed you didn't like getting dirty."

"Sometimes I don't mind."

Lou paused, watching him intently the way she had before. Like she was trying to measure him and hadn't quite decided yet. A flicker of annoyance appeared under Rich's returning calm. Who was *she* to judge him?

"That ... surprises me," she said.

He smirked. "Well, you don't really know me."

A blush rose up her cheeks and she dropped his eyes. Her reaction felt like triumph.

"No," she admitted. "No, I suppose I don't."

Lou reached for the clipboard to scribble a note. "I took a look at the engine," she said. "The issue isn't just the ignition timing. Sorry about that." She peeked over at him, frowning. "You didn't have someone else working on your car in the last couple weeks, did you?"

"No. Just you. Why?"

Lou tapped the pen against the clipboard. "Well, it looks like someone was messing around with it."

For a moment, the memory of the open door of the garage sur-faced, hair rising on Rich's arms.

"That, or you hit something hard enough to bust up the under-carriage," Lou finished. "The underside of the chassis is scraped to hell and it's leaking oil like a son of a gun."

Rich winced, remembering the pothole on the road to Red Rock. "I, uh ... think I know what happened. That one's my fault."

"It's not going to be an easy repair." She dropped the pen in her pocket, finally lifting her gaze. "And I don't have the right parts for this car. I'm going to have to order them."

Rich ran his hands into his hair, his regret sudden and intense. He wished he hadn't taken his anger out on his car. Wished he'd just told Amanda to cover for him and left Gabby behind. Wished he'd slowed down when it'd first started to roar. Wished he'd opted for a more reliable vehicle in Calgary. All of the options kept circling, fanning his anger back to life.

"Fuck!"

"It'll take a week or so to get the parts brought in," Lou explained, "or you could send the car out for repairs if you want." She stood and Rich followed. "That's up to you, but you should probably have it towed if you decide to send it to the dealership. In this shape, your car won't make it to Lethbridge. And my guess is that the place in Lethbridge would have to order in the parts, too."

Rich ran a hand across his forehead, oil smearing from his fin-gers to his brow. "I don't want to be stuck here!"

Lou reached up, then hastily pulled her hand back to her side. "If you're looking for a quick fix, it's not going to happen," she said. "But how you want to do it is up to you."

Rich glared at the car and then at Lou. Without it he couldn't get away from Waterton. He couldn't go *anywhere*! Even quick drives through the curving roads were gone. He was trapped with no escape.

"You can fix it?" he pleaded.

"Yeah, but I'll need a second set of hands to do it." She gestured to the tools at their feet. "I've got to figure out what's causing that idle problem, and then, when the other parts arrive, I'll have to deal with the oil pan and muffler you banged up. So, you willing?"

"I can help with the car," Rich said, "that's not a problem. But I've got a meeting in Lethbridge next week. Is there anywhere I can rent a car?"

"No. Waterton's too small for that, but if you need one, you can borrow my truck."

"What?"

"Borrow it when you need to go into Lethbridge," she said. "It's nothing fancy, but if you've got to be somewhere, it'll get you there."

He stared at her in confusion and then it struck him. "So what," he sneered, crossing his arms, "you rent me a clunker? For how much?"

"For nothing," Lou said. "You need it; I've got it."

"And what do I have to do for you?"

She gave him a sharp look that left him feeling like he'd just slipped down a notch in her eyes. "You pass the favour onto someone else."

Lou headed into the main gas station, waiting until Rich joined her at the till. He was unsettled by the offer. It left him feeling like she was trying to pull something past him, but he had no idea what. People didn't really do stuff like this. Did they?

Lou tore the completed bill off the clipboard, handing it to him with a tight smile. The price was, again, more than reasonable. He took his credit card from his wallet, putting it into her open palm. This time his fingers didn't linger.

"You're lucky you don't live in the big city, Lou," he said matter-of-factly. "People would take advantage of you if you did."

She set the card into the credit card machine. "Oh, I did," she said. "Lived in Edmonton, actually."

"Really? Why did you leave?"

She smiled, handing him back his card and receipt. "This was where I needed to be."

* * *

The two officers sat at the metal table, waiting as Lucas Sorenson was brought into the room and unshackled. He wore the standard orange jumpsuit of the Lethbridge penitentiary, but it was too bulky for his lean frame and he looked more like a kid than a criminal. Lucas's lawyer followed moments later. He pulled out the metal chair and took his place at Lucas's side.

"Are you ready?" Jim asked.

Lucas looked nervously from Jim to his lawyer.

"Whenever you are," the man replied.

Sadie tapped her photocopied notes on the table to straighten them. "We'd like to talk to you about the documents you took during the break-in," she began.

"Allegedly took," the attorney corrected. "Mr. Sorenson hasn't been to trial yet."

"Yes, but he was caught with the documents. And he's been charged with—"

"But hasn't been found guilty."

Sadie paused, taking a slow breath before continuing. "Alright, let me rephrase that. We'd like to ask you some questions about the papers that were discovered in the backseat of the car you were driving when you were pulled over by the police. The same papers that had previously been in Mr. Evans' safe but somehow got into your possession." She gave the lawyer a brittle smile. "Better?"

Jim bit his lip to keep from laughing. No one messed with Sadie.

"Now the last time we spoke to you," Sadie continued. "You refused the plea bargain that had been offered. Would you like to reconsider that now?"

Lucas shook his head mutely.

"Mr. Sorenson, I need your answer," she prodded.

The young man glanced nervously at his lawyer. "Um, no. No plea bargain."

"You'll go to jail for this if you're found guilty."

"I-I know that. But the answer's no."

Sadie frowned. "Why not?"

Jim cleared his throat, drawing Lucas's attention. "We believe you know who else was involved in the scam," he said patiently. "We know it wasn't just you cooking the books, Lucas."

"Allegedly altering the books," the lawyer said. "Mr. Sorenson hasn't admitted any guilt in regard to the—"

"You know who else was involved," Sadie interrupted. "We know that, Lucas. And the longer you sit here and pretend you don't, the worse it's going to be when you—"

"I don't know who it was!" Lucas cried, his voice loud in the small room. He dropped his gaze back to the table, fiddling nervously with the rolled cuffs of his prison uniform. His fingernails, Jim noted, were chewed down to the reddened quick.

Sadie leaned forward. "Who are you protecting?"

Her words were barely a whisper, but Lucas jumped at the sound. "I-I'm not," he gasped, his face pale and scared. "I don't know anything. I don't!"

His lawyer leaned in, whispering into Lucas's ear. Jim reached out, touching Sadie's sleeve, and she nodded, an unspoken message passing between them. When Lucas turned back, Jim smiled. He'd been a kid like this once, in and out of trouble.

"I just need you to help me out on a couple of details here," Jim said. "That okay with you, Lucas?"

The young man nodded.

"Good, good. I'm just trying to figure out how everything went, so any help would be appreciated." Jim paused, gesturing to the lawyer. "With your agreement, of course." The lawyer glared as Jim continued. "Now, Lucas, you already told the police who picked you up that you'd broken into the cabin, right?"

"Y-yes. I did."

"You took papers from the safe. Documents and such. That true?"

The lawyer opened his mouth just as Lucas nodded. Jim didn't wait.

"And that all makes sense," Jim said, steepling his hands on the table, "except for one thing. Just one little detail I need help wrapping my head around."

Jim could see Sadie watching him in his peripheral vision. Though her face was calm, her shoulders were rigid. Jim pulled the papers over in front of him, leafing through them until he found the photocopied deliveries schedule.

"This one here," Jim said, sliding it toward Lucas. "We found it in some of the filing from last year. Your name's on it."

Lucas paled. The lawyer leaned closer, putting on his reading glasses.

"That probably should've been in the safe with the rest of the stuff, but it turns out, Mr. Chan's filing system was a bit of a mess,"

Jim said with a chuckle. He put his finger down in the centre of the page, tapping on Lucas's signature. "Says here you were the one in charge of receiving deliveries to the Whitewater, but there are a couple places, every few weeks, where the deliveryman isn't listed at all." Jim waited until Lucas held his eyes. "I'm just wondering who that was."

Lucas swallowed hard, his Adam's apple bobbing. "I-I—"

"This has nothing to do with you, Lucas," Jim said quietly. "And I'm not accusing you of anything. I'm just wondering who that person might've been."

"I don't know."

"I just want a name," Jim said. "A name. Nothing else. You don't even have to testify. Just help me a little so I can help you out, too."

The young man's forehead crumpled. For a moment he looked like a little boy. "You can't help me," he whispered. "No one can."

"We can," Jim said. "We can give you protection, we can—"

"No one can protect me!" Lucas shouted.

"Constable Flagstone," the lawyer interrupted. "If my client and I could talk for a moment."

The young man wiped at bloodshot eyes. "I-I want to talk to my lawyer. I want to talk to him alone."

Sadie shook her head. She pushed the metal chair back with an ear-piercing screech and strode, stiff-backed, from the room. Lucas was slumped in his chair, the lawyer whispering animatedly.

Jim paused in the doorway. "Think about what I said. You help me, you've got my word we'll get you into protective custody."

Lucas Sorenson didn't look up.

CHAPTER SIX

Rich waited across the street from Hunter's Coffee Shop, his gaze on the people inside. As the first business on Main Street—Waterton's primary thoroughfare—the broad, glass-fronted café held an advantageous position, but unlike the other restaurants along the street, it also had the enviable feature of an adjoining parking lot. Rich scanned the flat roof-line and 1950s stylings, lips twisting in disdain. Like ninety percent of the town's businesses, the coffee shop was a throwback to another era. On the other side of the glass, red vinyl-covered booths marched past melamine counters, the faded decor borrowed from decades past.

From what Rich had gathered from Lou, Hunter's Coffee Shop was Waterton's unofficial meeting place of sorts; almost all the town locals could be found there a few times a week. But finding people wasn't Rich's issue. As his ill-fated meeting with Susan Varley had shown, getting them to talk was another matter entirely.

Rich scowled down at his watch before shoving his hand back into his pocket. He needed to arrange for the Calgary company which controlled the Whitewater's security alarms and sprinkler systems to do an assessment of the manager's cabin, but he could never find enough hours in the day to make the call. Rich had a growing suspicion that whoever had been harassing Jeff Chan the year before now had *him* in their sights. Little things—nuisances, mostly—had begun to draw his attention: someone coming onto his property when he was gone. The issue with the car's undercarriage that may or may not have been Rich's own doing; an unlisted number making crank calls to the Whitewater manager's office at odd hours, tools going missing from the garage and other items Rich knew he'd left in one place, showing up in another. All of it infuriated him.

He wanted to deal with the issue like an adult, but wasn't sure how. *Starting to sound as crazy as Chan,* Rich thought grimly.

Ten more minutes passed while Rich shifted from foot to foot. Besides the phone call to the security company he most definitely *wasn't* going to be making, he had a meeting with a Parks Canada representative at twelve-thirty regarding the satellite receiver issues. He wanted to talk to Hunter Slate before that started. Hunter had lived in Waterton for decades and owned property at the end of Cameron Falls Drive. If anyone knew who was running Borderline Industries, it'd be a Park old-timer like Hunter; getting his agreement on a satellite system might be enough to sway public opinion in its favour. But that only worked if Hunter was willing to talk.

Each attempt he'd made to contact the man had been a dead end. When Rich had come into the coffee shop, Hunter had told Rich point blank that he wouldn't talk to him during his work hours. Yesterday, Rich had driven to Hunter's cabin after work, but no one had answered the door. When he'd walked around the back of the house, a *'Private Property: Trespassers will be shot on sight'* sign on the fence had given Rich pause. If he didn't talk to Hunter soon, he'd end up going to his meeting cold, and Rich hated being unprepared. With a sigh, he lifted his eyes back to the shop. His breath caught.

A grey-haired man with a leathered face and plaid shirt appeared through the window. The door swung wide, bells jingling. "...thanks for all the help," a voice called as Hunter came through the door. "Appreciate you coming by."

"Not a problem, Colt," Hunter said. "Don't think that cougar'll be bothering your team anytime soon."

Laughter followed his words, swelling before being swallowed by the closing door. The old man strode toward the parking lot, his pace quicker than Rich expected. Rich stepped off the sidewalk. A horn blared. He jerked back, avoiding an oncoming minivan. Two more cars passed while Rich tapped his foot, his eyes on Hunter's receding form.

Hunter was halfway across the parking lot by the time Rich jogged forward. "Mr. Slate!" he called. Hunter reached the truck, searching inside his jacket pocket for keys. "Mr. Slate, can I talk to you?"

Hunter unlocked the door and tugged it open. He swung one leg into the truck, pausing with his hand on the wheel as if bracing himself for the rest of the motion. Rich sprinted across the lot, dodging parked cars.

"MR. SLATE!"

Hunter jumped at the sound, his expression sharpening into displeasure in a heartbeat. He dropped his foot from the vehicle and turned around.

"What's that?"

"Mr. Slate, I'm Rich Evans." He pulled a Whitewater Lodge business card from his pocket, holding it between two fingers. "I was wondering if we could talk for a few minutes."

Hunter took the card gingerly, putting it out to arm's length and squinting. "Talk about what?"

"About business, sir. I understand you know a great deal about the Park and its policies."

Hunter crumpled the card, dropping it onto the ground. "The Historical Society is just up the street," he said. "You should check there if—"

"The woman there gave me your name. She said you were the man to talk to, that you'd lived here since the sixties."

Hunter's expression darkened. "She did, did she?"

"It won't take long. Just a few minutes to get your thoughts on—"

"You're that Whitewater fella, aren't you?" Hunter interrupted. His nostrils flared in distaste.

"Yes, sir, I am."

Hunter put his foot back onto the floorboard, sinewy hand gripping the wheel. "Then you won't be gettin' any of my help," he said. With a grunt, he hoisted himself into the truck.

"But if we could just talk, sir, I'd like to—"

Hunter slammed the door and started the truck with a roar. "No, thank you!"

"But Mr. Slate, if you'll just listen, I'd really—"

The truck engine groaned as he popped it into reverse. Rich jumped back from the vehicle, avoiding the tires.

"Not interested!" Hunter shouted.

Rich watched as the truck trundled up the street, frustration welling inside him. "Dammit!" A flash of fuchsia caught his eye and he turned to discover Audrika Kulkarni watching from the sidewalk. She gave him a feline smile and lifted a jewelled hand to wave him forward.

"You're wasting your time with old Hunter," she said smugly.

"Oh?"

She rolled her eyes. "Hunter Slate doesn't know you from a hill of beans. And unless Hunter *knows* you, he won't help you with your project."

"You've heard about it, Mrs. Kulkarni?"

"Call me Audrika, dear. And yes, I've heard about your plans for the hotel."

"For the entire town," Rich corrected. "This isn't just for the Whitewater Lodge."

"Yes, yes, of course," she said, waving away his words with a manicured hand. "Snooping into lease agreements, wasn't it?"

Rich opened his mouth to argue, but laughed instead. "Yes, I suppose I was."

She nodded. "I make it a point to know what's going on around here. And you've caused quite a hubbub in Waterton already."

Rich frowned. "I have?"

"That should hardly be news to you."

Rich's smile returned. "Perhaps you and I could sit down sometime to talk."

Audrika's narrow eyebrows rose, her lips pursing in a moue of discontent. "Oh no, I'm much too busy with my shop to go visiting."

"Not a visit. A discussion about your thoughts on the town's progress. Business owner to business owner."

"No, I don't think so."

"Just a few minutes," Rich insisted. "That's all I'd need."

"I can't leave my shop unattended," she said, moving down the sidewalk.

"Mrs. Kulkarni, I—"

"Must run! I really should be getting back now."

"It'd only take a moment of your time."

"Another time!"

Audrika bobbed down the street and Rich watched the flash of colour recede until she reached the entrance to her shop. There, she turned and peeked over her shoulder, catching Rich's eyes. She smiled and disappeared inside.

* * *

Waterton was far too small to have a town hall, but for assemblies like tonight's Chamber of Commerce meeting, the Lions' Hall was used. The one-storey wooden building was located on Fountain Avenue in the centre of town, nestled between the Fire Hall and a small, rustic church. Behind it, the Whitewater Lodge loomed, surrounded by treed grounds. With his car in the shop for repairs, Rich had no choice but to walk. It was already dark outside, and with the meeting showing no sign of slowing, Rich missed his vehicle all the more.

"...and the Beargrass Festival is the highlight of the summer," a woman near him continued on, oblivious to Rich's upraised hand as he waited to take part in the discussion. "I think it only makes sense to keep it the same weekend."

"Hear! Hear!" a voice echoed.

"Well said," another replied.

Rich cleared his throat, but no one noticed. Susan Varley, head of the Chamber of Commerce, glanced cursorily through the room. "Would anyone else like to offer any insights?"

Rich raised his hand higher, waggling his fingers. Surely *now* she'd acknowledge him.

Susan's gaze caught for a split-second, then moved on.

"Anyone?"

"Yes," Rich said irritably, "I'd like—"

"I'll offer to bring the flyers in from the printers in Cardston," Hunter announced, his voice drowning Rich's words. "But I could use some help putting 'em up."

"Absolutely," someone agreed. "No problem," another answered.

The room was abuzz with offers.

"Thanks, folks," Hunter said.

"If I could just say something—" Rich said, but the voices didn't stop. Frustrated, he dropped his hands to his lap, gritting his teeth. He was being pointedly ignored, and without breaking protocol, he wasn't sure how to stop it.

"Excellent," Susan said, with a bang of the gavel. "Let's move on, shall we?"

Rich drummed his fingers against his pant leg, rehashing the night's events. Waterton's Chamber of Commerce was a pantomime. A horrible, pre-arranged piece of theatre, with Susan as director and her cronies as chorus, the group pushing the night's agenda through with well-rehearsed speed. Every small item Rich had attempted to bring forward had been diverted, his concerns ignored, items delayed. The third time Rich had tried to challenge a proposal and been sidetracked he'd belatedly realized that if Susan was directing this farce, he was here to play the part of the fool. *Well, I'm not playing your goddamned game,* he thought.

There were other ways to have his say.

Rich leaned back in his chair, waiting. Susan doled out favours to her group of favourites, smiling smugly at Rich as he stewed through the last few minutes of past business. She cleared her throat as the final discussion item was put aside. "And now that we're finished with the discussions," Susan said. "I'd like to open the floor to new business—"

Rich surged to his feet before she'd even finished. "I'd like a make a proposal," he announced, his voice reverberating against the pressboard walls.

Susan Varley turned in surprise, greying brows rising above her glasses. "Mr. Evans," she said, sucking his name through pursed lips. "*You'd* like the floor?

"Yes," he said. "I have a new proposal."

The chorus in the gallery hummed like an unsettled hive.

Susan smiled, but it only went as far as the corners of her mouth. "Go ahead then, Mr. Evans," she drawled, waving him forward with the mercurial indulgence of a dictator. "You seem *determined* to take the floor."

Rich strode to the centre of the room, drawing the attention of all present. There was a protocol to these meetings, and though the rest of them weren't necessarily playing by the rulebook, if he was presenting, they had to listen. He glared out at the crowd. In the sea of strangers, he recognized a few faces: Hunter Slate, Sam Barton, the man who ran the pharmacy, Audrika Kulkarni, and Louise Newman.

"It's time the members of the Chamber of Commerce updated the internet and cable access to the Waterton townsite," Rich announced. The uneasy voices rose. "This can easily be accomplished with a few alterations to the current—"

"What do you mean, update?" someone asked.

"The installation of a satellite dish," Rich continued, his voice vaulting above the others. "It'll help all the businesses in town. We'd have better cable, more channels, internet."

"Internet?" someone gasped.

"Impossible!" another retorted. The chatter of the room rose like a swarm of angry bees.

"I've already had an assessment done regarding the logistics of it," Rich explained. "It's a nuisance, but it can be done with relatively little—"

"It'll never work!" a man at the back shouted.

"It will," Rich retorted, "I've already looked into it!"

"This is ludicrous!" another argued.

More voices joined in the shouting. "A fool's errand—nothin' more!"

"You can't just bring in something like that!" The tone changed from shock to accusation. "Can't just change things!"

"Never!"

"No way! Absolutely not!"

"-won't let it happen!"

Rich's anger surged at the crowd's reaction. "I have already checked! It can be—" Voices drowned out his words. Rich glared over at Susan, waiting for her to intervene. It was her *job*, after all.

She smiled back at him with the warmth of a snake.

Infuriated, he swung back to the crowed. "I have the floor!" Rich bellowed. "And I *will* use my privilege!"

An uneasy lull followed his outburst. People whispered behind their hands.

"Now," he continued in a calmer tone. "My proposal is to share the costs of the satellite dish's installation between the businesses. If everyone in the Chamber would pitch in—"

The reaction was as violent as a spring storm. Calm one second, roaring the next. Rich shouted, but this time he couldn't even hear his own voice. People stood, shaking their fists at him. Snippets broke through the clamour.

"NEVER going to pass!" an elderly man in a cowboy hat barked.

"Can't just come in here and throw your weight around like some hotshot!" another bawled. "Who do you think you are?"

"I hold the floor!" Rich shouted to no avail. "Listen to me! Listen! I have the FLOOR!" But he might as well have been screaming into the roar of Waterton's wind. Around him, angry catcalls grew in volume.

"Bloody outsider! Thinking he can just come in here and take over."

"Bad as Chan was!"

"It'll never pass! NEVER!"

A jeering voice from the very back rose above the rest. "Why don't you run along home like your buddy Chan did!"

Rich turned to see who'd yelled, but the crowd was a sea, awash with movement. For a split-second he caught Lou Newman's eyes. She stared at him, slack-jawed and fearful; Rich was too furious to comprehend.

"Goddamned city slicker!" another voice echoed. "Crazy!"

"Go on, now! Git!" People spoke at once, enraged.

"GET OUT!"

Susan finally stood, interrupting the tirade. "Enough!" She banged her gavel down once, twice, and a third time. "Order!" she bellowed. "Order, I say!"

When the crowd's voice had dulled to a mere growl, Susan continued. "Mr. Evans, I thank you for your proposal. I now open the floor for—"

"But I'm not done!"

The crowd gasped at his impertinence. Susan shot him an icy look. "Your proposal is crystal clear," she hissed. "You want us to consider a satellite dish, and we *will*."

The hubbub grew in volume.

"But I haven't finished my propo—"

"Silence!" Susan yelled—to either Rich or the room in general—he didn't know, "The proposal has been noted in the minutes," she snarled. "I now open the floor for discussion!"

At her words, an explosion of discontent rocked the room, fury unleashed inside the confines of the Chamber of Commerce. Rich swore—inaudible above the din—and stalked back to his chair, already composing his rebuttals.

He hated this fucking town.

* * *

The Lions' Hall where tonight's Chamber of Commerce was being held was usually a place of merriment and community—Louise Newman's parents had celebrated their twentieth anniversary in the hall, and Lou had attended several wedding receptions there—but tonight it was anything but festive.

Lou sat at Hunter's side during the meeting, her knee bouncing nervously as the free-for-all continued. Friends and neighbours she'd known her entire life shouted angrily, Rich Evans' voice raising as he countered one accusation and then the next. After last year's troubles, Lou had hoped for a peaceful summer, but she wasn't going to get it. June was working itself up to be twice as turbulent as May had been.

In the eight weeks since Rich Evans had arrived, he'd paid the bill for an assessment by the Chinook Cable and Satellite Company. He now had a complete cost assessment for the satellite system overhaul, and the answer to everyone's question: "How can it be done?" It was surprisingly simple. A secondary satellite dish would be installed on top of the lower hump of Crandell Mountain, allowing cable and satellite connections to bounce through the mountain range instead of being deflected and broken up. The cost was reasonable if shared by the business owners, and Rich had proposed it be passed.

As soon as Susan Varley opened up the floor for discussion, a storm of arguments and accusations erupted. Grant, Hunter, and Susan spoke fervently against changes in the Park. Most people aligned with their friends while others refused to vote. Lou, trapped between the need to protect the community she loved and the urge to help Rich, forfeited her vote. Rich's accusatory glare left her wincing. With the vote undecided, Susan declared that there needed to be further investigation before a final decision could be made, and suggested that Rich organize a committee to undertake it.

Rich agreed, red-faced and fuming, and the meeting was adjourned. Lou tried to catch his eye, but he was absorbed in storing his projector and laptop in his carrying case.

"You ready to go, hon?" Hunter asked.

Lou gave him a weak smile. "You go on ahead. I just need to talk to Rich for a minute."

The lines of Hunter's face deepened. "So he's 'Rich' now, huh? Didn't realize you two were so close."

Lou put her hand on Hunter's arm. "Hunter, you've got to ease up on him a bit. He's just trying to do his job."

Hunter grabbed his coat from the back of the chair and turned away. "Likely story," he grumbled. "Just another bloody outsider."

When Lou looked back up, Audrika Kulkarni had stepped up next to Rich, her lipsticked mouth next to his ear. "If you want it done," she said, "you'll have to work on some of the holdouts."

Rich snapped the carrying case closed. "They aren't changing their minds," he answered coldly. For a moment his eyes caught Lou's, but he dropped her gaze just as fast. "That is perfectly clear."

Audrika glared at him. "It isn't clear at all," she said. "You're asking these people to pay for the changes and no one here has that kind of money to throw away." She lifted her chin defiantly. "So pay for it yourself."

He laughed mirthlessly, pulling the laptop case from the table. "I really don't see that as an option, Mrs. Kulkarni. I'm still dealing with the mess from last year. I don't have a hell of a lot of extra money to give away."

Audrika stiffened, her plucked brows dropping low. "If you want everyone to jump off the cliff, Mr. Evans, then you'd better be willing to go first."

Rich walked away without answering.

"Rich!" Lou called. "Could I talk to you?"

But he was already out the door, leaving her standing alone on the empty floor of the meeting hall.

*   *   *

The Chamber of Commerce meeting had dragged on for two solid hours, meaning it was well past ten by the time Rich started walking home. He was furious that after weeks of footwork and research the Chamber members had simply refused to decide. Now he was saddled with the impossible task of organizing a committee. Walking in the dark, with his thoughts muddled, Rich's foot rolled on an uneven patch of gravel. His ankle twisted and he yelped in pain.

"Shit!" He lurched sideways, the laptop case slamming against his knee, leaving him gasping for breath. "Need some goddamned streetlights!"

He stood, massaging his kneecap, waiting for the pain to recede. The street was barren, the town quiet. With the May long weekend over and June begun, Waterton had gone back to its early spring solitude. Most cabins were still closed for the season, windows boarded up. Its isolation was unnerving.

Somewhere, deep in the shadows, a branch broke.

Rich glanced around. There *were* streetlights here, but they were so far apart and surrounded by trees that light dropped away to solid black between them. The skin on the back of his neck crawled as he became aware of the darkness. He didn't usually walk around after nightfall, but tonight he'd had no choice without his car. The wind lifted his hair, leaving him shivering; a voice in his mind chattered nervously.

There was someone in my yard the other night...

Rich resumed walking, picking up a quick pace despite his aching ankle. Things he'd pushed aside in the rush to get the hotel up and running were back full force. There *had* been someone coming around his property the last few weeks. It was easy to blame that on troublemaking locals in the bright light of day, but alone, on the street, other thoughts intruded: the murderer still hadn't been caught.

The night was too black. The moon created an unearthly silhouette of the mountain range. Peering into the dark, he was aware of the sounds around him. There were things moving in the bushes, small skittering things running over cabin rooftops.

Almost there ... almost there!

Reaching the edge of another pool of light, he slowed, revelling in the feeling of safety the street lamp inferred. Here he was able to see the cabin surrounded by trees and children's bicycles propped against a garage wall. The tightness in his chest eased. He'd been jumping at shadows, Rich decided. Letting his imagination get out of hand. He smiled, his nerves settling as he walked under the streetlight. He wished now that he'd tried to talk to Lou after the meeting. He'd been furious when she'd refused to vote, but away from the angry crowd, those feelings had disappeared. Now he was just disappointed.

Waterton had no social life, and Louise Newman was one of the few people who'd give Rich the time of day. He'd found himself thinking about her the last few weeks; her laughter appeared in his thoughts at odd moments. He *liked* Lou. If he wasn't so damned busy, he'd try to do something about that. Rich was considering what excuse he could use to go talk to her as he reached the edge of the pool of light and stepped into leaden shadows.

A branch broke in the bushes beside him.

He jerked in surprise, the case banging against his knee again. He spun toward the source of the sound, but it was hidden by the trees.

"Hello?"

There was no answer.

Rich walked faster, heading into the centre of the road, as far away from the bushes that lined the sidewalk as possible. The wind rose, an eerie whistling sound that chased him through the trees. At his feet, dried leaves and pine cones rattled in the breeze.

Of all the fucking times for the car to be—

Something large moved through the brush, breaking branches and coming from the darkness on the other side of the road.

Not waiting to see what it was, Rich ran, his heart thundering. There was movement on either side of the street, followed by a flash of eyes in the darkness between the cabins. *The cougars!* his mind shouted in panic. Almost directly beside him, a moaning howl echoed in the night. It was a primitive sound, and his whole body reacted viscerally.

"Wolves!"

One hand was tight on the case, his legs pumping despite the stabbing pain in his ankle. He passed an open street and the creature from the shadows—large and canine—darted across, pacing his progress. At the very end of the road, the manager's cottage beckoned. He could see the roof with its cross-timbered peak, the cedar shake shingles, and the porch light surrounded by dancing insects. *Safety!* It seemed hopelessly far away.

He ran faster, chest burning. His ankle was now a white flare of pain, but he ignored it, pushing into an all-out sprint as he hit the property line. He needed to get back to the light!

Rich stumbled on an exposed root, almost going to his knees, righting himself before hitting the ground. The animal that was tracking him through the trees let out a snarling bark and the sound propelled him the rest of the way to the cabin. He had his keys out of his pocket as he hit the porch, the laptop and projector dropped indifferently on the stairs. In seconds, he was inside the foyer. His chest heaved, legs wobbling with the downward spiral of adrenaline.

"Jesus," he gasped.

A frustrated howl rose into the sky and the darkness fell silent once more. Rich slumped against the door, his cheek pressed against the wood. Through the panel, *another* sound left his chest heaving.

Under the faint rustle of wind, someone was laughing.

* * *

Lou stood in the pool of light on the veranda, her gaze on the heavy blanket of darkness out beyond the porch. A moment ago she thought she'd heard a dog, but now that she was standing outside, that certainty was gone. Wind whistled through the knot of trees that drew a line between her property and the next. There branches dipped and swayed, leaves twirling. But in the heart of the bushes, a single shadow remained motionless.

Lou stepped off the creaking porch and walked slowly down the sidewalk. There was the crackle of leaves as the bushes twitched from within. The breeze rose around her and a tremor ran up her spine.

"Hello?" Lou called.

The sound that echoed back wasn't a word, but a cough. If the shape in the trees wasn't so human, she would have guessed it was an animal. It waited in the oppressive cloak of darkness between the houses.

"I know you're out there," she said gently.

Her senses twinged. There was a faint scent in the air—wood smoke, and something else—the familiarity as subtle as vapour. Her fear rose alongside it. She took a deep breath and the other sense she'd had since childhood flared like a match lit in the dark, pulling her vision in two directions at once. Lou stood motionless at the bottom of her steps on the quiet street, while another part of her was someplace and sometime else...

She ran, blind, through the woods, twigs tearing at her bare arms and face. She wasn't alone. She could hear someone following—

Lou's vision recoiled, but the fading terror left her unsettled. It was another warning.

The shadow waited in the darkness.

"I-I can hear you," Lou said warily. "If you want to talk, I'm here."

She moved onto the carpet of grass, swallowing back a wave of unease. This new vision had a meaning, but she didn't know what. Last year, at the height of the furor over the Whitewater Lodge's construction, she'd felt something like this, but it wasn't nearly as strong as the panic which had enveloped her tonight. Something dark was coming, and she didn't know what.

Halfway to the trees, the shadow began to take form: a man's tall frame drawn in inky black. *Familiar,* Lou thought, *I wonder who—*

A dog howled.

The sound jerked Lou from her thoughts, attention shifting. Two streets away, someone was running, and Lou was briefly wrapped in *that* panic. The sound of branches breaking brought her back. The figure in the darkness was already in motion.

"Wait!" Lou cried.

She darted forward, stopping as she reached the edge of her yard. Like a flash of lightning, she knew why the figure was familiar. She'd felt the same type of foreboding last year when Jeff had stumbled into Hunter's Coffee Shop, ranting about being followed and the dead animals he'd found left on his porch. Lou had spent the weeks before he'd disappeared trying to uncover who was bothering Jeff, but she never had. Her hand rose to her mouth with a cry.

The trouble which had circled Waterton when Jeff Chan was the outsider in town was coming back to roost. And if it was anything like last time, the problems wouldn't stop until Rich Evans packed his bags and walked away.

* * *

Waterton's marina was located on the small jetty of land extending past Main Street out into Waterton Lake. Faded plank docks stretched out into the dark waters of Emerald Bay, boats moaning softly as they rocked against their moorings. The marina was the last, outstretched finger of the clasped hands of Waterton's business centre; this finger pointed back to the base of the mountains where the town's sole entrance lay. Unlike the marinas in larger communities, Waterton's waterfront had no life after the sun went down. The main walkway was bare, spectral shadows cast from the trees overhead dancing in the golden circles of street lamps. The shoreline, with its slope-roofed buildings, was eerily abandoned; a circular parking lot, bustling during daylight hours was empty save for a single motorcycle.

Mac stood in the oily darkness of the empty parking lot, glaring out at the slick black surface of Emerald Bay and the shimmering lights of the Prince of Wales Hotel reflected in it. The town was too small, in Mac's opinion. There were few places to meet without drawing suspicion. From his position near the marina, the sounds of the downtown streets intruded—people's laughter from the bar and strains of music—while beyond the trees, the steady chop of waves broke the silence. Early summer coolness clung to the air, leaving him chilled beyond what he'd expected for the last week of June. He waved away a small cloud of mosquitoes and took a long drag on his cigarette. The ember flared to life, revealing acne-pitted features and a prison tattoo which crawled up from the collar of his leather jacket around his neck.

The insects scattered as he exhaled. "Mother-fucker," Mac growled.

He glanced at his watch. Five more minutes and he was leaving. Ten more and he'd be out of the Park, back in cell phone range. Then Dax would get an earful. There'd been nothing but trouble with the transit system since the Whitewater's new manager had shown up, and they'd lost their connection to the border town. A few calls from Dax had supposedly 'cleared the air' with the contact, but the man who Mac had been assured was a 'sure thing' had just stood him up. The pipeline wasn't opening again, not tonight any-how. He dropped the low-burning cigarette to his feet and ground it out under his heel before turning.

A figure waited under the street lamp.

"What the fuck!" Mac grunted, his fingers reaching instinctively for the gun at his belt. "You scared the living shit out of me."

The man's features were lost in shadow, his hands weaponless at his sides. He crossed the lot slowly, footfalls echoing eerily. His insolent pace was another spark on Mac's short temper.

"You're late," Mac sneered.

The figure laughed, the sound bouncing forward across the wet pavement.

Mac's fingers tightened on his gun. "You think that's funny, asshole?"

"Relax," he said. "I've been here the whole time."

"Liar. I've been waiting since—"

"Midnight, and in that time you've smoked two cigarettes," the man said. "Your first was over there on the dock. I was waiting in the trees behind you. The second was right here a minute ago. You pulled out your phone twice, but couldn't get reception." He smiled, his teeth white against the darkness. "I've been watching since you arrived, Clarence. Making sure it was safe. Something *you* should do more often."

The hair crawled over Mac's scalp. He hated his given name, and he didn't need some backwoods asshole putting him through his rounds. The guy was Dax's connection, but that didn't mean crap-all to Mac. When the man reached Mac's side, he slid his hands into his pockets, rather than brushing back his jacket to posture with his gun the way most thugs would. The incongruity made Mac nervous.

Seconds passed.

"Do you have something for me?" the man asked genially.

"What?"

"If I'm reopening the border," he chuckled, "I'll have to have something to pay my guys."

"Uh, yeah. Just a sec," Mac muttered, walking back to his motorcycle. "I've got the money for the transport drivers, your cut included. Dax sent fifty G in unmarked—"

"Fifty?" The word was sharp.

"Yeah, fifty," Mac snorted. "And you should be happy you got anything at all after how long the pipeline's been closed."

"Fifty's never been the agreement."

"It is now." Mac tugged at the cords which tied the duffel to the back of the seat. "The deal's changed."

"And why's that?"

"Dax doesn't think it's a reliable route anymore," Mac said. "The Waterton line's been closed since May. That's a lot of stock with no market."

"I've got other connections for transport."

"Maybe so, but that big hotel's up and running again. There are people watching now. Too many tourists sniffing around."

"I told Dax I'd deal with it." The voice had grown very quiet, but engrossed in untying the knot, Mac didn't notice.

"Yeah, but the more people there are in town the more—"

There was the sound of scuffling, a single gasp, and the marina fell silent once more.

CHAPTER SEVEN

Audrika Kulkarni sat in the stiff-backed chair of Hunter's Coffee Shop, her green tea steaming on the table in front of her. Around her, a group of businessmen and women, busy with coffee and pie, chattered. It wasn't the entire membership of the Chamber of Commerce, but it was enough of them that it mattered. They'd sat like this a number of times last year, talking about the construction of the Whitewater Lodge. Today they spoke about Richard Evans.

"...Evans seems like a rabble rouser to me," Susan complained, a greyed brow rising up impatiently. "Internet, no internet. Who cares? Things work fine, they've always worked—"

"They don't," Audrika interrupted. "We've just learned to tolerate it. Perhaps you'd see differently if you asked your visitors what *they'd* like."

Susan stabbed her fork into her apple pie rather than answering.

"I think we should listen to what he's been saying," Audrika continued. "Times are changing. I'm not saying pull out our chequebooks, but I think we should consider the benefits."

"At what cost?" someone at the back shouted.

"Less than the cost of losing more business," Audrika replied. "If Canada Day was any sign, this is going to be a hard summer."

Around the group, there were a few nods, but more grumblings.

"No one in the Park at all. You'd hardly know July had started."

"...hasn't been this bad in years. No tourists, no money."

"I remember what it was like when the road was closed. We all suffered..."

"Can't just walk away and pretend it's not happening again."

"Not like then. Not even close."

The voices grew in volume as unhappy arguments sprouted amongst them.

"Leave it to the meeting," a voice offered. "We'll all vote on Evans' proposal."

For a few minutes, the group returned to their coffee and pie, the murmurs settling into contented sighs. Hunter moved from one person to the other, refilling mugs. He replaced the pot on the burner and turned to the group. "Not sure you've heard, but this Evans fellow is looking into the leases, too."

The murmurs grew in volume. "To do what?" someone asked.

Audrika opened her mouth to answer, but Susan was faster. "One of the girls at the Park Office told me he's not very happy about a loan Mr. Chan arranged. He's trying to track down who set it up."

"That's his problem," one of the business owners said. "Not mine."

"Ah, but it'll become your problem if he starts looking into the *rest* of the town's business," Susan retorted.

The chatter grew into a buzz of concerned voices.

"...that's why he was snooping around my shop!"

"I was wondering why he was asking about lease agreements!"

"Don't know why these city folk think they can come here and interfere!"

"...none of his business how we run things."

"...outsiders putting their noses into our business."

"We shouldn't talk to him!"

When the hubbub faded, Susan spoke again. "Evans is a strange bird," she said. "Always poking around, asking questions. Truth is, he's a bit like Chan was." Uneasy murmurs followed her words. "I don't care for him."

Audrika rolled her eyes. "Don't be so dramatic, Susan. I've only spoken to Mr. Evans a few times, but he seems like anyone else from the city. Arrogant, but harmless."

"You look at him and see a pretty face," Susan snapped, "but I know trouble when I see it." Conversation hushed as the other members of the group leaned in to listen.

"I think there's more to him," Audrika said.

"You *always* think there's more," Susan huffed. "But do you trust him?"

Audrika lifted the cup to her lips, blowing across her tea. "Mmm ... truth is, I don't trust anyone."

The crowd tittered with laughter, the sound cut off by the buzz of a walkie-talkie. Constable Flagstone stood from the table, taking several steps away from the group. "Goddammit!" he growled into the handset. "Alright. I'll be there as soon as I can." He tugged on his coat. "Gotta go, folks."

"Everything okay, Jim?"

Jim shook his head. "Some hikers just found part of a body floating in the water off Bertha Bay."

The group swelled into conversation.

"Heavens to Pete!"

"I can't believe it!"

"...another murder!"

"Might as well kiss July's earnings goodbye too."

"...weren't any murders before that Evans fellow showed up in town!"

"This won't help business at all!"

"...already having troubles getting tourists to stay!"

Audrika lowered her teacup. "Have they caught someone?" she asked, her smile like a cat with a saucer full of cream.

Jim tugged open the door, his hand dropping to the gun on his belt. "Not yet," he said. "But I'll be damned if I don't try."

Audrika dawdled at the table, waiting in growing irritation as another half hour passed. Colton and Margaret left, deep in conversation, the rest of the locals trickling out in fits and starts. She'd just finished her third cup of tea when Murray Miles picked up his faded newsboy cap and slapped it on his head. Audrika set the cup down with a clatter.

"Well, I should get going," Murray said with a nod to Hunter. "Add 'er to my tab, would you?"

"Just coffee," Hunter chuckled. "Nothing to add."

Murray touched the sweat-stained brim of his cap. "Thanks, Hunt. Appreciate that."

"Not a problem."

Murray had almost made it to the exit when Audrika slid into position at his side. He lifted an eyebrow in surprise. "You headin' off too, Audrika?"

"Oh, yes," she said, pushing the door open before her. "Wish I could stay longer, but I really should be getting back." She waited as Murray stepped past her. "I want to make sure I'm there if anyone comes in. First week of July is always my busiest time."

Murray snorted as if the thought amused him. "Wish I had your problem." He lifted his hat up, sliding his hand over his head before crushing it down again. His wavy hair was long enough that it curled over his collar and Audrika had half a mind to tell him he needed a haircut, but she bit her tongue. Murray Miles was a hippie at heart. He didn't take much to meddling.

"Closed the shop up for the meeting," Audrika said. "But I should get back." She flicked imaginary crumbs from her lapel. "Wouldn't want to lose any customers."

"The book store's been dead this summer," Murray replied. "Still haven't moved half the titles I ordered last year."

"Oh my," Audrika sighed. "That's too bad."

"Need some new inventory—people ask for certain writers, you know—but I don't even have the money for new stock."

"Yes, well, everyone's having trouble this summer."

"I guess so. Just wish..." Murray's words faded. "No use bitching about it. Just gotta do what I gotta do."

"Can I give you a bit of advice, Murray?" Audrika fluttered her lashes. "Friend to friend?"

Murray stumbled, his pace unsettled. "I, um ... I suppose."

"You need to modernize." She enunciated the word into three, crisp syllables. "You need to bring your store into the twenty-first century."

"How? It's a book shop."

Audrika patted his arm. "Ever been to that new fancy bookstore in Lethbridge? The one by the mall, with the coffee shop right there inside, and all the chairs and couches."

Murray's mouth tightened. "I have, but my store's hardly like that."

"I'm not saying sell out to a big chain," Audrika rushed. "I'm saying to think about what that store has, and yours doesn't."

"Like?"

"Internet access. Computer terminals. Email." She breathed the words like an incantation. "That's what people want nowadays.

Tourists are crazy for gimmicks."

"I haven't got the money to go setting up a bunch of computers."

"Aha!" Audrika chortled happily. "But you don't need the money. See? You just need to get the access."

Murray shoved his hands into his pockets. "It always comes down to money, Audrika. And there's no point. I don't have it."

"You wouldn't need cash, just connections," she said. "You could take a little help, you know." She tipped her head. "From me, for instance."

"Don't want to be beholden to anyone," he grunted. "Been in that situation before. Don't intend to be in it again."

Audrika's smile widened. So Murray *had* signed his store away. She'd always wondered but never known. Waterton's locals were bound by a code of pride. Suffering was done in silence.

"If you could get more business for the month of August," Audrika said, "how would you do?"

He shrugged. "Depends how much I got."

"I bet you could get enough to make the winter, and then you'd be in a better position for next spring. You wouldn't need to rely on anyone else."

Murray's eyes narrowed. "Except you."

"Oh, no. I'm looking out for everyone," she said, though, in truth, it intrigued her. "Just trying to keep the town on an even keel."

He glowered. "So you say."

Her mouth fell open. "What's that supposed to mean?"

"You're no better than he is. I do this for you, what'll you be asking me to do, Audrika? What'll I owe *you*, come next summer?"

She stopped walking and Murray did too, the two of them glaring at one another, pretence lost. "I'm doing this for everyone," she snapped. "I want to expand my store. I want things on my plate, in my bank account." Audrika sighed dramatically. "I've had my fair share of money issues in the past ten years—we all have."

"Hmmph..." Murray's gaze flicked out to the empty street. She knew he was remembering the same thing she was. In the early nineties the main route into Waterton had been a mire of mud and gravel. The government's replacement of the highway had cut off access to the border town, draining it of revenue.

"I almost went bankrupt," Audrika continued. It wasn't exactly true, but Murray would never know. "And I wasn't the only one. We've all gone through tough times, but that's behind us. I want to move forward. I can't do that alone."

Murray tugged at the brim of his hat. He was watching her with something like fear, and Audrika revelled in it.

"So what do you need from me?" he finally said.

"I need your vote on the satellite."

"But they aren't voting yet."

"Not yet," Audrika agreed, "but it's still on the table for discussion." Her words sharpened. "And when it comes to your vote, I need your word that I can count on you." She opened her mouth, wanting to say more, but changed her mind.

Murray caught the reaction and his expression darkened. "And?"

Audrika cleared her throat. "I've already talked to Margaret and Harold about it, but I was hoping you could convince Sidney and a few others to vote with us too."

Murray choked back an angry laugh. "So that's it, then. You, Harold, and Margaret are going to go up against Susan and the others. You're going to swing the vote."

Audrika smiled. "With your help," she purred, "and Sidney's, of course."

* * *

Rich was tallying the costs of the most recent water damage when the phone next to him rang.

"You have a visitor at the front desk, Mr. Evans," Amanda said, her voice lilting happily.

"A visitor?"

"Yes, and she'd like to talk to you in person. Are you available?"

Rich sighed with frustration. He'd expected Gabrielle to stay away this time. "Get rid of her."

"What?"

"Just tell her I'm out of town or something, I don't care."

There was a pause. "I'm sorry, sir," Amanda responded, "I thought that you'd—"

"You thought what, Miss Sloane?"

He heard the phone being muffled against her hand and Amanda's muted response: *"Sorry, I'm having trouble with the phone. Just give me a second here,"* as she walked away.

Rich glared at the reports on his desk. There had been another leak in the east wing plumbing, and drywall to repair because of it. Bills for the previous repairs were still unpaid. The Whitewater Lodge was a sieve; every hole he plugged was followed by two more.

"Mr. Evans, are you there?" Amanda's voice returned.

"Yes," he said wearily. "Now what's the problem?"

"It's just that Louise Newman is standing in the lobby, and I thought that since you were trying to get your car fixed and all, you might want to—"

"Well, why the hell didn't you say so?"

There was another pause. "Because you keep telling me that I talk too much when I call you, sir."

"For God's sake, Amanda," Rich said with an exasperated sigh, "this is *not* the time to start following my directions." The phone buzzed with stifled laughter. "Tell her I'll be down in two minutes."

"Yes, Mr. Evans," she said, another giggle bubbling through her words. "Next time Lou comes by, I'll keep that in mind."

*   *   *

Jim was winded by the time he reached the turnoff to Bertha Bay. The light that filtered through the lush canopy of trees was hazy, a veil of mist rising from the knee-high ferns of the ancient forest as Jim hiked the last half-kilometre. Sadie and one of the park wardens had already secured the scene; a line of police tape blocked off the entrance to the rocky beach.

As Jim arrived, Sadie jogged forward, her face pale and sweaty. "We've got another victim," she announced.

"I heard," Jim wheezed. "Sorry I'm late. Got here as soon as I could."

"Not a problem," she said with a smile. "Glad you made it."

"So what're we looking at?"

"Male, thirty to forty years old. Same M.O. as last time."

"Any identifying marks?" Jim asked.

"Nothing I could see, but the torso's in bad shape."

"Hands and teeth gone?"

"Body's been dismembered, same as the last one." Sadie's lashes fluttered closed and she took a breath through flared nostrils. "And the, um ... the rest of the body isn't here, so I'm not sure about the hands." She coughed, then opened her eyes. "Looks like he was dumped somewhere else, but a bear dragged the torso out to the beach to eat, and it ended up floating in the bay."

Jim scowled. "So this is a secondary site."

Sadie nodded. "I've got Jordan and a couple of wardens out looking, but I'm not sure we're going to find much. The torso's pretty mangled."

Jim stared out at the gentle lapping of waves on the pebbled beach. The black body bag on the shore was a glaring contrast to the pristine lakeshore.

"Whoever did this is seriously fucked up," he growled.

"Or smart."

Jim's face rippled in surprise. "Smart?"

Sadie gestured to the forest behind them. "A place like this is the perfect place to dispose of a body. Bears, wolverines, coyotes ... they'll all take a turn on a carcass given a chance."

"You think there are more victims?"

"Absolutely," she said with a bitter laugh. "C'mon, Jimmy. Think about it. He didn't have to leave him this close to town. He wanted us to find it."

"Sick bastard."

From the sloping mountainside came the sounds of hoots and shouts. Sadie and Jim turned as one to see Jordan Wyatt, the youngest member of the police force, waving frantically from the trees. "Jim! Sadie! We've found something over here!"

A few minutes later, they were back in the cool grasp of the primeval forest. A bright yellow ribbon marked off a section of underbrush. In the centre of the bed of bear grass and spongy ground lay a bloody arm, its hand severed at the wrist.

The scent of blood and decomposing flesh was overpowering, and Jim's stomach clenched in rebellion. Forcing back a wave of nausea, he inspected the remains. The upper shoulder and arm were stripped clean of flesh, but the wrist and lower arm were intact. Jim nudged aside a tuft of beargrass and his breath caught.

"Sadie, take a look at this!"

She knelt at his side. "Bastard just made his first mistake."

Jim turned, surprised by the fierceness of her tone. He still thought of Sadie as a rookie, but she was handling this as well as any vet on the force. "A tattoo," Jim said.

"That's our first identifying mark," Sadie said with a knowing smile. "If this guy has a prior, we'll have a name."

* * *

Lou and Rich stood side by side, the engine open before them. It had been years since Lou had worked on a car along with someone, and she had to admit Rich Evans was a quick study. He followed her directions meticulously, asking if he wasn't certain, never pretending he knew when he didn't. She smiled to herself as Rich passed over another tool, this time without being asked. He had a gift with motors.

They worked and talked, their words mixing with the sound of power tools and the voices coming in off the street. It was easy to be like this, Lou decided. It reminded her of working in the shop with her father years earlier, when everything could be simplified down to engine repair.

"If you're trying to figure out why something's not working," Old Lou had explained, *"just focus on the things that do work. Move through those things first and eventually you'll find the one part that's stuck."* Unlike so many other parts of her childhood, that particular memory left her smiling.

It felt, Lou decided, like things in her life were moving again. Like she'd been settled in one place for far too long—*stuck*, she amended—and she was flowing again. Standing in one place was steadying, but she had missed the exhilaration of wanting and being wanted. Having Rich at her side felt good, and that thought left her humming with anticipation. She knew the connection they had could go somewhere, but the future was riddled with uncertainty. Lou didn't do long-term. Long-term meant questions and answers she couldn't give, but short-term worked fine.

"...it seems like every time I get one problem dealt with," Rich complained, "something else around the place breaks. Sometimes I think it'd be easier to start from scratch." He handed her the damaged cable from the vacuum line. "Or maybe I need to win the lottery."

"And what if you did win?" she asked, taking the cable from his hands and handing him the replacement. "What then?"

Rich held the new vacuum line cable in place while Lou attached it.

"I'd stop working, I suppose."

Lou's bright laughter filled the garage. "You'd go crazy in a week."

He stared at her with the look she'd grown to enjoy, like he wasn't certain quite what to do with her. "Fine," he grumbled, "then I wouldn't do this."

"And what would you do? Hmmm...?" She tipped her head toward him and smiled. They were side by side, each holding the cable, their shoulders and arms touching. Suddenly *that* seemed very important.

"I ... um..." Rich's gaze dropped to the engine. "I don't actually know."

Lou tightened the hose in place. "Mm-hmm ... That's what I thought."

Beside her, Rich had gone very still. It was like he'd fallen into himself and was poised under the surface, waiting to come back. The part of Lou that read interactions like this—knew these things the way she knew how an engine worked—felt the urge to push, but this time she held back. She wanted to hear his untainted answer.

He turned to look at her, his expression fierce with sincerity. "I'd do things," he insisted. "I would, Lou! I'd travel the world, I'd go heli-skiing, I'd go back to the Caribbean and swim in the ocean, I'd climb Kilimanjaro, I'd—"

"You could do those things *now* if you wanted to." She leaned forward, her mouth over his shoulder, her breasts warm against his arm. "But I'm pretty sure they wouldn't give you a damned bit of happiness even if you did."

He let go of the cable like he'd been shocked, stumbling back from the engine and standing upright, his attention honed down to only her. "Wh-what do you mean?"

Lou's voice was warm and persuasive in the dim shop. "Win the lottery? Think about it. All you get is more taxes and people coming out of the woodwork to ask for money."

"True, but you could buy stuff, too."

Lou rolled her eyes. "Stuff," she repeated tartly.

He let out a coughing laugh. Lou was trying to read what he didn't want her to know, and she could tell Rich was trying to guess what game she was playing. The moment had dragged out just beyond the bounds of courtesy when she noticed Rich's gaze begin to alter, his attention shifting away from the conversation and onto her. She was standing just a little too near to him, and she knew it. But Lou wanted him to know she was there ... wanted him to feel it.

"And how about you?" he asked, uncrossing his arms and hooking his thumbs through the coverall's straps. "What would you do if you won the lottery?"

Her smile spread, the excitement she'd felt all afternoon rising in a warm flush. She wanted to touch him, but knew she shouldn't. A voice inside her was saying it was stupid—she was fixing his car, nothing else—but the low light of the stall and the faint scent of sweat reminded her that it'd been too long since she'd been with a man.

"I'd stay here, I suppose," Lou admitted. "I'd be doing exactly this."

"Working ... here?"

She grinned. "It's what I'm supposed to do."

He laughed, the sound full and confident, filling the garage and tugging her another half a step closer. Lou's heart pounded like she'd been running.

"No big plans?" he asked darkly. "No trip to Europe? No yacht? No designer handbags and Louboutin shoes?"

She gestured to the open car hood, smiling impishly.

"Hmm ... probably not those things," she answered slowly, "but maybe I'd pay someone to mess up the engine of the one hot guy in town and get him to stay."

She peeked at him through the fringe of her lashes, watching his reaction. His eyes widened and Lou knew he wasn't entirely sure if she was joking or not, but then he began roaring with laughter. Seconds later, Lou was cackling, too, as both were caught up in the craziness of the idea. By the time the sound faded, Rich's hand had somehow made it to her elbow and he held it there, stroking the small patch of skin, leaving her body alive and burning for the first time in more than a year.

"Let me take you to dinner," he said. There was no question Rich was used to getting his way, and he intended to get it here.

She nodded, feeling that sense of movement again. Lou wanted to take another step forward, but this time she held her place. She needed him to move, too.

"Alright," she said, "I'll agree to having dinner with you, but only if I get to choose the time and place."

"Okay..."

"My kitchen, next Saturday," she said. "I want to know if you can cook."

* * *

Rich grinned as he crawled into bed for the night. He pulled the blankets up his torso, feet rubbing against icy sheets in an attempt to get warm. In the darkness, his mind replayed the afternoon with Lou: their laughter, the shop, and the moment when he'd said what he'd been thinking for days.

Rich tugged the blankets over his shoulder, waiting for the first, hesitant warmth, as his mind flickered through a series of images—some remembered, some imagined—Lou in all. She wasn't what he'd expected when he'd met her, but then, nothing around Waterton was. Tonight, he *liked* the thought of everything he didn't know about her. He wanted to know the rest. Rich's eyes fluttered closed, the images blurring into a hazy blur of half-finished thoughts and unconscious wishes.

Sometime before dawn, he jerked awake, heart pounding. He'd kicked off the covers during the night and was shivering. Around him, the room was oppressively dark, his body panicked by ... *something*. Rich groped blindly, locating his cell phone by feel, flicking it on and squinting at the brightness.

3:08 a.m.

With a sigh, he flopped back, yesterday's events tumbling into place. He had a million things to get done tomorrow: the previous quarter's budgeting to oversee, next week's purchases to order, the—

Something heavy thudded onto the porch beneath the window.

CHAPTER EIGHT

Rich lurched upright. He flicked on the bedside light, kicking off the blankets and climbing out of bed. Dressed only in boxer shorts, he tiptoed downstairs, banging his head on the slanted overhang and swearing. Hunching lower, he jogged down the icy risers, reaching the foyer. He unlocked the interior door, pushed the screen door back, and stepped onto the porch, peering one direction and then the other. Seeing nothing, Rich lifted his gaze to the yard. The distant street lamp was too far away to illuminate the forested property; the light from inside cast a circle of light where he stood, but it extended no further.

"Hello?" he called timorously.

A blast of wind hissed through the trees, slamming the storm door behind him. Rich jumped at the sound, laughing nervously as he realized what had woken him. Shivering, he stepped back inside, latching the screen and shaking it twice to make sure it was locked. He headed back up the stairs two at a time, already planning the next day's work.

Rich was almost asleep when there was a new noise.

His eyes snapped open as he waited for it to repeat, the smothering darkness pulling close around him. Seconds passed, then minutes, as Rich struggled to hear. There had been *something*, he was certain of that, but it had been too brief to tell what. His senses spread out to the slow creaking of the house and the wind around the eaves. Another sound, something different—*scratching?*—was layered beneath. His heart began to pound. *Maybe there's a branch leaning against the window,* Rich thought. *It might—*

Thunk!

The certainty of the noise jerked any explanation away. Rich slid from his bed and crept down the stairs in the dark, his hand sweaty where it gripped the handrail. Reaching the bottom, he fumbled for the light and for a few long seconds stood undecided. With a rush of adrenaline, he jerked open the interior door, ready to confront the would-be intruder.

The porch was empty.

Rich shivered as cool night air wrapped around him. The streetlamps beyond the yard were dim, the night sounds loud. The wind rose and the screen door rattled. Rich looked down.

"Jesus!"

The storm door's latch dangled from its hook ... unlocked.

*   *   *

Warden Grant McNealy sat at the table, fingers tracing the handle of his coffee mug. It was a warm day, the scene outside the window picture perfect. Barring the sunshine that warmed his balding scalp, Grant barely noticed. Across from him sat Delia Rosings, a reporter from the Calgary Sun newspaper. She was petite, with a halo of golden hair like one of those paintings of angels that Grant and his ex-wife had seen three decades earlier on their honeymoon in Italy.

None of that fooled him.

The reports about Waterton's two unsolved murders had reached a fever pitch and damage control had to be done. The police had made an official statement, but were refusing all interviews. Parks Canada, in turn, was left dealing with the fallout. A firestorm of panic had ignited since the latest discovery. People were horrified by the idea of a serial killer using wild animals to destroy evidence. As much as Grant wanted to avoid it, someone had to make a statement and he'd been told, point blank, by Park Superintendent Sam Barton, that he *would* answer questions.

"Are you ready to go, Warden McNealy?" Delia asked, setting the recorder before him and clicking it on. "Would you like a glass of water, perhaps? Another coffee? We're in no rush here."

Grant's fingers tightened on the mug. "Nope, I'm fine, Miss Rosings," he assured her. "Just keep in mind, I can't say anything about the case. Just about the Park itself."

"Of course. Let's get started."

The first few minutes trickled by without incident. Delia's words came in short, choppy bursts, like gunfire, the pace picking up as she moved from the general hubbub about the murders into less familiar territory. If he paused to think about an answer, Delia immediately rephrased it. Altering the question slightly. Moving on to something else. The result was that he never really had time to consider his responses.

"Animals who learn to eat human flesh are particularly dangerous to people, aren't they?" Delia asked.

"Well, yes," Grant agreed, "but these animals weren't actually hunting anyone, they found the victim's remains and—"

"But the two bears located near the murder site were tranquilized and relocated into the mountains of Northern B.C. Is that correct?"

"Yes, as a pre-emptive measure to—"

"And Parks Canada has already started their own investigation, separate from the Waterton police," she said. "Is that true?"

"Yes, but that's simply to ensure that no more animals had—"

"I've been told there were three cougars seen in the town earlier this spring," Delia interrupted. "That right?"

"Yes," Grant said, "but there's no hint that cougars were involved—"

"But cougars *could* have eaten off the bodies that were discovered in the Park, right?"

"Cougars tend to hunt their prey; I really doubt that one would—"

"So they prefer live prey?" Delia prompted.

"Usually, yes. Cougars aren't carrion eaters."

"Is it true that cougars have been known to stalk smaller prey," she asked, "even here in Waterton?"

"Yes, of course, but cougars usually stay away from humans," Grant said, "and there's nothing to suggest they would—"

"But if they were already hunting, they might come into town?" she said.

"If they were hunting a rabbit or grouse—"

"Or a dog," Delia offered, teeth flashing.

"What?" Grant choked.

"Dogs," she repeated. "Don't cougars occasionally go after small dogs?"

"Yes, of course, but—"

"And children."

This time it wasn't a question.

"Yes, but—"

"In the last week, wolves have also been reportedly seen in the boundaries of the Park. Do you think the bodies have attracted them?"

Grant let out a weary sigh. "Miss Rosings, I really don't think wolves were part of the animals who'd been feeding off—"

"But you do have wolves in the Park, yes?"

Grant winced. Rich Evans had reported wolves chasing him back to his cabin, and no matter what Grant had said to calm Rich, he couldn't be dissuaded. The man was adamant.

"Yes, there are wolves in the Park, but I never confirmed that they were feeding off the two bodies that were found," Grant said. "Wolves are very rare, and though there are some in the back-country, they're deep in the mountains."

"Are you denying that there have been complaints about wolves in town, Warden?"

"No," he retorted. "Just ... to an untrained eye, a large dog and a wolf can look much the same."

Delia leaned forward and dropped her voice conspiratorially. "Now, you wouldn't be covering up information, would you, Warden? Keeping things calm at the cost of public safety?" She tapped her pen in a rapid beat, the sound like the rat-a-tat of gunfire.

Grant shot her an angry glare. She might have blonde hair and a twinkling smile, but with the hungry grin, she suddenly looked very much like his ex-wife. "Covering up what? We're a Park. There are wild animals here! Everyone knows that. And if animals find a carcass, they feed on it. It's a law of nature."

Delia's smile no longer reached her eyes. "That may be true, but according to Park records, a man by the name of Jeffrey Chan put in three animal complaints last year—"

"Who said that?"

"—and the police files," Delia continued, "show that Mr. Chan disappeared last fall, without any word of his whereabouts. Could *he* have been another victim, conveniently disposed of by the animals?"

"No! And I-I can't even talk about the murders. I can only tell you that the animals in the Park—"

"Mr. Evans, the new manager, has filed two complaints in the last month. One for wolves, one for cougars." She slid the recorder forward, her toothy smile widening until she looked like a crocodile. "Now, Warden, would you care to discuss any of that?"

Grant felt his face flush with heat, a trickle of sweat crawling down the side of his neck. He remembered this feeling from the day he'd walked into court with a house and car, and had walked out with half that. His ex-wife had smiled that day, too.

"No comment."

Things had gotten so much worse.

* * *

The decision had been on Rich's mind for weeks. If he was busy, the thought would fade for a time only to come back again when it was late, and his to-do list too high to count. *What's the point in staying?* he wondered. But for every argument, a counter-argument rose. Rich hated to lose, and that's what walking away from the Whitewater felt like. But the voice in the back of his mind remained: no job was worth this.

He wanted to succeed ... but Waterton itself seemed pitted against him. Rich found himself jumping at shadows, knowingly avoiding darkened streets unless he had to walk them. Double and triple checking the locks on his doors and windows. *Going as crazy as Chan did,* he worried. The broken latch was the tipping point.

Nando replaced the lock on the screen door the next morning, and the Whitewater's security company was contacted an hour later. Rich knew these were temporary measures. After his morning meeting with the day staff, Rich spent an hour closed away in his rarely-used office scrolling through job listings for Coldcreek Enterprises. Several caught his attention. There were postings for Waikiki Beach, Salt Lake City, and Bridgeport, a smaller co-management position in Atlanta, a district manager for the state of Arkansas, and a short-term mat leave at Coldcreek's New York office. All Rich needed to do was write up a final report on the situation at the Whitewater Lodge, file his official two week notice and turn in his resignation. Prischka Archer wouldn't be happy with his decision, but a phone call would smooth things out. After the mess that Chan had left behind, no one would even blame him.

Exhausted, Rich printed off the Arkansas and Waikiki Beach listings and headed out the door. There was no point in staying any longer.

A man waited at the front desk, a faded pageboy cap clasped in bony hands. Rumpled clothing, two sizes too big, hung on his rawboned frame, a 'Get Caught Reading' button pinned to his tweed jacket. Rich didn't know his name, but he recognized him from the Chamber of Commerce meetings. He often sat at the back of the room, watching but not speaking, a paperback folded over one knee.

"I'm sorry, sir, but I think Mr. Evans has an appointment in Lethbridge today," Amanda said cheerily. "I can take a message if you'd—"

Rich strode forward. "It's alright, Amanda. I've got this."

She jumped at the sound of his voice. "Mr. Evans! I didn't realize you were in the office."

"Just finishing up the staff charts before I left," Rich lied. He reached out a hand to the man at the counter. "Rich Evans. Manager of the Whitewater Lodge."

"Murray Miles," the man replied, shaking his hand and letting go at once. There was a slightly too long pause. Murray rocked on the balls of his feet, gaze skittering. He looked like he had just been caught shoplifting.

"So ... what can I do for you?" Rich prompted.

Murray cleared his throat. "I, uh ... was wondering if we could talk a minute."

"Certainly."

Murray nodded to the guests in the foyer. "In private, if you don't mind?"

"Of course." Rich pushed open the office door. "This alright?"

"Great. Perfect," Murray said, releasing a whistling breath. He bustled past Rich, disappearing inside. Rich gave Amanda a quizzical look and she shrugged in reply.

For a time, the two men made the requisite small talk about the unpredictable weather, the poor business, and the unsolved murders which still dogged the town. Little by little, Murray relaxed, his hands around the brim of his crumpled hat unclenching.

"I came by," Murray finally said, "because I heard you were having some troubles with the Chamber of Commerce."

"Trouble?"

"I'm not here to judge," Murray rushed to explain. "I'm just saying that's what I heard."

"Well, they haven't been helpful. No."

Murray set his hat on his knee, nodding. "But they *could* be."

There were times in meetings when Rich could read the person's pitch long before they gave it, but this conversation was leaving him off-balance. Murray crossed and uncrossed his legs, as if unable to get comfortable, repeatedly glancing at the door. His nervousness was unsettling.

"Not sure you ever heard how bad things were here in Waterton," Murray began. "How close we all were to going under. We, uh—That can't happen again."

Rich frowned. "You mean last year?"

"No, no ... long before that. This was back in the early nineties," Murray said. "The Park was changing. Waterton didn't have the same draw other places had, and the government—" Murray's nose crinkled in distaste. "—decided that the best way to fix it was to redo the road."

"Which road is that?"

"The highway from Cardston to Waterton. We'd been after 'em for years, but the damned government went and decided to do it all at once."

Rich blinked, his confusion growing. "But wouldn't that be a good thing?"

Murray snorted. "It would've been if they'd twinned the highway like the Chamber of Commerce had asked 'em to. They didn't. Just repaved it, and evened out some of the tighter curves."

Rich's lips twitched. If the new highway was the better one, he couldn't imagine what the old one had been like.

"For three summers in a row they worked on that road. Three bloody years to pave thirty miles," Murray grumbled. "Things got bad. Tourists had to wait in lines, had to drive on unpaved muck or sit in their cars for hours. Most of the day-trippers stopped coming. Just about did us all in. Stores were closing left and right. Business-es foreclosing. But there was a group of us that just kind of ... got through it."

"How did you manage?"

"Stubbornness," Murray said. "We buckled down and waited it out. The lot of us—all the ones who made it through—looked out for one another. Stuck together. And that feeling just sort of stays.

You know?"

"I guess..."

"There are old ties here in Waterton," Murray said. "Blood ties. Friends that've stayed together for a long time, but there are a few of us that're ready to move forward." Murray dropped his voice, hands tightening on his hat. "That satellite thing you were talking about. That could help us all."

"I've been trying to tell people that for weeks," Rich said with a wan smile.

"True, and change takes time ... But sometimes there's no other way." Murray tugged at his collar. "There are a few of us—we've been talking about what happened when the road closed and the tourists stopped coming—it's kind of like what's happening now. We've got to move on. The other way just—It doesn't work anymore." Murray stood, putting his hat back on and crushing the brim. "Your way might."

Rich followed him to the door, feeling like the floor had shifted under him in the last minutes. He still had the application papers in his hand, and he tossed them, forgotten, onto his desk. "Then I've got your vote," Rich said incredulously.

"Better'n that," Murray said, offering his hand. "You've got my word, Mr. Evans."

The two men shook hands, and Murray headed out as if pursued. Rich watched him through the window. He couldn't be more than forty-five, but Murray Miles was stooped, old before his time. The mountains of Alberta had the ability to bend those who lived here.

That, or it broke them.

* * *

The bells above the door chimed, and Lou looked up to discover a thin blonde woman coming through the doorway. In her shantung silk suit, high heels, and two-hundred-dollar haircut and colour, she didn't blend in with the decor of Lou's Garage.

"Siobhan!" Lou cried, running forward.

As the American manager of the Prince of Wales Hotel, Siobhan Andler wasn't a local, nor a tourist, but something in between. The six-storey Swiss structure she oversaw had been built in the 1920s, but it still held a faded charm, like an ageing beauty past her prime who attracted admirers nonetheless. The bathrooms were ancient and the rooms were small by current standards, but people came for the experience. In many ways, Lou thought, the Prince of Wales Hotel embodied Waterton far more than the Whitewater Lodge did.

In seconds, the two women were hugging. As someone who came to Waterton seasonally, Siobhan was separate from the world of Waterton locals and the tourists, but Lou's friendship with her spanned years. Lou knew, for instance, how Siobhan had been near to breakdown the previous summer, and how her husband's departure in the spring had nearly destroyed her. Siobhan had spent many hours last summer at Lou's side, working through the unpleasant details and emotions of a messy divorce. The woman who stood in the garage today had a lightness Lou had hoped for, but hadn't quite expected to see.

"I had a few minutes before my 'get your asses in gear' meeting," Siobhan said, "and thought I'd pop in to say hello."

"It's so good to see you," Lou said. "How are you?"

"With all this serial killer craziness, business has gone to hell, but I'm doing just fine," she said with a laugh.

Lou reached out, brushing dust off Siobhan's shoulder, her fingers tightening and then releasing. "I'm glad you came by," she said, "and sorry for the mess. I should know better than to hug someone after a day under the hood of a car."

"Doesn't matter," Siobhan tutted. "Just a little dirt." Behind them, the bells for the front door chimed. "And how about you? How's your garage faring with all this nonsense?"

"Things are alright," Lou said with a wink. "Everyone needs gas."

Footsteps interrupted her words, and she glanced over her shoulder to discover Rich waiting behind her.

"Sorry to interrupt," he said, "but I have that meeting in town today. I asked Mila about the truck, but she didn't have the keys. I wasn't sure what to do."

"Right, of course!" Lou said, shaking her head. "I was working and I totally forgot!"

"No problem," he said with a smile. "Again, sorry for interrupting. I know you're busy."

Lou flushed at his words, her chin dropping. The sound of a single footfall brought Lou's attention back to her friend.

"Siobhan," Lou said, "this is Rich Evans. He's the new manager of the Whitewater Lodge."

At his name, Siobhan's expression changed. Where there'd been warmth moments earlier, an icy mask resided. Rich reached out his hand, and Siobhan gave it a quick, angry shake. Her frosty gaze flitted over him, as if assessing the cost of a piece of knock-off luggage. "Your reputation precedes you, Mr. Evans," she said. "Lots of changes at Whitewater, I hear."

Lou felt her stomach drop.

A line of confusion appeared between Rich's brows, his eyes darting to Lou and back to her. "Sorry?"

"Let's just say that word travels fast." Siobhan smiled tightly. "I've heard plenty about what you've been doing this summer."

Rich's eyes darkened. "Wish I could say the same for you."

Lou positioned herself between the two of them, her heart pounding at the walls of her chest. She touched Siobhan's arm, but Siobhan jerked away, heading for the door. "It was good to see you again, Louise," she said without a backward glance. "I should go. I have to go prep my staff."

The clicking of her heels faded; Lou's eyes followed Siobhan as she slammed the sedan door and sped up the street. Lou's throat was aching, tears of frustration prickling her lids. She loved Waterton, but she hated this part of it.

"What did I do?" Rich asked.

Lou reached out and squeezed his hand. "Not a thing."

*　*　*

Lou waited through the sound of ringing, her hand tight on the receiver. She could feel events in the Park picking up speed, but the reason for the turmoil rested just out of her reach. The murders were the most obvious factors, but there were other issues, too. People were always distrustful of outsiders, and Rich had made enemies even faster than Chan had. Something *else* was going on underneath the town's surface, pitting Rich's efforts against the older generation. Panic had become a palpable force around the townsfolk. Their distrust verged on hatred.

Over the last month, Rich had mentioned a growing fear that someone was coming onto his property at night. The first time he'd said it, Lou hadn't given it much thought. Today he'd told her about an attempted break-in, and the unlatched screen door. Lou had shrugged off the broken latch as the wind, but Siobhan's behaviour had changed her mind. The woman had been seething, her emotion so visceral and unexpected that Lou hadn't known what to do. The confrontation in the garage had prompted Lou to make the call.

"H'lo?"

If anyone had a handle on what was going on, it'd be Hunter Slate.

"Hunter," Lou breathed. "Sorry to bother you, but I wondered if you had a minute to talk."

"Never a bother," he chuckled. "I keep telling you that, hon."

"Thanks. That's good to hear."

For a few minutes they ran through the usual courtesies before circling back around to the reason she'd called.

"I know something's bugging you, Lou, so you might as well be out with it."

Lou winced. Hunter wasn't going to like this.

"Siobhan was at the garage today. Seemed pretty riled up about Rich Evans for some reason."

There was a pause, and if Lou hadn't known Hunter as well as she did, she would have missed it. "You don't say?"

Lou forced her tone to stay light. "Just seems like things have been getting a little ... tense around town lately."

"Well, there's been two murders after all. You've gotta expect people to be scared."

Lou made a sound of agreement. "Yes, but it's more than that."

"Oh?"

"Just seems like people are being a little too nosey about other people's business."

"Nosey, hmm?" Hunter grumbled.

"There was a break-in at Rich's cabin."

"But they caught Lucas Sorenson, didn't they?"

"Yes, but someone tried to break into Rich's cabin again," Lou explained, "and I thought maybe with Rich looking into the leases around town you—"

"I had nothin' to do with that!"

Lou grimaced at his tone. She could hear the lie in the hard-edged shape of his words, but there was no way to say that to him and have him understand.

"I don't think you're the one who did it," she said carefully. "But I was wondering if you knew who did."

This time the pause was even longer before Hunter's voice returned in an angry growl. "I never said a thing to you about this."

"You didn't have to," Lou said gently. "But Hunter, if there is something going on, then I think you should let me—"

"It's not that simple!" he barked, and with that the phone went dead.

* * *

Jim Flagstone was heading up to Hunter's Coffee Shop for lunch when he heard someone shout his name. He turned around, lifting his hand to shade his eyes from the sun. Sadie sprinted down Main Street, braids flying, a crumpled piece of paper clutched tightly in hand. She came sliding to a stop in front of him, grinning like a child.

"You okay?" Jim laughed.

"It's here!" she gasped. "Just got it now!"

"Got what?"

"The guy. *Our guy!* We've got a name!"

She shoved the paper into Jim's hands and he smoothed out the edges, scanning through: *Clarence McCoy, AKA "Mac". Served five years of an eight-year term for homicide in the J-Unit of Mill-haven Correctional Institution, 1988-1993, Bath, Ontario. Paroled June, 1993. Outstanding warrants for breaking and entering (1995), drug-trafficking (1995, 1996, 1997, 1998), and attempted murder (1997). Should be considered armed and extremely dangerous. Mc-Coy is known to have ties to several high-level trafficking rings in the*

U.S. and Canada including to Darren "Dax" Xavier, a known felon. Anyone with information on his whereabouts or his crimes should contact the Bath Police Force.

"Nice guy," Jim snorted.

"Makes you wonder what kind of enemies a person like that would have," Sadie said.

Jim's hand tightened on the paper. "The kind that'd make a kid like Lucas Sorenson too scared to talk."

* * *

Rich's cell phone started buzzing the minute he passed through the Park gates. He headed east toward Lethbridge, moving out of the embrace of the mountains toward the open prairie. Reaching the highway, he pulled the phone from his pocket, glancing down at the screen in disbelief.

Forty-nine new voice messages.

He pulled the truck onto the shoulder of the road and parked, cell phone tight in one hand, his eyes on the landscape before him. From here he could see the foothills rippling out like a blanket from the ragged edge of the mountains. They spread in loose folds until becoming the flat expanse of prairie that crossed all the way to the Great Lakes. July's bounty was a brash flare of colour: wind combed through golden tracts of wheat and sun-bright canola so brilliant he had to squint.

The truck was balanced along the edge of an invisible wall which blocked Waterton from the rest of the world. He hadn't thought about how very *real* that barrier was; now that his phone was re-connected, it felt like a physical presence. He wasn't quite sure what he'd find on the other side. Rich sat in the idling vehicle, eyeing the phone in his hand. He'd been off the grid for so long that with it returned, he found himself overwhelmed. It struck him that the things he'd heard about addiction to technology might be true.

He clicked open the missed call list, glancing through the numbers. His mother; his sister, Kate; Stu, his college roommate; his optometrist; Brett, his running partner; someone he didn't recognize. The last one on the list left him scowling in frustration: *Gabrielle Rice*. A full half of the nearly twenty missed calls were from her. He listened to the phone messages one by one until he reached the last one.

Gabby's voice echoed shrilly in his ear. *"Fine, Rich. You've made it clear where you stand. Don't bother calling me when you get back to New York. It's over!"*

Rich slowly lowered the phone back to his lap. "Over..." he repeated, his voice abnormally loud in the empty cab of the truck.

The cell phone began to shake, and Rich noticed, in surprise, that his hands were trembling. He didn't know if he was relieved or furious. In fact, he didn't know anything except that he had no reason to rush back to New York now. This project with Whitewater could take as long as it needed to. There was nothing holding him to the rest of his life. And then another thought struck him, one that left him staring out at the prairie grasses, rolling like waves on a vast ocean.

If he left, he'd never see Lou again.

CHAPTER NINE

Rich wandered through the aisles of Fine and Fancy while Audrika finished ringing through customers purchases. A woman came up to the counter, purchases in hand, and Audrika greeted her by name. Rich glanced at his watch. He'd already been standing here twenty minutes, and he wanted to be back in time for the delivery truck. There'd been some mix-up with the transport contract. Chan's documents from the previous year showed a truck arriving twice a week, but this summer the cost for the same service had doubled. Rich intended to find out why.

The first customer left Fine and Fancy and the next came forward. "I don't mean to interrupt, Mrs. Kulkarni," Rich called, catching her eyes over the top of the woman's head. "But would there be a better time for me to talk to you?"

Audrika's expression curdled before returning to her affected warmth. "Hold on just a moment longer, dear. Just finishing up."

She rang the items through slowly, pausing to chat with the customer between each chime of the cash register. Rich shifted from foot to foot, fighting annoyance. He'd specifically worn the overpriced jacket Audrika had sold him the other day as he finagled an agreement for a meeting; he wondered if that purchase would be for nothing. She was all smothering interest if she was trying to sell you something, but there were claws beneath her silken paws.

The customer left the counter to the trilled "come again soon!" and the door to the shop closed. Audrika turned to Rich, hands on hips.

"You're a determined one, aren't you?" she said. Her gaze drifted from his toes upward, lingering for a long moment on his chest. "No wonder people are getting ruffled."

He bit back a smile, gesturing to the store. "Do you want to talk here or somewhere else?"

Audrika clucked her tongue. "Has to be here. I've got no one to cover the shop for me."

"Thank you for meeting with me," Rich said. "I appreciate the time."

"Well, I can't imagine what I say will be any help to you at all."

Rich gave her a lopsided grin. "Perhaps not. Then again, I've heard you're the one person who knows all the dirt around town."

Audrika rolled her eyes. "I think you've mistaken me for Hunter Slate. He's the town crier 'round here."

Rich's expression wavered. "But he wouldn't talk to me at all."

"You've rubbed him the wrong way," Audrika said dryly. "City folk do that sometimes."

Rich made a mental note: *Call Hunter again.*

"Do people from the city do that to everyone who lives in town, or just Hunter in particular?" he asked.

Audrika frowned. "Everyone, I suppose."

"Why's that?"

"This town is a quiet place but some people don't appreciate that. No one really wants change. Not really." She waved a bejewelled hand toward Rich. "Save for outsiders, that is. You and your satellite dish, for instance."

"It's a minor change."

She straightened the necklaces which criss-crossed her ample chest. "Too many changes and Waterton'll be ruined."

"That sounds very different from what you said the other night."

Her mouth opened and closed like a fish. "I ... I don't know what you mean."

"Yes, you do," he said. "You voted for the satellite dish at the Chamber of Commerce meeting, same as I did. Thank you for that, by the way." He narrowed his gaze. "But I'm more interested in why the other townspeople *don't* want the changes. Why all the secrecy? What's so important to protect?"

Audrika's expression cooled. "What do you mean?"

"There has to be a reason for staying closed off to outsiders. I want to know what you think it is."

"I don't know what you're implying but—"

"Let's not play games here, Mrs. Kulkarni," Rich interrupted. "The Whitewater Lodge is poised to transform this town ... to change it for the better. Now I can do it alone—I've done it before—but an ally could be a powerful thing." He shrugged. "But if you're not willing to help me out, I can't see why I should bother to help you out either."

The sharp look returned to Audrika's eyes. She stepped out from behind the counter and strutted through the shop to make sure it was empty. Satisfied, she closed and locked the front door and hung a *'back in 10 minutes'* sign.

When she turned around, her face was grim. "Don't tell anyone you came here. No one can know I said anything to you."

"Of course. I just want to—"

"And I'll expect Fine and Fancy to be featured glowingly in any local brochures the Whitewater Lodge puts out for guests. Perhaps a poster or two behind the front desk. One hand washing the other and all that."

Rich's smile widened. "Absolutely."

"Good," Audrika said as she strolled back to the counter. "Now then, what were you asking?"

Rich's pulse quickened. "I want to know why the townspeople are so against change. What are they afraid of? What's holding them back?"

Audrika settled regally onto her stool. "Waterton's not like other towns around here," she said. "It's tourists all summer but come winter this place is a ghost town." Her eyes flickered to the closed door. "It's a private sort of place."

"Why?"

Audrika inspected her nail polish as she spoke. "Well, I couldn't say for sure. I've never really—"

"It's about the leases, isn't it?" he said, weeks of frustration bubbling together in sudden insight.

Audrika's chin bobbed up. "My lease is just fine!"

"That's not what I asked." Rich pointed to the window and the people passing by outside. "Every time I've asked about the leases in the area from Cameron Falls Drive to Fountain Avenue, I get the run around, but almost all of them are owned by one company: Borderline Industries. Even the Park Office seems to be in the dark about them. There's got to be at least eight or ten business owners with connections to Borderline, but I can't get a word out of anyone."

Audrika's cheeks were flushed, her chest heaving. She looked everywhere but at Rich. "I, um ... I-I don't know what you mean."

"What's the connection? What are they hiding, Audrika?"

At her name, Audrika stood from her perch, moving out from

behind the counter and striding across the store. "You need to give this prying a break, Mr. Evans," she said irritably.

"And do what?" Rich laughed. "The Whitewater is why I'm here. If I can't get the lodge in order, I might as well quit now."

Audrika took down the *'back in 10 minutes'* sign and glared at him. "Go see the sights. Go hiking. Just ... go."

"Why in the world would I do that?"

Her eyes narrowed into slits. "Because if you don't, someone will give you a real reason to leave."

Rich stared at her. "Is that a threat?"

"Not from me," she said archly. "My lease and property loans were arranged with the Bank of Montreal in Pincher Creek and you can find *that* in the records. I have nothing to hide from you. Nothing at all."

"But someone else does."

She eyed him before unlocking the front door and pushing it wide.

"I have more questions," Rich said, gathering his newly-purchased coat and tucking it under his arm. "I'd like to continue another time."

Audrika shooed him out the door. "Off you go!"

"But you said—"

"Go hiking, Mr. Evans," she said, escorting him into the sunshine. "Waterton is lovely this time of year."

* * *

It was supposed to be a discussion, but Friday night's Chamber of Commerce meeting had degraded into shouts within minutes of opening up the floor. As an open meeting, all members of the public were welcome, and the room was hot with the press of bodies. In other cities where Rich had worked, meetings like this were dry, unsalted business, but in Waterton, every townsperson around attended. Murray Miles and a man Rich didn't recognize had nodded to him as they'd arrived. Audrika had given him an enigmatic smile as she took her place at their side.

Tonight wasn't the final vote, though Rich wished it was. It would be good to get the proposal back on the table; instead, it was another discussion. The satellite proposal was the centre of the storm of controversy. A number of business owners took the floor to provide opposition to the proposed satellite dish, while Rich scribbled notes for rebuttal. *Why keep the town closed? What does it gain to keep it separate? Who has the most to lose? It seems like an extreme reaction to normal progress.*

A sizeable faction of the townsfolk adamantly opposed the concept. Even with Murray, Audrika and their silent friend, Rich knew the vote at the next meeting would be close. Voices rose as the discussion continued.

"...will cause a change to the town's culture, one which can't be undone."

"It's one change," Rich argued. "And a minor one at that."

"One change *now*, but it's a gateway to others."

"I'm proposing a satellite dish, for Christ's sake," Rich said, "not a shopping mall!"

"If you don't like the way things are, Mr. Evans, you can always go home."

"You'd like that, wouldn't you?" Rich snapped.

There was a gasp from the crowd. Rich's shoulders were tensed, hands clenched. He couldn't see who'd shouted the taunt, but it was someone in the back row.

"No one's *making* you stay in Waterton," another voice chimed in.

"As long as there's a hotel to run," Rich sneered, "I'm staying right here."

A murmur of discontent rippled through the room.

"Then you best get used to dealing with us," a familiar voice bellowed. Rich turned, scanning the faces of the men and women who filled the front seats. They stared stone-faced at Rich. Reaching the last person in the lineup, he was shocked to find two flinty eyes looking back at him: *Hunter Slate.*

He gave Rich a withering glare before he leaned to the elderly man at his side and whispered something into his ear. Another set of eyes joined Hunter's before the second man turned to the next person, and the next. The hair on Rich's scalp crawled as the core of Waterton's community lifted their gaze to him, watching. Rich lowered his pen.

They were hiding something. He was certain of it.

* * *

Saturday, Lou's kitchen table was cluttered with the remains of dinner. Rich Evans hadn't bought take-out from the restaurant on Main Street, her first guess. Nor had he opted for something pre-packaged and frozen, her second. Instead, he'd brought in bag after bag of groceries and had cooked a meal that surpassed any she'd eaten in a month. It wasn't fancy: chicken sautéed in heavy cream, roasted beets and an herbed green salad, but it was savoury and filling.

"I'm impressed," she said with a wry grin. "I didn't realize you were a cook."

"Peasant food," Rich scoffed.

"Hardly. It was delicious." Lou tipped her head, expecting him to disagree. "Who taught you to cook?"

"My grandmother," he said without explanation.

Lou smiled and refilled their wine glasses, waiting for the rest. *A secret* ... Rich, it appeared, had just as many as she did. They'd been trading stories back and forth all night. Rich now knew that Lou's father had moved to Canada in the late sixties, though not why. Lou now knew that he was the eldest of two children, and that he had little to do with his ageing parents. Lou had wanted to ask him why, though she could sense his uneasiness with that question. In another situation, she might have brought it up, but she knew it would fracture the connection between them. Instead, she turned the conversation toward his trip to Lethbridge where he'd argued with the board of directors about further funding for repairs for Whitewater, the delays in getting copies of the surrounding leases, and then finally onto the confrontation with Siobhan Andler. A week after the event, it still bothered Lou.

"Sometimes people just have to learn things on their own," she explained. "I know Siobhan. Quite well, actually. And my guess is her behaviour had nothing to do with you at all."

"Really," Rich snorted, "could have fooled me."

Lou smiled and he smiled, the two expressions like parentheses on a single word.

"Yes, really," she insisted. "Everyone has their own life, their own experiences. And sometimes we get pulled into the experiences of others." She glanced to the kitchen window and the faintly visible mountains beyond. She didn't want to think about Hunter's brusque phone call. "Their karma, so to speak, bumping into us ... jostling us along the way. The lesson has nothing to do with us. It's *their karma,* not ours."

"Karma, hmm?" Rich scoffed, his eyes heavy with good food and even better wine, mouth in a crooked smile. "Sounds a little hokey to me."

Lou swirled the wineglass, lifting it to drink. When she lowered it, she caught him staring at the dampness of her lips. "I thought a lot about Siobhan this week," Lou said. "And I think karma was part of it."

"How does that explain what happened?" Rich laid his hand down on the table, palm up next to her elbow, an open invitation. A step halfway.

"Siobhan is dealing with ... *something.*" Lou lay her fingers lightly in his. Every nerve hummed with the connection. "How she treated you has more to do with the things she is working through than anything with you. It's her issue, Rich, not yours. But how you choose to react to her will affect your experience." Rich's thumb ran over the centre of her palm, and Lou shivered. Her fingers tightened around his, the moment unsettling in its intensity.

"I'm not sure I actually believe any of it, really," Rich said. "I mean, shitty things happen to good people, right? Karma's just a fancy way of trying to explain away the bad stuff."

"Or the good."

Rich chuckled, his fingers letting go of her palm to slide up her arm. "The good?"

Lou sighed at the feel of his caresses, imagining where else his hands might trail. "You've met Brendan Miles, right?"

"The kid who works at the garage with you?"

"Right. Well, Brendan's father, Murray, told me something that happened to him when he was a teen," Lou said. "He'd gone to work with his uncle, a prospector, and the two of them were on top of a mountain, following a vein of copper back to its source."

Lou slid her chair sideways so that the two of them now sat, knees touching. Rich's hand moved up her arm and he stroked the line of her shoulder, half-smiling.

"The way Murray tells it," Lou said, "he was bored to death while he waited for his uncle to finish, and he started wandering around. The mountain top was covered in rock, but there were several survey markers there—"

"Survey markers?"

"Small sticks, pounded into the ground, to mark the location of a survey line," Lou explained. "And Murray walked over and kicked a couple of them down. Just a dumb kid, not thinking," she said fondly, "but his uncle was livid."

Rich's fingers reached the nape of her neck and paused. "Why?"

"He explained that the survey markers were there so that anyone trying to locate the position on the mountain—geologists, or cartographers, or prospectors like him—could have a point of reference. He told Murray he had to think about his actions. To consider other people and how it might affect them."

"Karma," Rich said quietly.

Lou nodded, leaning back in her chair, lulled by the play of his fingers through her hair.

"Murray went to university, got married," she tipped her glass toward him with a grin. "Brendan was born. A few years later, Murray went to work for Trans Alta Utilities. One of his first projects was to survey a line across the same mountain range. The helicopter dropped him off on top of an open ridge, but he couldn't find the survey posts that were supposed to be there. He stood there, cursing up a storm. Finally, he got down on his hands and knees, brushing away the snow and dirt, until he finally located the broken stub of one."

Rich's fingers paused, a grin spreading like sunshine across his face.

"Murray realized that his uncle had been right, and he learned the lesson he was supposed to learn." Lou shrugged. "Karma."

Rich watched her, his fingers resuming their stroking. "Did that really happen?" he asked dryly.

"Mmm ... yes."

His eyebrows knit together, a crease appearing. Seeing it, Lou began to giggle.

"You don't believe me," she laughed.

Rich leaned forward, his breath warm with wine, near enough that it swirled the hair around her face. "I don't believe life's *ever* that simple."

She swallowed hard, her pulse quickening with his closeness. "I don't either."

Rich tugged her forward, the feeling of motion eddying around the two of them. Lou's hands slid up his shirt, looping around his neck. His eyes were on the curve of her breast and then the fullness of her mouth. Whatever she'd been trying to show him was now lost in the intensity of his gaze.

The decision hanging between them all night was made. Lou tipped in, Rich meeting her halfway. She gasped as his lips slanted against hers, the urgency of their connection shocking her. Lou had thought of this, imagined it a hundred times since meeting Rich Evans, but the realness of it was more than she'd hoped. She ran her tongue across his lips, tasting wine.

Rich's response was immediate. He slid the fingers of one hand into her hair, the other wrapping around her shoulders, pulling her half onto his lap. "Please," Rich gasped as he dropped his lips to her neck. Lou didn't ask what for, and he didn't offer; the two of them tangled together.

He pulled his hand from her hair, cradling her neck as he traced his way down her chest. He paused to undo each button while his mouth laid a path of kisses along the narrow column of her throat. "Want you," he panted, his teeth nipping her skin painfully, then soothing with his tongue. "Want you so bad."

Lou's fingers tightened on his shirt collar, pulling him closer. Her blouse hung open and Rich's fingers moved over the lace bra, teasing her through the thin fabric as he kissed her neck. She gasped as his tongue stilled and he moved back to her lips, his mouth angling over hers. All her thoughts focused down to the ever-tightening coil of desire between them.

"Wanted to kiss you that first day in the garage," Rich murmured, and Lou giggled. "It's true," he added, kissing away whatever response she might have given.

When the kiss had dragged on long enough that she was lightheaded, she put her hands on Rich's shoulders, pushing herself away. She could feel the heat between them, and straddling his lap, there was no question of how much he wanted her too. Rich's eyes were dark with desire, one hand still kneading her breast, the other tight against her waist.

"What?" he panted.

She fought down the urge to drag him to her bedroom, smiling coyly instead. "You should go," she said quietly.

His face rippled in shock and then disappointment. "But..."

Lou leaned closer, unable to stay away. "I like you, Rich," she said simply. "I do. But tonight's just too fast."

His chin dropped in embarrassment, the hand on her breast sliding to her waist. "Sorry if I—"

"Don't be sorry," she said, pressing a gentle kiss against his closed mouth. "I enjoyed tonight. I'd like to do it again sometime."

Rich leaned in, kissing her gently, his disappointment disappearing. "I liked this too."

He moved closer a second time, and this time Lou dodged the embrace, clambering off his lap. She walked to the kitchen door, pulled it open, and waited. Rich followed, brushing against her as he stepped onto the porch.

"Don't push your luck," she teased.

"Later then," Rich chuckled. He headed down the steps, waving before turning away.

"Night," Lou called, her eyes staying on him until he reached the end of the lot, heading, oddly, into the centre of the street as he walked home.

Lou turned back to the kitchen, glaring at the dishes waiting to be done. She was woozy, but not tired, her body buzzing with unquenched need. Smiling, she walked to the sink, putting in the plug and waiting while it filled. Her gaze lifted and she looked out at the shadows beyond the window; the mountain range a slash of ink across dark parchment. For a long while, she let the feeling of contentment wrap around her.

She put her hands under the sudsy surface, swirling slowly through the water. In the back of her mind she wondered what *she* was supposed to be learning from this, and if Rich would have a story to tell about her, someday.

The thought left her smiling.

* * *

When Hunter heard the telephone ring, he knew it'd be Lou. He'd been far too brusque with her on the phone, and the old guilt wouldn't let it rest. He'd picked up the receiver more than once, meaning to call her, but he didn't know how to apologize without explaining what he'd meant, and *that* he couldn't do.

The phone rang again and Hunter lifted the receiver from the wall, an apology already on his lips. "Was hoping you'd call, hon," he said.

"Waiting for someone?"

It wasn't Lou.

Hunter's smile flickered before disappearing. "Yes ... no," he faltered. "Sort of." He cleared his throat. "I talked to Louise Newman the other day," he said. "She's been asking a lot of questions."

"Oh?" The tone was flippant.

Hunter felt his irritation ignite. He knew Lou ... loved her. And he didn't like being caught in the middle. "She was asking questions," he said. "She knows."

"She *thinks* she knows."

Hunter ran a hand over the back of his neck, grimacing. "It's starting again," he said hollowly.

The phone echoed with laughter.

"You know as well as I do that it never ended."

CHAPTER TEN

Audrika Kulkarni stood at the window to her shop, her attention on the tourists on the sidewalk. There were people moving around town, but not enough buyers for mid-July. She frowned as she pushed open the door and bustled down the street to the shop next door.

"Margaret?" she called from the doorway. "You in here?"

The owner popped up from behind a rack of t-shirts. She had a ticket-gun in one hand and a roll of red stickers in the other, her glasses askew. "Over here!" Margaret called. "Just pricing down the left-over Canada Day shirts."

Audrika glanced at the almost-full rack and the empty store. She obviously wasn't the only one struggling for business. One part of Audrika was relieved by the thought, another part concerned. "Well, don't stop working on account of me," Audrika said, "I'm just here to ask if you'd heard the news?"

Margaret's chin bobbed up. "News?"

Audrika took a deep breath, her chest swelling like a ship with wind in its sails, then launched into her story. "Well, Jordan told Silvia, who told Hunter, who told me they've identified one of the bodies. A really nasty fellow, it turns out." Her voice dropped dramatically. "A hardened criminal!"

"You don't say!"

"Oh, but I do," she said with a smug smile. "It turns out the victim they found at Bertha Bay was a drug dealer. Had ties to the Hell's Angels and everything. Waterton's never going to live this down!"

"Oh my!" The older woman's eyes widened behind thick glasses.

Audrika clasped her hands together in excitement. "With all the bad publicity from the *last* murder, Sam Barton is absolutely fit to be tied!"

"Bad press, again. That won't help business. If I can't get this inventory moving, I'm going to have to get another loan to—"

"Yes, yes, dear!" Audrika interrupted. Gossip was not Margaret's forte. "That's terrible, but this thing with the drug dealer is so much worse than that!"

"Worse than a murderer running around?"

Audrika's mouth puckered in discontent. "Well, no. Of course *that's* the biggest concern, but having the *'criminal element'*..." She made air quotes around the words. "...so entrenched in Waterton is a blow for us all." Audrika's mouth curled up like a cat. "And there's more!"

Margaret's hand rose to her throat. "Oh no!"

"Oh yes!" Audrika chortled. "Seems there might be some connection with the Sorenson fellow who broke into Mr. Evans' place."

"The one who took all those leases and such?"

Audrika's smile wobbled. "Well, I can't say I know anything about *that* end of things, but rumour has it that the Sorenson boy was doing some off-the-record deliveries, and with this fellow showing up dead, the police are thinking that this guy might've been the one he was meeting with."

"Well, I never!"

"It's just too bad we don't have something else to offer," Audrika

said, gesturing around the silent store. "To bring in the tourists before it's too late for all of us."

"Something like...?"

"Why, the satellite system, of course!"

Margaret blanched. "I— well, I hadn't really thought about it."

"You mark my words," Audrika said. "It's going to come down to
a vote. You should think about it before it does."

"Oh dear," Margaret murmured. "I don't think Susan would be
happy if I—"

The chimes above the door rang and Audrika eyed the street. If
people were shopping she really should be going. "Just don't go saying I talked to you about any of this," Audrika called over her shoulder. "Wouldn't want people saying I was trying to swing the vote."

"Of course not, dear," Margaret said distractedly, already busy
with her first customer of the day.

* * *

Rich was late.

Lou tried not to let that bother her. There was always a reason,
she reminded herself. Since he'd cooked her dinner, they'd rebuilt
the scoured bottom of Rich's car and the last few days had been
filled with finessing the finer points of the engine.

"For a high-end car, it's a bit of a lemon," Lou'd teased him.

Rich tugged her closer. "But a lemon that got me into your shop."

"Yes, it did."

The undercarriage had been a mess, and it was on the tip of Lou's
tongue to tell Rich someone *had* been messing with it, but his presence at her side was a boon, no matter how it happened. They'd
been circling each other for months, the connection blossoming in
time to the appearance of wildflowers, desire rising alongside heady
July blooms. Now they were finding reasons to be in one another's

space. Excuses to stay.

Repairing the engine was a slow process that left them plenty of time to talk. Today they were going to replace the engine control circuits ... if he arrived. She stood in the doorway to the garage, her eyes on the streets beyond. With the stillness of the air, the sun was a heavy blanket on her shoulders, the unyielding glare burning her scalp. The Whitewater Lodge was visible in the distance, austerely modern in contrast to the crumbling buildings which surrounded it.

Lou could imagine Rich hiding within. She closed her eyes, letting her mind wander, search, and finally focus on him. *Hurry up, Rich,* she thought. Feeling the tug of connection, a thrill of anticipation ran up her spine. Lou didn't let herself nudge events often, but she did it today. *I'm waiting.*

An hour later, he still hadn't appeared. Lou finished replacing some minivan spark plugs and was just about to head home when she heard the garage door open. Rich stood in the doorway, tie askew, still wearing his suit.

"I'm so sorry, Lou," he panted. "We had a plumbing backup." He walked forward, putting his hands on her shoulders. "I called a couple times, but there was no answer in the store."

"Brendan's in front today," she said with a laugh. "He gets flustered with the phone, so I told him to turn off the ringer. If it was a real problem, I figured the caller would come over in person."

"I came as soon as I could."

Lou had laid out the parts for the circuitry control system on the workbench. "Feel like getting your hands dirty?"

Rich nodded, peering wordlessly around the room.

"What do you need?" she asked.

"You got something for me to wear?" he asked. Lou pointed to a tattered pair of coveralls. "Just let me switch into those, and I'll be right back."

Grinning, he yanked them off the hook and headed to the washroom at the back. The realization hit Lou in the centre of her chest: Rich *wanted* to be there.

They worked slowly through the manual, conversation drifting from their individual days to the controversies embroiling the Park. The police had identified the second victim: a criminal wanted for a long list of crimes. It was a shocking discovery and Waterton was on high alert until the murderer was located, the streets nearly barren. Given the sharp drop in trade, a number of businesses were looking at year-end losses. Some, Lou knew, might close forever.

The issues with the Whitewater Lodge were small in comparison, but Rich grumbled about the never-ending to-do list. His request for funds had been turned down by the board of directors and an audit of the prior year's budget had been announced regarding Chan's unexpected loan and a series of undocumented workers. Any hopes of having Chinook add a secondary satellite dish were momentarily on hold.

"It just feels like I'm stuck in quicksand," Rich grumbled, pausing while Lou soldered wires together. "Every time I fix something, it's followed by two more problems: fix the electrical, but the plumbing fails. Get access to the property reports, but can't find the holding company for the leases. Keep meaning to program the cabin's new security system, but never have time to go through the manual. I just—"

"You having more trouble around the cabin?" Lou interrupted.

"Yeah. Little things mainly," Rich said. "Seems like someone's been hanging around ... trying to scare me."

"What?!"

"There've been little things disappearing. Other things moved." Rich's hands went still, his jaw tightening. "Get the feeling someone's watching me sometimes. Seems like someone wants me out."

Lou's eyes widened. "Rich, you need to report this."

"I don't want to worry you with it," he said. "Christ, I just wish I could get my hands on them!"

"Don't," Lou warned. She held the wires in place, her eyes pleading. "You don't know who is doing this ... what they're like." The memory of the figure in the dark taunted her. She couldn't explain her fear, the words wouldn't come. "Just ... Just tell the police about what happened. And be careful, okay?"

"I did make a police report." He winked. "Scout's honour."

"Good," she breathed, tension easing. "I'm glad."

Rich chuckled wearily. "Back when Lucas broke in, the police told me to put up a fence, but I just haven't gotten around to it. Seems like every second is eaten up before I begin."

Lou murmured agreement, reaching for the next pair of wires. Rich lifted the soldering iron. "Thanks," she said, taking the tool from his hand.

"When things go wrong—and *everything* has been going wrong lately—it's like I can't turn my brain off. Can't sleep sometimes. Just keep going over and over it in my head. Worrying."

Lou nodded, moving to the next set of wires.

"You need something else to focus on." She smiled to herself as the solder began to heat, the beads like quicksilver. "You need an escape, Rich."

"Like what?"

She shrugged. "Depends what you like, I suppose. A hobby's a good place to start."

"What's your escape?" he asked.

Lou raised her eyebrows, taking in the dim garage and her tools. "I fix things."

"And people," he added.

She jerked like she'd touched a live wire. The statement was too close to the truth, and it left her feeling bare and exposed. "No, I don't," she said with a nervous laugh.

"Yes, you do," he insisted. "I see how you are with people: Brendan and Mila, Hunter ... and that woman from the Prince of Wales—"

"Siobhan."

"Right, Siobhan," Rich said. "I see how you are with them, Lou. You don't just talk to them, you tell them stories and they're different because of it."

She shifted uneasily. This wasn't something she'd talked about since her mother had died. Rich Evans was much more perceptive than she'd given him credit for.

"You help people," he repeated. "You do."

Lou leaned in to inspect the engine again so that she didn't have to hold his eyes. "Maybe I help them," she mumbled. "But I certainly don't fix them."

Rich's hand brushed her lower back, and Lou glanced up, catching sight of his look of concern. He was closer to understanding than he should be, and that upset her. "Helping ... fixing ... how's that different?" he asked.

Because I know things I shouldn't, she thought. Lou's throat was tight, her nerves strung taut. She hadn't told anyone since childhood, and even then, her father had never understood. Old Lou Newman had been a good man, but he'd laughed outright at her declaration.

Rich stood, waiting.

"If I fixed them," she answered cautiously. "It'd be like working on an engine. Replace this, and the problem is solved. People aren't like that. I can share a story that helps them, but they still have to do the work themselves."

Rich nodded, waiting for her to continue.

"When someone has a problem," Lou said. "I just talk to them." She laughed nervously. "I guess I just like telling stories."

"Hardly," he scoffed. "You're like some kind of ... of..." He grinned. "Some kind of guru, sitting in the mountains, handing out advice to unsuspecting tourists."

Lou crossed her arms. "That's not funny."

"But it's true!"

"It's nothing like that."

Rich's grin softened, laughter drifting into uncertainty. "Oh, now don't be mad, Lou. You know I'm just teasing you."

"That's *not* what I do."

"Hey, don't pull away," he said softly. "I'm sorry. It was a bad joke."

Lou nodded.

"So what do *you* do?" he asked. "Who do *you* talk to when things get hard?"

She took a shaky breath, trying to smile and failing. "It used to be my mother. But now..." She shook her head sadly. "Now I usually just disappear into books."

"Ah," he said with a gentle smile. "That's where you find all your stories."

She swallowed against the lump in her throat, wondering at how much it meant to her that he understood this.

"Everyone has a story," she whispered.

*   *   *

It was a lonely trek from Glacier Park, Montana to the lake head of Waterton Lakes. Nate set up a neat campsite at the Kintla Lake campground, chopping wood he wouldn't use and inflating an air mattress he'd never sleep on. He left a note on the dash of his truck: *Gone fishing. Back Wednesday. Nate.* Before dawn, he tied a fishing rod and tackle box to his pack and headed off.

The trail was one he took ten or more times a year until winter snows closed the route. Few travelled these mountain paths. Of those who did, most were hikers. Some, like Nate, were another kind of traveller. He'd run into these other mules a few times in the last five years, but he gave them wide berth and they did the same for him. Each man was separately contacted and outfitted, unable to identify the rest. With a transport system this elaborate, it was worth the cost. Nate knew only a handful of his contacts, and he liked it that way.

High in altitude, and barren except for the most seasoned back-country hikers, the trail was a desolate, gruelling climb which took a full eight hours at the best of times. It took Nate along the south face of Mount Custer, through Boulder Pass, and over the continental divide, the mountains rippling off either side like the waves of a frozen storm. He took regular breaks as he walked, adjusting the straps on his pack and checking that its contents were sealed. Inside his backpack was nearly eighty pounds of cocaine. In his jacket pocket, a handgun.

Arriving at Thunderbird Glacier, Nate ate a hurried lunch, slaking his thirst with the melted water of the last ice age. The trail swung down at this point, taking him past Lake Francis and along Olson Creek. His legs were weak and shaking, but he didn't slow. There was a good chance of running into Park officials at this point in the journey, and he fingered the forged driver's license and fishing permit he carried in his pocket. The firearm was a last measure.

Reaching Goat Haunt mid-afternoon, Nate timed his arrival alongside a passel of tourists from The International, a boat tour from Waterton. While the tourists mobbed the beach, drawing the attention of the border crossing guards at the end of the lake, he slipped past, taking the hiking trail up to Boundary Creek. There were a few Canadian hikers embarking on the long winding trail to Summit Lake and from there to the Alderson-Carthew trail, but unless Nate saw wardens or border patrol in their numbers, he wouldn't follow. He waited until the last hiker had disappeared around the bend, then pulled on his pack, setting a quick pace along the rocky beach.

After another two hours he'd reached the turn off. A nondescript trio of rocks marked its place, otherwise invisible, along the shoreline. Nate scanned for people before he moved into the trees. Filled with dense brush, this was the most difficult part of the climb, and his back was slick with sweat when he located the rock. It was larger than any boulder you'd expect here, an erratic left over from glaciation when a kilometre of ice had sliced off a massive chunk of the mountain, pushing it down the slope to its base. On one side of the limestone slab, centuries of water had dug out a sizeable hollow. It was hidden by shrubs and thin-branched saplings. Behind the barrier of foliage, Nate took one last surreptitious look over his shoulders.

Alone.

He slid the backpack off weary shoulders and dropped it into the hollow next to the other five: the only evidence of the other mules. Hundreds of pounds of illegal drugs filled the hole, ready for the next step in transport. Nate didn't know who did it or how, and he didn't care. Finished, he headed back through the trees, making it to shore in less than an hour. He scanned the length of the lake with field glasses. The meeting point was a secluded inlet, tucked in the wrinkled folds of Mount Richards. Nate strolled the shore, checking his watch now and then. He was forty minutes early, but his contact would be here on schedule. The man was fastidious in his habits, and drug running was a business where details mattered.

For the first time in eight hours, he sat down to rest.

Nate had started to stiffen from his lengthy hike when, like clockwork, a smudge of white appeared on the mirrored surface of the lake. Breath held, Nate lifted the binoculars, waiting as the boat came into focus. Recognizing it, he let out a whistling sigh of relief. There'd been once, last summer, when a boatload of tourists had shown up, inadvertently interrupting the meeting, and Nate had been forced to hike all the way back to Kintla Lake rather than coming into town and catching a ride back. The two-way hike wasn't something Nate wanted to do again. He was grateful that today he didn't have to.

With a groan of exhaustion, he headed to the rocky beach. He thumbed the safety of his gun. He'd known the contact for more than two years, but a person could never be too careful. Dax was angry about something that had gone down in the last two months, though he'd never told Nate what. One of Nate's friends—Clarence 'Mac' McCoy—who'd introduced Nate to Dax, had disappeared. Nate guessed this was part of the reason for Dax's ire. One thing was certain, however, things were moving on this side of the border.

The speedboat spun into the shoreline, coming to a stop in the shallows of the pebbled beach. The rasp of stone against the bare hull sent a shiver up Nate's back.

"Good to see you, Nate," the man at the helm called amiably. "Want me to give you a hand?"

"No, thanks," Nate said. "I'm fine."

He waded into the shallows. Despite the heat of the afternoon, the lake water, fed by snow-melt, numbed his feet to the bone. Groaning, he caught hold of the rocking boat. With his eyes on the driver, Nate hitched one leg over the side, tumbling awkwardly onto the floor. The man smiled and turned the key without comment. The engine started with a roar, and Nate slumped in the passenger seat, exhausted and shivering.

"Any trouble getting past the border?" the driver asked.

"Nope."

The speedboat headed out onto the wide lake and the two men fell into silence. Nate knew he ought to follow Dax's orders and leave things alone, but Mac was his friend, his disappearance too fresh to ignore.

"You haven't seen Mac around lately, have you?" Nate suddenly asked.

The man looked up in surprise. "No. Was he supposed to be coming down this time?"

"Not sure. Dax doesn't tell me anything."

"Me neither, man," the man laughed. "Me neither."

Nate smiled, tension easing. "Well, if Mac *does* show up, tell him Dax is mad as hell."

The man snorted in good humour. "I can imagine."

The boat buzzed along for a few minutes and Nate's eyelids grew heavy. It was a fifteen minute ride back to town, but five minutes into it, the boat slowed.

Nate peeked over the edge of the boat, watching for the tell-tale white line marking a submerged tree stump beneath the inky surface. "What's going—?"

* * *

By the time the engine control system was replaced, it was almost eight. Most of the restaurants on Main Street were closing for the night, but Hunter's was open. The sound of a boat's engine could be heard echoing down the lake, but other than that, the late evening was calm and quiet. Rich held the door for Lou and they headed in side by side. The grill was already turned off, the server explained, but anything cold on the menu could still be ordered.

"The grill's off and the restaurant's open?" Rich said in disbelief.

Lou grinned. "You're not in Kansas anymore, Dorothy."

Scanning their meagre options, they placed their orders and the waitress left them to talk. Rich decided it was good to just be here, next to Lou. She made him feel settled in a way he hadn't felt in years. Being around her was like coming home to a place he never knew he missed. *Like the farm,* an inner voice whispered, but Rich didn't listen.

"You grow up around here?" he asked.

"My mother's family is from Macgrath," she said with a nod. "You passed it on the way into Lethbridge." She giggled. "Mind you, if you blinked, you may have missed it."

"One of those towns, hmm?"

"How about you, Rich? Where'd you grow up? Tell me about that."

In minutes they were laughing and talking. Rich found himself telling her things he didn't intend to: memories of visiting his grandparents' farm in the summer and spending every weeknight in high school rebuilding the engine of a '78 Mustang.

"I always knew you loved working on cars," Lou said as their food arrived. "You're too quick a learner otherwise."

He chuckled. "God, I loved that Mustang. It gave me everything I wanted as a teen. Freedom ... power..."

Lou leaned forward, her voice a growl. "Sex?"

Rich choked on his sandwich, coughing while Lou cackled.

"Let's just say," he laughed, "it helped a certain scrawny seventeen-year-old get a few dates."

"I'll bet the backseat of that car could tell a few stories."

Rich snorted, trying to think of which story he could share.

"You loved that work," Lou said. "Taking it apart, rebuilding it."

He sighed, remembering. "God, did I ever."

Lou's smile melted into something dimmer. *Care-worn.* "So why did you stop? Why aren't you doing *that* for a living?"

The stories running through Rich's mind faded away, leaving only a sense of longing behind.

"It wasn't gonna happen," he answered with a shrug.

She bit her lower lip, waiting. "Why?"

Rich fiddled nervously with a fork. There was more to the story. Too many arguments with his parents. Too many slammed doors and forgotten promises. The farm that was his escape, long gone.

"I just..." His hand tightened around the fork's handle. He stared at his plate, trying to remember the reasoning. It came back to him in his father's words. "It wasn't a good career choice," he said coldly. "There's no money in being a mechanic, you know."

He lifted his eyes, realizing, belatedly, that he'd just insulted Lou. She was watching him, but she wasn't angry. Instead she looked terribly sad.

"I'm sorry," she said quietly.

"Me too."

He choked down his sandwich without tasting it, wishing he'd never spoken of his past. He didn't usually talk about that part of his life with anyone. The coffee shop was closing; a waitress was lifting up chairs and setting them precariously on empty tables. It felt like something had changed between them, and he wasn't sure how to get back to where they'd been before. He reached out his hand, and Lou stared at it for a heartbeat before putting her fingers in his.

"I didn't mean that about you," Rich said.

She squeezed his hand.

"There's a story," Lou began, "about John D. Rockefeller. At the time he was the richest man in the world." Her gaze drifted to the window. The long shadows of late evening were fading into murky gloom. "A man asked Rockefeller, 'how much money is enough?'" She looked back at Rich, her voice soft. "And do you know what he answered?"

"No."

Lou smiled, but this time it held no happiness at all.

"Just a little bit more."

CHAPTER ELEVEN

Hunter didn't like how the unofficial meeting in his coffee shop was going, but he had no idea how to change it. Everyone was at one another's throats.

"It's that murderer!" a voice at the back shouted. "Until he's found, none of us are safe."

"It's not my fault the numbers are down," Jim said.

"Troubles all started with Rich Evans, I tell you!"

"Can't expect tourists to come when that killer is still out on the street."

Jim's brows dropped low over his eyes. "Sadie and I are working the case," he growled, "I'm not sure what else you expect us to do."

"Do?" Susan retorted. "Your job, for a start!"

"Relax, Sue," Colt said. "We've still got August. I'm sure business will pick up."

"Hardly! I'm doing worse this summer than the one I opened. Can't even blame it on inexperience."

"There's still time," he insisted.

"Easy for you to say," Susan retorted. "You've got your back-country hippies to drag around. They'll come no matter what. My guests aren't like that."

"They're customers, same as yours, Sue." Colt shrugged. "All I care is that they pay."

With a sigh, Hunter moved around the table, refilling coffee mugs. Even the most easy-going of their group was on edge today.

"I'm certain Jim and Sadie are making excellent progress," Audrika said, drawing the attention of the group. "But we should really be talking about the next Chamber of Commerce meeting. Evans is going to present the findings of the Chinook satellite sub-committee tomorrow. He'll bring it to a vote."

"...more changes!"

"Losing money hand over fist..."

"Nothing but trouble since Evans arrived..."

"...snooping in everyone's business."

"No one but Evans even wants the change," Susan railed. "I'm sure no one else wants to—"

"I want it. My customers want it," Audrika interrupted. "And I'll bet that as soon as Whitewater starts stealing the tourist trade away, you'll want it too."

"Well, I for one, haven't got the time or money," Susan argued. "And I'm certain no one else does either!"

"Really?" Audrika said, "I'm pretty sure I could name a few people sitting at this table who'd make a liar out of you!"

People were suddenly entranced by their coffee, refilling cream and sugar or lifting their mugs for more. Susan huffed, her face pinched and angry. Hunter's eyes grazed over the silent group, his suspicions confirmed.

The door to the coffee shop swung open and Lou walked in, stopping as she saw the others. "'Morning everyone," she said uncertainly. "I ... I didn't realize there was a meeting today."

Susan Varley was the first to stand. "There's not!" she shouted as she stalked away. The others stood, mumbling goodbyes and following Susan out until only Hunter, Sam, and Lou remained.

Lou looked down at the empty table, cluttered with cups. "What's going on?" she asked, her face ashen.

Sam stood, his gaze shifting uneasily from Lou to Hunter. "I, um ... I oughta be going too," he said with a nervous smile. "See you 'round, Louise." He practically jogged out the door.

Lou stared in confusion. "Hunter?"

He picked up the bowl of creamers in one hand and the coffee pot in the other. "You've gotta decide where you stand, Lou."

"And what's *that* supposed to mean?"

Hunter's expression was steely. "Means Rich Evans is an outsider. Simple as that."

* * *

Rich sat in the Campfire Lounge, a list of contractors' reports in one hand, a bottle of beer in the other. If there had ever been a reason to drink, it was this damned hotel. In light of the Whitewater's most recent crisis—a burst pipe in the Aspen suite—he'd missed his standing car-date with Lou Newman. Luckily for him, Mila relayed his regrets. The leak in the east wing and the ensuing repairs was going to cost the lodge a good portion of its pitiful July profits. Tile work and panelling was being pulled out tomorrow. And that was before dealing with the rest of the problems. There were soffits to be installed, finishing of the west wing millwork, and the often-stuck elevator in the main lodge.

Throwing good money after bad, his father's remembered voice chided. That had never been more true than today. Rich sighed, sipping the ale. It was always one step forward and two steps back where the Whitewater was concerned. He set the bottle back down with a thunk, lifting the papers. *Just need one day ...* he thought wearily. *A single day when nothing new goes wrong and I'll—*

The lights went out.

Rich glanced around. He waited ten seconds, then twenty, wondering when the emergency lighting would turn on.

It didn't.

There were no windows in this room. Faintly, he could hear someone shouting in a hallway above him, followed by several doors opening. The hallways, Rich knew, had no windows either. Fumbling through his jacket pockets, he located his cell phone, turning it on in lieu of a flashlight.

In minutes he was down in the lobby where Amanda had assembled an entourage of guests, assuring them the issue would be resolved immediately and ordering the bellhops to add extra wood to the fires. The room had a cozy, cabin feel, and if Rich hadn't been seething, he would have appreciated her tact in calming the guests.

"Where the hell are the backup lights?" he hissed. He had a Chamber of Commerce meeting in an hour, and he didn't want to be late. "I don't have time for this!"

Amanda took his arm, steering him to the front desk and out of the earshot of the guests. "The guys are working on it," she answered calmly.

"Working on it," Rich snapped. "It's the backup, for Christ's sake! They're supposed to be on as soon as the power goes out! What the hell happened?"

"Well, sir, I'm not exactly sure. But Nando's got his guys on the main floor right now. We'll have the guests back in their rooms in no time at all."

Fernando was the most senior of the Whitewater's maintenance officers and it gave Rich a small amount relief to know that someone he could trust was already looking into the issue.

Amanda reached out and patted Rich's arm. "Look on the bright side, Mr. Evans. At least no one's in the elevator."

"Yeah, great," Rich mumbled. "Now, the outage. How long does it usually take for crews to get the power back up in town?"

Amanda pointed to the windows that framed the room. "The power's not out in Waterton, sir," she said. "Just here at Whitewater."

Rich stared out the windows in alarm. Just as Amanda had said, the lights in the houses beyond were twinkling. If he didn't solve this fast, he'd miss the Chamber of Commerce vote, and there'd be no chance in hell for the satellite system.

"Dammit!" he snarled. "Does this happen very often?"

"No. In fact we've never had issues with the power at all." She laughed shrilly. "We would have known the backup lights weren't working otherwise. Right?"

"Right. Just another problem." Rich stepped behind the desk, yanking open drawers in aggravation. He had no idea where to find a flashlight. "Just another thing that doesn't work," he muttered. "Another issue. God, I don't have time to deal with shoddy electrical too!"

"I'm sure the electrical's fine."

"I highly doubt that," he snapped. "There's no reason to think anything works around here."

Amanda started giggling and Rich paused to stare at her.

"What?"

"Well, we always had trouble with the pipes, that's true. But the electricity has *never* been an issue." She eyed him. "I'd vouch for the wiring, sir."

"And how do you figure that?"

Amanda leaned in, her voice dropping breathily. "I was dating the head electrician last year. He had no reason to rush through the work, and he took his time at it." She winked. "Double checked *everything.* I'm certain it's just a tripped breaker or something. I'll run downstairs and check."

Rich shook his head. There were people milling around, and if Amanda Sloane had one gift, it was chatter. She'd keep them content until the lights came back.

"No," he said. "Stay here with the guests; I'll check." He closed the last drawer, massaging his temple. He could feel a migraine coming on. "Do we have a flashlight?"

"Of course, Mr. Evans," Amanda said, reaching into her pocket. "I've got it right here."

Rich took it and headed for the door. "I'll go down and see what happened. Send Nando down when he finishes up."

As he walked down the metal stairs to the basement under Whitewater's main building, Rich couldn't help but remember his grandparents' farm in Minnesota. The house was a beautiful, two-storey stone and wood structure, its high-ceilinged rooms filled with the smell of borscht and perogies. Rich had loved everything about the place except for one thing:

Unlike his parents' suburban home, his grandparents' house had never had a proper basement.

Where Rich's city home had a ping-pong table and a washing machine, the century-old farmhouse had a root cellar, accessible only from outside the house. When staying with them for the summer, his Baba would send Rich to get potatoes and carrots from the cellar. It was a task young Rich had learned to hate. The room, with its moist, cobwebbed walls and low ceiling, had no electricity, and his imagination ran rampant as he climbed down the wooden stairs. Tonight, the same thrill of the unknown ran up his spine. "One more fucking disaster," he hissed through clenched teeth as he followed the lines of wiring into the bowels of the hotel.

The Whitewater's basement was a far cry from the root cellar, but with the power out and no emergency light, it was easy to fill in the darkness with childhood fears. He made his way around piles of neatly stacked boxes, the flashlight's beam bouncing as he searched for the breaker box. The mechanical room was cluttered with discards: the unmatched chair and table that had once been part of the entrance furniture, a cluster of beer pitchers, and a water-stained mattress leaning against the wall. The long shadows seemed to dance. He stepped past, pushing two boxes aside. Nearby was the circuit breaker box. The door hung unexpectedly askew, the interior panels open. Rich scowled at the line of circuit breakers, his mind giving him an answer he didn't understand.

This wasn't an accidental outage. *Every one of them had been thrown by hand.*

"What the...?"

In the darkness behind Rich, a shadow moved. A single footfall echoed.

Rich jerked in surprise, spinning around to locate the source of the sound. His free hand tightened into a fist as he swung the flashlight back and forth in panic.

"Who's there?" he shouted.

Rich's ears were filled with the sound of his own frantic breathing, and then, horrifyingly close, a box toppled into his shoulder, knocking the flashlight to the floor. His chest constricted, adrenaline pulsing like lightning through his veins. Rich dropped to his knees, scrambling to grab the rolling flashlight before it disappeared under the hollow triangle formed by the mattress.

"Fuck!" Every childhood monster in his memory was suddenly real.

He swung the flashlight up, the beam catching on the edge of something large and black running past him. Rich didn't think—didn't have time to. He lurched backward in horror, hitting his head against another box. This crate was full of metal room service trays and they clattered behind him like thunder. Rich yelled in terror. There was another noise in the darkness as something was shoved aside; the intruder was heading into the labyrinth of rooms under Whitewater. The growing panic tightened like a noose around Rich's neck.

This time, he didn't follow to see who or what it was. All his past and present fears of the unknown figure lurking in the shadows launched him forward. He sprinted for the stairs, distant footsteps echoing behind him. He was almost to the top when the door swung open. The light beyond was blinding, and he lifted his arm, shielding his eyes.

"We heard yelling," Nando said. "Are you okay, Mr. Evans?"

Rich stumbled up the steps and into the hallway, now lit by the emergency lights. He put a trembling hand out to the wall, his legs wobbly and weak.

"There's somebody down there," he gasped. "They took out the power on purpose."

*   *   *

Alone in the silence of her cabin, Lou suddenly lowered the book she was reading, listening not with her ears, but her thoughts. Someone was outside.

Someone dangerous ... her mind whispered. She rose, book forgotten in hand, as a bubble of fear filled her chest.

It was the same person from last year.

She didn't know where the idea came from, but once it arrived, it lodged deep inside her. She'd felt this same trepidation the night before Jeff Chan had shown up in Hunter's Coffee Shop raving about the dead animal smeared across his porch. Lou had been sitting in her living room, reading—same as she was tonight—and she'd had a vision of tentacled darkness spreading over the townsite like a claw.

A noise interrupted her spiralling thoughts and Lou dropped the book to the hardwood floor, heart pounding. There were footfalls on the pavement outside; a person was nearby, running. Stepping over the book, she flicked on the porch light and swung the door wide.

A shadow sprinted down the street, coming from the direction of the Whitewater.

"Hello?" she called.

Hearing her, the figure jackknifed across the road, switching directions as he bolted for the shadows. Lou gasped. The silhouette passed out of the porch light and into a heavily wooded area, disappearing like frosty breath.

Lou's hand was icy where it gripped the glass knob. It was a local, but who? Lou couldn't say. The figure was long gone, the night's calm returned. *I'll talk to Hunter tomorrow,* Lou thought. *He'll know.*

Decision made, Lou took a deep breath, forcing her fears away. The air was full of the scent of pine and rain. Around her, the lights of Waterton twinkled like a chain of fireflies. Each link was a home or business, shining cheerfully. Each one—

Lou's breath caught. Far in the distance, one link in the chain was broken, leaving a void in its place.

The Whitewater Lodge was wrapped in darkness.

* * *

It had been a long night and even longer morning, but Constable Sadie Black Plume had no time for sleep. She sat in the sunlit office, squinting at the computer screen. The results for the prints she'd lifted from the break-in at the Whitewater Lodge late last night were here, and she was eager to see them. She drummed her fingers in annoyance, waiting for the email from the Pincher Creek police station to download.

Loading ... Loading...

With a sigh, she turned her attention to the notes inside the case folder. The investigation into the break-and-enter of the Whitewater wasn't really a high-priority crime, not with the Park's murderer still at large. But between combing through gruesome crime-scene photographs and searching for information on Clarence "Mac" McCoy, Sadie needed a break. *Besides,* she thought wearily, *the rest of the town has problems, too.*

She peeked at the screen once more: *Loading...*

Sadie was reasonably sure they wouldn't find the culprit. Last year there had been a rash of break-ins at Whitewater Lodge. Jeff Chan had been convinced the crimes were malicious, but Sadie figured it had been due to transient seasonal staff. With people coming and going all summer, those types of crimes were relatively common in Waterton. Given what could have happened last night, Rich Evans had actually done pretty well. No one had been hurt, nothing stolen, and the culprit had been scared off before doing any damage. Throwing the breakers was just mischief. A boon, in the grand scheme of things, especially when there was a killer out there.

The screen flickered as the email popped open: *Complete.*

Sadie slid forward, her braided hair brushing her shoulders as she skimmed through the document. Most of the prints had been identified as those of Nando Rodriguez, though there were a number of unknown prints along the top of the box. These, Sadie figured, were likely the installer's. A second series of prints had been lifted from the support beam in the basement as well as on one of the metal trays which had been knocked down. These were the ones flagged in the email as having a match. She smiled grimly, gaze narrowed on the screen.

"And that's our key," she murmured. "Who are you?"

According to the email, these prints were part of an open investigation. Sadie popped open the email's link, waiting as the computer chugged to download the file.

Loading ... Loading ... Loading...

"C'mon, c'mon."

Complete.

The pdf appeared, images of another gruesome murder scene filling the screen. Swallowing bile, Sadie read through the report. *"John Doe", Caucasian male, age 25-30, identity unknown. Body found in a forested area near Colter Peak, Yellowstone National Park, September 1992. The death was originally filed as an 'animal attack' by Park officials. After the discovery of a weapon (see article 2.58) with three partial prints, located a short distance from the attack site, the case was reopened. In October 1992 an autopsy noted the seration of rib bones and the case was deemed a homicide.*

The perpetrator is, as yet, unidentified.

Sadie stared at the screen in shock. This information changed everything. Reaching for the phone with shaking hands, she dialled the front desk.

"Hey, Liz," she said, "can you find Jim for me? Tell him we've got a bigger problem than just a break-in."

CHAPTER TWELVE

When Hunter Slate was in his restaurant, he was at work, but that didn't stop him from visiting too. He'd known Louise Newman since she'd been a toddler, and as she walked into the coffee shop, she had that look that always warned him she'd be asking questions he didn't like. The ones that got him thinking about doing the 'right thing' rather than the 'easy thing', whether he intended to or not.

He knew this would be one of those days.

Hunter poured a cup of coffee, grabbed a handful of creamers and carried them to the table by the window. Lou was frowning as he approached, her gaze on the tourists outside on the street. Reaching Lou's side, he set the coffee and a spoon in front of her, dropping the creamers in the centre.

"Looks like you've got something on your mind, hon."

She lifted her eyes to him, expression tired. Guilt tightened around him; Hunter still hadn't apologized for telling her to pick a side. Hunter's friendship with Lou had once been the easiest thing in the world, but Rich Evans had thrown everyone off-balance.

"Yeah, Hunter, you could say that," she said, gesturing for him to sit.

He slid into the seat across from her. There were pale blue rings under her lashes, making her seem fragile. A wave of affection rose in Hunter's chest. *If that damned Evans is to blame,* he thought irritably, *I'll tan his hide.*

Lou glanced up. "What did you say?"

Hunter laughed uneasily. "Not a thing."

She nodded, attention drifting back to the window.

"So how've you been holding up?" Hunter asked.

Lou sipped from her coffee, peering at him over the rim. "You heard about the break-in at Whitewater Lodge?"

Hunter sighed. So there it was. Lou wasn't going to dance around her questions; they sat on the table in front of them. "Everyone's heard about it," he said noncommittally. "It's in the Cardston paper already. There'll be reporters here in no time, should anything come of it."

The lines on Lou's face deepened. "Rich says the police found prints in the basement. They match an unsolved murder in Yellowstone."

Hunter paled. "Another murder?"

"Yeah, another one, just like the two they had here in Waterton." Lou pressed her lids closed as if the thought wounded her. "All of this is draining the town. Won't be long and everyone's going to just up and move away."

Hunter reached out, patting her arm. "I'll still be here," he said. "But how about you? Looks like your garage is doing alright."

For a few minutes, they talked business. With the only gas station in town, Lou Newman was assured a living by necessity, whereas others weren't. As for Hunter, he was content either way. He'd owned the coffee shop for decades, and with the skeleton staff able to manage it, he did fine no matter how small the trade. Not everyone else in town had that comfort.

"I heard Susan saying there weren't enough people to make up for her June and July losses," Lou said wearily. "The reporters are keeping the hotels afloat right now, but it won't stay that way."

Hunter shrugged. "So the town's a little quieter. I'm just as happy without the tourists, to be honest."

Lou scowled, making her seem much more like her father than made Hunter comfortable. He owed old Lou Newman more than he wanted to admit.

"There's no harm in quiet," Lou said, "but there's a lot of harm if someone's killing people to keep it that way."

The corners of Hunter's mouth turned down at her words. "We've gone through troubles before; we'll ride 'em out again."

"It's the same as what happened last year. People around town hated Chan, and he left without a word to..."

Lou's mouth hung slack as the unspoken possibility appeared between them. Hunter averted his eyes, engrossed in the checker-board tablecloth. Lou had been circling around the issue ever since Rich Evans had shown up in the spring, and it looked like she was heading down that road again.

She hunched forward, hands splayed on the table. "What if the murderer is doing it for a reason?" she whispered. "What if he's picking off people because he *wants* to keep the tourists away?" Her face was aghast.

When Lou looked at him like this, she reminded Hunter of her mother, Yuki. Hunter swore that woman had been able to see through him. *Perhaps,* he thought, *her daughter can, too.* Today he refused to flinch.

"Nice and quiet suits me fine."

"Oh, Hunter," Lou moaned. "Please don't tell me you know who's been—"

"The Park's changing, Lou," he said, standing up. "I know that as much as anyone else does." He reached out, laying a heavy hand on her shoulder. "But I'm not gonna hurry it on its way."

* * *

Susan Varley stormed away from the Chamber of Commerce meeting at the Lions' Hall, jaw clenched in mute fury. Everything she'd fought against for the last two and a half months had been for nothing. Friends and neighbours she'd *thought* she could count on had shown their true colours. Lou had been the only person who'd refused to vote, but her decision hadn't changed a thing.

The proposal for a secondary satellite dish for the community had been passed.

"Susan...?" Lou called.

Varley didn't slow. Sam Barton would take the application from Chinook to Parks Canada. There'd be an environmental assessment soon, and there was every chance it would be passed. Satellite dishes like this already existed in other Canadian parks.

"Susan, wait!" Lou shouted, panting as she ran after her.

"What?" Varley snarled, turning to face her.

"I wanted to make sure you were okay," Lou said gently. "You ran out of there so fast, I was worried."

The older woman jabbed Lou's chest with her forefinger. "Don't pretend like you care!" she barked. "You stood there and let the vote go through!"

Lou glanced down at Susan's finger, surprised by the accusation. "But ... but I didn't vote," Lou said. "I never do."

Susan made a disgusted noise. "That was all it took, wasn't it?"

Lou shook her head, but Susan wasn't done. Countless frustrations—the dwindling tourist trade, money troubles nudging her toward possible bankruptcy, Audrika and Murray siding with Rich Evans—bubbled over.

"You— you stand there," Susan yelled, "and you *act* like you care about this town, but you're no better than the rest of them!"

Lou stumbled back, wide-eyed. In the back of Susan's mind, she knew this wasn't entirely true—Lou had been a voice of kindness and support when Susan had struggled her way through a decade-long gambling addiction—but that voice was far away. Behind Lou, the door opened and Rich Evans appeared.

Susan's temper combusted. "Traitor!" she shouted. "You want to sell out, just like Kulkarni and the others!"

"That's not true," Lou said.

"It is!"

Rich marched toward them. He was coming up behind Lou, but Susan could see him perfectly. He glowered. Minutes earlier, Susan had verbally attacked him and now she revelled in the thought of his response.

"You know I love Waterton," Lou said patiently. "I grew up here, Susan. I care every bit as much as—"

"Liar!" Varley roared. "You're in it for yourself and your ... your ... goddamned *boyfriend!*"

"My what?" Lou gasped. Behind her, Rich paused in his tracks.

Susan moved in, hands rising in clenched fists. She'd seen the looks between Lou and Rich; had run into them together in Hunter's any number of times. Now she couldn't help her words. "Your lover!" she bellowed. "You think it's some kind of big secret, Lou? Everyone knows what you're up to!"

Lou pushed forward, placing herself directly in front of Susan. Her presence, as much as her words, interrupted the tirade.

"It's not like that!"

"And what *is* it like?" Rich's voice echoed.

Lou turned in surprise. "Rich," she choked. "I only meant that..."

Her unfinished words faded to nothing. Susan laughed angrily as she headed for her car. She heard Lou plead: "Rich, please let me explain."

"It's fine!" he snapped.

Susan pulled open the car door and climbed inside, watching through the windshield as Rich turned and strode away.

* * *

Lou settled down onto the floor of the garage, leaning against the wall. At her side was Rich Evans, his hands loose in his lap. Lost in thought, he stared out the doorway, which framed the mountain and street corner beyond. Lou hadn't been sure he was going to come today after the confrontation with Susan the previous night. But four-thirty had rolled around, and he'd been standing outside, same as usual.

Angry, but willing.

They were nearly finished repairing the engine. Lou was glad they'd had fussy work to keep them busy; adjusting the cooling systems had given them plenty of time to just 'do' instead of talk. The awkwardness had worn away until they were at ease once more. Feeling the tension drawing out, Lou started to speak. The story she chose was an old one from Japan, and it had been passed mouth-to-ear through Lou's family for generations.

"There was a blind beggar who lived near a monastery," she began. "He heard the people of the village come and go, following them through the sound of their voices." Lou peeked at Rich through the fringe of her lashes. He watched her, unsmiling. "Every day he sat with his cup in his hand, listening to those around him, and over time, his ears became his eyes, until he could finally see in a way that no other could."

"By eavesdropping," Rich added coolly.

"He listened to everyone," Lou explained. "He heard the voices raised in anger, and those lowered in grief. In time, the blind man found that he could judge the characters of those around him by the tone they used. Some people, the blind man said, used words of congratulations for their friends' success, while their voices were secretly filled with envy. Other people used words of condolence for hardships their friends had endured, while their voices were secretly filled with satisfaction that it hadn't happened to them."

Lou shuffled sideways until her shoulder was pressed up against Rich. They'd stood like this all afternoon as they worked on the car, but sitting here on the garage floor, it felt different. *Important.* His arm was warm, and though he didn't slide it around her shoulder, he didn't pull away either.

"The Zen master, Bankei, was one of the monks who lived in the monastery," Lou said. "When he died, one of his acolytes came to talk to the blind man. He asked: *'What did you hear in my master's voice? What secrets did his voice tell?'* The blind man smiled, as if he could hear Bankei once more, his voice full of joy. *'Bankei's voice,'* the beggar answered, *'was the one I loved most of all.'* The monk asked him why. *'Because when he spoke of happiness,'* the beggar said, *'all I heard was joy, and when he spoke in sorrow, all I heard was his grief. He only ever spoke with one voice.'"*

Lou sighed, her mother coming to mind. She hadn't understood this story as a child. She did now.

Next to her, Rich sat in silence.

"What does the story mean?" he finally asked.

"It depends on what you heard last night."

He grimaced and said nothing. For a long time, they sat without speaking. The air outside was filled with the lilting sound of sparrows, the buzz of traffic on Main Street, and under that the faint lapping of waves on the lakeshore. Lou smiled. It wasn't the same, but it was better.

And better, Lou thought, *is a start.*

* * *

Amanda Sloane had worked in Waterton since she'd left Winnipeg at the age of eighteen, moving out of her mother's trailer one early July morning. She'd brought along a high school diploma, a wad of cash stolen from the coffee tin, and a backpack full of clothes. Amanda had never looked back, and her mother hadn't come to find her. That summer had marked a new beginning in her life.

She'd made her way across the prairies to Alberta—a place that was as far away from Winnipeg as eighty-four dollars in crumpled bills and a willingness to hitchhike could get her. Amanda had gone door to door in Waterton, asking for a job. Louise's father, old Lou Newman, had been the first to say 'yes'.

She hadn't left Waterton since.

Over the slow pass of winters and summers, Amanda had grown to understand the cycles that made up small-town life. She knew that fewer tourists meant easier work for the staff, but fewer tips for the servers, and less chance of picking up extra hours. A busy summer kept everyone hopping and the tills full, but it also shifted the steady pace of life, tugging it into a frenetic rate.

The final days of July had been relatively busy compared to the previous months. Some people, like Audrika Kulkarni, thought it was because the furor over the two murders was finally passing; Rich Evans' interpretation was far less optimistic.

"They're vultures," he'd grumbled to her one afternoon.

"Sir?"

"They're here to see how bad things really are."

It made sense, Amanda decided. People thrived on the misfortunes of others: her mother was the perfect example of that. *Can't see a car accident,* she thought, *for wanting to climb inside and join in.* But guests were guests, and for the first time since it had opened last year, the Whitewater Lodge was doing decent business, even if half of them were news crews.

The ringing phone at the desk pulled Amanda from her daydreams. She sat up, reaching for the handset. She couldn't count how many times Mr. Evans had called unexpectedly to check up on her.

"Whitewater Lodge," she said cheerily, "how might I direct your call?"

"Amanda?" Nando said. "Is Mr. Evans around?"

"Just a sec, I'll check."

She leaned back in the rolling chair, sliding away and pushing open the interior office door with her toe. It was empty. Rich had a desk, but rarely used it. "Not in his office, no," she answered. "You want to leave a message?"

Nando snarled something under his breath, leaving Amanda giggling. She might not speak Spanish, but she certainly knew the *tone* of what he'd said.

"Not gonna work," he said. "I've got to talk to him right away." Nando swore again. "Look, have him call me. I'm in the east wing: Aspen Suite."

"Another pipe break?"

"Wish it was. We've got a bigger issue."

Amanda's lashes widened. "Something bigger?"

"The guys repairing the tiles in the Aspen suite just found something behind the sink."

"More mould?"

"Worse."

The front door opened and Rich walked in, laptop case in hand, a clipboard under his arm.

"Mr. Evans!" Amanda squeaked, covering the receiver with one hand and waving at him with the other. "Mr. Evans! You're needed right away!"

"...tell Evans he's gotta call the police," Nando finished. "We found dried blood—*a lot of it*—behind the sink and under the floorboards we pulled up."

CHAPTER THIRTEEN

Jim and Sadie stood in the en-suite bathroom of the Aspen Suite, surveying the crime scene. A dried puddle of flaking blood, unobserved for most of a year, had been discovered behind the column of a pedestal sink. The linoleum had been pulled up to reveal blood-soaked floorboards. Droplets under the millwork and blood splatters along the toe-kick of the door showed there'd been far more than that at some point. Seeing it reminded Jim of the old barn where his uncles processed meat from hunting, the floor stained black from years of blood. He turned away, stomach roiling.

"The bathroom's not the murder site," Sadie announced. "The blood pattern isn't an attack; it's someone moving a body. Dismembering it."

"We need to locate Jeff Chan and find out what the hell happened here," Jim replied grimly. A deer hung on meat hooks to 'drain' appeared in his mind's eye and he swallowed bile. "Bastard could be our killer."

"Or maybe Jeff Chan *is* what happened here. Maybe this is what's left of him, " Sadie said, gesturing to the stained floor. "Won't know until we send the blood for DNA testing."

She paused as Jordan and another member of the team passed by.

"Are we ready for the blue light?" Jim asked.

"Just a minute longer," Jordan said. "Team's prepping the room now."

"Sounds good." Jim turned back to Sadie. "We don't just have a murder here," he continued, "we have a conscious effort to hide it. If it was Chan who died in the room, then someone else would've had to dispose of his body and conceal the crime. When Chan didn't show up for work, Amanda was on the phone filing a missing person's report that same day. You and I did a walk-through of this whole hotel. I'm sure we were in this room."

"I'll double check that, but yeah, I don't remember any unfinished work in this wing when we came through," Sadie agreed.

Jim scowled. "This happened before Chan left."

"Then our victim is someone else. Someone who disappeared and was never found."

"We'd only get a missing person's report if their family knew they'd travelled here," Jim said. "Could've been a drifter or someone from the wrong side of the tracks."

Sadie turned in a circle, her gaze taking in the marked floor and splashed tiles.

"Lots of people come to Waterton on the spur of the moment," she said. "Lots who are just passing through. So the killer could have lured them up to this unfinished room and done away with them." Her fingers played with the end of her braid. "We just need to figure out who was working here when this suite was being finished."

The rest of the team was blacking out the windows; Jim and Sadie stepped aside as they passed. "The files Evans gave us show the millwork in this room was finished last October," he said. "No crew members listed. No details."

"Files can be changed."

"True enough. But the head of maintenance, Nando Rodriguez, said he couldn't remember who was working in this section of the hotel." Jim said. "He swears he never did any work in here. Amanda and a couple others who were here last winter can corroborate his story."

"Whoever did it knew how to install tile and lino."

"Not very well, according to Nando," Jim chuckled.

"Do the files list the other people doing maintenance in the hotel that month?"

"Not sure."

"Give me a second." Sadie disappeared around the corner, returning a moment later with a clipboard full of papers. "Jordan says the Luminol's almost ready," she muttered, flipping pages.

The papers were curled and tattered, several torn in half. Whatever Jeff Chan's managerial skills had been, filing hadn't been one of them. "September twenty-eighth, twenty-ninth, thirtieth..." Sadie murmured. She turned another page. "October first, second, third ... Bingo!" She looked up, grinning. "We've got our guy."

Jim came around beside her, bumping shoulders as he peered down at the documents.

"Lucas Sorenson," he said dourly. "Now *that* explains a few things."

* * *

Rich paced the hallway, burning off his anxiety through constant motion. The police had been in the Aspen Suite for over an hour, individual staff members being pulled aside for questioning one after the other, but there was no sign of an end. The crime scene investigations unit from the Lethbridge police force had arrived to assist with the homicide investigation. Rich figured he wasn't a suspect—the crime had taken place long before his watch—but the fallout would impact his ability to bring the struggling hotel together. Even with Amanda's tact, moving the guests from this wing of the hotel had been an ordeal. He knew there would be talk, and that, come morning, some guests would be gone.

That was the least of his fears. Rich would have to close this wing until the scandal blew over. The first priority was damage control, but he wasn't sure how to manage it. *When it hits the papers,* Rich thought in dismay, *we're screwed. Fuck! Fuck! FUCK!* Every possible thing that could go wrong with this hotel had gone wrong, and today's discovery would only make the situation worse.

The door at the end of the hallway opened and Rich spun around.

"Mr. Evans?" Constable Black Plume called.

"Everything alright?" he asked.

Sadie's brows knit together, and she stared at him for several seconds. "No, Mr. Evans. Things are *not* alright."

"Yes, of course, I just meant..." Rich ran his hand over his face. "I don't know what I meant. Just wasn't thinking. It's been a hell of a day." He dropped his hands to his sides, forcing the rat-in-a-maze thinking away. "What can I do for you?"

"We're going to have to pull up the carpet. See where the blood stain stops." The officer nodded toward the half-open door and Rich followed her gaze. There were people with cameras, areas of tape marking spots on walls. The door to the bathroom hung wide, the disturbing trail of black smears spread across the subflooring. A strong chemical smell invaded Rich's nostrils and he fought the urge to vomit.

"Yes, of course," he said numbly. "Pull up the carpet. Right."

"If there's anything you can think of which might help us to find the person who did this—anything at all—I need you to let us know."

"Wasn't here last year," Rich said. "Jeff Chan was the manager." He swallowed against a dry throat. Someone had drawn a series of circles across the toe-kick near the tiles, marking blood droplets. Nauseated, he couldn't pull his eyes away from the scene.

"But if you can think of anything you might have heard or seen since you took over," Constable Black Plume continued. "Something that stuck out in your mind. No matter how small, I want to hear it."

A woman wearing a face mask stepped across the threshold, evidence kit in hand. She carried a swab aloft in a plastic bag, the end marred orange-brown. Rich took a slow breath, and another waft of the chemical invaded his nostrils. His stomach clenched. He needed to think his way through this but he couldn't get past the fact that someone had died in the hotel. It didn't make sense, unless—

Rich's heart leapt. "There was something going on with Jeff Chan!" he announced, words tumbling out in a rush. "He had a loan, but no one seems to know what it was for. A loan with Borderline Industries. Coldcreek looked into it, but the company isn't properly listed. I've tried to find the contact information. Nothing! It's like the whole thing is a front."

"What company is this?"

"Borderline Industries," Rich said. "It's a holding company, one based in the States. The company controls the leases for a number of cabins here in town. I've been trying to find out—"

"Properties here in Waterton?"

"Yes! Properties all across town. Jeff Chan owed Borderline Industries money—the Whitewater Lodge *still* does—and the hotel's listed as collateral. The board's lawyers are trying to locate Borderline but—"

"Sadie!" a voice from the other room shouted. "We're ready to go, if you want to see."

"Hold that thought," Sadie said, turning away from him. Rich followed her retreating back into the Aspen Suite. The room's windows had been blocked off, a camera on a tripod set up in the middle of the room. Blue-light fixtures on stands were placed in each corner, wires snaking back to a central hub.

"Let's give it a try," someone said, and the last light flicked off. Encased in darkness, the terror Rich had felt in the basement returned. In a shimmer, the room relit in tones of blue and grey, bright spots of bluish white glowing ominously across the wall.

"My god," someone gasped.

Splashes of blood marred every wall. The pristine 'cool grey' paint had been cleaned, but the Luminol had revealed a macabre last scene. Rich's gaze caught on a single hand print. It trailed downward in a smear of lines. He swallowed convulsively, his eyes drawn from one splash to another. *So much blood,* his mind chattered. *So much fucking blood!* Rich's ears were ringing, throat tight.

"Jimmy," Constable Black Plume said. "You see this message?" Her voice had changed in the last seconds. The brusqueness gone, breathless excitement in its place.

Rich peeked around the door frame to the room beyond. A frisson of fear ran up his spine to lodge deep in his chest. "No!" he cried.

The words "GET OUT!" were smeared in foot-high bloody letters across the wall.

* * *

Jim stood, hands clasped behind his back, inspecting the inside of the Whitewater Lodge's ascetic main office; a few steps away, Sadie was finishing her interview with Rich Evans. The manager of the

Whitewater Lodge had lost his smooth façade. Hair rumpled, eyes wild, he paced circles in time to her questions.

"...and was Jeff Chan the manager at the time the Aspen Suite was completed?" Sadie asked.

"Yes, that's right."

Sadie scribbled into a notebook. "He would've been the one to oversee any clean-up?"

"I'm guessing so," Rich said. "But I don't know for certain. I wasn't here."

More scribbling. "You ever meet Mr. Chan before you came to Waterton?"

"No."

"You sure, Mr. Evans? Not even once?"

Jim perused the white walls and unfinished trim in the office, happy to let Sadie do the questioning. He was itching to get back to the station so he could go through the discoveries from the Aspen Suite, but with the revelation that Jeff Chan had been paying an unexplained debt to Borderline Industries, pinning down facts was the most pressing matter.

"Definitely not," Rich answered. "I was living in New York until this spring. Chan was here last year."

"Was this the same Mr. Chan who signed the loan you mentioned?"

"Yes, yes," Rich said, tone sharpening. "I told you that before. Chan signed for the loan himself."

Sadie added another note. "Coldcreek's management was okay with that?"

"They didn't know about it 'til after the fact," Rich said, feet slowing. "And no. The board of directors was *not* okay with it."

Sadie raised an eyebrow, catching Jim's gaze. "What was Mr.

Chan's loan for, exactly?"

Rich ran his hands through his messy hair. He looked, Jim decided, like he'd been on a bender, so different from the self-assured man Jim had met earlier.

"He didn't have enough money to finish the millwork in the main wing, so far as I could tell."

Jim's gaze skimmed over the missing toe-kick and unpainted quarter-round on the ceiling. Even now the hotel wasn't finished.

"So far as you could tell?" Sadie prodded.

The pacing started again. "The books are a mess," Rich grumbled. "I've tried to figure it out, but there are things missing. Details that I know should be there, but aren't..."

While Rich's list of complaints continued, Jim scanned the office. It looked like it was waiting for its rightful owner to return. No coffee mugs with "Number 1 Boss" or other platitudes cheered the tidy desktop. The standard "Word a Day" calendars and sports paraphernalia were unexpectedly missing. In fact, the only thing on the otherwise empty walls was a dry-erase board with staffing charts written in a terse hand. Even the corkboard was devoid of photographs. Jim rolled onto the balls of his feet, considering what wasn't there. *Doesn't let his work mix with his life,* he thought. *Or doesn't intend to stay.*

Jim wondered which.

"What information are you missing, Mr. Evans?" Sadie asked.

"The details of the loan, for one, information on Borderline ... And that's only one of Chan's many mess ups."

Sadie made another note. "There're more?"

"I've got a delivery schedule from last year that doesn't match up. Can't find the vendors for some of last year's deliveries. Half the staff don't—"

"Deliveries?" Jim interrupted. His mind, which had been drifting seconds before, was now sharply attuned.

"Yes." Rich nodded. "There were a bunch of deliveries last summer that were marked for carbon-copying, but no one knows to whom. I've got files that—"

Another knowing look passed from Sadie to Jim. "More than the ones you sent us?"

"Well, yes," Rich said. "I found a few others that had to do with—"

Jim stepped forward, clearing his throat. "We're going to need those files."

Rich looked from Sadie, to Jim, and back again. "Oh ... okay."

He rustled through the top drawer of a filing cabinet, bringing them forward. "This is what I've found so far." He didn't hold Jim's eyes as he said it, just shoved the pile of documents into the officer's hands.

"Bring the rest when you get them," Jim said dryly. "You know, the *other* ones you found."

Rich's eyes widened. "I'm not involved."

Jim straightened the file and tucked it under his arm. "I never said you were."

"Then why?" Rich asked, voice rising. "Why are you treating me like I'm a suspect? I wasn't even living in Canada when this happened!"

"We're covering all possibilities," Jim replied.

"But this isn't about me!" Rich shouted. "It's about Jeff Chan!"

"Sir, calm down," Sadie instructed.

The direction seemed to infuriate him. "It's Chan!" he shouted, gesturing wildly. "It's always been Chan! He's the one who got the loan! He disappeared! You've got to find him!"

Jim widened his stance. "Mr. Evans, you need to lower your voice." Rich's rant stumbled to a heaving stop.

"For now, you aren't a suspect," Jim said. "But we can't risk anything that might impact the case. The mess in the Aspen Suite..." Jim pointed out the door to where two other officers were talking quietly to Amanda Sloane. "Whoever did that, whatever happened that night last year ... It's going to get messy. And when we find the person responsible, I want our case airtight."

Rich stared at him.

"Do you understand what I'm saying?" Jim asked.

Rich's throat bobbed. "Do I need to call my lawyer?"

Sadie flicked the notepad closed with a snap and Rich flinched. "That's up to you, Mr. Evans," Sadie replied "For now, you're not a suspect. As you said, you weren't even in Canada at the time. But we need to see anything you've found. All the files, all the leases. Whatever you've got."

"Exactly," Jim nodded. "Just leave the investigating to us." He ambled to the door. "You ready to go, Sadie?"

The two of them walked through the lobby where Amanda stood flirting with Jordan, and headed out to the police cruiser.

Sadie tugged distractedly at her braid. "You really think Evans was involved?" she asked.

Jim winked. "Doubt it. Just letting things play out. Seeing where the pieces fall."

"Fair enough." Sadie climbed into the cruiser and slammed the door. "You notice how he was acting in there? Panicked ... crazy even."

Jim snorted. "Sounded a lot like that Chan fellow did last year. Paranoid."

"But why?"

Jim stared at the multi-million dollar Whitewater Lodge, the biggest building in the entire Park, but a minuscule structure compared to the peaks that rose up around it. "Not sure," he admitted, his smile fading. "Seems like the mountains do that to city folk."

* * *

Lou had a small backpack slung on her shoulders, scuffed hiking boots on her feet. The water bottle clipped to her pack sloshed in time to her footsteps as she headed up the first leg of the Alderson-Carthew hike. The trail head was high in the mountains, starting from Cameron Lake, which still had snow lingering in the shadows of the far end, and up the mountainside to the bowl of a valley and a series of summits. Even in the sullen heat of early August, the hike was one of Lou's favourites.

She hadn't been planning to take the entire day off, but her mind was too troubled to be trapped indoors. The murders in the Park gnawed at her calm, leaving her wondering whether her friends and loved ones were safe. There were other issues, too. Rich Evans had been marked as off-limits by the townspeople. Barring Mila and Brendan, the locals had grown oddly distant with Lou the last few weeks. Hunter had come into the gas station to fill up his truck yesterday, and when she'd tried to make small talk, he'd accused her outright of fishing for information. Lou was experiencing ostracism she hadn't known since childhood when she was 'different' and hadn't known how to hide it.

Nearing the summit, the tree line grew sparse, sunshine spreading through the canopy until Lou was walking along the rocky path draped in heat. She sifted through stories she'd read and heard, looking for an answer to what was happening. A tale of three boys lost on the mountain flickered in Lou's mind, but before she could pull it forward, her worries tugged it away. Far below, in one of the other valleys, someone had a campfire. A tendril of smoke moved past, carrying with it an unexpected memory. Lou's vision shimmered. *She was hiking along a narrow trail with the rest of the peasants, a sack of grain hoisted up on one shoulder. The fields were burning to stop the invaders from—*

She stumbled, the mountain's edge precariously close. Lou's thoughts were jumbled, calm undone. She'd lived hundreds of lives, remembered snatches of them all. From her earliest childhood, the echoes had risen and fallen like ripples of light seen through water. The one today felt the same as the ox on the muddy road.

It scared her.

Perhaps, a voice inside her whispered, *Rich is on the right path and you're the one who isn't.* She shivered despite the warmth of midday. With the discovery of the murder scene at the Whitewater a week before, Rich Evans had all but disappeared from Lou's life. The feeling of distance worried her. There was chaos unfolding in Waterton, and Rich was at its heart.

Around her, hikers took their rest in rocky outcrops, others posing in front of lake-filled vistas that hung like the footprints of giants across the horizon. Unsettled, Lou walked on, reaching the trail that descended north and then east, back to town. As she turned the corner a line of tourists on horseback appeared in front of her, a man on a dappled mare leading them. His expression contracted in surprise and then joy as he saw her.

Lou stopped. "Colton Calhoun," she said, a careworn smile crossing her face. "It's been too long."

* * *

Mila was working the till when Rich stopped by the garage. "Lou around?" he asked.

The teen shook her head, pointing to the landscape beyond the window. Outside, the late afternoon light was painting the mountains red and gold. "She's hiking Alderson-Carthew today," Mila explained. "I dropped her off at Cameron this morning."

Rich's shoulders slumped. He'd been so busy with the drama at the hotel he hadn't been down to Lou's garage for almost a week. The police investigation had kept him at work until midnight for the last three days in a row. He knew it made no sense to be irritated that she wasn't here, but it still rankled him. He needed someone to talk to!

"That a long hike?" Rich asked, already knowing the answer.

Mila gave him a sympathetic smile. "Six to eight hours," she said. "And knowing Lou, she's not rushing."

Rich gritted his teeth. He longed to see Lou today. It wasn't just about fixing the car; he needed her advice on other things, too. With the discovery in the Aspen Suite and the obvious cover-up, questions had arisen about the original building inspection. Rich had been certain it would be in Chan's files ... and it had been, only there was doubt about the inspector's qualifications. A new building inspector from Lethbridge had done a thorough examination of the building after the police had left and Rich was horrified by the findings. The inspector had insisted that Rich close two of Whitewater's three wings "effective immediately" or shut down the lodge entirely.

Rich had slept less than six hours in the last forty-eight. He was so tired he couldn't think straight, unexpected fears pushing him into a spiral of paranoia. There were items he was *certain* he'd left in his office, inexplicably moved the next morning. Other issues—the broken lock on the Whitewater's supply shed and the muddy footprints going inside—couldn't be blamed on his own exhaustion. That was malice. That was intent. And it wasn't just at work, either.

Two days ago, Rich had again heard someone on his porch, but they were gone by the time he opened the door. He followed Lou's advice and called the police. Jim Flagstone drove by, checking the property under the swooping glare of a flashlight.

"Might've been the wind," he told Rich.

"It's not! I've told you before, someone's harassing me!"

Jim gave Rich a level stare. "I'll write it up," he said. "But unless there's evidence, my hands are tied."

"How many times do I need to report it," Rich snapped, "before you have enough to do something, huh?!"

Jim glowered at him. "Just once," he said, "with proof," before walking stiffly away.

Proof or not, someone *was* coming onto his property at night. The certainty Rich was being taunted by someone in the small community had grown into all-out panic. While the newly-installed security system on the cabin assured him that he could sleep in peace, his property wasn't fully secured. Today when he'd left for work, he'd found a window in his garage had been broken during the night, further infuriating him. It was yet another thing he didn't have time to deal with. Another report the police wouldn't believe.

All Rich could think about now was that Lou should be here at the garage, and wasn't.

"Do you know when she'll be back?"

"Not sure," Mila said, glancing at the clock. She frowned. "Actually, Lou should've been back an hour ago."

"What do you mean?"

"I'm sure it's nothing, Mr. Evans. Lou's probably just late." She smirked. "She's not a tourist, after all."

"Right." With a murderer on the loose, the assurance didn't make him feel any better.

Mila nodded to the windows. The light was starting to change as day eased toward the lazy twilight of the mountains. "You could walk to the end of the trail if you want and see if she's there," she said.

Rich shifted uncomfortably. This would be a great suggestion if he had any idea at all where the trails were located. "Mila, um ... do you happen to know where the Alter-Alder..."

"Alderson-Carthew," she prompted.

"Right. Do you know where the trail is?"

Mila pointed to the map next to the door. "Of course," she said. "Just walk up the road until you reach the movie theatre, then turn right and walk toward the mountains. The trail comes down right next to Cameron Falls."

Rich's stomach tightened into a knot. That was where he'd seen the cougars.

CHAPTER FOURTEEN

Sun-warmed and smiling, Lou and Colton stood talking like the old friends they were, Lou's earlier worries pushed aside.

"Take one," Colt insisted, gesturing to the line of horses. "Ride back with me."

Lou grinned. "There's no room."

"I'll move the packs over. C'mon. It'll take five minutes."

"I can't ride one of your horses. They're for paying customers only."

"With the way business has been all summer?" he chuckled. "You should definitely take one back to town. We can divide up the saddlebags with the other horses."

Lou rolled her eyes. "I'm no good at riding. You know that."

"I'll help you up."

He smiled warmly and Lou looked away. They'd never dated, but she still found Colt's attention too fierce, like looking up into the hot afternoon sun. The man was nothing if not persistent.

"I'm fine," Lou said. "I like hiking."

"And I like company. C'mon, Lou. It's already afternoon. You're gonna be hiking in the dark by the time you get back." Colt's expression shifted, worry weighing down his otherwise happy features. "Waterton's changed this summer, what with the murders and all.

If you were out here alone, I'd worry." He reached out to touch her hand and she pulled away, crossing her arms. There it was again, that feeling, only this time it was tinged with annoyance.

"I know how to keep care of myself," she said stiffly.

"Uh-huh." He smirked. "Heard that before."

Lou knew, without him saying it, he was remembering any number of times in their childhood days when he'd covered for her transgressions. Young Colt had a guileless face and he'd often used it to his advantage.

She fought down a smile. "I *do*, Colt."

Colt hooked his thumbs in his belt loops, watching her for a few seconds as if deciding something. "Lord above, you're as stubborn as a mule, Louise."

For some reason that struck her as particularly funny and she snorted happily. "Nice, Colt. Real nice." He laughed and Lou began to giggle. "Bet that approach does real well with the ladies."

Colt shook his head, looking backward to where the last of his horses and their riders were disappearing around the bend. "Well, I should get moving. Gotta lead these city slickers on back to town before nightfall." He sighed. "Wish I could stay and talk, but I gotta make hay while the sun shines, you know. This summer's been bad."

Lou's smile disappeared. "It's been bad for everyone," she said, the worries of earlier settling on her shoulders.

"You sure you don't want a ride back?"

She shook her head. "You go on. I'm fine."

He hooked the toe of his cowboy boot into the stirrup and grabbed the pommel, swinging his right leg up over the saddle in a graceful motion. At one with animals, Colt made riding seem easy, but Lou lacked his finesse. "Was good to see you again, Lou," he called, leading the pack horse back down the trail. "Stay safe, alright?"

"I will," she said, forcing a smile.

In seconds he'd passed from the bright sunlight of the trail into the shadow of the trees. Only then did his words start niggling at her. It was stupid to be out here by herself and Lou knew it. They hadn't caught the killer yet. He could be anywhere. Seconds passed as Colton's silhouette grew smaller and smaller on the trail. She chewed her lower lip, fighting the urge to shout out.

Colt was a dot in the shadow of the tree when another thought appeared: *Walking out here by myself, I'm the perfect target.*

"Colton, wait!" she hollered.

He stopped and Lou jogged to his side. "I'm coming!" she called. "Just wait."

"Happy to oblige," he said, tipping his hat.

She grinned, though the smile wasn't really for him. Lou was already late getting back to town and Rich was waiting for her. She didn't question *how* she knew, she just did. Travelling by horseback was twice as fast as walking.

"Don't you dare tease me about my riding," Lou warned.

"You go as slow as you want," Colt said. "I'll follow behind you and..." He gave her a devilish smile. "...enjoy the view."

Lou felt a blush crawl up her neck. She shook her head.

"Colton Calhoun, you are the worst."

He winked. "But you put up with me anyhow."

*   *   *

By the time Rich reached the trail head by the falls, the street-lights had started to come on. Rich's body tensed as he remembered the cougars. Walking over the bridge straddling Cameron creek, his palms were clammy, nerves strung tight. He paused at the sign Park officials had posted with a warning for cougars.

C'mon, Lou, his mind pleaded.

The bushes were thick and heavy. He couldn't hear anything above the roar of the nearby waterfall. Swallowing the first hint of panic, he forced himself to walk up to the end of the first switchback.

Lou wasn't there.

Rich glanced in one direction and then the other, undecided, then made himself keep walking. He reached the end of the next switchback just as two riders on horseback, followed by a long string of horses, appeared on the trail above. Catching sight of Lou, he grinned in relief, but the expression quickly faded.

There was a man riding next to her, his knee almost touching hers as their horses walked side by side. The group they led was far behind them and Lou leaned toward her unknown companion, touching his arm as she laughed.

"What the hell?" Rich muttered.

The irritation that had bubbled under Rich's skin for days was at the surface. His hands clenched into fists as Lou and her companion rode down the trail toward him. Lou's face was bright with laughter, hair tumbling over her shoulders, unbound. His gaze flitted to her companion. Barring the mountain setting, Rich thought in annoyance, the man looked like he'd climbed off a movie poster. A white cowboy hat shadowed a lantern jaw, faint stubble only adding to the affected casualness. The man's shirt was pressed neatly despite the heat of the day, the collar open to show a 'V' of muscled chest and a silver chain. Lou said something and the man laughed aloud, baring straight, white teeth. The whole effect seemed too perfect, too poised to be real. Seeing them together, Rich had the completely insane thought that the man had *no right* to be that close to Lou.

As if hearing him, Lou lifted her eyes and frowned. Her body stiffened as she caught sight of him watching. "Rich!" she shouted. "What're you doing here?"

She slid off the side of her horse and bounded forward, throwing her arms over his shoulders. His fingers tightened against the fabric of her shirt. It'd been too long since he'd last touched her.

"I came by the garage," Rich said, "but Mila said you'd gone hiking."

He glared over her shoulder at the man. The stranger sat atop his mount, smiling down at them, though his expression was different now. *Forced.* Both hands were tight on the reins, his posture wary.

Lou sighed happily as she moved out of Rich's embrace. "I was hiking," she said. "And I ran into Colt and his group. He offered me a ride back." She caught Rich's hand and held tight. "If you have some time, we could grab a drink or something."

At first Rich was relieved, but then he caught sight of the stranger again, and his temper soured. "It's alright," he said, tugging his hand away. "Looks like you and your *friend* are busy. I'll talk to you later."

Lou's eyebrows pulled together in confusion; she stepped up to the other man, urging him forward. "Sorry, Rich. I didn't realize you two hadn't met. This is Colton Calhoun. We went to grade school together. He runs the stables."

Behind them, the other riders rounded the switchback, plodding nearer.

"I heard you speak at the Chamber of Commerce meeting the other night," Colt said, giving Rich another white smile. He nudged the horse forward with his knees, leaning down to hold out his hand rather than getting off his mount. "Good to meet you," he said, offering his open palm. "I go by Colt." He winked at Lou. "Colton sounds like I'm in trouble for something."

Lou laughed and another flame of annoyance joined the first. Rich shook the man's hand once, letting go just as fast. "Rich Evans," he mumbled, "Manager of the Whitewater Lodge."

"Rich has really brought the lodge together," Lou said. "Don't know if you've been inside, but the changes since last spring are amazing. The place is quite breathtaking."

Rich was torn between Lou's generosity and Colton's faint smirk. "I've ridden past the Whitewater a number of times," Colt said. "Very grand indeed. I'm sure it's the pinnacle of luxury."

Rich fumed. It felt like Calhoun was saying something altogether different.

"You still living down in that little cabin by the stables?" Lou asked.

Behind them, the placid line of horses came lazily down the trail, stopping a stone's throw away from the trio. The tourists took photos as they waited for the trail ride to continue.

"Cabin might be a stretch," Colt chuckled, "but it's good enough for me. No frills. No fluff." His eyes flicked to Rich and then back to Lou. "You can really breathe here in the mountains. Can really feel alive without all the extras."

Rich fought the urge to groan. This guy really put on the whole one-with-nature act. "As long as you don't mind living like you're camping," he grumbled.

Lou turned back to Rich. "So do you want to do something tonight?"

An hour ago he would have jumped at the chance. Now, his answer sounded petulant, even to his ears. "I suppose."

She turned to Calhoun. "Come along with us, Colt. It'll be fun!"

Rich grimaced at the suggestion but Colton raised his hands in defeat.

"Thank you, Lou, but I have to say no. Got to get the tourists back and earn my day's bacon." Colt winked at Lou and she smiled at the unspoken joke. "I'll let you two catch up, and be on my way."

"Another time then," Lou said. It irritated Rich to hear her disappointment.

"Absolutely," Colt said with a smile. He touched the brim of his hat, nodding to each of them. "Lou speaks very highly of you, Rich. It was an honour to meet you."

"Likewise," Rich said through clenched teeth.

* * *

Rich and Lou walked down the quiet street, the shadowy bushes alongside the road adding to Rich's tension. The summer cottagers had trickled into town over the last few weeks, and warm light poured out of the windows of the houses. No matter. The memories of the cougars, and of the wolves—*or dogs, if you believed McNally*—were still crisp in Rich's memory. He *wanted* to be walking in the centre of the road where he could see into the darkness, but Lou was here beside him. The blood in the Aspen Suite of the Whitewater, the unsolved murders, and the disturbing increase in the trespassing on Rich's property flared to mind, increasing his discomfort. He'd grown to hate Waterton.

"You okay?" she asked, sliding her hand through the crook of his arm. "You seem a little tense."

He shrugged. He was in a terrible fucking mood, but he didn't know how to claw his way out. "Just tired," he muttered. "And sick of being stuck in this town." She looked at him with concern, and he felt a twinge of guilt. "With all the issues, the building inspector forced me to close two wings, effective immediately. For everything I fix, something else breaks. Feels like a trap!"

"I can imagine."

Rich grumbled in discontent, and they continued along the road in silence. On the south side of the street was an old school which had been converted into a community centre. Like many older buildings in Waterton, it was cross-timbered, with stonework around the base. Tonight, in the darkness, it appeared strangely new; like a snapshot out of an old album. *Out of time,* his mind whispered. The town really *hadn't* changed over the years.

"Hunter told me an interesting story about that hike I was on," Lou said. "He heard it from the man he bought the restaurant from when he moved to the Park. The man was an old-timer, but in the forties and fifties, he'd had three little boys. When the story happened, these kids were five, seven, and nine, and one summer afternoon, they decided to hike up the Alderson-Carthew trail together."

"Alone?" Rich scoffed. "That hardly seems safe. God, there are cougars there, Lou. What if they'd been attacked? They could have been killed."

Lou giggled, leaning her head against his shoulder. "Shh ... Rich. I'm the one telling the story."

He looked down to find her grinning and his chest tightened at the sight. In the darkness Lou's features shifted from pretty to breathtaking: her face was a moon, and her hair a swath of black night. Rich ached to kiss her.

"Unless you have a story?" Lou teased.

"I'll be good."

Lou laughed and a crooked smile pulled at Rich's mouth. Even in his sour mood, Lou made him want to grin.

"The boys went fishing at Cameron Lake and were walking back to town with their fishing poles. Partway through the hike, where the trail crosses the creek, the youngest boy set down his fishing pole and forgot it. The three boys walked on, and a few hours later they realized the mistake."

Lou and Rich were nearing the town's business area, the lights of the movie house sparkling, laughter coming from people wandering the streets. Rich could imagine the three boys running along the street next to them, the town of fifty years ago much the same as it was tonight.

"Now the boys knew that their father would be angry if they came home short one fishing pole, so they turned around and walked back the way they had come. When they got to the creek where the pole had been left, it was sundown, and by the time they started back down the trail, night had fallen."

A shiver ran up Rich's spine. "They were alone on the mountain."

"Yes ... all alone," she agreed. "Mind you, they'd grown up in Waterton, and there were three of them, so they weren't that worried. The boys kept following the path in the dark."

"Fuck," Rich muttered. He didn't like the dark at the best of times. He remembered the feeling of terror in his grandparents' cellar. But this—lost in the mountains—was a different thing altogether. The horror was tangible.

Lou unlinked her arm from his, looping it around his back instead. "For the longest while," she said, "everything seemed fine. The boys weren't concerned, because they were together, and they knew the way. As the moon began to rise, they reached the switchbacks that should have led them to the townsite. They could see the town twinkling in the distance, and knew they'd be home soon." Her voice dropped dramatically. "And then, without warning, the trail ended."

"Ended?"

"It made no sense to them either. They'd walked this way any number of times, but this time the path just stopped on the edge of the wild. Confused, the boys backtracked the way they'd come, following the switchbacks upward until they were *certain* they were on the right trail. This time they came down the path much more slowly, following it together, hand in hand." She smiled mischievously. "And the trail ended in the same place."

Rich frowned. "They'd gone the wrong way again."

"That's a possibility, I suppose," Lou chuckled. "That's what Hunter thinks, too, but I'm not so sure. You see, there are no other trails up that way. Not even today. The boys *couldn't* have gotten onto the wrong path, but it ended all the same. The boys knew this, and for the first time, they started to get scared."

"Jesus," Rich said with a shiver, imagining himself on the mountain, lost and in the dark.

"The three of them got down on their hands and knees, crawling along the end of the trail, searching for where they'd gotten lost. The eldest boy had matches, and the boys burned them, one by one, trying to find where they'd missed the path."

Lou's voice dropped lower, and Rich felt himself drawn toward her, the way he always was.

"What happened then?" he asked.

"They left the path," Lou said, "and started walking straight into the forest, searching for a way down. The boys could see the town's lights and they figured if they headed toward the creek they could find their way back."

Rich pulled Lou to a stop, his jaw tensing. "This isn't going to end well, is it?"

Lou gave him a sideways hug, walking once more. "You might think that," she said, clucking her tongue. "The boys' father certainly did. He went searching for them. He walked the Alderson-Carthew trail three times that night, calling out for them until his voice was hoarse. He was certain they'd fallen into Cameron Creek and drowned. The boys' mother stood at the falls until dawn, watching and waiting for their bodies to come over the waterfall."

Rich shuddered, the image abruptly too real. The mountains here held death as well as life.

"So what happened?"

Lou snuggled closer. They were nearly at the bar.

"The boys were halfway down the mountain when the eldest stumbled and fell over a small cliff. It had been invisible in the dark." She gave a one-shouldered shrug. "The boy wasn't badly hurt, but it scared his brothers. The three of them huddled against the bottom of the embankment, waiting through the long night."

"What about their father?" Rich asked. "Wouldn't they have heard him?"

"Perhaps they were too tired," Lou said. "Perhaps there was another reason ... but they never heard him calling for them. And they slept the night away, finally waking up the next morning."

Lou stopped, Rich following her movement without thinking. They stood in the shadowy alcove of one of the buildings on Main Street.

"When they awoke, everything was as they expected. The boys stood up and there was the trail, visible through the trees. They'd slept through the night within sight of it."

Rich pursed his lips. Lou always had another reason for telling her stories, but he was having trouble with this one.

"But the trail had disappeared," he insisted. "It wasn't there."

"Yes, that's right."

"And it was right there that morning. They could see it."

"Mm-hmm..."

Rich grimaced, trying to fold his thoughts around this story.

Lou slid her arms up his chest as she leaned in on tip-toe. His arms wrapped around her, his attention on her mouth as much as her words.

"Sometimes," she whispered, her lips brushing his cheek, "you need to be lost in order to be found."

* * *

Lou and Rich had been dancing for hours. The pulse of the music was alive, the notes wrapping around them, driving away thoughts of the day. Lou's body was loose and pliant, her thoughts muffled by alcohol as she navigated the crowded dance floor of the Watering Hole. Nearby, Mila and her girlfriend Lucy rocked along to the rhythm, while along the side, a number of locals perched on stools, engrossed in conversation.

As Lou lifted her arms, swaying to the beat, Hunter caught her eye, frowning.

Don't care, her mind hissed. *I'll do whatever I damn well please.*

She moved deeper into the crowd, dragging Rich along with her. Mila bumped her shoulder, grinning, and Lou laughed aloud. The press of bodies was tight, the space sauna-like. Lou wove and spun in undulating circles as Rich followed her lead. His eyes were dark, hinting at what else he wanted to be doing.

Maybe later, she thought with a smirk. *But not until you've blown off that foul mood of yours.*

Rich had been annoyed on the trail, something Lou didn't totally understand. At the bar, he'd suggested a line of shooters, and she'd agreed. She'd downed one to every three of his, then pulled him out onto the dance floor. Lou writhed against him, her eyes half-closed, as she let the music drag her away. Each rhythm took her to a different place in herself. Somewhere, under the electronic notes, a plaintive strum of strings rang out—*Lou stood, violin in hand, in front of a small group of listeners, her fingers sweating. She wasn't supposed to know who they were, but as she lifted the child-sized violin to her chin, her attention was drawn to a man at the front. His clothes and the jewels on his fingers announced his rank even as—* the music changed, and the memory rippled and disappeared. This song was faster, with a heavy salsa flavour. Lou grinned as a memory—*a woman dancing, castanets in hand*—flared like a candle and winked out. She ran her hands down Rich's arms. His annoyance had faded, replaced by desire.

The upbeat music shifted into a slow, steady song.

"Careful of my feet there," she teased.

Rich's movements were languid, his smile fuzzy. "Sorry, but it wasn't your feet I was looking at."

Lou looped her arms over his shoulders, settling in for the song. It felt good to be held; to want someone who wanted her back. She pressed her forehead against his neck, revelling in the feel of him tight against her. Rich was warm and solid, the lines of muscle tangible under her fingers. She breathed deeply, comforted by the faint whiff of sweat and cologne, a scent she recognized from the weeks when they'd worked on overhauling his car.

His fingers trailed over her ribs. "I like you, Lou," Rich whispered against her hair. "I like you a lot." She giggled at his slurred words and he tipped up her chin. "I want to know you better," he said. "I want to know everything."

She swallowed hard. They'd dated a bit over the last few months—if you could call one homemade dinner, a couple restaurant visits, and making out in her kitchen "dating." And they'd rebuilt an engine. Hardly the foundation to a real relationship.

"Y-you do know me," she said, forcing her tone to stay light.

"I want to know more."

His hands were warm where he touched her, but Lou hesitated. She'd learned to hide her differentness over the years. The truth was on her tongue, but she bit it back. That wasn't a conversation she knew how to start, and certainly not here, on the dance floor of the bar.

The couples around them moved apart as the music picked up a hard rock beat. Mila and Lucy laughed and twirled nearby. Lou and Rich clung together. He leaned in and Lou was certain he was going to kiss her. Her body tightened in anticipation. Instead, he ran his fingers into her hair, his mouth hovering next to her ear.

"You want to get out of here?" he murmured.

"Where?"

"Outside for a walk. It's too warm."

"Yeah," she said, smiling. "I wouldn't mind getting some air."

He grinned, and Lou's stomach tightened. He was beautiful tonight, his hair sweaty and unkempt, his good shirt wrinkled, the sleeves rolled up to his elbows.

"Just let me grab our stuff," he said, kissing her forehead.

Rich clumsily dodged his way through the dancers to the empty table where she had dropped her backpack. Lou turned to walk off the dance floor, wondering when Rich's emotions had become so integral to her own happiness ... and stopped.

There, on a line of stools, the town's locals sat watching, their faces masks of indignant disapproval.

CHAPTER FIFTEEN

Hunter and Sam glared at Lou from across the room. *Goddammit,* she thought, *I don't have time for this right now!* Before she could turn away, Hunter waved Lou forward. Her heart sank. Lou's mother had caught Lou sneaking out of her second floor bedroom in high school. She felt the same way now, and looked forward to this discussion just as much.

As Lou reached them, the music's roar dropped to a reasonable din. She forced a smile. "Hey, Hunter. What's up?"

He opened his mouth to speak, but Sam beat him to it. "You still messing around with that Evans boy?"

Lou coughed in shock. "He's hardly a boy," she said, "and you're not my father."

Hunter's expression was pained. "Now, Lou," he said, "I'm sure that's not how Sam meant it, we just—"

"Don't like him," the superintendent finished.

"Really?" she said calmly. "Well, thanks for clearing that up, Sam. I couldn't tell." She turned to go, but Hunter reached out, stopping her.

"Lou, hon—"

"Don't you 'hon' me," she snapped. "You've already said your piece."

He recoiled as if slapped. "But, Lou, we just want you to be careful."

"Why?" On the other side of the room, Rich was searching the crowd, trying to catch sight of her. Lou wanted this conversation over *now*.

"Because he's not one of us," Sam said. "He's not from around here."

She stepped closer, heart pounding. "Everyone comes from somewhere," Lou said. "So what if he's not from around here? Most of the people from Waterton aren't." She glared at Hunter, daring him to disagree. He surprised her by lifting his chin, defiant.

"You're right," he said. "But I still don't trust him."

"It's not your call," Lou retorted. "Because I do!"

Behind the group, Rich appeared, the backpack slung over one arm. A groove of concern etched his forehead as he caught sight of their expressions. "Everything okay?" he asked.

Lou took his hand, yanking him away without looking back. "Everything's fine," she said tightly. "Now let's walk."

* * *

The figure stood in the shadows at the side of Main Street as the townsfolk came and went. No one saw him watching. When the last passersby had moved on, he moved closer, positioning himself next to the Historical Society building.

Twenty minutes passed.

His gaze rested on the door of the Watering Hole, unwavering in its intensity. On another night, if Rich had been alone, the man might have come inside, but Lou was sharper than most. She sensed things others didn't—a fact which kept him at bay. Eventually, his patience was rewarded. The man took a hissing breath as Rich and Lou left the bar, arm in arm.

Fighting the urge to make chase, he forced himself to wait. The couple moved slowly up the street, pausing beneath a streetlight, laughing at some private joke. Even from a distance, he could see the brightness of Lou's smile, the flush on her cheeks as Rich leaned down and kissed her. When the embrace ended, Lou took Rich's hand and led him away, smiling.

The man counted to ten, then followed.

* * *

They were heading back toward Lou's cabin, but they'd hardly gotten past the business district before Lou changed directions.

"Where are we going?" Rich asked.

Lou pulled him toward the school field. "Short cut," she said.

"But why?"

"I think someone's ... I just want to, okay?"

"Sure."

Rich didn't know how moving away from the straight lines of the sidewalk was supposed to help. His vision swam, his gaze caught on the curve of her waist and the heart shape of her ass as she pulled him along. He stumbled, the mountains pivoting on an impossible axis.

"Wait!" he laughed. "Hold on Lou, I'm gonna—"

He tripped and went down hard, momentarily winded.

Lou crouched beside him. "Shit! Are you okay?"

"Fine," Rich moaned. "I just ... Oh god, feels like I'm spinning."

"You're drunk, Richard," Lou giggled.

He smiled as she leaned over him. Like this, Lou became the sky. He ran his hands up her arms, cupping her chin, his attention lost in the dark pools of her eyes.

"God, you're amazing," he murmured.

Her grin softened. "You are, too," she whispered as she leaned in and kissed him.

Soon they were wrapped around one another, lips sliding together. He tasted whiskey on Lou's tongue, and something else. *Ginger?* Everything about her was new, the whole world full of the details that were her. He wanted to feel every part of Lou, taste every inch of her skin.

They lay in the dark field, but for once, the shadows didn't scare him. He was too entranced by her low moans, the feel of her on top of him. Lou's lips were gentle but her hands were firm as they teased the flat plane of his stomach. He tried to pull her down, but she kept her perch. The layers of cloth between them felt ready to burn away and part of Rich's mind was acutely aware of how little effort it would take to have her here and now.

The embrace dragged on until both were struggling for air. Rich broke the kiss and fell back against the cool grass, aching to be inside her. Lou's hands moved over his navel and hips, her mouth trailing the line of his neck to the muscles of his chest and down to his abdomen.

Her fingers had just started working at the button of his pants when Rich grabbed her shoulder, stilling her. "My god, Lou. Look at that!"

She lifted her head in surprise, following his line of sight above the tree line. Beyond the distant peaks, a green and blue symphony of lights had begun. It rippled and shimmered like sunshine on water, leaving Rich blinking back tears. He'd read something about this but had never seen it before.

"It's the aurora borealis," Lou said quietly. "Northern lights."

She lay down on the grass at his side, twining her fingers through his. The mysterious glow pulsed and moved, colours shifting as they travelled the sky.

"Amazing..." Rich breathed, his fingers tightening around Lou's. He meant both the spectacle they watched, and the woman next to him.

Lids slowly drooping, he wondered if he'd looked up at the night sky in Waterton before, and if he had, if he'd ever really *seen*.

* * *

The radio was playing a raucous Celtic beat while Sadie sat in the dark, too tired to turn on a light and too keyed up to sleep. She'd spent a gruelling week working all angles of the Whitewater Lodge murder case, rising at five each morning so she could be at the station hours before anyone arrived and staying until exhaustion sent her home each night. She couldn't keep the pace up forever, but she didn't know how to let it go.

The murderer's still out there, her mind warned.

Sadie's body was a heavy weight, but her thoughts buzzed with questions. Wired, she caught the flicker of movement outside the window at once. By the faint light of the street lamps, a shadow loped across the street, disappearing into the trees.

She flicked off the radio, waiting for the figure to re-emerge from the shrubbery. *Someone walking home?* she wondered, *or a teen taking a shortcut?* It had to be one of those. Half a minute passed as Sadie scanned the woods, but the figure didn't reappear.

"Goddammit," she growled, squinting into the night. Her breath caught as the shape suddenly reappeared near her fence—a man— darting into the overgrown caragana hedges and poplar trees. She surged to her feet. "What the hell?!"

He was headed into her backyard.

Sadie strode to the porch—losing sight of the figure as she crossed the kitchen—and pulled open the door with a squeal of hinges. She left the light off so she could see. Her body was vibrating with anger, the last cobwebs of sleepiness gone.

"You, out there in the trees," Sadie ordered. "Come out now!" She combed the bushes with piercing eyes. "If there's someone out there, you best show yourself!"

Nothing moved.

Seconds drew out like a bow. The night was calm, quiet. Wind rose and fell like the breath of a great beast. She crept across her backyard, wondering if she was being stupid, if she'd imagined the person there, but the fear was alive inside her, reminding her of the truth. *Should have grabbed the flashlight!* a voice inside her chattered. *Should have grabbed the gun ... It could have been the killer.* The hair rose on the back of her neck at the thought.

"Anyone here?" Sadie called uncertainly.

Two streets over, a dog howled and Sadie jumped. "Someone walking their goddamned dog," she said with an uneasy laugh before heading back inside the cabin. But she checked the lock twice before going upstairs to bed.

* * *

After the aurora faded, Lou navigated a very inebriated Rich back to her cabin and guided him up the steep stairs to the bedroom, disappointment rising. She was certain he'd be asleep in minutes. He wove unsteadily to the bed, falling loose-limbed to the coverlet.

"Come here," Lou laughed. "You can't sleep in all that."

Rich's shoes were easy enough, but the jacket proved much more difficult. Trying to take off both shirt and jacket at once, he ended up tangling his fist in the cuff.

"Goddamned jacket," Rich grumbled. "Too tight ... to get ... off." He pulled at the sleeve with his free hand and tumbled sideways on the bed, groaning. Giggles bubbled from Lou's lips.

"Oh god, Rich," she laughed. "Just stop. Stop!"

She moved closer, peeling off the layers of his clothing. With each dropped piece of fabric, she expected Rich to flop down and fall asleep. Instead, he waited through her care, his skin rising in gooseflesh where she touched him. When he was naked, she paused and looked up. Rich was watching her. The ferocity of his ardour scared her.

"Thank you," he murmured. His hands slid up her arms. "For this. For ... everything."

The mood of the room had changed, laughter gone. Lou could barely breathe, her heart a bird pounding its wings against the cage of her chest. Rich's hands fumbled uncertainly as he undressed her, but they were a spark to the tinder of her emotions: *desire, impatience, uncertainty.*

Warmed by his focus—on her and nothing else—the room seemed to fade. Lou's body was a wire, his touch the connection. She felt alive for the first time in years. She shivered as Rich nuzzled closer, his breath warm against her bare breasts.

"You're cold," he whispered.

"So are you. Here, let's get under the covers."

Icy sheets greeted them. Rich struggled onto the pillow, bumping his head on the headboard in his rush. His mouth dropped against hers while his hands found their way under the blankets to her bare skin. There was too much to feel, too many tumbled emotions to consider. For years she'd been alone.

She wasn't now.

The kiss grew bolder, fanning her eagerness. She wanted his weight against her tonight, tethering her to this spot, and this now ... *their* now. The cabin and the garage, and the car they were so close to fixing, and the life she imagined even though she knew

Rich would leave her behind some day. Tonight, she allowed herself to want ... to need ... to imagine all of those things she couldn't have. The word 'love' flickered like a shooting star against the darkness of her mind, but she didn't allow herself to go further.

Love was too dangerous to consider.

Lou sighed, forcing her fears into the background. Rich dropped his mouth to her neck; her lashes fluttered closed as he reached her breasts. His mouth was a single point of white heat, burning through her remaining hesitation. She wanted him, and knew he wanted her too. Lou ground herself against him until she could feel Rich's heat. There was a fire between them, a line of pleasure stretched between her mouth and her breasts and her core.

"Please..." she moaned.

Rich kissed his way back to her lips, stopping for a moment to look at her. She could sense his intent, feel his emotions, raw and true, riding over them both. *Love.* She could read it in his eyes, smouldering with desire. Rich reached up to cup Lou's chin, kissing her at the same moment their bodies met. She gasped as desire exploded from flames to a raging wildfire. Suddenly Rich's yearning was her own, his desire redoubling with her own rioting emotions.

Her eyes closed as he moved, each pant, each touch adding to the swirl of sensation. *It's been too long,* she thought. *Too long!* And her body was greedy for release. It was like burning alive, but with pleasure rather than pain. Each nerve ending pulsed where he touched her. Her legs jerked in shock as the pace increased. Like a cliff diver, Lou's body stretched out on a wave that hung, perilously, for one endless moment, then toppled into crashing release.

"Rich!" she shouted, and he dropped his mouth against hers, kissing away the rest of her cries.

He thrust hard a few more times, before shuddering and going still. He slid sideways, pulling her into the circle of his arms, and Lou laid her head against his chest, listening to the steady thud of his heart. Lou's eyes prickled with unshed tears, her chest inexplicably tight. *I want this man ... This life.* The admission frightened her.

Outside the windows, the wind rose until it filled the room with the sound of whispering pines. Throat tight, Lou's lashes closed. Rich's warmth and the steady rush of sound, the cool sweetness of the air, all wrapped her in comfort.

Most nights, Lou's dreams were a mesh of incoherent memories, leaving her unsettled in their passing. But tonight when she dreamed, she dreamed only of Rich.

* * *

Amanda liked working evenings. By the time she came on, most guests were already checked in and, barring a call for room service, it left her long hours of downtime. Tonight her shift ended at four a.m., the deepest lull of the twenty-four hour schedule which governed working life at the Whitewater Lodge. She signed out of the guest registration software, tapped her I.D. number into the staff scheduler, and waved goodnight to Nando before heading out the side exit into the inky predawn gloom.

Clouds filled the high mountain valley. The sky above was a solid, starless black; land and sky knit together into a vast shawl. Amanda's gaze trailed along the dimly lit sidewalk. There were security lights at intervals along the building, but a heavy layer of branches overhead and untrimmed bushes on either side broke the cast of light into a scattering of puzzle pieces, strewn across the ground.

The snap of high heels mixed with the whisper of leaves and creaking night-going insects, the pulsing crescendo pulling the cloak of darkness closer. Amanda's mind hummed with leftover snippets of the night's events. The ceiling tiles in the front entranceway had a new water stain and would need to be replaced yet again. The elevator in the main lodge was being ornery; it had broken down twice, and there was a complaint from the elderly couple who'd been trapped inside it for an hour. Mr. Evans would have to deal with them this morning. As she walked, the night sounds faded until only the clicking of her heels remained, but the change went unnoticed. Amanda had done what she could about the guest complaint; a note sat on Mr. Evans' desk, a message on his voice mail. Nando had promised to tell him personally if he saw him, but she knew she'd have to deal with the aftermath. Her shoulders slumped. She'd think about it tomorrow. For now, she needed sleep.

Reaching the end of the main lodge, she turned the corner, passing the now-vacant west wing. In the distance, the staff parking lot appeared, lit by a rectangular orange glow of security lights. Something was different tonight. Before her confused eyes, a patch of darkness broke away from the rest, a knee-height hump of shadow crawling along the ground. The clicking of her heels stopped almost before Amanda realized why. Heart pounding, her legs tensed, ready to run.

There was something moving between the lodge and the tool shed, but the night had eaten away its details, leaving only a shapeless void trundling backward. Amanda squinted, but could get no sense of what it was. *A dog?* she wondered, but it wasn't moving right. *Maybe a cougar.*

Her fingers tightened around her car keys, forming them into a claw. She stepped backward, the sound of her heel a staccato snap. The form abruptly shifted shape, a head lifting up from the bulky body. Backlit, the animal had become a blocky, amorphous shape.

It stood, doubling in size.

With a terrified cry, Amanda spun, sprinting back the way she'd come. Her shout transformed the night. The darkness exploded. Bushes broke. Footsteps—*my god, footsteps!*—pounded on asphalt. Amanda ran without cease, reaching the side exit and slamming herself bodily against the release handle.

It didn't open.

"No!"

At 4:05 a.m., the access was exit only. Behind her, the faceless man rounded the corner and paused, searching. Seeing her, he began to run, his shadow growing arms as he did. He held something in one hand. Amanda shrieked and sprinted away, aiming for the front of the building and safety. Bushes rustled behind her. She peeked over her shoulder only to trip, knees slamming down with force enough to elicit a grunt. She clambered up, one shoe falling off as she limped down the sidewalk, leaving it behind.

The overgrown foliage which surrounded the main lodge was a trap. Bushes snagged her arms, twigs clawed her face. She reached the manicured front garden to the Whitewater Lodge's main entrance, tears streaming down her face. The windows next to the doors glowed like a movie screen. Amanda could see the morning staff moving about, could hear a vacuum humming faintly.

"HELP!" she screamed.

Footsteps closed in as she ran. Her foot twisted, the second shoe fell off as she threw herself against the main doors, pushing them wide with the force of her fear. The crashing stopped. She saw, in slow motion, the morning clerk turn, her mouth drop open. Amanda struggled, half-limping, half-running the last steps into the foyer before collapsing.

"Miss Sloane!" the clerk cried. "What happened?"

Amanda slumped to the floor. Her knees were bloodied, her palms pock-marked with gravel.

"Th-there was someone out there," she sobbed. "Someone waiting in the dark."

CHAPTER SIXTEEN

Rich woke in an unfamiliar bed, head throbbing. He groaned, propping himself up on his elbows and squinting into the sun-bright room. The Shaker furniture was simple and sturdy; the bed in which he lay, covered in a patchwork quilt. Outside a dormer window, Waterton had dawned bright and windy, the leaves of nearby aspen trees slapping merrily at the panelled glass. Next to long white curtains, a backpack leaned up against the wall, a pair of broken-down hiking boots tossed next to it.

He swung his head the other way, catching sight of a dresser and several framed prints; a close-up of a tiny purple flower, another, sepia-toned, looking down at Waterton Lakes, mountains rising on either side. Between them was a faded colour photo. Its yellowish tones revealed a little black-haired girl perched on top of a man's shoulders. The girl was grinning, her mouth open in silent laughter.

"Lou," Rich breathed in surprise.

She wasn't here with him, but it was clear she had been at some point. A hollow dip marked the second pillow; wrinkles lined the sheets and blankets. Rich struggled to remember exactly what had gone on between them. He grimaced, snippets of the night before coming to mind. He could remember kissing her, touching her ... and the sky alight with colour.

"Northern lights," he mumbled, swinging his feet out of bed.

After that, his memory was hazier. He remembered Lou's face in front of him telling him he had to walk, that he was "too damned heavy to carry." Rich winced. He'd fallen *up* the stairs at her house. He rubbed his left knee. *Yup, not my classiest move.* There were a few scattered memories of the two of them laughing like children, Lou's body silver in the moonlight, Rich moving on top of her, and then one final memory of lying in the dark with her tucked into the crook of his arm, warm and sated.

Smiling despite his headache, Rich pulled on his discarded clothes and staggered out of the bedroom. A clock on the wall announced it was nearly one p.m.; he'd slept at least twelve hours. Rich was late for work for the first time in his life. Swearing, he located a bathroom, cleaning himself up as best he could. His jaw was shadowed and dark circles ringed his eyes. *Look like shit.* There was no doubt he'd been up partying. Late or not, he'd definitely have to head home before going to work.

By the time he emerged, the floor plan had resurfaced in his memory. Lou's house was one of the old, chalet-style cabins with the stucco and stone exterior. A snippet of conversation from the previous night emerged.

"The first owners named it Whispering Aspens when they built it."

"Named it?" Rich had scoffed.

"Yes. Every cabin in town has a name."

That had seemed like the funniest thing in the world. Rich remembered falling onto his side in gales of laughter.

"Your cabin has a name, too," she'd insisted.

"Really?"

"It's the old Pattison place, but everyone calls it Windy Pines."

Rich headed for the central stairwell dividing the house into two sides. He walked gingerly down the risers, head throbbing in time to his footsteps. He recognized the kitchen from the night he had cooked Lou dinner. It, too, was empty. Rich's shoes sat on the mat next to the back door. A note was tucked inside his left shoe; he grinned seeing it.

Rich,

Had to open up the garage this morning, but didn't want to wake you. (Figured you could use the sleep.) Make yourself at home.

Lou

Rich's smile faded. He didn't expect her to write, *'Love, Lou'*, or to wait around all day for him to awaken. That just wasn't her. But it still bothered him. His hand tightened around the paper, guilt twinging.

Leaving before a woman awoke was something he'd done too many times himself.

* * *

Lou tried to tell Rich the truth about herself when they had dinner, but everything kept conspiring against it. Rich was dealing with the attempted assault of one of his staff. He'd spent an entire afternoon going through the scant security footage and arranging for the installation of security lights along all the Whitewater's pathways. Arriving at the garage almost two hours late, Lou was ready to cancel, but Rich insisted they go out to eat. The Prince of Wales had a restaurant and Rich wanted to compare the food choices to those at the Whitewater. Lou couldn't think of an excuse to say no, and so a long, uncomfortable meal began.

The tinkling of crystal, white tablecloths, and black-suited servers did nothing to put Lou at ease in her faded jeans and work shirt. She leaned in twice, with every intention of bringing up the conversation about visions and past lives, but then someone stopped to say hello, and the time for admissions was lost.

Bravado failing, Lou asked Rich about his week.

"The hotel's a disaster," he said bitterly. "I'm sure everyone's heard about the murder in the Aspen Suite."

"Yes, Audrika mentioned it once or twice." She reached out, placing her fingers on top of his. "I'm sorry you're dealing with that."

"Two wings closed. Too many things going wrong."

"Will it take long to repair?"

"It'll take at least six months, and that's if I can even find contractors willing to work during the fall and winter." He glowered. "The ones from Lethbridge laughed when I suggested it."

She couldn't help but feel relieved. Lou still wasn't letting herself think too far ahead, but it gave her inexplicable relief to hear he'd be staying after the summer.

"I'm sure you'll get it figured out, Rich," she said, squeezing his hand. "Look at what you've accomplished since you arrived."

"A waste of time!" he grumbled. "I sometimes think it'd be better to just raze the whole thing and start over."

Lou opened her mouth to answer, but the server returned with hors d'oeuvres, and that opportunity was lost, too. Being open with him was proving harder than she'd expected.

Two nights after their uncomfortable dinner, Lou showed up at the Whitewater Lodge to invite Rich out for a drink. Again, she struggled to make the words. Barring her mother, she'd never been able to tell anyone about her dreams and memories except her father, who'd never believed her. She'd spent too long hiding what she was. That night she didn't get to find out if Rich would react differently to an admission because they were interrupted by Amanda Sloane. She'd come to tell Rich that the kitchen staff had found mouse droppings in the walk-in cooler. He needed to deal with it before the health inspector arrived the next morning. Lou gave a half-hearted smile, watching Rich and Amanda leave.

The opportunity to talk kept slipping further and further away.

* * *

Jim and Sadie waited in the industrial grey waiting room of the Lethbridge penitentiary, the only decoration a line of documents on one wall. It had been a long drive out, and Jim's nerves were frayed. He'd received a tip from the Lethbridge Police force that Lucas had posted bail this morning, surprising everyone involved in the case. Jim had pulled a few strings to get one final interview before the noon release. He glanced nervously at the clock.

They had less than an hour to get their answers.

Jim knew Sadie was worried about this turn of events. She was restless, moving from the windows to Jim's side and back again. He wished she'd stand still for a moment; he couldn't think when she was pacing and there were too many variables he needed to consider. Rich Evans' tip about Borderline Industries had been a dead end. The company *was* listed on a number of leases in town, but as far as Jim could tell, it was a benign American holdings company with shares in a variety of Waterton businesses. He'd asked Susan Varley, head of the Chamber of Commerce, about Borderline and she'd passed along their contact information. The phone number directed him to an automated answering service. None of Jim's messages had been returned. Frustrated, he had put in a requisition for details of the company's management and organizational information, but he didn't have time to wait for an answer.

They had a murderer to find.

The numerous prints they'd taken from the Aspen Suite had two matches: Lucas Sorenson and the unknown perpetrator from the

Yellowstone case. Jim had been through Sorenson's room in White-water's staff quarters: a futon, black and white television, and an old gaming system were the only items. Not the kind of set-up for someone with cash.

"Didn't think he'd make bail," Jim said.

Sadie glanced up. "He's got a rich friend, that's for sure."

"A rich *something*," he replied. In Jim's opinion, a friend would've dug up the money beforehand, but a relative might let him stew in jail just to teach him a lesson.

"Lucas knows the killer," Sadie said. "I'm sure of it."

"Probably."

"Probably?" she scoffed. "He has to."

"Lots of people came in and out of that room at Whitewater," Jim said. "Let's not jump the gun here."

"There were only two sets of prints. Both in blood. That's no mistake."

Jim sighed. She was right, of course, but that wouldn't make this any easier. "We've got to handle things carefully," he said. "I don't want to spook him, alright?"

"Fair enough, but the kid's an accessory to murder."

"Maybe so," he said slowly. "But it's not gonna help us if he won't talk. Let's just go easy this time."

Sadie nodded. "Got it."

A moment later, the door opened and an officer from the Leth-bridge police force appeared. "They have Mr. Sorenson in a holding cell," the man announced. "Are you ready to head down?"

In minutes they were face to face with Lucas Sorenson. He looked harder than the last time they'd visited, the lines of his jaw tight and unwavering. A newly-healed scar marred his left eyelid, a faded bruise crossing one cheek. *Prison life's been tough on him*, Jim thought as Sadie's interrogation began.

"We found the blood in the Aspen Suite," she said. "We know there was a murder there."

"You *suspect* there was a murder," the lawyer corrected. "There's no body so—"

"The second set of prints match a known murderer," Sadie continued, unhindered. "That isn't being disputed. The rest of the situation is."

Jim cleared his throat, drawing the attention of everyone at the table. "Lucas, we need your help here," he said patiently. "I've seen the blood. It's just a matter of time before we have enough evidence to lay charges. You've got to tell us what happened in that room."

"Don't answer," the lawyer said. "You're not—"

"Who was killed in the Aspen Suite?" Sadie asked. Her voice was icily calm, probing.

"I ... I don't know."

"We know you weren't alone," she insisted. "We need a name."

"I told you, I don't know."

"C'mon," Jim urged. "Help us out a bit here."

Lucas's shoulders slumped. "I can't."

Sadie's gaze flicked to Jim, the barest hint of a smile curving her lips. The boy *did* know something. "Why not?" she asked.

"I-I just can't."

Jim opened his mouth to ask a question but Sadie was faster. "How did you kill the victim?"

Jim winced.

"Constable Black Plume, I must insist!" the attorney interjected. "Mr. Sorenson has not been charged with this crime!"

She turned on the lawyer, dark eyes flashing. "But he knows," she snapped, her cool composure slipping into contempt.

"I didn't do it!" Lucas cried. "I was just there for the clean up."

Jim felt like he'd plunged through the surface of a half-frozen lake, all air sucked from his lungs. "You cleaned?" he repeated breathlessly.

"Chan asked me to," Lucas gasped. "There was blood ... blood everywhere! But no body."

"Did you say *Chan* asked you?" Sadie asked. "As in Jeff Chan?"

"He found the— the mess. The blood on— on the walls," Lucas stammered, his voice coming in halting gasps. "But Mr. Chan couldn't call the police. He couldn't!"

"Why not?" Jim asked.

"Because he knew what would happen if he did!"

Jim frowned in confusion.

"What?" Sadie asked.

"The hotel would be shut down," Lucas said. "If there'd been a murder there—a murder like that!—the whole hotel would be closed. He couldn't let that happen."

"Did Jeff Chan murder someone?" Sadie asked.

"I don't think ... I don't—" Lucas took a sobbing breath. "I just don't know," he hiccoughed. "I got called in after it was all over. I-I got paid. Paid a *lot* to clean up that room. Washed the walls, repainted them, fixed the floor." He rubbed tears from his eyes, wincing as his hand crossed his bruised cheek. "I figured it was easy money. I didn't know. Didn't think..."

Jim waited until Lucas's sobs faded. "Look, Lucas," he said, "we're going to offer you a deal. Tell us—"

"My client has *not* been charged!" the lawyer shouted.

Jim's jaw clenched in annoyance. "But there will be charges laid at some point," he retorted, then turned back to Lucas. "Tell us what happened, and you'll only be charged as an accessory. Don't talk, and that's it. The murder charge falls on you."

"But I didn't kill anyone! I didn't—"

The suited attorney interrupted him. "Mr. Sorenson, as your lawyer, I insist that we discuss this in private before you say anything which may further incriminate you."

"Take all the time you want," Sadie replied coolly, already heading to the door, "but remember that this is the best offer you're going to get."

Jim waited until Lucas looked up at him. "Think it through," Jim said quietly. "Just do the right thing. Alright?"

Lucas dropped his eyes to the table rather than answering.

Outside the room, Sadie chewed the edge of her nail as she walked circles in the narrow corridor. Jim leaned against the wall. He had a throbbing headache, and the sound of her footsteps on the tile floor was snapping against the nerves in his forehead.

"You think he'll take it?" She sounded less certain than she had in the interview room, more like the rookie that she was than the collected detective she pretended to be.

Jim massaged his temple. "He's stupid if he doesn't."

"Stupid or scared."

The door opened and a guard gestured them back inside. Lucas was ashen-faced, his hands clasped tightly together on the table.

"Mr. Sorenson is not willing to provide names," the attorney announced stiffly. "He declines the offer of a plea bargain at this time."

"What?" Sadie gasped. "Christ, Lucas! You're gonna go to jail for this guy."

Lucas recoiled. His face was pale and terrified. "I only cleaned!" he cried. "I didn't kill anyone. I only—"

"But you were receiving deliveries at the Whitewater Lodge," Jim said, his mind leaping like a spark between the two crimes. "You know who the unnamed person on the deliveries schedule is. That's a name you could give us."

Lucas's eyes widened until they were saucers. "I can't," he whimpered hoarsely. "I-I just can't."

"If you tell us who you were helping," Sadie pleaded. "We can help you."

"No!"

"Lucas, listen," Jim said. "Tell us whose name was on those delivery files and let us figure out the rest. We can help you, but you've gotta help us, too."

Lucas slumped against the table, pressing the heels of his hands against his eyes. "No one can help me now."

"I believe this interview is over," the lawyer said. He stood, offering his hand across the table. Jim shook it. Sadie stared contemptuously at his open palm for a few long seconds, then followed suit.

The lawyer nodded to the clock. "It's three minutes past noon. Mr. Sorenson is free to go."

Jim felt his heart sink. "If you change your mind, Lucas," he said, "the offer stands."

Lucas shook his head mutely and followed his lawyer from the interrogation room.

* * *

The first heat wave of August began, but it drew no tourists and the town was empty for the first time in Lou's memory. With the Whitewater in the midst of a renovation and police investigation, Rich's schedule was packed from morning until night. Lou's time with Rich dwindled, their moments frenetic and harried. They spent one last afternoon finishing his sports car's overhaul, but Rich was quiet and withdrawn as they closed up the chassis. Lou assumed it was because Rich, like her, had realized they wouldn't have the same excuse to spend time together. It tugged at her like a faded ache.

With the engine repair complete, they began cleaning up for the night. It was then Rich finally spoke.

"The police think I'm involved," he said as he pulled off the soiled overalls.

Lou dropped the wrench into the toolbox, the metallic bang glaringly loud. "W-what?"

"They didn't use those words when they talked to me, but that's what they think."

Lou wrapped her arms around herself, the memory of the figure running through the dark street rising in her mind. "No," she said quietly. "That can't be right."

"Tell that to Constable Flagstone," Rich said with a weary chuckle. He hung the oil-stained fabric on the hook, his motions slow. Rich had grown thin in the last weeks, stress whittling him down to bone and lean muscle. "He's the one who told me to back off. Let *him* do the investigating is what he said."

"But there's no reason to think you're involved," Lou insisted. "You weren't even here last year. Chan was."

"Unless I'm trying to cover something up," Rich sneered. "I gave them the files they asked for. The ones I put together."

Lou reached out, touching his arm. "Files?"

"On Borderline. On the lease agreements. On all the goddamned shit I've been trying to figure out for months."

Lou held tight to keep her fingers from shaking. Rich's fear and anger were a combination she didn't understand. "It's going to be alright," she murmured. "You'll get through this."

His shoulders slumped and Lou almost missed his next words. "Didn't give them all the delivery reports though." He looked up, a wry grin ghosting over his mouth. She recognized the expression:

arrogance and intelligence at odds. "I'm close to figuring that part out," Rich said, "and when I do..."

Lou wanted to ask him *'what then?'* but her throat was blocked. She could feel danger here, but she didn't know how to fix it or explain.

Wiping his hands on a greasy rag, Rich's expression loosened, a real smile finally taking the place of the grimace. "It feels good to be done with the car," he sighed. "I think we just about took it down to the frame and put it all back together again."

Lou quelled a feeling of melancholy. There was no more excuse to set aside time each day. No reason to expect him. "I've double-checked everything," she said, forcing her words to stay light. "Bring it back in, and I'll be convinced you're doing it on purpose."

Rich pulled her into his arms. "Don't need an excuse now, do I?"

"No," she murmured. "No, you don't."

He caught her lips in a heady kiss, only pulling back when both were breathless. "It's a little late for dinner," he said. "But do you want to grab a coffee or something?"

"Yeah, I do."

August sunsets came late in the mountains, and the town was gilded pink as they emerged from the darkness of the garage. They headed to Hunter's Coffee Shop, as had become their tradition. Hunter, as always, was behind the counter, and he poured two mugs of coffee before walking over.

"Would you like to see a menu?" he asked.

"No, thanks," Lou answered. "Just here for coffee and pie, if you've got it."

Hunter nodded. "I've got apple, saskatoon, huckleberry—"

"Huckleberry," Lou said, raising her hand.

"Coffee's fine," Rich replied.

Usually that would be enough to send Hunter on his way, but this time he lingered. Lou lowered the cup from her lips in concern. Hunter's arms were crossed, hands in fists.

"I heard that Sam Barton took that proposal of yours to Parks Canada."

Rich peered up at him. "Yes, I'd heard that."

Hunter's bushy brows dropped low. "Then you might be interested in knowing that the area where Chinook wants to install it is untouched. It's virgin land ... animal habitat. *Wild*."

Rich glanced at Lou and then back to Hunter. "And?"

Hunter made a choking sound. "And that makes it worth preserving. You go and put a satellite dish up there and—"

"Look, Mr. Slate," Rich said tightly. "It's not my issue. I'm just saying we need things to work around here, and they don't."

Hunter leaned down, his posture menacing. Lou's eyes widened.

"Fine and dandy to say it's *'not your issue'*," he snarled, "but it'll affect everyone!"

"Hunter," Lou interrupted, reaching out to touch his arm, "maybe you could bring this up with Sam?"

"Already did. Wrote letters to the government and everything, but I wanted Mr. Evans here to know what he's gonna cause."

"You know," Rich said acidly, "the committee did their research when they were—"

"I wasn't asked to be on your fancy committee," Hunter snapped, "but I still care!"

Rich's eyes narrowed. "Why *don't* you want people installing that satellite, Mr. Slate? Is there something out there in the woods you're trying to hide?"

"You bastard!"

"Hunter!" Lou gasped.

He scowled at her, then shook his head. "I'll get your pie," he grumbled. As he wandered away, she was certain she heard him muttering "got to take a stand."

Lou's gaze followed Hunter's stooped back as he headed into the kitchen. The feeling of being an outsider was exacerbated as her relationship with Rich became more visible. She hadn't felt such exclusion for years.

"You okay?" Rich asked. He brushed his fingers over her wrist. "We could go somewhere else."

Lou's features tightened in pain, their growing connection soiled by Hunter's outburst. "I *like* Hunter," she said quietly. "I don't want to go somewhere else."

Rich stared at the checkered table cloth, his fingers smoothing a seam over and over. The silence had just moved out of the range of comfortable when he looked up again. His blue eyes were troubled.

"I'm sorry I bother him, Lou," Rich said quietly. "I know you two are friends, but I'm just trying to do my job."

"I know you are."

Rich reached across the table and she laced her fingers through his. "I'm not trying to destroy Waterton, *I'm not*." He turned to the window, his mouth settling into a weary smile. "It's one of the most beautiful places I've ever been."

Lou found her throat aching at the admission. What a change from describing the Park as a trap!

"It really is," she said thickly.

Rich's brows drew together in the look of obstinacy she knew so well. This was the other side of Rich. *Stubborn.*

"I just need to get the Whitewater off the ground, Lou," he explained. "Without things like internet, what've I got to sell it? No cell phone reception. No cable. No contact with the outside world."

Lou leaned forward, breath quickening. "So you sell *that*."

"What?"

"Just what you said. The isolation. The experience. The exclusivity."

"But that's no different than what Andler is doing with the Prince of Wales," Rich argued, "and she's got seventy years on her side. I can't compete with her if I don't change that. If I don't try to bring in the new."

Lou shook her head. "I think you're wrong."

Rich frowned, but didn't argue. Lou gestured to the mountains above the storefronts.

"Before the murders this summer, people wanted to be here. It wasn't just hype," she said. "Use that as your talking point. There aren't many tourists—even less now—so the market's just waiting to be opened up. Like Hunter said: the wilderness here is untouched. Unlike the Prince of Wales, the Whitewater Lodge is a modern hotel. That alone will bring people. But it's the experience that you've got to sell. It's something that very few places could possibly offer. That's the key."

Rich's face shimmered as the words sunk in. "You're right," he said. "I *could* sell that!" He turned back to the window. This time Lou could see him taking it in with different eyes. Rich pulled her hand toward him, pressing a kiss to her knuckles. "You're really good at this," he said with a chuckle. "You'd fit right into a boardroom."

"Nah," Lou snorted. "It's too damned busy in a city." Hunter emerged from the kitchen, and Rich let go of her hand. "I like it just fine here," Lou added.

As Hunter set the pie in front of Lou, she almost missed Rich's next words, but later that night, she played them over in her mind.

"I like it here, too."

* * *

He picked up the phone on the first ring.

"Hello?"

There was the crackle of a long-distance connection, and a man's growling voice emerged. "Lucas is free."

"Glad to hear it."

"Kid posted bail this morning," the voice continued. "Got outta jail around noon."

"He say anything to anyone?"

"Nothing, far as I can tell," the man answered. "Kicked off his newfound freedom with a night on the town. Still sitting in the bar, actually. Just saw him." Laughter, mean and angry, crackled through the phone line. "Stupid fuck just bought a round of drinks for everyone there."

There was a long pause, filled with the sound of heavy breathing. "And...?" The single word was a warning. A hint of what would happen if his rules were not followed.

"And he won't make it home," the man said darkly. "It'll be done tonight. You have my word."

"Good."

* * *

Rich and Lou parted ways in the parking lot outside Hunter's Coffee Shop, kissing once again, heedless of onlookers. Breathless, Rich waited under the buzzing street lamp, watching Lou skip her way across Windflower Avenue and disappear into the dark alley behind Lou's Garage, her silhouette fading until it was only a ghost, and then nothing but an after image lost in the dark.

"'Night, Lou," Rich murmured. Even her name was magic. With

a sigh, he climbed into his now-finished sports car, heading back toward the Whitewater Lodge. While he wouldn't have missed their final garage-date for anything, he couldn't go home yet. There was simply too much to do around the lodge before the night was over.

The engine's purr was a low rumble, the car's controls under his hands smoother than he'd known since the day he'd bought it. It struck Rich as he pulled into the lot that the vehicle hadn't had trouble on the first trip down from Calgary; it had only been since he'd moved to Waterton. The hair on the back of his head crawled at the thought. *What if the car was the first hint of trouble...?* The idea that someone had been messing with the engine was a standing joke between him and Lou, but sitting in the dark outside the lodge with the looming bulk of the mountains beyond, the idea held macabre undertones. Perhaps the car hadn't been a lemon. Maybe someone had tried to kill him with it.

Rich's stomach clenched uneasily. He hadn't had any trouble around the cabin since he'd had the security system installed, but the garage had nothing more than an old padlock on the outside. Rich made a mental note to have a security system added there too. As always, it came down to finding time.

Three hours later, the thought had slipped his mind under the avalanche of unpaid bills and receipts. Rich yawned and turned his computer off. The hotel was quiet, the faint murmur of the furnace the only sound besides the wind outside. Rich turned, staring back at a reflection of himself in the office window. The image jerked away the wan tendrils of exhaustion. From outside, anyone could see him.

With trembling hands, he closed the blinds, reminding himself to close them when he worked late. (There was something *else* he was supposed to remember to do, but he could no longer recall what.) Scowling, Rich slumped back into his chair, staring for long seconds at the dimmed monitor. He was too wired to sleep now, but he didn't relish the thought of more paperwork. There were certain ones that just didn't make sense, or—

"Invoices," Rich breathed. *That* was what he was supposed to remember.

He pushed aside the pile of monthly bills and flicked open the tattered folder from the summer of 1998. Jeff Chan's spidery handwriting greeted him like a familiar voice, and Rich scanned the listings of deliveries sent to Lethbridge. There were regular items— recycling, machinery needing repairs, the few things that couldn't be done in-house—but something didn't make sense. There were simply too many outgoing trucks. Rich unfolded the papers, scanning for clues.

"There has to be something..."

His finger paused atop a scribbled note. The attendant was listed as Lucas Sorenson. Under 'special instructions' the handwritten carbon copy had been noted, but there was no name beside it. Rich moved to another week's deliveries. It had the same attendant and mark. And the next five, too.

Exhausted, Rich considered the now-black computer screen, but didn't bother restarting it. *Need to call Coldcreek,* Rich thought, *and see if Chan's emails have been purged.* If Chan or Sorenson had sent copies to someone, then that person might be able to help. Rich scribbled a note on the memo pad on his desk and tore the page free. He was about to leave when sudden inspiration had him adding one last reminder: *Call Lou. Set up another date.*

With that, he tucked the paper into his pocket and headed out of his office, smiling.

* * *

It was past two when Lucas stumbled from the oppressive heat of the bar. The rush of nighttime air was a shock. It doused the sweat on his back into an icy layer, his hair drying into peaks before he'd made it five steps down the street. Lucas dragged the faded leather jacket up one arm, missed the arm hole, and swung past it twice before succeeding. The coat was bulkier than usual, and he patted his breast pocket fondly. It was full of fifty dollar bills—there were more sitting in a duffel at the hotel room he'd booked downtown—a payout for his silence and more cash than he'd seen in his lifetime. Grinning, Lucas wove unsteadily toward the crosswalk and teetered on the curb.

Across the street, a square patch of forest—Galt Gardens—waited, silent and foreboding. He'd crossed the downtown park numerous times when he'd been in high school as he walked home from the Park Place Mall. The occasional drunk would hassle him for a cigarette, or homeless teens would grift for spare change, but Lucas had never had trouble. Galt Gardens was too open to be dangerous. Tonight it gave him pause. There was something foreboding about the rustle and heave of swaying pines, the whisper of elms in the shadows. On instinct, Lucas turned and went back the other way.

The downtown streets were empty save for the occasional commuter passing in the isolated bubble of his car. *Maybe I should buy a car,* Lucas thought cheerfully. The money wouldn't last forever, but forever was a long goddamned time. He smiled, his steps following an awkward, meandering pace. *Yes,* Lucas thought, *a car would be good.*

He staggered as he walked, catching himself against the nearby bricks every few paces. Unexpectedly, the wall stopped. Overhead, signage from another era announced "Men and Boys' Wear," but there was nothing beyond. Like a missing tooth, the next building had been pulled out, replaced by a gravelled lot. This stretch of 5th Street was an echo from Lethbridge's heyday, when the town had been known as Coalbanks and the bars that lined this road had been filled with fur-traders and rum-runners. The missing building was a ghost; a dark, unlit stretch of pavement with cars blocking his view. The hair rose on Lucas's arms as he lurched past.

He kept his gaze on the end of the parking lot and the start of the next building, where a cobbler's sign hung. He was halfway past the parking lot when a figure stepped from between two parked cars, blocking his way. Lucas stumbled to a stop. The streetscape shimmered like a ribbon across his vision.

"Spare some change," the stranger slurred, hand outstretched. He was one of the hardened destitutes for whom the downtown core was home. His clawed fingers were knobbed and sinewy.

Lucas recoiled in disgust. "I got nothing, man."

He tried to step around him, but the man matched his step, the two of them moving into a circle of streetlight. Here, Lucas could see the man's face: wrinkled, weathered skin; eyes faded by cataracts. He wore the indeterminate age of alcoholism and homelessness like armour.

"C'mon, man, be a pal," he said, giving Lucas a gap-toothed grin full of rotten teeth. "Whatever you can spare."

Lucas's hands rose in fists. "I got nothing," Lucas lied. "I'm broke." The need to run had his legs twitching. It struck him that the wad of bills was visible through his jacket, and he cursed himself for bringing so much along.

"You sure?" the man persisted, the waft of alcohol and fouled flesh rising as he inched nearer. "Just a loonie or two. That's all I need. Lil' bit to hold me 'til morning."

The alcohol in his veins made Lucas bold. "I said 'no,'" he barked.

"Now fuck off!" He shouldered past the beggar, knocking him back between the cars.

Lucas jogged a few steps, but the sidewalk was too uneven without the wall at his side to hold onto, and he slowed almost at once. Faint footfalls paced him—the man, he guessed—and he increased his pace into a tottering stagger. He didn't want to get in a fight, but if he didn't get away from here, he might. Street people were unpredictable; mostly harmless when alone, but you could never tell. *Fucking dumb thing to do,* Lucas thought. *Should've crossed the park.*

Lucas had almost made it to the end of the parking lot when he heard the scuffle of footsteps. He spun, hands upraised.

"You need to fuck OFF!" he bellowed. "Or I'll ... I'll..."

The unsmiling man who faced him was a head taller than the unkempt one who'd asked for change. He held a tire iron in one hand, but there were no cars parked on the street. Lucas's sluggish mind struggled to piece together a web of discordant thoughts.

The Whitewater Lodge appeared.

"Hey," Lucas slurred, "aren't you that guy who—"

With the speed of a striking snake, the tire iron swung in an arc, smashing into Lucas's temple and bringing him to the ground.

CHAPTER SEVENTEEN

The office of the Waterton Police Force had transformed in recent weeks. Where posters of the Beargrass Festival and Chili Cook-off had once filled an entire billboard, an array of photographs from the various crime scenes was now posted, Rich Evans' notes pinned along one side. Today Sadie added a new item: the official statement of Lucas Sorenson. She held the photocopied document in place with a tack, glaring at the incomplete picture it provided.

"Stupid kid," she sighed. "Should've talked."

"He's scared," Jim said. "You could see that as well as I could."

Sadie muttered something under her breath that sounded like "he should be."

"We're getting closer," Jim continued. "The prints from the Aspen Suite match the unknown perp from the Yellowstone case."

"And the others match Lucas Sorenson," Sadie added.

"Based on Lucas's reaction to the question about the deliveries," Jim said, "I'd say it's a pretty fair guess that person is either our killer, or knows who is."

Sadie played with the end of her braid, rolling it over and over. "Lucas knows the guy. Maybe even helped him commit the murder."

"Could be, but he's not the person who killed the last two," Jim continued. "He was in custody when they were murdered. So we've got a serial killer with links to the States. What'd bring him up here to Waterton?"

Sadie scanned the macabre images. "Quiet town with a large transient population in the summer. Only a few locals in the winter." She shrugged. "It's almost like the place is designed for someone who doesn't want to be found."

"And he's still here," Jim said.

"That's my guess." Sadie flicked Lucas's statement with her nail. "Lucas is involved. He knows who it is. He's protecting him. Question is, why?"

"A drug ring moving product across the border?"

"Possibly. Makes me wonder who the other victim is."

Jim didn't answer. He eyed a photo of the mangled torso of the drug dealer, the silence dragging out. *The bodies were left as a warning, but a warning to who?*

"I think Rich Evans' information is more important than we realize," he said.

"Trespassers on his porch at night ... People rattling on his windows?" Sadie smirked. "You sure *he's* not the crazy one?"

"Might be, but I'm starting to think someone's trying to scare him away."

"Like they did with Chan?"

"Exactly," Jim said. "But the bodies are a warning, too."

She frowned. "You think there are more out there?"

"Yeah, I do."

Sadie scanned the grainy black and white images. "Two in the woods. And the message in blood in the Whitewater Lodge. A third body there, whether we found it or not."

"Still think there's more," Jim insisted.

"What makes you so sure?"

"C'mon, Sadie. Waterton Park is almost five hundred square kilometres. That's a hell of a lot of hiding places for a body."

"If there's anything left to find. Animals did most of the guy's handiwork for him. Evans' statement clinches it: We've got to reopen the missing person's case for Jeff Chan. He's—"

A knock on the door interrupted her.

"Jim, Sadie. You have a second?" the receptionist asked, a faxed printout in hand. "I didn't want to bother you two, but this came through a minute ago. It's marked high priority."

Sadie read the documents, her skin growing ashen.

"Who's it from?" Jim asked.

She didn't answer.

"Sadie? What's going on?"

She looked up, her face caught in a tangled expression of pain-filled fury. "Lucas Sorenson is dead."

"What?"

She took a slow breath, holding out the fax with shaking fingers. "He was found in an alley near Galt Gardens this morning, bludgeoned to death."

Jim grabbed the papers from her hand, scowling as he read. "Goddammit!"

Sadie reached out for the back of a chair, catching herself against it. She held on, white-knuckled. "We should've gotten him protection even if he didn't talk," she said shakily. "The kid was scared and—"

"Stop it."

"I should have done something," Sadie insisted. Jim put the paper down and reached out for Sadie's arm, but she tore away. "I should have known!"

"No one could have known this would happen."

Sadie paced like a caged animal. "We've got a killer out there—a killer with connections to our town—and he's going to keep doing this until we stop him." She went to move past Jim, but he blocked her way. "He's going to go after everyone who threatens him," Sadie hissed. "You. Me. The rest of Waterton."

Jim put his hand on her shoulder, waiting until she lifted her gaze and held his eyes. "So we find him," he said grimly. "Before he kills anyone else."

"How?"

"We investigate everyone in town, one by one, until we find him."

* * *

Audrika was in an excellent frame of mind. The rest of the patrons of Hunter's Coffee Shop might be grumbling about the murders looming over the town, but she sat at the table preening. After the first request for the satellite dish had been declined, a new proposal had been brought forward by Rich Evans, and it had passed ... *barely*. Despite any misgivings he might have had about bringing the Park into the twenty-first century, Superintendent Barton had presented the satellite dish request to Parks Canada. The final decision wouldn't be made any time this year, but at the morning's coffee shop meeting, details were emerging. *Another step closer!* Audrika thought with glee.

She glanced around, smothering a smile behind her hand. People were deep in conversation. At a lonely table near the back, Hunter tapped a spoon on the tabletop. Louise Newman sat next to him, expression tight. Yesterday, Hunter had argued that Lou should be invited to attend the meetings again. Much as she might disagree, Audrika couldn't think of a reason why not. But that didn't mean she had to like it. Lou lifted her gaze, catching Audrika's eyes and holding them. There was a question there, and an awareness that made Audrika uncomfortable. She turned away with a huff, her composure ruffled. Audrika's distrust of Lou had only grown this summer.

"I think we should start considering what the satellite dish might do for next year's business," Sam announced. "I'll be bringing up the idea of a town revitalization committee to the next Chamber of Commerce meeting."

Yes, she thought merrily. *This year is a turning point.*

"That satellite thing still a go?" Colt asked. "Thought it was on hold."

"Looks like we have enough people to check into it," Sam said. "So if any of you want to talk to me beforehand, I'd like to hear your ideas."

"Maybe you should talk to Evans and get some of his thoughts," Audrika suggested. "He seems to be full of ideas for improvements."

Hunter made a sound of disgust. Nobody had argued for Rich's inclusion in today's meeting. He was moving through the town like a gale force hurricane, every upset followed by another upgrade. Audrika didn't know if he could keep it up, but she admired his tenacity. In the aftermath of the murder scene his staff had unwittingly discovered, the Whitewater had been forced to shut down two wings, but the main lodge was still open. It was booked solid for the remainder of the summer. No other business in town could boast that.

"I'll work on your committee," Susan offered, "I'm sure we can find a way to make improvements without being so..." She turned, glaring at Audrika, "radical in our approaches."

Before she could respond, the door to the restaurant opened and everyone turned. Audrika half-expected Rich Evans. He seemed to be everywhere lately. But the figure who came through the doorway was Constable James Flagstone, ruddy-cheeked and wheezing. He sat down with them while Hunter brought coffee and pie to the table.

"Any news on the murderer?" Audrika asked.

Jim tugged at his collar. "Not yet."

"I don't know about you," Audrika said, "but if one more person asks me about the serial killer in town, I'm going to give them a piece of my mind."

Jim took a swig of coffee. "We're getting closer," he assured her. "Picked up a few stray fabric fibres at the last site and we've got a few other leads." He winced. "Mind you, it's not a certainty until we actually get the guy."

"It sure doesn't help tourism any," someone grumbled.

"...business just isn't what it should be this time of year!"

"Just been a bad year altogether," another added.

"Don't hurt mine none," Hunter said.

Susan scowled at him. "We're already in August and I haven't brought in half of what I took in last summer."

Audrika smirked. *That* was an interesting tidbit of information.

Hunter raised a bushy eyebrow. "Maybe it's just you," he chided. "For Chrissake, woman, would it kill you to smile once in a—"

"Hunter!" Lou choked, "that's not helping."

"Me'n Sadie are doing what we can," Jim said. "But there've been some issues with the case."

"Issues like what?" a voice at the back shouted.

"Why haven't you caught this guy?"

"...there's a murderer out there on the streets!"

"Not safe!"

The noise rose until Hunter finally stood. "Enough!" he bellowed. Everyone fell silent. Hunter glanced warily at the few tourists watching the interaction then back to the table. "Whatever you're trying to say, Jim, you better spit it out. I've got other customers, you know."

Jim rose from his chair. "Look, everyone," he said, hands lifting. "It's a formality for now, but I want you to hear it from me directly. Sadie and I are extending our investigation outward until we catch this guy. I know it's an inconvenience, but we're going to go through as carefully as we need to. We don't want someone like this wandering the streets. We're checking everyone." He paused. "Even locals."

The hubbub returned tenfold. Sam, the Park superintendent, was the first to stand. He stormed out, cheeks flushed, Murray and the others following until only Lou, Hunter and Audrika remained.

Audrika took a final sip of her green tea and dabbed her lipsticked mouth with a napkin. "I suppose I should go, too," she said, falsely bright. Things like this didn't bother her as long as she was in the know, and lately she felt like she was holding all the cards. "Have a good day, Hunter." She pulled her handbag off the chair's back, smile fading. "Lou."

Lou didn't look up as Audrika headed to the door. She was staring at the scattered mugs on the tabletop. "What the hell is going on?" she asked.

Hunter reached out, laying a comforting hand on her shoulder. "Nothing good."

* * *

Lou had every intention of leaving things alone. But when she came out of the café, she headed south on Main Street, rather than north, her feet carrying her down past the stores of friends and neighbours until she arrived at the entrance to Fine and Fancy. It had been years since she'd passed through the doorway, and with good reason. She and Audrika Kulkarni were like oil and water.

Lou steeled her shoulders and pasted on a smile as she came inside. *Audrika already hates me,* she thought wryly. *What's the worst that can happen?*

Audrika was sitting behind the counter, a tabloid celebrity magazine in one hand. "Come on in!" she called. "How can I—" Her words stumbled, the false smile turning icily polite in an instant. "Why, Louise," she said. "Whatever brings you in here?"

Lou came to the counter slowly. "I wanted to talk to you a minute, if you have time."

"Well, to tell you the truth, I'm a little busy right now."

Lou looked around. The store was empty. "Oh?"

"But I suppose just a minute won't hurt," Audrika said, her tone sharpening. "So what's this visit about?"

"Rich Evans."

"Oh really...?"

"Yes, he's been having trouble around his place," Lou said. "Things moved and broken." She waited for a reaction that never came. "You heard anything about that?"

Audrika uncurled herself from her perch and leaned against the counter. "Why in the world would I know anything about that?"

"Because it's the same kind of thing that happened to Jeff Chan last year."

The seething mask dropped for a split-second. "What's Chan got to do with this?"

"Chan knew you," Lou said. "He told you he'd—"

"I don't know what you're talking about," Audrika interrupted. "I didn't even know Jeff Chan!"

"He talked to you. I remember it, Audrika. I was there in Hunter's that day, too."

Audrika's mouth popped open, then snapped closed. She returned to her perch on the stool, distrust in her kohl-rimmed eyes. "I don't remember that," she said.

"We were all there, but Chan wanted to talk to you privately," Lou continued. "I remember that. I'm not asking for details..." Lou gave a weak smile. "But whatever happened with Chan last year seems to be happening with Rich now. And it's scaring me ... I— I don't know how to stop it." She closed her eyes, fighting for control. "I need to know what Chan came to you about."

"This is ludicrous!" Audrika retorted. "I don't even remember talking to that—that lunatic! How should I know what he was after?"

"If anyone knows, it's you," Lou said placatingly. "You have connections no one else does. You know everything going on around town." The older woman's expression thawed under the glow of Lou's praise. "Please, Audrika. I need to know what Chan asked you about."

"I don't—"

"Please," Lou pleaded.

For a few seconds, Lou was certain Audrika was going to deny it and tell her to leave. The older woman peered around the store, then leaned forward, voice low.

"Chan was asking about getting a loan to finish the lodge. For a city boy, he was quite the dud. Mismanaged everything! Couldn't float the costs anymore." Her hooded gaze grew stony. "I couldn't help him, of course, but I knew a company that could."

"Borderline." The word was a stone dropped into the stillness of the room.

Audrika's face blanched under her makeup. "Yes ... that's right," she said cautiously. "I didn't realize you knew about that."

"I don't, really," Lou said. "But I've heard the name from a few people around town."

Audrika smirked, arms crossing on her ample chest. "Well, I have no part in it either," she announced. "I've never needed the help."

"The help?"

"Oh goodness, Louise. Don't be such a goose. Everyone needs a foot-up sometimes. Borderline was offering help and a lot of people needed it." Audrika rolled her eyes. "You don't look a gift horse in the mouth."

"So you put Chan in contact with Borderline?"

Audrika looked down at her ringed fingers. "I might've mentioned Borderline to Chan ... not sure," she said, spinning a square-cut zircon. "Like I said, I've got no part of Borderline. I've never needed the help, you see. My business has always done just fine."

Lou nodded. She'd never heard of Borderline either, and that worried her. The townsfolk were her family; their lives, her life. "I never knew a thing about Borderline before this summer," she admitted. "But I've heard it's got leases all around town."

Audrika sighed dramatically. "Well, it's a big company, dear, and I'm certain it has holdings in lots of places. Not just here."

"But *I've* never heard of it," Lou repeated.

"Perhaps you just never asked the right people," Audrika sniffed. The edges of her lipsticked mouth sharpened into daggers. "Or maybe no one wanted to tell you about it."

Lou shook her head. "But someone had to introduce Borderline to the business owners. Someone vouched for the company's ownership."

"And...?"

"Locals are wary of outsiders. They wouldn't have signed on without reason. I want to know who brought the proposal forward,"

Lou said. "It wasn't at a regular Chamber of Commerce meeting. I'd remember that."

"I don't know what you mean."

"Someone vouched for Borderline," Lou pressed. "And I want to know who."

Audrika shifted in her seat. "Well, I couldn't say ... I'm not sure I..." The door opened behind them, and Audrika gave the young couple a bright smile. "Welcome! Welcome!" she trilled. "Come on in—I'll be right with you"

"It was one of the locals, wasn't it?" Lou said.

Audrika's attention jerked back to Lou, her jewelled hand fluttering to her chest. There was anger in her gaze now. "Things were a lot different five years ago," she said sharply. "A lot of people would have gone under, Lou. That's all I'm saying."

"I was here, too," Lou replied. "I should have been told—"

"You're one to talk," Audrika sneered. "A gas station does fine no matter what. Others weren't so lucky. And if you were never told, it was because people didn't want you to know. You've no right to judge what you don't understand!"

In a swirl of gaudy silk, Audrika joined the customers over at the sales rack, dismissing Lou with her turned back. Disappointed, Lou headed from the store. Up the street, the windows of Hunter's Coffee Shop gleamed. Seeing the café, a wave of concern rode over her. If Audrika had known about the agreement with Borderline, that meant Hunter'd known about it too.

And he'd never said a word.

* * *

Amanda Sloane was working nights again, any lingering fears from the near-attack assuaged by an expanded sense of self-importance. In the days that had followed, Rich had arranged for caretakers to cull back the overgrown shrubbery along the walkways, and Nando had installed five new security lights along the path. A 'be street smart' poster now hung in the staff room reminding staff to walk in pairs, and a panic release button had been installed on all exits. Jim Flagstone had never given Amanda a second look before that terrifying night, but when she'd given her statement to the police, Jim had patted her hand and told her she was "a brave young woman." She liked that part best of all.

Amanda smiled, thinking of the two romance novels she'd picked up from the drugstore today. The teenage boy behind the till had smirked as he rang them through, but she didn't care. Since Mr. Evans had removed the television behind the counter, Amanda had been looking for a new distraction.

The door to the back room opened, and Nando headed into the lobby. He wore jeans and a plaid shirt, his wavy black hair slicked down. Amanda's mouth curled knowingly as he passed. Out of his work clothes, the guy definitely had potential.

"Heading off, Amanda," he said with a wave. "See you tomorrow."

He went to step past her, but she leaned forward, her breasts propped on her arms where they rested against the counter. Amanda knew how to use her best side to her advantage. Seeing it, Nando stumbled to a stop.

"Stay and talk a minute before you go," she purred.

Nando glanced behind him, looking for the person she was talking to. Finding no one, he turned back, expression wary. "I, um … I…" He swallowed hard. "Okay."

"You doing something tonight?" she drawled.

His eyes dropped to her chest and then jerked back up, cheeks colouring. Nando was a nice guy, and Amanda had belatedly started to appreciate that in a man.

"I, um..." Nando's chin bobbed again. "I, uh ... there's a pool tournament at the Watering Hole, and me and a couple of the guys from the Prince of Wales are meeting up."

She tipped her chin, fluttering her lashes. "No girls allowed?" she pouted, twirling her fingers through her long hair.

Nando's blush deepened until the tips of his ears were bright pink.

"No! I mean, yes! Yes, women are allowed." He laughed nervously. "Of course they are."

"That sounds real nice," she said, leaning closer. "Wish I could go."

He swallowed hard, his eyes moving around the room rather than settling on her. Amanda bit her tongue to keep from laughing.

"I, um ... well, I suppose you could," Nando stammered. He looked, she decided, like a deer in the headlights.

"Problem is ... I don't get off until midnight," Amanda said petulantly.

Nando's gaze jumped back to her. "Why don't you come then?" he suggested with a toothy grin. "Tourney will be half done, but we could grab a drink."

"Would you mind?" she cooed. "I mean I'd just watch." She reached out, running her fingers along his arm. "Unless, of course, you wanted to teach me."

Nando made a wheezing noise, his hand wiping nervously at his forehead.

"Yeah ... yeah, I could do that, Amanda." His eyes dropped to her breasts, mouth agape. "If you wanted."

"Up here, Nando," she giggled, putting a hand coyly over her décolletage.

His eyes jerked back to her face. "Oh, Jesus, so sorry," he gasped.

Amanda squeezed his arm. "No problem." She winked. "And I'll see you after twelve. Okay?"

"See you," he called before leaving. He looked, Amanda thought, like someone who'd just found a fifty dollar bill tucked into a wallet they'd assumed was empty.

Yes, she thought smugly. *Nando will do just fine.* She reached in her bag, pulling the first novel out. The cover showed a woman with flowing red hair standing on a cliff, a bare-chested man with long dark hair, wrapped around her. If Amanda squinted, she could almost imagine Nando in the role.

She opened to the first page.

As the eldest daughter of the Chieftain Lochlan Noch Ruin, Mistress Selena had always known she was destined for greatness...

* * *

Hunter was on his front stoop picking burrs from his youngest dog's fur when the phone rang. Duke barked, pulling free of Hunter's hands. "Goddammit!" Hunter snapped as the overgrown hound bounded away from him, skittering into the house and sliding across the linoleum.

The phone rang again and the dog's barks grew louder.

Hunter groaned as he hoisted himself to his feet. "I'ma coming, I'ma coming," he sighed. The other dogs had joined into the chorus, a cacophony of sound filling the kitchen. "Quiet now!" Hunter shouted. All the dogs settled, except Duke, who turned in circles, whining. "Go on!" Hunter grumbled as he picked up the phone. "H'lo?"

There was the faint sound of breathing, nothing else.

"Hello?" Hunter repeated. "Anyone there?" He was just pulling the handset away when he got his answer.

"I'm going to do it," a voice announced.

Hunter put the phone back to his ear, pulse racing. "Do what?"

"I'm going to get rid of Evans once and for all."

Hunter reached out for a wooden chair with trembling fingers. He dragged it toward the phone and sat down. The house felt unnaturally quiet. "Now let's just talk about this before you do anything," Hunter said. "I'm not sure you should—"

"It's time to make a stand!"

For a second, Hunter couldn't speak. He closed his eyes, pinching the bridge of his nose. "Maybe ... but this isn't the way. I need you to stop and think about this a minute." Duke lay down at his master's feet and put his head on his paws, looking up at Hunter with solemn eyes.

"I'm done thinking. Scare him enough, Evans will turn tail and run."

"Not sure about that," Hunter sighed.

"I need your help. Yes or no."

Hunter put his elbows on his knees, fighting for calm. "Forcing the situation will make it worse," he said. "There's already trouble."

"Are you saying no?"

"I'm saying I need a minute to think about this. Alright?" Hunter's voice was constricted and tight. Duke cocked his head to one side, whining.

Laughter, dark and angry, filled the receiver. "There was a time you used to help your friends. You've gotten soft in your old age. You've changed."

Hunter let out a defeated sigh. "Leave it alone for a while," he said. "I don't think this—"

The phone clicked off and a dial tone filled his ear.

Deflated, Hunter hung up the phone and stood from the chair.

Things were coming undone at the seams. Too much was going on.

The dogs followed Hunter into the living room. When he pulled on his jacket, the two older dogs perked up their ears, joining him at the door. Duke ran circles around his legs, yipping happily. Hunter reached down, running a hand over the loose skin of the dog's neck and ears.

"Yes, Duke," he said tiredly. "You can come too."

* * *

Rich came by to pick up Lou after work, inviting her out for a test drive of the sports car. With the warmer weather finally arrived, Rich itched for an escape from the confines of the town. He'd missed the rush of driving. It gave him a release few things could compete with.

"Sure I'll go for a drive," Lou laughed. "But I might need to grab something to eat first. I missed lunch."

"A short drive then," Rich said. "And dinner after."

"Fair enough," Lou said with a grin, "but this time I cook."

Rich pulled her into a kiss. "Done."

The two of them drove up the looping road to Cameron Lake, chasing the receding sunlight that fell in soft bands of crimson over the mountain peaks. Unlike Gabby, who chattered on her phone while they drove—ignoring Rich altogether—Lou left her palm open beside her on the seat, and Rich wrapped his fingers around hers. They drove with the windows open, enjoying the cool that came with dusk in the mountains. The gloaming was what Rich's grandfather had called the purple haze of half-light. The mountain peaks had narrowed to flat cut-outs, the sky a smoky lavender burnishing to blue. Another half-hour and it would be solid black, but for now, time hung in that lazy hour between night and day.

"You seem quiet," Lou said as they reached the turn-around at

Cameron Lake and started back toward town.

"Just busy," Rich answered. Lou's silence, and the gentle grip of her hand against his, pushed him to explain. "Nothing serious," he assured her. "Still trying to figure out Chan's mess."

"This about the deliveries again?"

Rich nodded, swinging the car around another curve in the road and tapping the brakes. For the first time in months the vehicle handled perfectly. "Even with half-full trucks, there's only so much to send out. I've got the invoices, but I can't find out who he sent them to. All Chan's emails were purged before he left." He laughed tiredly. "It can't ever be easy."

Lou smiled up at him. "I'm sure you'll figure it out. It's got to be there, right? I mean, someone knows."

"You'd think so, but I tried calling the people I had names for, and even the driver's number is disconnected. No one seems to know anything." Rich shook his head. "Anyhow, I'll get it done, but for now—" He released her hand, dropping the car down in gear as they neared a sheer drop. In the back of Rich's mind, a thought appeared: *If I'd been driving here when the gears didn't shift, I couldn't have made the turn.* But the engine lowered with the purr of a contented cat, and the tension eased from Rich's shoulders. "Tonight, I want to focus on us."

Lou released a contented sigh. "I like the way that sounds."

Reaching Windy Pines, Rich parked the car on the street under the unwavering eye of the street lamp and led Lou to the porch. He tapped in the code for the security system and they slipped inside.

"Any more trouble?" Lou asked.

"Same kind of things. Broken window in the garage. Things moved. But I'm having a security system set up for the garage as soon as..." He didn't even finish the sentence. There was never enough time.

While Rich flicked on lights and turned on music, Lou foraged through the limited groceries for inspiration, rifling through the drawers like she owned the place. In minutes she was pulling out items and dropping them onto the counter. Rich grinned; it was different to see her here. Settled and homey. It left him thinking of other places she might live; other roles she might don. Daughter, friend, peacemaker ... *Wife and mother,* a secret voice inside him added. Yes, he could definitely see her in that role, too.

Lou put her hands on her hips, grimacing at the scant offerings. "You're going to end up with scurvy if you don't start eating vegetables," she said disapprovingly. "This is a sorry choice of food."

Rich chuckled. He came up behind her, looping his arms around her waist and putting his chin on her shoulder. "We could head over to the Whitewater," he suggested. "The dining room's still open."

Lou twisted so she could see his face. "Not a chance. You're mine tonight. And you are *not* working."

Rich pressed a kiss to her neck, amazed at how good it felt for her to claim that. She shooed him away and began to pull dishes from the cupboard.

"You can help," she said, "but no distractions." Rich groaned, and Lou's grin widened. "Until after," she amended.

Lou announced that dinner would be breakfast: coffee without cream, as Rich had none, and pancakes smothered in butter and maple syrup. He basked in the nearness of her as she cooked. Things were moving forward with Louise Newman, but it was like the two of them were on different pages of the same book. He wanted more from her ... and he wasn't certain she wanted the same. The vague answers she gave left him squirming, and every time he tried to move things forward, he found circumstances inexplicably blocking the way.

He sighed, wondering when in the world he'd allowed himself to go and fall in love with Lou. Rich *knew* he had it bad.

"Are you happy living alone?" he asked, leaning against the counter as she ladled homemade pancake batter into the pan.

"Sure, I'm happy. And I'm not *really* alone, Rich. Yes, I live by myself, but I have lots of friends in Waterton."

"Not hoping to settle down some day?" A hot flush of embarrassment ran up the back of his neck; Gabby had asked him that question more than once.

"Not sure marriage is in the cards for me," she said, flipping the pancake over. "I'm pretty content on my own."

She turned away from the stove, reaching out for the butter and carrying it to the table while Rich glowered. *That was his line.*

After dinner they sat in the living room Rich never used, instrumental jazz echoing in the background. Unlike Lou's cabin, with the framed photographs and worn furniture, Windy Pines looked like it was still waiting for its rightful owners. The white couch on which they sat was a modernist piece; a lacquered black coffee table sat in front of it. The furniture contrasted starkly with the antique room. The faded wallpaper had shadows where photographs had once hung. The wood panels covering half the wall spoke of generations of visitors. Now it felt uncomfortably empty.

Rich was entranced by the woman on the couch next to him. Lou's hair spilled around her shoulders, falling forward whenever she laughed. She seemed brighter tonight. *Or maybe,* Rich thought, *it's just that we're finally alone again.* He'd barely touched her since the first drunken night when they'd come together.

"God," she said. "I haven't heard Ella Fitzgerald in forever."

Rich slid closer. "I never knew you liked her."

"You never asked."

"Tell me what you like," he whispered, mouth brushing her ear.

She glanced up, concern reflected in the crinkle between her brows. "Like what?"

Rich smiled. "I don't know, Lou," he laughed. "Anything. Everything!"

She tapped her fingers against her lips, leaving Rich aching to kiss them. "Hmmm ... Everything, huh? That's gonna take a while."

Rich's hand moved into her hair, combing through the heavy strands. She closed her eyes, settling against the couch as the music wrapped around them.

"What's your favourite food?" Rich asked on a whim.

She opened one eye quizzically. "You serious?"

"Yes, I am," he chuckled.

She closed her eyes again and Rich went back to stroking.

"Well," Lou began, "I guess my favourite would be water."

"Not a food."

She glared at him before her lashes fluttered closed again. "Fine then," she said wryly. "If it has to be a food, it's huckleberries."

"Huckleberry what?"

She shook her head. "Just the berries. Nothing else. You ever had them?"

"Uh-uh."

"Mm..." Lou murmured, settling deeper. "We'll have to fix that sometime."

Rich grinned; he liked her making plans for him. The sound of music rose from the stereo, filling the room with song.

"Favourite smell," he prompted, kneading her neck.

"Smell? Probably lilacs, or—no, wait!" she said, lashes flaring. "You know when you've been away for the day, and you drive back to Waterton, and you open the truck door, and you take that first breath: water and clean air, and the trees and sap." She sighed. "That smell exactly."

"Never noticed."

Lou poked him in the ribs and he choked back laughter. "You should breathe next time you come back," she chided. "It's amazing."

Rich caught her fingers, stroking the inside of her palm and her expression shifted, awareness in the amber depths. "I'll do it next time, just for you," he said quietly. He leaned in, and Lou's mouth parted slightly. "Promise."

For a moment, it seemed like something might happen.

"Next question?" Lou prompted, her gaze skittering away.

"What's your favourite memory?"

Her expression became slightly pained. Before she could answer, a keening howl rose outside the window. Rich stood up, the hair on the back of his neck rising.

"Jesus!" he hissed. "That's the wolf I heard!"

"The what?"

"The wolf!" he snapped. "That night when I came home from the Chamber of Commerce meeting, two of them followed me."

He strode to the windows, pulling back the curtains and peering into darkness. With the lights on inside and the sky scudded with clouds, the night was solid black.

"Rich," Lou said behind him, "I don't think that's a—"

Without warning, another howl rose, this one louder, and Rich jerked back, bumping directly into her.

"Fuck!" he hissed. "It's in the yard!"

CHAPTER EIGHTEEN

Outside the cabin, howls rose into the air, and Rich stumbled against the couch. Terror coursed through his veins, leaving him reeling.

Lou took his hands. "It's not a wolf," she said calmly. "It's a dog, Rich. A dog."

"That doesn't sound like a dog to me." His voice sounded panicked, even to his own ears.

"It's probably a cougar hound," she said. "A few people in town have them, and when they get going, they're pretty loud."

"Really?"

"Yes," Lou said with a gentle smile. "Hunter and Colt and—"

An unexpected whine came from outside the front door, magnifying Rich's fear.

"What the fuck?!"

She walked away from him, unlocking the door.

"Don't!" he hissed.

Lou glanced over her shoulder. "Trust me." She pulled open the door an inch and a dog's auburn muzzle appeared. It snuffled her fingers, whines growing. "You lost, buddy?" Lou asked. She used her knee to push the dog's snout away from the door frame and back outside. "C'mon, let's figure out where you came from."

Lou leaned down, catching the dog's collar. She cooed and it began to make happy whining noises. Rich felt his chest ease. It wasn't a wolf after all. While he watched, Lou tugged the animal away, walking down the porch steps. Through the half-open door Rich could see the red-coated dog dancing happily at her side, its tail slapping her legs.

Rich waited in silence, embarrassment replacing his fear. He walked forward stiffly, flicking on the porch light before heading outside. Lou half-walked, half-dragged the lunging mutt to the end of the property, stopping beside Rich's car. She peered up the road, her gaze focused somewhere in the distance.

"Where are you supposed to be, buddy?" she muttered. "Where's your owner gone?"

As if in answer, a distant whistle echoed from across town. The dog jerked away from Lou, running back into the shadows. Lou reached up and massaged her shoulder.

"So much for finding your owner," she laughed.

Rich waited for her on the steps. Behind him, a small swarm of insects swirled around the porch light, pinging and bouncing. As Lou reached his side, Rich pulled her into his arms. He was trembling as his panic faded, but touching her, he felt the tremors ease.

"You okay, Rich?"

He leaned in, his words spoken against her lips.

"I am now."

* * *

The man moved through the wooded area between the buildings in silence, heading toward the bright patch of townsite which marked the boundaries of the Whitewater Lodge. The lights of the grand hotel sparkled in the darkness, a chain of diamonds against a velvet dress. He followed the deep shadow along the east wing, dodging the motion-sensitive lights as he traced a path back to the basement entrance. Hidden by the overhang, he dropped to a crouch and tested the windows. While the one from weeks earlier had been resealed and barred off, there were others along the wall which remained poorly locked. He smiled, teeth gleaming.

The oversight was the perfect opportunity.

Lifting a blade from his pocket, he shimmied it along the seal. With a faint pop it released. The man glanced around one last time, then pulled the window open.

It was time to settle the score.

* * *

Rich and Lou were tangled together on the couch, long kisses interposed with snippets of conversation. Lou sighed as Rich's mouth paused against her pulse point. Her lashes fluttered closed, a soft moan escaping her lips. Rich knew how to touch a woman. His tongue ran along her collarbone and then stopped. Lou opened heavy lids to find him looking at her.

"I was wondering," he said quietly. "You'll tell stories, but never about yourself. Why?"

Lou's hand on his arm became clammy. "There's nothing to tell," she said, leaning forward to kiss him. *That* she could do without guilt.

He pulled back, his finger tracing her lips. "I don't believe that."

Lou shifted under him, uncertainty beginning to push forward. "Why?"

"Everyone has a story," Rich said. "I wasn't kidding when I said I wanted to get to know you."

"You do know me," Lou insisted. "I live here in Waterton, I own a garage." She smiled mischievously. "I like the smell of air."

Rich chuckled but didn't move. He was staring at her the way he had when they'd kissed under the stars. His eyes were bluer like this; more determined.

"What...?"

Rich leaned toward her ear, his breath swirling the hair against her cheek. "Those are facts, Lou," he whispered. "But I want to know what matters."

Her eyes widened. She turned to look up at him, her body abruptly aware of just how near he was. She felt unable to breathe.

"Like what?"

He leaned in and kissed her hard. Lou couldn't think of anything except the taste of him under her tongue, the feel of his hips, angled against hers and the heat growing between them. His fingers ran under her shirt, tracing her ribs. "I want to know what excites you, Lou," he murmured, his tongue flicking against her collarbone. "What scares you..." His mouth moved lower. "I want to know what you care about..." He drew a line of kisses over the curve of her breast. His fingers tugged down the fabric, her nipple pebbling in the cool air. "I want to know what you love the most..." He drew the pink peak into his mouth, leaving Lou biting back moans.

"I, um ... I..." she panted.

The words wouldn't come. Lou wanted to tell him her secrets, but didn't know how. Everything was too raw tonight, because she *did* want Rich to understand, and was afraid of what he'd say. Her father's remembered words taunted her from the shadows: *"It's all in your head, Louise! These dreams are utter foolishness. Nothing else!"* She wished she could believe that.

Rich unhooked her bra, his mouth sliding to the other breast. Lou gasped as his free hand moved down her ribs and fumbled with the button on her jeans. "I ... I like being with you, Rich," Lou panted. "I like *this* ... tonight ... I like..." She gasped as his fingers moved past the barrier of her panties, stroking over her wet heat. Everything she was supposed to say was lost in the feelings wrapping around her. "Oh, Rich, that feels so good."

At her words, everything changed. If there'd been a spark between them, now there was fire, and they were both too close to avoid being consumed.

"Please, Lou," he said. "I want you."

She nodded. "Yes."

* * *

An hour after Nando departed, Amanda was still reading. She had just reached the part when the Viking invader pulled the struggling woman into his arms when her reverie was rudely interrupted by a blaring alarm. She dropped the book, wincing. Around the hotel, doors opened and people moved in the hallway. With a groan, Amanda moved to the security panel behind the desk. The entire board was blinking with yellow lights.

"Motherfucker," she snarled.

She typed in the security code, searching for where the fire was located. East Wing: *Clear. West Wing: Clear. Central Wing: Clear.* Amanda lifted an eyebrow as the system's response appeared. *Smoke Detection Units A-L: Air Quality Consistent. Fire Alarm System: Alarms 2, 8, 11: Engaged. Alarms 1, 3 ,4, 5, 6, 7, 9, 10, 12, 13, 14: Ready.*

She sneered as the last item appeared: *Sprinkler Systems: Ready.*

"None of the sprinklers are on. That makes no sense." The realization hit her like a slap to the face. Someone had tripped the alarms by hand. "Of all the dumbass things to do!" she hissed.

People were beginning to file down to the main lobby. They stopped at the desk, asking in worried tones about the fire.

"Just go outside," Amanda answered tightly. "I'm certain it's nothing, but we can't be too careful."

The phone at the desk rang. Amidst the racket, Amanda picked up the receiver. "Whitewater, this is Amanda!" she yelled.

"This is Walter at the fire station," a familiar voice responded. "I've just put the call out, and we'll be there as soon as we can. Five minutes. Maybe six."

Amanda groaned. Waterton didn't have a standing fire crew. This meant every one of the volunteers had just been awoken to respond to what Amanda assumed was another prank.

"It's fine, Walt," she said. "I'll get everyone out of the hotel."

"Get below the smoke, and hurry up."

"There *is* no smoke," she snapped, then put her hand over the receiver, glaring at the confused guests. "You need to PROCEED to the PARKING LOT!" Amanda bellowed. "This is a FIRE!"

People jumped to follow her orders. She ran a hand through her hair, staring at the security panel in fury. *Sprinkler Systems: Ready.*

"There's no smoke so far," she shouted into the receiver. "Honestly, I don't think this is even a real—"

"Get everyone out," Walt ordered. "We'll be there in a few minutes to check it out."

Amanda grimaced. *So much for my night!* she thought in annoyance.

In two minutes, the hotel was empty. Amanda glanced into the hallways of the main lodge, double-checking for guests; everyone was out, the corridors empty. There wasn't even the faintest whiff of smoke.

"No fucking fire! Just stupid fucking kids playing stupid fucking jokes," she muttered as she jogged down the basement stairs to reset the breakers and turn off the alarm.

Reaching the mechanical room, she paused. Something was

hissing. She took a slow breath and coughed. There was a smell she could remember from her childhood. She blinked, her mother's stove appearing in her mind.

"It's a gas leak," she gasped.

A nearby hot water heater flared to life. The whoosh of flames that surrounded Amanda erupted through the bowels of the building, exploding outward with the force of hell unleashed, quelling her first screams before they'd even started. In a flash, the mechanical room was gone, the entire hotel aflame.

Amanda Sloane was dead.

*   *   *

When the couch's confines grew too limited, Lou and Rich made their way up the rickety stairs to the bedroom, hand in hand. They rolled under sheets that crinkled with cold, their combined warmth a pool of comfort.

"Sorry," Rich said, teeth chattering. "I haven't figured out the furnace yet."

Lou snuggled nearer, kicking off the rest of her clothes and throwing them into the corner. "I'm not complaining," she laughed. "You're warm." Her cold nose pressed up against his neck and she sighed.

"This okay?" he asked, his mouth against Lou's cheek. He wanted her to be here. Wanted her to want him, too. No more drunken fumblings he could barely remember.

"It's better than okay," she sighed, her chilly fingers moving over his bare chest. "Stop worrying, alright?"

Rich leaned forward, mouth bumping roughly against hers. Now that he held her in his arms, the room didn't feel so frigid. He ran his tongue along her lips, drawing out the first seconds of a kiss. This time felt more real, more settled, his body humming in anticipation.

He shifted closer, one leg sliding between Lou's knees, marvelling at her silken skin against his. Her fingers slid down to touch him, and Rich gasped. With a groan of frustration, he pulled her hand away, kissing her breathless, before moving his mouth to her neck. His fingers played over Lou's skin.

"Feels so good," she gasped. "So good..."

Rich's body convulsed at the sound of her voice. Lou moaned and with that, the embrace lost all timidity. The long-banked fires that had built over the spring and summer were now blazing, burning away all thought. All Rich knew was that he wanted Lou, needed her more than he'd needed any person in his life. His caresses grew bolder, fingers and tongue moving in time to her panting breaths. He lifted his face, catching sight of her laying wanton before him. Her hair was a stormy swirl of black; a sheen of sweat covered her upper lip. Rich edged forward until he was barely inside her, his hand tangling in the sheets as he fought for control. Lou's fingers slid into his hair, dragging him into a drowning kiss, and with that, he was lost.

He drove forward. The wave of emotion and sensation tore him away from a world which now balanced on its axis. *Lou ... Lou ... Always Lou.* She was everything to him, all he wanted in life. Rich did everything to slow down: counted backward from ten, tried to remember the exact layout of his college apartment ... but there was no point. Lou was already rocking under him, rolling her hips, grinding herself closer.

They fell into motion as one, ecstasy twining them together. Somewhere in the distance, a sound like thunder rolled through the valley. Neither noticed. Rich's pace quickened and Lou met his thrusts. She arched, her head falling back onto the pillow.

"Rich!" she shouted.

Her cry pulled him over. Sensations redoubled as Rich tumbled into the abyss. A swirl of colour exploded behind his eyelids; Lou's gasping filled his ears. It was like flying or falling, the motion everywhere at once.

Spent, Rich slid sideways, pulling Lou close. She laid her head in the crook of his shoulder, lashes fluttering closed. Outside the windows, the whine of sirens rose, but Rich ignored them. He was filled with a sense of peace he hadn't known for years, his body sated.

"Love you, Lou," he said.

He didn't consciously think about the admission; it bubbled out on a wave of contentment. But once it was spoken, the weight of what he'd said appeared. It was true. *Rich loved her* ... and had for weeks. The words were too heavy to undo and he waited for the havoc they'd unleash.

Lou lifted her chin, gazing at him with warm, knowing eyes. "Love you, too," she replied. She leaned in, sealing her words with a gentle kiss.

The sirens grew louder. Rich's eyelids drooped; Lou's warmth, the creaking house, and the cool sweetness of the air wrapped him in comfort. *She loves me too* ... his mind whispered, a smile tugging up his lips. Eyelids half-closed, the faint sight of lights dancing along the horizon drew his attention. They were gold and orange instead of green.

"Northern lights," Rich murmured.

"Hmm?"

"Outside," Rich replied, then closed his eyes. "The light."

Lou slipped from the bed, pulling on his discarded shirt and walking barefoot to the window. She gasped, one hand pressing up against the pane of glass.

"Oh no!" she cried. "The Whitewater's on fire!"

* * *

The blare of sirens pierced the night with sound. The Whitewater Lodge was a pyre in the centre of the town, shouts of onlookers mingling with the crackle of burning wood. Billows of black smoke rose into the sky as the fire overtook the first floor, and then the second, burning faster. Flames, which had nibbled tentatively up the walls, now jumped from window to window like angry sprites, tearing the hotel apart. In the sky above Waterton, the smoke had doused the stars, but sparks rose to take their place.

The smart thing to do was to leave. He knew that. Still Colton Calhoun lingered.

The guests from the hotel huddled at the far edge of the parking lot, milling like the sheep they were. Other people were arriving. Tourists stumbled from cabins, aghast at the sight greeting them. A woman near the hotel wept, and a young man put his arm over her shoulders. The flames were night-blooming flowers, bulging outward as another explosion rocked the building. The crowd screamed.

A wicked smile spread across Colt's face as a dormer fell inward in a shower of sparks, his skin tightening under the wave of heat. It was over. The Whitewater Lodge was gone! And with it, the town was his once more. It was another step in Colt's plan, another chess piece moved into place. He was breathless with excitement. A step at a time, he'd build an empire.

More people were arriving, locals now. He waited, caught between duelling urges to witness, and to hide. Hunter and Margaret appeared on the street, talking in hushed tones, and Audrika strode forward, her face unnaturally bare without makeup. Nearing his side, she turned, catching his eyes.

"My god, Colton," she said breathily. "What's happened?"

Fear made his throat tight, but he fought it down. "Not sure," he said with a calculated shake of his head: part worry, part shock. "Just got here myself."

She turned back to watch the growing flames, her hand rising to cover her mouth. "Such a waste," she murmured.

Colt bit his cheek to keep from grinning. "Terrible," he agreed. "Absolutely terrible."

CHAPTER NINETEEN

Beyond the bedroom window, flames rose like a bonfire into the sky, the fire truck's siren a constant scream. Lou and Rich dressed in horrified silence, and when Rich headed to the car, Lou followed. They drove halfway to the hotel, but could get no further. Rich parked the car and shoved the door open, sliding out to head past the roadblock into the crowd.

"Rich!" Lou shouted. "What are you doing?"

He didn't turn back. Lou climbed over the gear shift and settled into the still-warm seat. She eased the vehicle up to the curb, parked, then followed.

Rich had already disappeared.

The streets surrounding the Whitewater looked like a war zone. Shattered glass was strewn across the sidewalk; ashen-faced people stood sobbing. Others, smeared with soot and blood, wandered in a daze. The closest hospital was forty minutes away, so a triage unit had been set up on the front lawn of a cottage. People lay across picnic blankets, paper towelling and tea towels pressed against lacerations. A gloved man wearing plaid pyjama bottoms and a bright "I'd Rather Be Fishing" t-shirt was taping a wound on the forehead of a small girl.

"Lou?" a familiar voice called. "You alright?"

Hunter stood on the sidewalk, his arm over Margaret's shoulders, Colton a few paces away. Audrika stood next to the trio, her hands pressed to her mouth. They weren't the only locals there. Grant McNealy and Sam Barton were part of the growing crowd. Sam was hissing at Grant, but his words were too faint to make out. Susan Varley stood by herself, whey-faced and silent as the building burned.

"Lou, are you alright?" Hunter asked again.

Murray joined Hunter and Margaret on the sidewalk. Siobhan Andler came out of the crowd, stopping next to Grant and Sam. The two men stopped speaking as she approached.

"I'm fine," Lou said. "You seen Rich anywhere?"

Hunter pointed up the road. "Saw him heading to the parking lot. The police were having trouble getting a head count on White-water staff."

Lou scanned the street. The east wing was now completely engulfed in flames, great billows of smoke rising into the air as the inferno spread to the main lodge. The volunteer fire force was unable to do much other than keep people out of the way and prevent the fire from spreading to the nearby cabins. Crews from Cardston and Pincher Creek were on their way, but they would be too late to make a difference. The Whitewater Lodge was already lost.

The horror overwhelmed her for a moment, and suddenly the dream was there, too. *The hemp rope tore through her hand as the ox thrashed in the driving rain ...* A sound like a gunshot echoed from the interior of the building, and the crowd gasped. Lou's head bobbed up in shock, the memory reversing. The west wing and main lodge were still semi-intact, but the east wing looked like a bomb had been detonated inside it. A large portion of the wall slumped inward and great tongues of flames licked their way up the exposed beams to the roof.

"Step back to the barricades!" Constable Black Plume shouted on a megaphone. "We need everyone to step BACK from the building!"

The staff of the Whitewater Lodge stood in the far parking lot, wide-eyed and stunned. Some were holding one another, weeping, some sat silent and weary. A young man holding a pool cue wove through the crowd, calling out for someone. Others stared, open-mouthed, at the entrance to the dying hotel.

That's where she saw Rich.

He was arguing with Walter Phillips, the fire chief, Rich's arms gesticulating wildly. As Lou watched, Rich tore away, sprinting toward the main doors.

"No!" Lou screamed. She pushed her way through the crowd, catching up to Rich at the same time two firefighters did. Walt and another man each grabbed an arm, and Rich hung between them, roaring. He thrashed madly, his panic palpable.

"You CAN'T go back in!" Walt bellowed. "That section's gonna come down too!"

The air was a wall of heat. Rich screamed incoherently. He lunged, and Lou's mind flashed to the tugging dog in the yard, jerking against her arm.

She stepped in front of him, blocking his view of the hotel. "You need to stop!" she cried. "You can't go in. You'll die."

"Let me GO!"

Behind Lou, the remaining windows shattered with a silvery sound, bits of glass peppering the back of Lou's pants. The heat intensified, the skin on her arms crawling.

"Hold him!" Walt ordered. They tugged Rich backward, his legs coming out from under him.

"You know this guy?" the other firefighter snarled.

Lou nodded as they dragged Rich to the lawn with the other wounded. He slumped to the ground. Somewhere far in the distance, faint sirens could be heard. The other fire teams were arriving from Cardston and Pincher Creek.

Rich gasped in great heaving breaths. She crouched next to him, her arms wrapping his shoulders. She wasn't sure how she was supposed to stop him if he tried to get away, but she'd try.

"I need to get inside," he wailed.

"Shh..." she whispered, tightening her grip, "it's only stuff, Rich. It can be replaced."

He began choking again, the tears wetting her neck. "No..." he croaked. "I can't find Amanda Sloane."

* * *

Hours later, Constables Flagstone and Black Plume stood in the shadows of the pine trees, conducting interviews of the hotel staff and witnesses. It was just past ten, and the hotel's former glory was reduced to a smouldering pile of ruins. Blackened beams reached up into the morning light like praying hands, a snowfall of ashes blanketing everything.

Jim knew he should be listening to Sadie's questions as she pulled aside yet another staff member to interview, but after so many hours on his feet, he could barely think. The sight of the devastation left him sick to his stomach; the town was broken. He glared out at the crowd that lingered. *A goddamned sideshow,* Jim thought, *for everyone to watch.*

Despite the hour, the streets were busy with curious sightseers and for the first time since being called to the fire, Jim had time to notice just how many there were. They milled at the edge of the police tape, jostling for position. The arson squad from the Leth-

bridge police force had arrived just after dawn to assist Jim and Sadie with the investigation. The team had located a woman's body in
the basement, the charred remains hidden under melted platters
and downed beams. Jim watched them bring her out, shrouded in
a body bag. The discovery changed things: the fire had taken on a
sinister tone.

A young woman was called forward, and Jim wobbled in place,
exhaustion threatening to topple him.

"Please state your name," Sadie said.

"Grace. Grace Blessington."

"What did you see tonight?"

Sadie's words were a dulled hum in Jim's ears, other words and
other people drawing his attention. He blinked gritty eyes. A few
yards away, a young couple clung together. "My god," the woman
sobbed. "I just saw her yesterday."

The young man patted her back. "She was going to come play
pool with us after work. Never showed."

Jim swallowed against the stone in his throat. At his side, Sadie's
interview continued: "And how exactly do you know Mr. Evans?"

"I don't know him personally, not really, but I thought I should
mention..."

Behind Jim, a siren flicked on and a police car neared. He turned
to follow its passage, catching Sadie's eye as he did. She scowled in
unspoken frustration, and Jim grimaced. He ran a hand over bleary
eyes, bringing his attention back to the woman standing in front
of Sadie. She had a Prince of Wales Hotel name tag on her white
blouse and she twirled a strand of her auburn hair around her finger
as she talked.

"I, um ... maybe I shouldn't say anything," she said anxiously.

"If you think it's relevant," Sadie urged, "then we need to hear it."

The young woman shifted uneasily, her fingers twisting tighter. Jim forced himself to listen, but there were too many things going on. The flashing lights. Blue smoke rising in the air. The dirty-looking man at the barricade, two steps closer than he really ought to be.

"I, um ... I just ... it was something I heard," the woman said.

"Go on," prompted Sadie.

"Well, I work at the Prince of Wales in the dining room," she said, her voice dropping low, "and the manager of Whitewater..." She paused, her eyes darting uneasily through the crowd before coming back to them. "Mr. Evans, that is. Well, he and his girlfriend were having dinner the other night and he said something strange."

Jim's gaze caught on a man in the crowd. His leather jacket with the painted skull and silver studding was out of place, but it was his expression that demanded Jim's attention. He was rapt with interest, a cunning smile on his pockmarked face. *Listening in,* Jim thought. *Trying to get close enough to hear what the girl's saying.*

"What did Mr. Evans say?" Sadie prompted. "What were his exact words?"

The man took another step closer to the barricade and Jim's pulse jumped up a notch. The man's hands were loose at his side, but there was a bulge in the right hand pocket. *A concealed weapon!*

"Mr. Evans said it'd be easier to raze the hotel to the ground and start over," Grace answered.

"Interesting," Sadie murmured.

The man on the other side of the barricade smiled with yellowed teeth, and Jim marched forward, clearing his throat.

"You need something, sir?" Jim asked loudly.

The man stepped back. "Just passing through," he mumbled, as two people stepped into his place. "I'll just be on my way." He started walking away.

"Jim?" Sadie called.

"That guy there," Jim said, moving toward the barricade. "The one in the leather jacket. He was listening in." The man melted back into the crowd, other people blocking Jim's view.

"Where is he?" Sadie asked.

Jim jogged forward, searching the mob. For a moment, the man appeared. "You there, in the leather jacket!" he shouted. "You need to STOP!"

The man's gaze flickered back. He held Jim's eyes for a split second, then bolted. The crowd between the two men had thickened into a knot and Jim struggled to get past. "Out of the way!" Jim roared, his sight-lines blocked by the growing numbers of voyeurs. "Move back! Move BACK!"

The crowd parted, but the man was already gone.

*　*　*

Rich walked, shell-shocked, around the remains of the Whitewater Lodge. He'd spent most of the morning on the phone with his boss, Prischka Archer, from Coldcreek Enterprises. Two hours ago, Amanda Sloane's burned body had been pulled from the rubble. This wasn't *just* an accident. Rich paused in front of what had been the main entrance. He could remember walking in the doors in the spring, his feet icy with slush. Amanda had been sitting behind the desk. *"We were told you'd be in tomorrow morning ... I didn't realize flights came into Lethbridge this late."* Her voice returned and sudden tears blurred his eyes.

Rich took a choking breath as he stared out over the empty husk of the once-proud building. Only the uneven rockwork of the fireplaces remained.

"Mr. Evans," a woman called. "A moment of your time."

He turned unsteadily. Hunter was walking three of his dogs past, while Audrika held court on the lawn across the street, a bevy of her friends listening as she regaled them with the night's events. It made him want to scream. They would be celebrating his failure. Revelling in it.

"Mr. Evans?"

He looked back the other way, finding Constable Black Plume standing at his side.

"Sorry, what?"

Her expression was a neutral mask, indifferent to the chaos. "We need you to come into the station with us, Mr. Evans."

"For what?" He had been awake too many hours in a row, and nothing made sense.

"We need an official statement from you," she said evenly.

"But I ... I was off work. I was out with Lou and—"

"Mr. Evans," she interrupted. "Under the Charter of Rights and Freedoms, I need to advise you that anything you say to me can be used against you in a court of law. You should seek legal counsel at this point. If you cannot afford legal counsel, legal counsel will be provided for you."

"Wh-what's going on?" Rich stammered. "Am I under arrest?"

"Not yet, Mr. Evans, but that's certainly a possibility." She pointed to the police cars that now filled the Whitewater's lot. "I need you to come in and make a statement. You'll be talking with Captain Nelson. If there are charges or a summons, he'll let you know."

"Captain who?"

"Captain Steve Nelson from the Lethbridge Arson squad," she said grimly. "In light of the incidents at the hotel this summer and the discovery of Miss Sloane's body this morning, the Lethbridge Police Force is treating Miss Sloane's death as suspicious."

"Lethbridge Police Force? I don't—" He shook his head, struggling to clear it. "Wh-what's happening?"

Constable Black Plume put a gentle hand on his arm. "Mr. Evans," she said in a grim voice. "Call a lawyer. If you are charged, it will be for arson causing death."

* * *

Constable Flagstone stood outside the interview room, his attention on the two men behind the glass. Captain Steven Nelson was reading through the official statement he'd drawn up based on Rich Evans' interview. It was one of many they'd taken today. As Jim watched, Nelson pushed the paper and a pen toward the other man. Evans' lawyer had joined them from New York via conference call and Rich muttered something into the receiver, then picked up a pen and signed the bottom of the statement.

The two men stood up from the table and shook hands just as Jim headed to the back office. Lacking solid evidence, no arson charges had been laid, but Rich Evans had been given an appearance notice for an upcoming preliminary hearing. If there were charges, it would happen at that point, but for now he was free to go.

In the last hours, the crime investigation billboard had taken on a new layer of gruesome images. A black shape was curled into a half-C. Jim knew it was Amanda Sloane, but it was easier to pretend it wasn't. There were other photographs too: the hotel in flames, dazed people, the rubble of the aftermath. Now they just had to figure out who'd done it.

Behind him, the door to the interview room opened. "Call if you remember anything else, Mr. Evans," Nelson's voice wafted forward. "And don't leave town for now. We'll likely be in contact again." Jim hid a smile behind his hand. Fancy lawyer or not, Evans wasn't getting any special treatment.

"I'll do that, Captain," Rich said, his footsteps receding.

Captain Nelson had spoken to Rich Evans for over an hour. It seemed clear Rich had been nowhere near the hotel for most the night. *Not that it means he wasn't involved,* Jim's mind argued. Rich's story was conveniently corroborated by Louise Newman. Her interview had taken place earlier, no lawyer requested, all questions answered in full.

Rich hadn't been nearly as forthcoming.

His lawyer, via telephone, had refused to allow him to discuss anything until the preliminary hearing occurred. Each of Nelson's questions regarding the Prince of Wales hotel conversation had been a dead end. Jim peered at a photograph showing the east wing of the Whitewater. The image showed a gaping hole marring the side of the building, fire tearing through it the way a flame from a match ate through paper. Rich's refusal to discuss the "raze it to the ground" comment made him seem guilty, even if he wasn't.

The case was now being overseen by the Lethbridge Police force, but Jim and Sadie were part of the main investigation. Though Nelson's investigation was firmly fixed on Rich Evans, Jim and Sadie had been given the task of generating another list of potential suspects, backup in case Nelson's suspicions proved unfounded. Many locals would benefit by the Whitewater's destruction; each of them was now on the list.

The prints from the original break-in were connected to the unsolved murders, and it seemed that this new crime might be related, too. The arson squad had found evidence that the valves to the gas lines had been tampered with prior to the fire. Footage from the closed-circuit security cameras had been destroyed by the intense heat, but the parent company had been able to relay the technical data from the security system computers. Three fire alarms had been pulled minutes before the building went up in flames.

"So why would a killer want to bring down an entire hotel?" Jim said. "Why burn it to the ground?"

Sadie looked up from her desk. "To hide his tracks," she said. "The Aspen Suite case hadn't been solved. Maybe we were closer than we thought."

"Maybe," Jim said, scratching his chin. "But it still doesn't make sense why he'd clear out the hotel beforehand."

"Unless he was just trying to destroy the hotel, not kill someone."

"So we've got a killer with conscience?" Jim snorted. "Likely story."

"Or he had his own reasons." Sadie gestured to the pictures of the crime scene. Several included blurry images of the crowds that surrounded the building. "There was that guy in the crowd when we were talking to witnesses," Sadie said. "No one got any pictures of him. I already looked."

"Yeah, I remember. Seemed a little too interested in what we were doing." Jim tapped the list with his forefinger. "He took off."

"Exactly," Sadie agreed. "No reason to do that unless he was up to something he didn't want us knowing about. I've got to file these statements, but if you've got a minute, do you mind seeing if you can scrounge something up?"

Jim was already halfway to the door. "We've got an hour before Nelson's meeting," he said. "I'll talk to the locals. See if they remember the guy." Jim grinned. "Hunter Slate seems to know everyone."

* * *

Exhausted, Rich staggered down the sidewalk to the manager's cottage. After almost two days awake, he needed a shower and a shave and at least a few hours of sleep. Twice he'd pulled out his cell phone before remembering that there was no reception in town. The police station had allowed him to use their phone to contact his lawyer for the conference call, and for that he was grateful. Stu Calaghan might charge five hundred dollars an hour, but he was well worth it in a situation like this. An appearance notice wasn't the same as being charged with arson, but it was a hell of a lot closer than he liked.

Rich grimaced as he neared the manager's cabin. The sidewalk in front of his house was teeming with people, white vans from a variety of different television channels cluttering the street. Rich slowed, catching sight of reporters in the unfenced yard. Some were filming; others were clearly waiting for an opportunity to begin.

"Oh, for Chrissake." He turned to head back the way he'd come.

Rich had left his car keys behind when he'd taken off last night, so he couldn't drive. He didn't have his wallet, so he couldn't very well get a hotel room somewhere else. With a sigh of defeat, he turned toward Windflower Avenue.

Maybe Lou would help.

*　*　*

Cell phones were Seth's usual approach, but with no reception in Waterton, he'd been forced to contact the main office in Seattle on a landline.

"Did you take Calhoun out yet?" Dax asked, his voice buzzing hollowly through the receiver.

"Not yet," Seth said. "But I will."

"Don't wait too long; I want him dead."

There was ice in Dax's words, an anger that only Seth and a few of Dax's closest advisors truly understood. Seth remembered when the first hints of trouble had begun. Everyone, including Dax, had assumed it was just a mess up on the Canadian side of the border. It had happened last year when the town had been overrun with contractors. But construction teams, and the chaos they brought, were a tiny matter in comparison to the murders that had made the tiny border town front page news this summer. The infamy had brought the drug transport pipeline to a grinding halt in a matter of weeks.

"I know you do," Seth said, "but I gotta wait for the right moment. Can't rush into this. Calhoun's too smart." He pushed the hotel's curtains aside, peering nervously past cottonwood branches heavy with flossy seed pods. Waterton's Main Street was eerily silent, but sirens could be heard in the distance. "The police are all over this fucking place."

"This about that Sorenson kid?"

"Nothing to do with him," Seth replied. "Far as anyone knows, Lucas was killed in a bar brawl. Don't even think the police are looking into it."

"Then what's the holdup? Calhoun kill someone else I should know about?"

Dax's words were scathing. No one messed with the cartel and lived to talk about it. Colton wouldn't either. Three mules had disappeared this summer; no explanation, just gone. Colton claimed he wanted the border open, but this summer had proven him a liar. There was something else behind his actions—greed, stupidity, or plain old insanity—it didn't really matter. Colt was a danger to everyone's livelihood and he needed to be stopped.

"Not sure what happened exactly," Seth said. "There was a fire at that big hotel last night. Some girl died."

"The Whitewater?" Dax scoffed. "That's got to be Calhoun."

The previous summer, Calhoun had expanded the transport of drugs into the Whitewater's trucking system: moving more product faster. But he'd lost his connection a few months ago, and the pipeline had abruptly stopped. Seth knew he was frustrated, but burning the entire place down seemed an extreme measure, even for him.

"Coulda been Calhoun," Seth said. "Not sure." An ambulance trundled slowly up the street and Seth let the curtain drop. "Tried to get close enough to the police to find out, but I think I spooked 'em."

"You what?!"

Seth cringed. "I was just checking things out, but one of the cops saw me. No one knows it was—"

"You stupid fuck!" Dax bellowed. "You know what you're there to do! Get rid of him! Do it now!"

Seth's fingers tightened around the receiver. "I know how to do my job," he said stiffly. "I'm just covering my bases." The cartel was a giant machine; each person, each connection, a small part of a bigger whole. Every once in a while, one of the cogs in the mechanism slipped out of place and Seth's task was to put them back in order. It was about balance, but it was also about being smart.

"He's taken out three of our top guys and one of his own," Dax snapped. "This isn't someone to screw around with!"

"But I thought you told me to be—"

"Don't think! Just get it done!" Dax interrupted. "Calhoun can't be trusted. You know what he did to his partner in Yellowstone. That was what he did *last time* someone messed around with him … and that'll be us if you don't stop pissing around and kill him!"

Everyone in Dax's circle knew Colton Calhoun had been a cartel guide for years, travelling the high Rocky Mountain trails that few knew, and fewer still followed. The rumour was that he'd taken his last post by force, but no one knew for sure. This summer's events hinted that the same thing was underway. Seth's job was to stop the coup before it happened.

"Fine," Seth grumbled. "I'll kill him tonight."

CHAPTER TWENTY

Jim stood at the counter of Hunter's Coffee Shop. "So d'you remember the guy?" he asked. "Average height, dark hair and eyes. Long-haired. Was wearing a leather jacket with a skull on the back. Looked like a biker."

Hunter's gaze drifted to the customers lingering at the back table. "Not sure," he said warily. "Can I ask what this is all about?"

Jim eased nearer. "There were a few people around the Whitewater Lodge when it burned," he said in a low voice. "Most of 'em are already on our interview list, but there were a few new faces." He raised an eyebrow. "This guy was one of 'em."

Hunter wiped his hands on a towel. "Ah ... that makes sense."

"So do you know him?" Jim asked.

"I don't, but I've seen him around."

"Where?"

Hunter shrugged. "In town. In the restaurant the other day." He cleared his throat. "And at the fire, like you said."

"Any idea who the guy is?"

Hunter lifted the coffee pot, preparing to do another round. "No idea," he said without holding the officer's gaze. "But I'll call you if I see him again."

Jim frowned as Hunter walked away. "You do that."

* * *

Colton was grooming the horses when he first sensed something was wrong. It wasn't a concern he could put into words, just a feeling of unease. There was a hush to the stables, a heavy silence that hadn't been there an hour before. The horse nearest him whickered nervously, and he ran a steadying hand up her neck.

"Easy there," Colt murmured. "Easy."

The mare settled and he went back to currying her, his arms moving in relentless circles, silent and meditative. Before he finished, he checked her legs and hooves. Colt couldn't risk a horse throwing a shoe while he was on the trail. The drug smuggling business required reliable horses to get the product into town, where the transport system took over, moving the product out via the delivery trucks of respectable businesses. *Trojan horses,* Colt thought smugly. That was the trick: move your product with legitimate means, in trucks where no one would think to look. He smiled to himself, the brush slowing.

At least that had been the usual plan.

This summer had wrought changes upon the town, and to Colton. Some he'd expected. Some he hadn't. His hand stilled atop the brush, lids growing heavy. The killing had been an ... *unexpected shift,* but not a bad one. Not really. He'd killed before, but it had always been in the heat of the moment. Killing to take charge. Killing to fend off intruders. Killing to protect. But this summer he'd allowed himself to indulge in a secret joy, one he'd spent his entire life trying to shove away.

Guilt rose in his chest and he opened his eyes, the motion of the brush restarting. *It's only people who won't be missed,* the dark voice of his mind argued. *Not anyone who matters.* Even now, standing in the warmth of the barn with the faint smell of manure and horseflesh, he knew that wasn't entirely true, but he let himself believe it anyhow. The other choice was too disturbing to consider.

The horse bobbed her head, drawing him from his reverie, and Colt finished the last few strokes. Today had been a good day in a string of them. He'd brought in the last shipment from the border and cached it deep in the mountains. Now he had everything he needed to start anew. *Except for the new transport connections,* he thought. *Got to work on that part.* Vehicles were the last link in his expanded operation. The remaining Waterton businesses were too small to have their own fleet like the Whitewater did; Hunter and the others only brought in supplies a few times a season and Colt's business had outgrown them. But there was always another way. Someone would build in Waterton eventually. Someone would come to him for help. And when they did, he'd be ready.

Until then, he'd focus his attention on the other players.

Colt had a trip to the States planned for the last week in August. "A bit of time off," he'd told Hunter and the rest of the coffee crowd yesterday. "Just need to get out of town for a while." (He'd said the same thing in '92, and they'd believed it then too.) Colt's upcoming trip would knock the final player from the board.

Outside the wind rattled the door of the barn and the horse danced uneasily. Colton patted her neck, his mind lost in dark, unnatural thoughts. He could already imagine the slippery warmth of blood on his hands, the copper tang in his nostrils. It left him smiling in anticipation.

Dax would be next.

* * *

Lou was closing up the garage when she felt the first twinge that Rich was coming back. It was an itch at the back of her mind, a subtle brush of his thoughts through hers. She dawdled, offering to wash the floors for Brendan so that he could go home early, the steady swish of the mop calming her. As expected, there was a tap on the glass window just after nine. Lou lifted her gaze to see Rich waiting outside in the darkness. Treetops bobbed and swirled behind him, a storm brewing in the dark sky. Rich's hands were shoved deep in his pockets, his clothes marked with ashes.

"I'm sorry I took off on you after the fire," Rich said when she unlocked the door. "I just ... I wasn't thinking."

"It's okay," she said. "Everyone's had a shitty day."

"That's an understatement."

Lou nodded, setting the mop aside and moving into his arms. She rested her face against his chest, letting herself be comforted. Rich smelled of smoke, his clothing stiff under her fingers. For a moment, the vision of the burning fields flickered to mind, but she pushed it aside. She didn't want to think of that. Rich was here, and he was real.

"There are reporters camped out around my house," Rich said. "The hotel's gone, and I ... I can't go home." His voice faded, his hands running over her hair and shoulders.

Lou lifted her chin. Rich's eyes were red-rimmed, wrinkles she'd never noticed before marring the corners. The confident man she'd first met was gone, an older version of himself trapped in the lines of his face.

"You okay?" she asked.

"They're investigating me. They— they think I— I—"

Lou's fingers tightened in his jacket. "What?"

"They think I burned down the lodge," he choked. "I got a sum-mons to attend a preliminary hearing. That's when they'll decide if they're going to charge me." His voice broke. "If there's enough evidence to go to trial."

"Oh, Rich. I'm so sorry."

"I— I didn't know where else to go," he said brokenly. "Everything's gone, Lou. It's all just ... gone."

Lou smiled, feeling a prickle of tears at his words.

"I'm glad you came to me."

* * *

By the time Colton left the barn, the wind had risen into northerly gusts which whipped past the ragged mountain peaks to suck the heat of the day away. Lower Waterton Lake, visible in the distance, was capped with white-horses. A storm was coming. The mare's nervousness made sense.

The cabin was a short walk from the stables, but heading into the brewing storm, it felt longer. The wind bellowed and jerked the door against Colt's hand as he opened it, banging his knuckles before he could get inside. He slid off one arm of his coat and lifted his head in surprise.

His dog wasn't there to greet him.

Heart pounding, Colt let go of his jacket and reached for the sheath at his hip, fingers wrapping around the hilt of his knife.

"Don't move," a voice from the darkness ordered.

Colt froze, his pulse redoubling. There was someone waiting in the shadows, but he couldn't see where. Colt squinted, seeking out the familiar shapes of the couch and rabbit-eared television, the mound of the recliner visible in the wash of moonlight. A second passed and another as he waited for a shot that never came. He might not be able to see, but if that was true, neither could the man waiting in the dark. Hope bubbled beneath Colt's panic.

He took a hesitant step to the left.

"You've caused a bit of a problem this summer," the voice in the shadows growled. "Three good men, all gone. Stupid, that." The shadow laughed coldly. "Dax wasn't sure it was you, 'til that Sorenson kid got killed. Then he knew you were behind it."

Colt didn't answer. He inched sideways, his gaze on the murky nest where he was almost certain the hired gun waited. If he could get out of his range, then he had a chance. Waiting in place was death.

"Dax wants the border open again. That can't happen with his boys showing up in pieces," the voice continued. "He wants it nice and quiet. Ready for deliveries."

Colt's mouth twisted bitterly. He'd done what he had to do. No one stole from him. Not even Dax. Whether or not he took pride in it—*enjoyed* it even—wasn't really the issue. These men weren't like him. They were criminals, each and every one. He smiled at the rush of memory, crimson and bloody; Colt had done the world a favour by killing them.

"Dax knows what you did, boy. What you've done before. This isn't some backwoods smuggling op you're dealing with. The cartel's international. Bigger than Dax and his men. Hell of a lot bigger than one little man with a grudge."

Colt took another sliding step, avoiding the places on the hardwood floor that squeaked. This wasn't the first alliance he had broken, and it wouldn't be his last. He'd been a carrier long before he'd taken the reins of Borderline. And with each link he severed from the chain, he was a little closer to having control of the entire area.

"You don't bite the hand that feeds you ... and you don't just walk away either. You can't."

Colt's fingers tightened on the hilt of the knife. He just needed to survive long enough to deal with the fallout. Then he'd bring down his own vengeance. Blood would flow.

Leather squeaked as the man moved. "Turn on the lights," the voice ordered. The man shifted in place. Now Colt knew with certainty where he was. Four steps away, at most five. With the knife in hand, the darkness became Colt's weapon, one he'd used many times before.

One step took him to the sideboard.

"Calhoun? What the hell are you doing?"

Another step onto the rug.

"Calhoun?"

Two more, and he was at the man's side.

"Turn on the fucking lights!" the man growled. "I know you're in here!"

There wasn't time to think about his reaction, Colt just *did*. In a rush, he attacked. There was a flash of light as the gun went off. *Seth*, Colt thought absently. A flare of pain spread through his ribs. He slashed blindly, across the throat like a hunter with a deer—*another explosive flash*—and then down into Seth's gut. The two men fell to the floor, caught together; predator and prey. The gun went off a third time, though it was strangely quiet in Colton's ears. This time, a shower of plaster sprinkled down on them. Seth flailed as Colt knocked the weapon to the side, the gun clattering across the floor.

Climbing on top of him, Colt stabbed Seth again. He jerked the knife upward until he felt the muscle give and the wet slipperiness of intestines release over his hands. The warmth brought a rush of pleasure. Seth jerked like a fish on a line, struggling to get away. Colt's ears were ringing, the sound of Seth's screams muffled and indistinct, but the excitement had arrived. *The ecstasy; the high!*

Colt staggered sideways, holding the wound in his side, and turned on the lights. The room appeared in an explosion of light and colour. Seth lay gasping on the floor. His belly was a mass of snakes, purple and knotted where they tumbled onto his legs.

"You bastard," Colt said coldly. "You think you can come into my town and push me out?" He wiped bloodied hands on his shirt, grimacing at the spreading pool on the floor. This wasn't how he liked to do it. He liked killing in the woods. *Clean.* The way a hunter took down an animal. No mess. No remains. Only the purity of action and release. Hunter and hunted, perfectly balanced. "I control the border here," Colt said darkly. "No one but me! And Dax better fucking learn that!"

Seth took a gurgling breath. His mouth was full of frothy red bubbles; a trickle of crimson drew a line from the side of his mouth to his ear. "Someone knows about Borderline," Seth croaked.

Colton leaned forward, lip twisting in an angry sneer. "No one knows about Borderline! No one has any—"

"Someone does." Seth smiled with bloody teeth. "You're fucked."

Colt felt his body still, the anger shifting into uncertainty. "How?"

"Leases," Seth choked. "Dax said—" He fell into a fit of coughing. "Lawyers are checking..."

Colt grabbed his shoulders. "Who found the leases?" he barked. "Who!"

"Fuck ... you," Seth wheezed, his eyes rolling.

"Tell me!" Colt shook Seth harder, but the other man's body was limp and heavy. Seth choked wetly, blood pouring from his open mouth. "Goddammit, you tell me who!" Colt roared.

Seth's hand fell to the side. His lids were half-closed, tongue protruding from bluish lips as his chest rattled and went still.

Colt loomed over him, breathing in ragged gulps. Adrenaline coursed through his limbs, the urge to run fighting with the urge to stay. He needed to think things through. Needed to think rationally. He had covered his bases! Every person who rented from him owed him something: money, drugs, or illegal favours. Colt's connections were everywhere: from Susan Varley, who'd first tipped him off to Rich Evans' plans for modernizing Waterton, to the numerous business owners Colt had saved from bankruptcy in the 90s and whose holdings in Borderline Industries gave him the cover to launder his drug money, to the dealer who'd killed Lucas Sorenson on Colt's command. Even Jeff Chan had been part of the empire. He'd borrowed money from Borderline last summer, long before he'd known who Colt was. The cash was a bargain deal for easy access to the Whitewater Lodge's transport trucks, and a way to move the drugs out of the Park. And when Chan had refused to pay, Colt had taken a stand. One dead hitchhiker—easily disposed of in the woods—and a message left in the Aspen Suite of the still-unfinished hotel.

Keep up your end of the bargain or "GET OUT."

Even if any of the people in Waterton suspected Colton might be the killer, they'd never tell. Every local in town, every friend he'd made, had their own dark secrets and would cover for him to the bitter end, because he knew *their* secrets too. Waterton was the perfect hiding place because everyone here had something they wanted to hide. There was no way someone would bring their suspicions to the police. No way he'd be betrayed, unless ... The realization was a muzzle flare, lighting the darkness.

Unless the person who'd found the leases was Rich Evans himself.

With a roar of frustration, Colton grabbed the gun from the floor and headed into the night.

* * *

Rich slept until midnight in Lou's bed, coming awake in a rush of panic. *The fire!* With that thought, the last hours came back, leaving his heart pounding. He lay in the darkness watching the minutes crawl by on the clock. There were too many things on his mind to let him fall back to sleep. *"A preliminary hearing isn't a trial,"* Stu Calaghan, his lawyer, had explained. *"It's to see if there's enough evidence to follow through with a trail. You'll be fine, Rich. Just fine."* But in the darkness, that assurance felt like an empty promise. Too many uncertainties hung in the balance. A sleepless half hour later, he finally crept from Lou's side, dressing in the dark.

The bedroom door creaked as he opened it and Lou stirred. "You're leaving?" she asked, her voice husky from sleep.

Rich's heart tightened at the disappointment in her voice. He came back to the bedside, his hand cupping her cheek. "I need to get back to the manager's cabin before the reporters do," he whispered. "There are papers there. I need to contact Coldcreek in New York. Give them an update."

She turned into the hollow of his hand, her breath warm against his palm. "You want me to come along?"

"No, you stay here and sleep," Rich said. "I'll catch up with you in the morning."

Lou's lashes fluttered against his fingers. "Love you, Rich."

He leaned in, kissing her gently, his chest tight with emotion. "Love you, too." He'd said the words before, but they'd never meant the same thing as they did when he said them to Lou.

In minutes, Rich was driving down Waterton's empty streets. The entire town felt like a stage devoid of actors, the ruins of Whitewater ghostly in the moonlight. For a second, Amanda's laughing face shimmered to mind, and Rich turned his gaze away. Forcing the thoughts aside, Rich sped down the last half-block to his cabin.

He never saw the figure waiting for him in the shadows.

* * *

Lou stood in the mud of a rural road, the rain sluicing in heavy sheets around her. She lifted her gaze, only to catch sight of another

monk standing across from her. At their feet, a heaving ox laboured in
the knee-deep mud, eyes rolling in anger and fear. The rope in Lou's
hand began to slide, and her fingers clutched reflexively at it.

"Keep it steady!" the other monk shouted. "Pull harder!"

His voice was unexpectedly familiar, and Lou squinted against the
rain, catching the other monk's eyes.

'Rich...?'—

With a jolt, the image receded, leaving Lou gasping for breath,
entangled by the linens on the bed. Panicked, she kicked the sheets
away, fumbling for the light. The vision waited in the depths of the
familiar bedroom, the smell of mud and sweat and blood sharp in
her nostrils. Groping blindly, she located the switch and clicked it
on. The shadows peeled back.

The wallpaper and framed photographs were just as they'd been
when she'd fallen asleep, her sturdy bedroom furniture a sudden
comfort. She took a shaking breath, knowing she wouldn't sleep
again tonight.

"Rich, I had the craziest dream—"

She turned, expecting him to be there, but his side of the bed
was empty. Seeing it, her panic surged. She stumbled out of bed,
rushing to the window. The treetops bounced under an unrelenting
torrent of wind. Rain snapped against the window panes.

Rich left, she realized.

"No, no, no!" Lou cried. The sky beyond was an inky black lit
by a dim scattering of stars. Limbs quaking, she dressed. In minutes she was downstairs, but as she put her hand on the doorknob,
she stopped. Lou headed back to the phone and dialled, waiting
through four rings.

"H'lo?" a sleep-thickened voice answered.

"Hunter," she gasped. "I ... I need your help."

She heard the old man moving around, covers rustling. "Lou? What's going on, hon?"

"I, um..." She frowned, uncertain how to explain. "I think something's wrong."

"Wrong?"

"With Rich."

There was a pause. His voice was cooler when it returned. "What d'you mean?"

She felt her throat contract. This was what she could never explain. Not to Rich, or anyone else. Even her own father had never believed her. "I had a dream," she said in a tight voice. "A dream about Rich. Something bad's going to happen to him, Hunter. I know it."

He coughed in disbelief. "Lou, what in Sam Hill is going on with you and that Evans boy?"

"I'm going to find Rich," she said. "And in case something happens to me, I want you to know I went over to his cabin. Alright? I'm leaving now."

"Lou, wait. You can't just—"

She slammed the receiver down without a goodbye and pushed out the door into the night. Waterton's streetlights were few and far between and she sprinted between them, heart in throat.

For the first time, the town scared her.

* * *

Rich sat at the table, flipping through the last few files he'd unearthed over the summer. It wasn't most of them, or even half—the majority had been submitted to the police weeks earlier—but a scattering remained. Rich thumbed the corner of a deliveries list, with the hand-written 'cc' in the corner. Waste of time. *Never did figure out who Chan was carbon copying,* he thought, shoving it aside. *Now it's too late.*

Twenty minutes later, he was carrying boxes of files into the kitchen when he heard the door handle rattle. Rich smiled to himself, shifting the box into one arm as he checked that the alarm was disengaged. He reached for the doorknob.

"I should get you a key, Lou," Rich said, pulling the door wide. "There's no reason you can't..." His words trailed away.

There was a gun pointed directly at the centre of his chest, Colton Calhoun on the other end of the weapon. In the strange other-sense of waking dreams, a number of details jumped into focus, each one distinct and unsettling: There were two horses standing in his yard. The wind was making the trees rock and sway. And, most confusing of all, Colton held a coil of rope in his free hand.

"What the...?"

The men's eyes met, and in that moment, Rich knew. The 'cc' didn't mean carbon copy at all, but "Colton Calhoun." The one lingering clue Rich had never understood—the numerous delivery trucks scheduled to visit the Whitewater last summer—now made perfect sense. There were twice as many because they were transporting something—*illegal goods?*—out of the Park. Calhoun's trail guiding service was the perfect cover. When Jeff Chan had gotten too close to the truth, the murder in the Aspen Suite had been a warning.

Colton Calhoun was the murderer.

"Turn around and put your hands behind your back," Colt ordered.

Rich dropped the box and lunged behind the barrier of the door, fumbling for the security panel. Colt was faster. With the speed of a snake, Colt slammed his shoulder against the door, the edge of the wood plowing into Rich's temple.

"Lou," Rich mumbled as the darkness overwhelmed him.

CHAPTER TWENTY-ONE

Rich groaned, his headache pulsing in time to his heartbeat. He was on the floor. He knew that, but beyond it, nothing made sense. He rolled sideways and fought the urge to vomit. His mouth was stuffed with a soiled dishcloth, his hands bound behind his back. A shadow passed in front of the light and Rich squinted upward, catching sight of Colton jogging down the stairs, papers in hand.

Rich thrashed futilely, but Colt barely appeared to notice. He dropped the papers into a plastic garbage bag, then headed back up the risers, coming back a minute later with another handful. Rich knew without seeing what Colt carried: it was the remaining documents for the Whitewater investigation. There was no question what Colt had planned; he would destroy the papers and kill Rich, destroying the last of the evidence. *No one will ever know it was him,* Rich thought in growing distress. *Not even Lou!*

Rich went still as Colt came back into the room. He was favouring one side, as if he'd pulled a muscle in his back. Colt shoved the last papers into the bag and tied it tightly. When he headed out the door, Rich began to jerk and pull like a bound calf, struggling desperately against the ropes. The rough fibres cut into his wrists, a trickle of blood drawing a sticky path down his forearm. Colt came back inside, a gust of wind bringing with it the smell of rain. Rich froze as Colton knelt at his side. The man's face was ashen, a splatter of dried blood and a bruise across one cheek.

"I'm going to untie your legs," Colton explained, icily controlled, "and you're going to walk to the horse and I'll help you climb onto its back."

Rich shook his head in denial and Colton's expression darkened. "You *are* going to get on the horse," he said, pulling a blade from his pocket and trailing it across Rich's neck, "or I'm going to slit your throat first, and then put you on the horse. I don't give a damn which way we do this, but you *are* coming with me."

Rich swallowed against another wave of illness, his mouth thick with the musty taste of old washcloth.

"Do you understand what I'm saying?"

Rich nodded slowly.

Colt reached down and started to work the knots. "Should've walked away when you had the chance," Colt muttered. "But you just had to go digging." His forehead was beaded with perspiration, and he worked in short spurts, pausing now and again to press his hand to his side. A growing blood stain marred the jacket under Colt's fingers. He jerked at the knot and Rich winced, stars appearing behind closed lids. "If you'd just let things be I wouldn't—"

The door opened behind the two men, the wind swirling around the room like an uninvited guest. Rich craned his neck sideways in alarm.

"Colt?" Lou gasped, her face ashen. "My God! What are you doing?"

* * *

Colton Calhoun had grown up with Louise Newman. She'd laughed and talked with him, walked Waterton's trails at his side, and turned down his romantic advances any number of times. The sight greeting her just didn't make sense. His eyes were mean and hard, like an animal draped in Colt's form. She blinked, the lathered ox from her dream appearing for half a second, then disappearing just as fast. Rich was tied-up on the floor, thrashing, Colton standing between them.

"Y-you're the killer," Lou stammered.

Colton smiled, the gentle expression unnerving against the backdrop of the attack. "Now, Lou," he said patiently. "This isn't how it looks."

Rich bucked and kicked, fighting against the knots which held him. Lou's attention dropped to him and then back up.

Colt was a step closer.

"Y-you burned the Whitewater," Lou gasped. "You killed those men. It's you. It's always been you!"

"I only did what I had to," Colt said. His voice was warm and inviting, the approach he so often used when talking himself out of trouble. Tonight it left Lou nauseated. "I did what I had to do to protect Waterton. Just doing what *you* do. Keeping care of things in your own way." He moved nearer, halving the difference between them. "Same thing entirely."

Behind her the wind gusted against the window panes, the sound jerking her out of her thoughts. Lou stumbled back, grabbing hold of the doorknob with shaking fingers.

"It's not the same," Lou argued. "Not at all!" She wanted to look at Rich, but didn't dare. Colton was too close now, and she needed to save Rich. "I help people, Colt, no matter who they are. You kill."

Somewhere, Lou heard a dog howling. She swung open the door and lunged out into the night. The wind was a deafening roar, the rain like needles against her face as she sprinted away from the house.

"LOU!" Colt bellowed, following her without a backward look.

The sound of dogs barking was the only thing she could hear over the gusts. Tormented by a summer of tragedy, Waterton was a ghost town. Cabins were boarded up the way they'd be mid-winter.

"Help!" Lou screamed. "Someone, please, HELP!"

No one answered.

She ran without pause, swerving and dodging around parked cars, weaving through backyards. The sound of footsteps grew nearer, the downpour chilling her to the bone.

"HELP!" Lou shouted, but at this time of night, the streets were silent, no stragglers lingered in the shadows. She dashed through the trees. If she could get home, she could phone the police. If she could get to the garage, she could get inside. If she could—

A hand caught her jacket and she fell to the ground, screaming. The sound of barking grew louder. *Someone's walking their dog!* The thought sent Lou into a sudden frenzy.

"Police!" she screamed, the wind dashing her words away. "I'm being attacked! HELP! I'm being—"

Her screams were smothered by Colton's hands around her throat. "Colt, please," she choked. The words disappeared as his fingers tightened. Caught, Lou jerked and twisted, fighting for breath. The light of the street lamps above her seemed to grow in size, the halos expanding as Lou's windpipe contracted under the pressure.

"Just ... stop ... screaming!" Colt grunted.

The lights faded. Seconds passed. Lou felt the warmth of sleep wrapping around her. It'd be so easy to let go, so easy to—

Colt's fingers released and air rushed to her lungs. Rain caught in her throat and Lou turned to the side, gagging. In seconds, Colt had his arm around her neck, the muzzle of a gun pressed against her side.

He dragged her back up to her feet. "Walk!" he ordered.

"Stop, please, Colton, I—"

"Keep walking," he growled. "Stop and I'll shoot."

The two of them moved through the dark band of foliage between the lakeshore and cabins, avoiding the streets. Lou's mind scurried from one thought to another. If she could get away, she had a chance. The police station was only two blocks away; she might be able to make it. Lou tugged sideways but Colt's arm around her throat tightened as he dragged her back onto a path only he could see.

"Where are you taking me?"

The gun bruised her ribs as he jammed it into her side. "Walk!"

There was no patience to this version of Colton, no kindness. It was like a mask had been pulled away from his face, uncovering a monster hidden beneath his friendly façade. She realized she had seen this monster once before, decades earlier, when they'd both been children.

They'd played together all summer, but she only realized what Colton had done when he brought out the length of twine to play with. Louise had seen that piece of rope before, over and over again, in her recurring nightmares.

"You tie this end to your can," Colton said happily. "And then I'll tie the other end to my can, and it'll be a telephone."

He reached out, offering her the dangled end of cord, but she didn't take it.

"You did it," Louise whispered.

"Did what?" Colton asked, an easy grin brightening mischievous features.

"You killed Buddy. Your rabbit."

His smile stayed the same, but his skin paled under his tan. "Don't know what you're talkin' about Louise. Buddy ran away. I told you that."

She shook her head. "That's what you told everyone, but it's not true."

Colt's smile faded into nervousness. "Is too."

"Liar."

Colton's lip began to quiver. "You're crazy, Louise," he said. "Everyone knows it."

"Am not."

"Are too. You're always saying weird stuff." His face darkened angrily.

"Colt, you're my friend but—"

He dropped the twine, standing up and backing away. "Nut-job, nut-job! Nut-job Newman!" he sang.

"Stop it!" Louise cried, following. "I know what you did. I saw you!"

Colton staggered back, his eyes glittering with unshed tears. "I didn't do it," he shouted. "You're wrong! It wasn't me!"

She touched the arm of his jacket but Colton tore out of her grip. "I had a dream," Louise insisted, "a REAL one, Colt. I know what you did!"

"I didn't kill Buddy!" he sobbed. "You've gotta believe me!"

But Louise could see it playing out before her. "You killed him and then got scared. You buried him behind the shed," she said. "He never ran away from you, he never—"

Colt pulled her from the trees onto a narrow path and Lou's memory jumped back to the present. In horror, she realized Colt was guiding her to the docks. The grass and brambles grew thinner as they passed between the wooden walkway and a copse of trees, streetlights appearing up ahead. She could see her garage, but there was no way to get there with the gun pressed to her side. Lou had a moment of frustration. Why hadn't she known it was him? They were friends, but she'd only talked to Colton once or twice this summer, and she *had* dreamed of him, but it had come painted in echoes of another life. With Rich drawing her attention, she hadn't understood what it meant. There was no time to consider it now.

Colton paused as they reached the sidewalk, his breath hot where he panted against her neck. He was almost as winded as she was, and Lou wondered why. Colt was a back-country guide, hiking and horseback-riding each day.

A dog barked and Colton shoved her forward impatiently. "Keep going," he grunted. "Down into the boat."

Lou took a step and slipped on the rain-slick dock. Thunder clapped overhead, and the image of the ox trapped in the mud flashed in the darkness of her mind. *He's trapped and he's scared*, she realized, *and when an animal's scared, it'll do anything to survive.*

"Move it!" he shouted.

"No, Colt. You can't—"

His grip tightened painfully. Beside them, the water beneath the dock's edge loomed, black and swirling. It struck her that if she got into his boat, he'd take her with him and she'd never get back.

"Get into the boat," Colt ordered, "or I'll—"

From behind them came a plaintive howl, the same sound that had terrified Rich the night he'd stayed at her cabin.

"Let her GO!" a voice shouted.

The dog bellowed again, the sound mingling with the keening wind. Lou turned in surprise. A few feet away, Hunter Slate held a rifle at eye level, his wrinkled face chiselled with fury.

"Get away from her," Hunter snarled. "Or I'll shoot you where you stand."

"And hit Lou?" Colton scoffed. "Doubt that."

"You've hunted with me before. You think I'll miss at this range?"

The first wail of a police siren echoed in the distance. Colton's expression rippled, fear appearing for a heartbeat, then twisting into anger. "I've got no issue with you, Hunter. None at all."

Hunter's gentle eyes narrowed. "No, but I've got one with you," he warned. "Now let her go."

Hunter's finger tensed on the trigger and Lou realized he *would* shoot Colt ... that as much as he abhorred violence, he'd do what he had to do.

"Go home," Colt said, lifting his handgun. "Forget you ever saw me."

"Not without Lou."

Lou peeked over her shoulder. Colt's gun was at eye level. Ready.

"No!" she cried. Her heart was a bird trapped in her chest, her breath so fast she could hear it whistle. Someone was going to die tonight, and she couldn't stop it. *Just run!* Her mind screamed out a desperate prayer. *Get away while you can! Run! Run! RUN!*

Sirens filled the air, a ribbon of blue and red appearing at the far end of Main Street. Without warning, Colt shoved Lou away from him and she tumbled forward, knocking Hunter onto the dock. Colt sprinted for the boat. Lou sat up just as an engine sputtered, the hum rising alongside the cry of police sirens. Hunter lay on the dock in the rain, two of his three dogs whining as they danced beside his legs. Lou watched as Colton spun the boat out across the narrows of the bay, swerving back along the lakeshore, heading south.

"Is he gone?" Hunter groaned.

Lou's eyes filled with tears as she helped him to his feet. "Yeah, he's gone."

"Good." Hunter slung an arm over her shoulder. "Just hope the police get here in time."

"Police," she repeated dully. The word didn't make sense.

Hunter nodded to where Colton's boat was moving across the surface of the dark lake. "Called 'em soon as I got off the phone with you."

Lou followed his gaze, peering out at the whitecaps on the water. The storm had settled into the deep 'V' of the mountains, the fury of nature released. A scribbled flash of lightning lit the looming bulk of Vimy Mountain, a deafening thunderclap following half a second later. No sane man would be out on the water tonight. She shivered, remembering Colton as he'd been when they were children. Lou had never fit in, and Colt hadn't either. He'd been an outcast ... different.

Now she knew why.

"Let's hope they catch him before he gets to the end of the lake," Hunter said, leaning heavily against Lou.

"*If* he makes it to the other end," she whispered, not sure why the idea made her want to cry.

* * *

The boat jumped and slapped against the water, riding up the flat plane of each wave and slamming back down on the other side. Colt was cut through by shards of wind, hands numb, but the wind was behind him and that gave him an edge. Nearing the halfway point, he peered over his shoulder, searching for lights. The police weren't out on the water yet, but it wouldn't take them long. Their boat was heavier. That made it steadier in rough weather, but slower.

Colt would reach the end of the lakes, and America, long before them. There, hidden in the ragged underside of a tree stump, he had a backpack full of camping supplies. It wasn't his only backup.

Tucked under the boat's canopy was his last payment from Dax. More importantly, six full backpacks of drugs with a street value of more than a million dollars were hidden deep in the backwoods at six separate locations in Waterton Park. It would take time to retrieve them and build a new network of buyers, dealers and mules, but with time, he'd do it. For now, he'd lay low. It would be a gruelling walk out through Glacier Park, but he'd be safe in Montana long before the police could reach him. The money would get him far from here, and once he was off the radar, he was safe. Borderline was an international company. Colton might lose his cartel connections with this fiasco, but it would only slow him down, and when things had died back down, he'd come back again.

Then Hunter Slate would pay.

Colt smiled grimly as he gunned the engine. The Whitewater Lodge had been a burr under his saddle for months. Rich Evans' arrival and his insistence on modernization had brought with them the risk of increased tourism to Waterton. It was the kind of change that could—*and had*—upset the delicate workings of the border system. A pipeline this extensive only worked when it was in balance; a quiet border town with just enough tourists to keep the few local businesses going. Businesses who were struggling, always on the edge of going under. Owners who had no one else to go to. These connections to Borderline allowed Colton to launder his illegal drug money while the network of transport trucks got his product out of the Park without drawing attention. It was a system as fragile as it was effective, and Rich Evans had undone all of that. That Colt himself had exposed the town to outside attention through his pleasure killings was a furtive whisper at the back of his mind, easily ignored. His teeth gritted as he knocked the throttle into high gear and the hull shuddered. *Those men deserved it,*

Colton thought bitterly. *And others do too...*

It might take another year, but Richard Evans would pay. A thrill of excitement ran through Colt, his lips pulling back in a macabre leer. Colt would give Evans the kind of long, lingering death he was so good at.

Between the roar of the wind and the motor, Colt's ears were filled with sound, even the slap of waves disappearing. Each shudder rocked the boat, but he didn't slow. The whitecaps came at him, line after line. He knew he shouldn't be out in this weather, but as long as he headed straight into them, he wouldn't capsize. *Get out. Get control. Come back.* He'd done it in Yellowstone in '92. He'd do it here, too.

Past the inlet that led to Hell Roaring Falls, the north wind eased. He was almost there, almost safe. The sun was on the horizon behind him, the American border, cut into the tree line, greeting him as he passed over. Colt's hand dropped from the wheel to the throttle just as a gust of warm westerly wind—the chinook so common in the Rockies—whistled down over the peaks and nudged the side of the boat. At any other time, at a lower speed and in better conditions, or with both hands solidly on the wheel, Colt could have handled the shimmy of the boat's trajectory, but he was weak from blood loss and cold, his reactions dulled.

The port side tipped low as the boat came over the other side of the wave, catching the prow in a deep furrow. Before he could brace himself for impact the boat flipped, scattering Colton and fifty thousand dollars in unmarked bills across the water.

* * *

Lou, Rich, and Hunter sat in Lou's kitchen, a steaming pot of tea before them. With Rich's cabin officially a crime scene, the three of them had gathered here to give their statements to the police. Now that Jim and Sadie were gone, they sat quietly, lost in thought. Rich rocked the cup between his hands while Hunter brooded in stony silence. Lou sipped lukewarm tea. *They'll either find Colton or they won't,* she thought gloomily. *And there's no use worrying about it until it happens.* She lowered the cup, her fears rising again. *But if he does come back...*

She glanced over at Rich to find him staring down at his hands. His wrists were wrapped in gauze, but red slashes of abraded skin were visible at the edges. *Maybe it'd be safer if he just left.* Lou's heart contracted at the thought and she looked back to the window. At the low edge of Waterton's bowl where the mountains met the prairies, the sun was a ball balanced on the horizon. Somewhere, out there in the early morning sunshine, Colt was on the run. Caught up in the summer's unrest, Lou hadn't recognized the danger until it was almost too late, but months ago she'd stood in this kitchen and dreamed of the monks on the road, the ox between them. Last night that vision had come to pass. She watched the sun break past the tree line and start its slow rise. Red and gold clouds dissipated under its unwavering glare, the night's tempest fading into late summer splendour.

"Why'd you know to call me?" Hunter asked. His voice was rough with disuse, eyes red-rimmed, weary.

Lou tipped her head, considering her words. She had a lie on her tongue, but the truth fell from her lips instead. "It's like I said: I had a dream," she said quietly. "A *real* one."

Rich looked up at her. "A dream?"

"Yes."

"About what?" Hunter asked.

Lou forced herself not to flinch. It was so simple, yet impossible to say. She looked over at Rich. His face was ravaged, one eye almost swollen shut, and for the first time in many years everything made sense. Lou had always believed she was meant to be alone, but the truth was, she just hadn't met the right person yet.

"It was about Rich," she said tremulously. Hunter took a sharp breath, but her gaze didn't sway from Rich's face. "I knew something was wrong last night. I could feel it."

Rich reached out, wrapping his fingers around hers. Lou half expected him to ask her what she meant, but he said nothing.

"How?" Hunter croaked.

Lou shrugged. "How do we ever really know anything for sure?" she said with a nervous laugh. "I just had a dream—a crazy, crazy dream—and when I woke up, I was certain something was wrong." Her gaze drifted to Hunter. He was staring at her with something akin to fear. This was the reason she couldn't tell anyone. This was why it was easier to lie.

"A dream," Hunter repeated hoarsely.

"When I woke up, I called you and then went to find Rich."

Rich lifted her hands, pressing a kiss against her battered knuckles. "Glad you came," he murmured.

Lou's eyes were trapped by Hunter's distrustful stare. She'd been on the receiving end of this type of judgement many times before, but never from him. She opened her mouth, meaning to soften her admission with a half-truth, but found she couldn't. She was glad she'd gone to Rich, even if it meant exposure.

"I did what I had to do," Lou said.

Hunter's scowl deepened.

"Why did you call the police if you didn't believe me?" she asked.

Hunter stood from the table, pushing the wooden chair back with a squeal. "Had enough of this foolishness." He crossed the room, putting his hand on the doorknob. "Dreams," he grumbled.

"Bunch of New Age nonsense."

Lou's words stopped him. "No, Hunter, I'm serious. If you didn't believe me, then why bother calling the police? Colt was your friend. Why step in the way?"

Hunter didn't move; his hand remained tight around the door handle. "I just..." His words faded and for a long moment the only sound was the sighing breeze outside the windows. When he spoke again, his voice was barely audible. "I called 'em because you were the one in danger, Lou. No other reason. Just you."

And with that, he pushed open the door and walked away.

* * *

The lake was fed by melted snow and glacial runoff, and even mid-summer, the chill of the water was a force unto itself. Colt re-surfaced, sputtering. His body trapped in a cold so deep he could barely breathe or move. Each kick of his legs took concerted effort, his lungs heaving with every gasping breath. *Just get to shore,* his mind chanted. *Get the pack. Start a fire. Get warm.*

If he stopped moving, he'd die.

The waves caught and pushed him along, hands of water rising over him and slapping him down like a toy. Reaching the lakeshore, he stumbled and fell, then stood again. The sun had begun to rise, but it would be another few hours before any heat would come of it. By then, he'd be dead.

The torrential rains had altered the shoreline. Where there'd once been calm beaches and easy walking, mud now thickened the path into mire. Colt staggered forward, tremors coursing through him. Somewhere along the way, he lost one of his boots, but he didn't stop. He could see the path toward his cache, and the tree stump beyond. *Just a little further,* he thought, *and I'll be safe.* He staggered through the tree line, catching himself when he stumbled.

The game trail leading to the cache was treacherously muddy and he slipped and fell a second time, roaring in frustration. He'd grown up in the mountains, but this morning the wilds seemed to be pitting themselves against him, making every step a test.

Sick with cold, Colt reached the exposed roots of the tree, but a small mudslide had dragged a pile of debris down the side of the mountain during the night.

"Goddammit!" he bellowed, staggering forward on unfeeling limbs.

He tugged futilely at the tangle of branches and twigs, searching in desperation for the pack he'd left behind.

"Sh-should be here," he said through chattering teeth.

In his stupor, the forest had begun to change. The sounds were confusing, his eyes blurring in his exhaustion. He tugged another branch out of the way, gasping as a jagged twig poked through the palm of his hand, momentarily catching there. The pain was almost an afterthought, his fingers no longer working effectively. He paused, panting. He was so tired he could barely think. If he could just stay here and rest a while, things would be better. Easier. *Just need a moment to rest,* Colt thought, wobbling on his feet. The broken branch dislodged and he staggered backward, pain bringing him momentarily to his senses. *Need the matches to light a fire. Need to do it fast,* his mind warned. *Hypothermia's starting. Can't stop now!*

With a cry of anger, he launched himself against the tangle of branches, pulling debris out of his way with clumsy hands. Behind him, something large moved in the darkness of the forest, but Colton was too busy searching for the pack to notice. He fell to his knees, working with panicked fervour as he pushed mud and roots aside. Suddenly the hollow beneath the stump appeared. The pack was there!

"Oh, thank god," he cried as he caught hold of the mud-stained canvas. "Just gotta—"

An angry roar cut off the rest of his words.

CHAPTER TWENTY-TWO

The hollow buzz of the phone connection rang in Rich's ear. "I'm sorry, Ms. Archer," Rich stammered. "Could you repeat that? I thought you said—"

"You're being given a severance package," she said tightly. "Given the arson investigation and the destruction of the Whitewater Lodge, your position at Coldcreek Enterprises has been terminated."

Rich's vision swam. "But the Whitewater is going to be rebuilt, isn't it? I mean, you'd need someone to oversee that. You'd need—"

"The Board of Directors decided this yesterday," Prischka interrupted. "Given the hotel's failures for *various* reasons—the murder, the contracting fiasco, the disappearance of Mr. Chan, and this fire in particular—the board felt it was time to cut their losses." She cleared her throat. "The investigation has tied our hands for now, and the board felt that a decision to rebuild would be yet another..." Her words trailed off. "Poor management decision."

Vertigo overtook Rich entirely and he slid down to the floor, blood rushing in his ears. He leaned his head between his knees, cradling the handset against his shoulder. "I ... I'm not sure what to say," he faltered.

He heard Prischka sigh. He could imagine her staring down at him as she had at his interview, ebony-skinned and indomitable, her hijab lending her a queenly presence.

"You say thank you for the opportunity," she snapped. "And then you move on."

Rich took a steadying breath before answering. "Sorry if I don't," he said. "I did *exactly* what was asked. This fire had nothing to do with my abilities."

There was a tense moment.

"Look, Richard, I made this call myself for a reason." The ice in her voice thawed. "You deserved to know why. If it helps, I argued against liquidating, but I wasn't the only one voting. Waterton's a sinking ship, one with too many holes. Satellite issues, building issues ... the whole murder scandal." She sighed. "But the arson investigation was the clincher. For what it's worth, I actually believe you."

"Thanks," he said tiredly. "I appreciate it."

"In case you're wondering, the board consulted your lawyer before we proceeded with the severance package. Mr. Calaghan spoke very impressively on your behalf. So, wait out the investigation and the trial. Get your affairs in order," Prischka said matter-of-factly. "And when this is all over, you can reapply with Coldcreek..." She paused. "...if you want."

Rich glowered. And there it was; the thing that wasn't being said. He was going to be the fall guy for this shit-storm. "I think we both know that I'll never get hired on again."

Prischka cleared her throat. "There are other companies, Richard. I'd be happy to refer you. Now then," she said abruptly. "This call is to give you official notice that we'll be putting the manager's cottage up for sale, and you'll need to vacate the premises as soon as possible."

Rich laughed bitterly. "Just when I thought this week couldn't get any worse."

* * *

The edge of the lake was scattered with debris. Water-soaked bills, bits of paper marked by police tape, and numbered labels appeared in pockets along the gently lapping shore. Sadie and Jim stood at the edge of the tree line, watching the team of police officers and Glacier Park rangers secure the scene.

"They found Colt, or what was left of him, in the trees," Jim said. "The American authorities are looking into his death. Out of our hands for now."

"At least they get stuck with the paperwork," Sadie grumbled.

"Not such a bad thing," Jim laughed.

"Yeah, but we'll have enough of our own."

"Oh?"

"Jordan and the others are tagging the murder scene at Calhoun's cabin," Sadie said. "Hell of a mess in there."

"S'pose that's a fitting ending for the guy," Jim said.

"I guess..."

A technician carried a tray of evidence out of the forest and the two officers fell silent. Jim could make out a jagged shard of bone, nothing else. Sadie scowled and turned away. She kicked at a stone, watching as it rolled into the water.

"You alright, Sadie?" Jim asked, bumping her shoulder.

"Just feels like we should have been able to bring him in," she sighed. "Made him pay for the murders."

Jim shrugged. "Well, he won't do it again and that's more than you can say with some cases."

Sadie shook her head, a wry smile tugging the corners of her mouth. "You ever get tired of looking on the bright side?"

Jim winked. "Not yet, but I'll let you know if I do."

Sadie snorted with laughter just as Grant McNealy emerged from the shadows. With Colton's death on the American side of the border, the criminal investigation was out of Sadie and Jim's hands, but Grant's knowledge of the animals in the area meant he was part of the team of Waterton-Glacier wardens. Seeing him, Jim waved, and Grant headed to their side.

"Any news?" Jim asked.

"The scene's pretty bloody," Grant said. "Only bits and pieces of him left, but it's definitely him."

"You sure?"

"Whatever attacked Colt came at him from behind. Wasn't much of his body left, but his face was ... *mostly* intact." Whey-faced, Grant unbuttoned the collar of his shirt. "It's Calhoun. No question."

"Any idea what killed him?" Sadie asked.

"Teeth marks on the back of the skull make me think the initial attack was a grizzly, but uh..." Grant turned, glancing nervously behind him. "The other rangers aren't so sure. Cougars maybe. And I think there might've been wolves working at him, too."

Jim's mouth dropped opened.

"But wolves don't attack people," Sadie said. "You told me that yourself."

"I, um ... yeah. I couldn't really say for sure, but if they found a body out here..." he nodded toward the shadowy woods, "and there was nothing to stop 'em."

"Or if they'd been fed before," Jim said.

Grant winced. "Look. You never heard any of that from me. I'm just saying whatever got to Colt did a hell of a job cleaning the bones. Could have been anything, really." He brushed his hands on his pants. "Either way, I'm just glad this whole mess is over."

"Me, too," Jim nodded.

* * *

Lou was under the belly of a Dodge Caravan when she heard the footsteps come up next to her. She bit her lip, forcing the smile that was trying to pop out back under a layer of calm. Lou knew Rich had been down at the police station this afternoon, identifying the papers discovered floating in the lake, but she'd sensed for an hour that he would show up at the garage after he finished.

The polished shoes stopped next to the side of the vehicle, and then Rich's voice broke the silence. "Lou, can I talk to you a minute?"

She slid out from under the minivan, smiling up at him. Rich wasn't in a suit. Today he wore jeans and a black t-shirt, his hair, usually neat and tidy, unkempt and hanging in his eyes. The change unnerved her.

"Hey, Rich," Lou said. "What're you doing here?"

He shrugged. "I'm screwed," he said, giving her a lopsided smile. "They fired me."

Lou's breath caught in her chest. The danger she'd been worrying about all summer was gone, but a new one had just blindsided her. *He's going back to New York!* her mind screamed. She stumbled to her feet.

"What?" she cried. "But why? Why?!"

Rich caught her arm, steadying her. "They're closing down the lodge for good. There isn't going to be another Whitewater."

"No!"

"It's true," he said. "They're even selling off the manager's cabin. I'll be moving to Lethbridge to wait for the preliminary hearing."

"But I thought Colt started the fire."

"I'm sure he did, but in the end it doesn't matter. They haven't found any evidence yet, and I'm an easy enough suspect to pin it on." He shook his head, glaring out at the street. "I got the official summons from Captain Nelson today. Preliminary hearing is set for the first week of September."

"But I don't ... I..." Lou's voice trailed away, her mind awash with fear. This couldn't be happening. Not now! Not when she was finally willing to risk the truth.

"I've already started packing," Rich said. "I'll be out of your way in a couple days."

Lou opened her mouth to say one thing, but something else came out.

"Stay here with me!"

"What?"

"You've got to live somewhere until the hearing, right?" she said. "Why not here?"

His hand tightened on her arm, his expression tumbling from surprise to elation to uncertainty. "Are you sure?"

She swallowed her fear, her hands coming up to his chest. "Yes, I'm sure," she answered, voice wavering. "You're practically living with me now."

Rich pulled her into a hug. "I'm sorry about that." He kissed the top of her head. "When the preliminary hearing is over, I'll get out of your way."

Lou's eyes swam with unshed tears. "It's no problem, really. What're you going to do in the meantime?"

The expression on Rich's face shifted, his gaze drifting outside. The warm August air was heavy with cottonwood seeds, the distant mountain peaks hazy in their perfection. "I dunno," he said. "I guess I hadn't thought about it."

She wrapped her arms around him. "I could always use a hand in the garage."

"You joking?"

Lou laughed, her worry lifting. Rich *wanted* to be here. She could feel his excitement blooming outward and filling the air around them. "Not joking. I could use help with oil changes and things." She winked. "Besides, we worked together well enough before."

Rich nodded, cupping her chin. "I thought so, too."

*   *   *

Sadie and Jim sat at a back table in The Watering Hole, a half empty pitcher of beer between them. Neither was on duty, but they'd met here by habit.

It was seven-thirty and the bar was still reasonably quiet. Hunter and Grant were perched side by side on barstools, an aerial map of the mountains laid out on the bar between them. A short distance away, Susan Varley sat at a video lottery terminal, her foot tapping along to the music. And at the tables near the doorway, a scattering of seasonal and year-round staff, Mila and Lucy, Nando and Zuan, were whiling away the night with a drinking game. Each of them had a card stuck to the middle of their forehead, their laughter rising and falling with each round. With the murders solved and the controversy dwindling with each passing day, the tone of the entire town had changed, the lazy hours of late summer passing at a slower pace.

"Penny for your thoughts," Jim said.

Sadie gave a half-hearted smile. "The preliminary hearing."

"What about it?"

"It's a waste of time. There's never going to be a trial."

"Nelson thinks there will be," Jim said with a grin.

"Nelson can think whatever he wants," Sadie said dryly. "But there's no way any arson charge against Rich Evans is going to stick. All Nelson has going for him is accessibility and one waitress eavesdropping."

Jim took a sip of beer, his eyes narrowing on the bottom of his glass. "Wouldn't be so sure about that," he said. "Evans has a lot to gain by the hotel burning."

"Had," Sadie corrected. "I'd hardly say an arson charge is help-ful."

"True," Jim chuckled, "but I'm sure someone who commits arson doesn't expect to be caught."

Sadie nodded, her gaze following a group of young men and women coming in off the street. They came up to the bar, talking loudly. The bartender glanced over at the two officers before asking all of the patrons for ID. Amidst groans, they complied.

"If the place had just burned to the ground," Jim said. "They would've been able to rebuild from scratch." He tipped his empty glass toward Sadie. "Just like Rich Evans said."

"I don't think that was the point of the fire," she argued. "If Evans had done it, he would've done a better job hiding it. The guy's not dumb."

Jim reached out, refilling his glass from the pitcher. "Would've been easy to make it look like wiring," he mused. "That would've been the thing to mess with, not the gas."

"Exactly. Those alarms were pulled *before* the fire. Evans would've known that'd show up on the security system's files. With two empty wings, he could've set the fire there, and still got the guests out with plenty of time to spare."

Jim's brows drew together until a deep groove appeared between them. "Whoever set it didn't know that ... Rich did."

"Bingo," Sadie said. "Which means the arsonist wasn't Rich Evans. It was Calhoun."

Jim snorted into his beer.

"What?" Sadie asked.

"Colt was crazy as a barn owl," Jim said. "I'll give you that. He killed a bunch of people, and had a lot of questionable friends—but that doesn't mean he was the arsonist."

Her dark gaze sharpened. "Oh yes, he was."

"You sure about that?"

"Yes, I'm sure!"

"What'd Colt have to gain by burning that hotel down?"

Sadie took a swallow of beer before answering. "Ah, but he wasn't trying to get something." A cunning smile turned up the corners of her mouth. "He was trying to get something to go away. Something bigger than the Whitewater ... Something *huge*."

"Go on," Jim chuckled, nudging her with his elbow. "I know you got something, so spill it."

Sadie reached in her pocket, pulling out a folded piece of paper. She tapped it once against the table before holding it out to Jim. "This got faxed to me this morning."

Jim lowered his glass, taking the paper from her fingers and unfolding it. "What is it?"

Sadie flicked the paper with her nail. "It's a list of names. People who were temporary help for the Whitewater Lodge. Unlisted workers, people who weren't on Chan's official staff roster."

"Temps?"

"Nope. Deliverymen. Moving in and out of Lethbridge with company trucks, delivery 'goods' that no one seems to account for. There were too many deliveries. See? Things that should've tipped us off. Whitewater was moving more goods *out* than they brought in, and the guys moving it were unlisted for a reason. Rich Evans was right: Colton Calhoun was running drugs. My guess is Chan got involved before he knew what he was getting into. When he found out, he tried to back out of the deal and..." She sucked air through her teeth as she ran her finger across her throat. "Goodbye, Mr. Chan."

"So that's it," Jim laughed. He banged his fist on the table, glasses clinking. "That's the last piece!"

"Yeah ... I just wish we'd jumped on it as soon as Evans gave us his statement after Calhoun's attack." Sadie rolled her eyes. "Lethbridge Drug Enforcement took in a guy last night. They figure he's the one who killed Lucas Sorenson. The guy named Calhoun right away. It's out of our hands."

Jim snorted, then began to laugh aloud.

"What?" Sadie asked.

His cackling grew.

"No, seriously, Jimmy. What?"

Jim wiped at the corners of his eyes, laughter fading into contented sighs. "Only you would be pissed off that a case was solved so quickly."

"I'm not mad," Sadie huffed. "Just wish I could take credit for it ... not Evans."

"Be happy it shook out the way it did. Coulda been a hell of a lot worse. Done is done, right?"

"I guess."

A few seconds passed before Jim gave her a Cheshire grin. "But that doesn't mean Evans wasn't the arsonist."

Sadie began to laugh but ended up choking on her beer; Jim pounded on her back, chuckling good-naturedly. When she could speak again, she croaked: "Hey! You're my partner. Aren't you supposed to *help*, not harass me?"

"Yeah," he said happily, "But I've tried both, and it's more fun bugging you."

Sadie laughed. "Well, it's a good thing I like you then."

"Oh you *do*, do you?" Jim said with a wink.

She lowered the empty glass to the table with a thunk, smiling to herself.

"Maybe."

Jim tapped her foot with the toe of his boot. "Maybe is good enough for me."

The music had picked up tempo in the last minutes, and Mila and her friends moved out to the dance floor. Hunter folded the map and tucked it into his lapel pocket, heading for the door. He raised a hand in greeting as he passed, and the two officers returned the gesture. Sadie sighed, relaxing for the first time in months.

It was a good way to end the summer.

* * *

Darren "Dax" Xavier sat in his Seattle office, listening with half an ear as his assistant read off the news that had arrived. Some of his sources were legal news agencies, others private investigators. All provided new facets to the puzzle that was Dax's daily business dealings.

"The police have closed all leases connected to Borderline, reverting control back to Parks Canada," she said. "All business partnerships with Borderline Industries have been dissolved, loans waived. The company's assets have been seized. It appears none of the business people who signed on with Borderline had any idea what was going on."

"Mmph," Dax grumbled. At least Calhoun'd had some sense. "Anything else?"

She flipped open the dossier in her hands, passing him a yellow memo. "Your team in Kalispell wants to know when you'll be sending them a new transportation coordinator for the Canadian side of the Waterton-Glacier transfer."

Dax pursed his lips, glaring down at the note. "I won't."

Her eyes widened in surprise. "Sir?"

He crumpled the paper up, tossing it into the garbage can. "I'm closing that part of the border," he announced. "We need to reorganize. Get things figured out before we move again."

She nodded, making notes. After a moment she glanced up. "Do you want me to transfer one of your teams from the Northwest?"

He shook his head. "I want everyone out of Montana altogether. Send someone to clean their warehouse. Get rid of any evidence. Buy out the local police if there's any trouble. The Waterton-Glacier system is closed."

His assistant didn't argue, but her prolonged silence was question enough.

"There's too much police presence in the area these days," Dax explained. "They'll be checking those trails after this. Waiting for it to start back up. Any chance we had of putting things to rest were screwed the second Calhoun died on that lake. Bastard left too much evidence behind."

"Understood, sir," she said briskly. "I'll arrange for the Kalispell and Great Falls teams to be moved back to Spokane."

"Good. And make sure it's done without any attention."

"Of course, sir. Understood."

Dax glared down at the map in front of him. Canada had the largest undefended border of any country in the world. It had a peaceful relationship with the United States, and that meant its borders were controlled with less diligence than many other nations. While Waterton was a good location, it wasn't the *only* location. This was a hiccough, nothing more.

"Is there anything else you'll be needing before I go?" his assistant asked.

Dax flipped the folder closed, pushing the documents aside, but leaving the map in place. "Not for now," he said. "I think this mess is finally solved."

"Then I'll see you tomorrow morning," she said brightly. "Goodnight, sir."

"G'night."

Dax watched as she pulled the door closed behind her, then spun the map around, scanning the coast of British Columbia. He had connections in Vancouver. Friends who knew people who knew people. Dax smiled.

It was time to start thinking about the future.

*   *   *

It was a quiet Wednesday afternoon, and Hunter's Coffee Shop was empty except for a small group of locals huddled at the back of the sunny café. Not everyone was present—Lou, for one, was absent—but those who attended were the central core of the business community, the heart of Waterton.

On the street outside, a few solitary tourists wandered by, the last trickle of visitors to the now quiet town. There was a softness to the light beyond the windows, a calmness captured in the purple shadows which crisscrossed Main Street. These were the last lingering moments of late August. Summer's dying days. Sunlight cast bright cut-outs under trees. Birds sang. In the branches above, the uppermost leaves were already brushed with a glimmer of gold, the first hint of changing weather.

"Got my new lease today," Hunter said. He sat at the table, his hands cupped around a coffee mug that seemed too small in his raw-boned grip. "Parks Canada has resumed control of the leases around town. Borderline Industries is gone."

"Gone?" someone at the back asked. "For how long?"

Nervous whispers rustled through the room like autumn wind.

"Forever, far as anyone knows," Hunter said. "Colton Calhoun's dead, after all."

An uneasy murmur followed his words. People were still reeling from the discovery that there'd been a murderer in their midst. Colt had been a keeper of secrets, among other things, but few had guessed his knack for business and willingness to help friends had gone to such dark lengths.

Hunter stared down into his cup, a frown pulling his brow into a point of concentration.

"Dead or not, they'll know our businesses were part of Borderline," Susan muttered sourly. "Jim Flagstone was already asking me about it. They've got a list. We're all on it."

People shifted uneasily. The mutterings rose.

Hunter blew over his steaming mug and took a sip before speaking. "It was a holdings company," he said tiredly. "Nothing else. As long as we all stick to the same story, there's no problem."

The rumble of discontent rose until it was the hint of a storm brewing on the horizon.

"Calhoun was the only thing keeping me afloat."

"...he lent me money last year."

"Could've used more..."

"What if they find out about my payments?"

"...sent him a cheque every Friday."

"...let him use my pickup when I ordered supplies."

"Will it be linked back to us?"

"Do the police know?!"

Audrika set down her teacup, clearing her throat to draw their attention. Hunter lifted bushy brows in surprise. Audrika had her finger on the pulse of most things, and had needed less of Colton's help than the others. "Borderline's under investigation, yes," she announced. "But none of us are part of that."

Hunter felt a wave of relief and disbelief. He lowered his coffee. "You sure about that?"

She buffed her fingernails against the sleeve of her blouse, a knowing smile on her lips. "My sister-in-law works at the Bank of Montreal in Pincher," she said archly. "Colton only deposited cash and cashier's cheques. Any links to our businesses were directly to Borderline, not to Colton Calhoun himself." She nodded sagely at Hunter. "It's like Hunter says: we all tell the same story, everyone's safe."

Hunter leaned back in his chair, setting down his mug. Fingers trembling, it clattered against the saucer. "A new start," he muttered hoarsely. "For all of us."

The room's tone shifted with his words, the worried buzz changing into a bubbling rush of excitement. Happy laughter filled the café alongside the sound of cutlery tinkling in cups. Audrika rose and picked up the half-full coffee pot from the burner behind the counter, refilling cups in Hunter's stead. Reaching his side, she squeezed his shoulder.

"It's fine," she murmured.

Hunter blinked rapidly. "Thanks for, uh ... checking in on things," he said gruffly. "Appreciate that."

She waved away his words, then refilled his cup. "Friends stick together," she said lightly. "You'd do the same for me."

Throat aching, he nodded and turned his gaze to the windows.

The light outside had begun to dim. Shadows stretched from one side of the street to the other, reaching up the walls like fingers as the street lamps came on. In the north, a bank of dark clouds was building above the ridge of mountains, the tops of Buchanan and Crandell already fading into misty half-light. The last pigmented bands of sunset gilded the sides of buildings in orange light, but the rattle of wind against the panes of glass brought with it a promise of rain.

Autumn was coming, but no one save Hunter Slate seemed to notice the change.

EPILOGUE

The storm rolled in late-afternoon. Down the lake, the first low rumble of thunder began, the tentative taps of intermittent drops arriving on the roof minutes later. The shower started off slowly, gradually building to a constant drum roll. The storm punctuated Rich and Lou's dinner, growing in fits and starts. Insolent wind whistled past the window panes, chased by arpeggios of rain. By the time the two of them climbed the stairs for the night, the downpour had grown to a steady hum.

"The temperature's dropping," Lou said through chattering teeth.

Rich took her hand. "I'll keep you warm."

The bed in the upstairs bedroom of Whispering Aspens was slightly smaller than Rich's tall frame required. His sock-clad feet stuck off the end, elbow bumping the raised edge of the sagging mattress. The bed was cold, the cotton sheets like crisp folds of parchment under his cheek and against his arms, but with Lou tucked against his side and the blankets piled atop them, he was content. With Lou he could forget the summons and all the rest ... he could relax, and just *be*.

"Love you, Rich."

He smiled and pressed a kiss to her temple. "Love you, too."

Rich's eyes rose to the angled ceiling which stretched up from behind the bed to the far reaches of the peaked roof. The only sound which reached his ears was the thrum of rain. There were no tourists in town to break the night-time calm. Four months ago, the thought would have left him fretting, but tonight it brought a sense of contentment. *Home.* He wondered when he'd started to think of Waterton that way.

Lou curled into him, icy toes sliding along his calf, and Rich smiled. "Tell me a story," he whispered.

She glanced up at him, her eyes dark pools reflecting moonlight. "Which one?"

"Something about Waterton," he said, leaning in to brush his mouth against hers. "Something for the end of summer."

She closed her eyes for a long moment before she began. Rich wondered if he should have asked for a story about *Lou.* She so rarely included herself in her stories, and he wondered why. Lou's lashes opened the second Rich thought it.

"When Hunter Slate first came to Waterton, he'd never actually been hunting before," Lou began. "He worked on a ranch for a time, and grew to be friends with the owner, Levi Thompson."

"Thompson ... I know that name."

"Levi's a Park old-timer. He's the grandson of Ephraim Thompson, the settler I told you about," Lou explained. "Now Levi had grown up in the woods, and he took young Hunter under his wing. Wanted to show him what it was like to track an animal. That September, he and Hunter got tags for two deer, and headed out to the forest reserve to hunt. It was clear and sunny when they left, but partway through the day, a storm blew in, much like the one tonight. It was too far to walk back to Levi's truck, so the two of them took shelter in the hollow of a 'V'-shaped gully that was filled with blow-down."

"Blow-down?"

"Trees and broken branches. There'd been a snow-slide sometime before which had filled up the 'V' in the hill with dead trees. The blow-down gave Levi and Hunter a fairly good shelter, and plenty of wood to burn. The two of them started a fire and waited out the storm. By the time it passed, it was almost midnight and far too dark to walk. The two men sat and talked, watching the embers of the fire." Lou paused, smiling mischievously. "And then Hunter heard it..."

"Heard what?"

Lou's grin widened. "There was something above them in the blow-down: An animal moving through the tangle of trees and branches, trying to get down."

A shiver ran up Rich's spine. "A bear?"

Lou shook her head. "They turned away from the fire, waiting until their vision got used to the darkness, and then they saw the eyes. It was cougars—three of them—and they were climbing down through the maze of broken tree trunks toward them."

Rich's memory of the night by the falls returned. "Shit!" he hissed.

"Now cougars are curious," Lou continued. "They're big cats, really. And they wanted to know what kind of animal had stumbled into their den. Old Levi knew how dangerous they could be. He fired the first shot up into the bracken, but in the dark, he couldn't see. The shot went wide. He hoped it would scare them off." Lou paused. "It didn't."

Rich found his fingers had tightened into a claw in the sheets and he forced himself to relax. "What happened then?"

"The cougars came closer, screaming and—"

"Screaming?"

"Hunter told me they sounded like a woman screaming," Lou said. "I don't really know; I've never had a cougar hunt me. But that's what happened to Hunter and Levi. A bit of karma, if you think about it," she said with a giggle. Rich tried to join in her laughter, but the sound was tight and constricted. "So, Hunter and Levi spent an endless night watching the tangle of branches above them, keeping the fire at their backs, waiting for the attack. They used up all their ammunition just before dawn."

Rich's lids were weighted, the story weaving a spell around the bedroom. "That's messed up," he mumbled thickly. Lou muffled her laughter against the pillow.

"Old Levi was ready to set the entire mountain on fire by that point," she said dryly. "But when the sun came up, the woods went silent. The cougars had gone. Hunter and Levi grabbed their gear and practically ran back to the truck. They never did get the two deer they had tags for. After an endless night, they were finally safe."

Her voice faded, the story disappearing like smoke; there for a moment, then gone.

"Why that one?" he murmured.

Lou rolled toward him. "What's that?"

The bed was warm, the clean smell of rain mixing with night air and cedar: a smell as heady as incense. Sleep beckoned, but something niggled at Rich's mind. "That story," he yawned, eyelids closing. "What does it mean?"

Lou's fingers slid across his chest, resting over his heart. "Sometimes you have to wait out the night," she said quietly "Morning always comes."

Rich tried to answer, but his words were thick on his tongue, swallowed by sleep. He was surrounded by softness: the quilts, the rain, the green smells of the forest and the musty warmth of the cabin. The storm outside rolled closer, moving in slow steps across the great expanse of lakes. From the bowl of the mountains came thunder, the voice of a long-ago giant from childhood days, or perhaps from Lou's stories. The thought made him smile.

"Night, Rich."

Goodnight, he thought, but didn't say.

He drifted into slumber, wrapped in the cozy embrace of the bed and Lou's arms. The house was snug and warm, the storm held at bay. The rain might drown the world, but Rich didn't care.

He was safe. He was home.

The End

ACKNOWLEDGEMENTS

The writing of Edge of Wild has been a lengthy process, but I could not release it without expressing my sincere gratitude to the many people who have shaped it along the way:

Thank you to my husband, my most enthusiastic collaborator, for reading aloud every iteration of this project from beginning to end, so that I could make sure the language sounded 'just right'. Thank you also to my children, for tolerating long periods when I couldn't play, as I wrote, and rewrote, and rewrote again. I owe you one.

Thanks to Morty Mint, for being the first to believe this book would be published and for his unwavering support every step of the way. Thanks also to Dinah Forbes, for providing a lifetime's worth of editing prowess as she reshaped the story into something far greater than I'd imagined.

A very enthusiastic thank you to Netta Johnson, Julie Yerex, and the entire Stonehouse team, for their tireless efforts in bringing the project together. Edge of Wild is yours as much as mine.

Finally, a special note of appreciation to my fellow authors, editors, and artists: Amy, Anamarya, Angel, April, Barry, Becca, Candice, Cecilia, Clare, Claudia, Dave, Deb, Deborah, Deena, Elaine, Elizabeth, Emily, Emmalie, Erin, Eugie, Fiona, Greg, Heather, Jen, Jenevive, Jennifer, Jill, Jordan, Joseph, Karen, Kate, Keith, Kerri, Lana, Lexie, Liz, Lynn, Madi, Manik, Mary, Megan, Melissa, Michael, Monti, Naz, Nicole, PS, Rachel, Ray, Reshma, R.

D. K. STONE is an author, artist, and educator who discovered a passion for writing fiction while in the throes of her Masters thesis. A self-declared bibliophile, D. K. Stone now writes novels for both adults (*The Intaglio Series, Edge of Wild and Ctrl Z*) and teens (*Icarus, and All the Feels*). When not writing, D. K. Stone can be found hiking in the Rockies, planning grand adventures, and spending far too much time online. She lives with her husband, three sons, and a houseful of imaginary characters in a windy corner of Alberta, Canada.